BLOOD & INK

Brett Adams was raised in country Western Australia, and lives in Perth. He has a PhD in Computer Science that taught him to love puzzles, and a family who taught him to love stories (or vice versa). He writes fiction across a range of genres, and has been known to plant an easter egg or two.

BLOOD & INK

Brett Adams

 FREMANTLE PRESS

For Elisha, Cayley, and Jos. And for Tara, who still isn't complaining. I can't imagine life without you.

'The purpose of literature is to turn blood into ink.'
—T.S. Eliot

PROLOGUE

Any fool can hold a gun.

For proof, I offer myself. Crouching in the shadowed stoop opposite the café, I held the Glock raised before me, gripped double-hand. Easy.

Fully loaded, a Glock 17's steel, brass, plastic and propellant totals nine hundred grams. Weighs less than a can of beans. And any fool can hold a can of beans.

What's more, if the Glock is typical—built, as it was, by a man with no firearms experience to win a contest by the Austrian Ministry of Defence—any fool can design one too.

But to fire one at a human being?

That, it turns out, takes a devil.

It's like they say: pressure can make a diamond, or a stain. It all depends on what's being squashed.

Squatting there in the shadow, one shoulder braced against a dirt-encrusted brick wall, trying to keep the Glock's sight trained on the kid's chest as he sauntered to the café entrance, I was beginning to fear I was from Stainsville.

The problem wasn't the occasional yellow flash of a taxicab, or the stink of rotting trash wafting out of the gutter. I had clear sight across the street. There was no wind to speak of. I knew the chambered hollow point round would expand when it punctured his flesh with a good chance of smearing an artery or organ.

Everything was ready.

Except me.

My hands were jittering like a junkie in withdrawal.

Maybe it was nerves? I know it wasn't guilt.

No, I wanted a tight bead on his chest. I wanted my bullet to tear him a new hole. Was *giddy* to see him ragdoll to the ground, and watch his blood sluice onto the street.

Those are the perks of an Angel of Death on an avenging mission.

My real fear was that my body was falling apart. That the stresses of the past weeks had caught up with me, and the flesh-machine named Jack Griffen had finally thrown a cog. That deep down, part of my constitution had ruptured. Now, when I needed it one last time.

Maybe murder took more than a professor of literature had—particularly a forty-five-year-old professor of literature with a diabolical heart condition and a fear of needles.

Why not? Everything else had broken.

I strained again to still the tremble in my arms. Just one more shot.

Because—*oh, boy*—I meant to murder. Just once. First and last on my scorecard.

My one hope was that before he died, he had the presence of mind to look for me. I wanted him to know I made it. Me, Jack Griffen. I played his game. And he lost.

1

Fifty-six days earlier

The knife was six inches long.

Its handle was hardwood wrapped in brass wire, its blade acid-etched with a Native American icon of a snake. A scalping knife.

Hiero laid the blade across the palm of my hand just above the first knuckle, on the fleshy part of the fingers.

In hindsight, it probably should have concerned me more when he burst into my office brandishing the knife, quoting Homer, 'The gods are hard to handle—when they come blazing forth in their true power!'

But to be honest, in the months I'd known Hiero, I had come to expect anything.

'Describe it for me, Professor,' he said.

'*Professor*?' I said. 'You haven't called me that since the first day you walked in here.'

'Maybe I'm feeling nostalgic.' He leaned toward me across my desk. 'Come on. How's it feel, the blade's touch? Like a line of fire?'

This close, I noticed the livid skin of a graze on Hiero's normally immaculate forehead. But the feel of razor-keen steel on my skin left no room to consider its significance.

Fighting the urge to flinch, I shut my eyes. In the darkness I tried to shrink my world to the feel of that line of pressure on my skin. The smell of his aftershave was overpowering.

From somewhere outside a shriek of laughter echoed through the grey buildings of the English Faculty. The campus was slowly draining of students on a post-exam high.

'It feels …' I said, groping for the right word. 'Wet.'

My eyes snapped open, fearing for a moment that the blade had drawn blood.

'*Wet*?' he said, voice flat. 'That's the limit of your imaginative reach: *wet*?'

I nodded, a trifle guilty, and the scratch of his pen on a notebook was the only sound for a moment.

He put the pen down, and with the ghost of a smile, shifted the knife blade. He lifted it and rested the last two inches of steel across the base of my index and middle fingers.

'Now you have a choice: two fingers, or—' He angled the blade, moved it down. 'One thumb.'

Not exactly Sophie's Choice, but my mind refused to work with the blade touching me, so I stalled.

'Last time you made us drink that bottle of five-dollar wine.' (A shattering hangover eclipsed the fun of trying to write how *that* felt.) 'The time before you punched me in the neck. When are you going to threaten me with donuts?'

He withdrew the knife and sat back. From a box on my desk, he took a chocolate, popped it into his mouth, and chewed. The aroma of chocolate wafted past me. They were a gift from a failing student, but I never ate them. Hate chocolate.

I snatched my hand back, and noticed the glimmer in his eye dim a little.

But only a little—it never quite died with Hiero. He lived high octane, as crazy as that sounds for a kid meeting in the cool evening hours with a crusty professor of literature.

I watched him scratching in his notepad, and wondered if I'd miss our talks when he returned home. He was on exchange, and semester had almost finished. The next day he was flying back to the US.

'You told me to research, Jack.' His hand rested on a leather folder he'd laid on the desk, his touch almost a caress. The folder had been with him for weeks now. Its cover was brown and worn like a sailor's skin.

Research? I had. Three weeks ago. Straight after he'd told me his secret: he was writing a novel.

'Not just any novel,' he'd said. Hieronymus Beck only had one novel in him, but it would be a cracker. A *Catcher in the Rye*. An immortal novel.

When I pressed him about it, he said he didn't want to spoil it, but confessed it was a murder mystery. And since then, he'd remained uncharacteristically coy.

Tonight was my last chance to grill him, face to face. The teacher in me wanted to convince him that it was the details—the *verisimilitude*—that made a novel ring with truth. Made it endure.

More than that, I'm ashamed to admit. There was a rare spark in Hiero. If this novel did, against all odds, turn out to be a bestseller—or, God forbid, a classic—this was my last chance to be the guy who coached him to greatness.

Selfish, I know.

I took a breath and dove in. 'Who's the victim?'

His gaze settled on me again. Behind those eyes I fancied I could see his mind calculating whether or not to entrust me with his baby.

Then—

'This guy,' he said.

Progress, at last.

'How does he die?'

'Death.'

'Hilarious. Knife wound?' I said, glancing at the knife, which he had thankfully set down.

He shrugged.

I pressed. 'Bullet, strangulation, poison? You must know.'

'All of the above,' he replied, deadpan.

Gen Y—always want all the options.

He took a sheet of paper from his folder and wrote again.

'What about forensics?' I said. 'Murder always leaves a mark on the world.'

I hunched forward onto my desk, tried to coax a tell from his poker face.

'What trace evidence will your medical examiner find? Is it poison? It's poison, isn't it.'

He didn't deny it, so I latched hold.

'Poison offers plenty of ways to fork the reader's attention, but you need to be precise. Hemlock isn't arsenic.'

'Hemlock,' said Hiero, 'causes dilation of the pupils, dizziness, trembling, paralysis, whereas arsenic causes headache, drowsiness, diarrhoea, white patches in the fingernails.'

'Wonderful!' I said. 'But cold. Here's the twist: hemlock grows by the side of the road in Washington; arsenic looks like cholera in Haiti. See the potential?'

'My novel isn't set in Washington or Haiti.'

'Don't be obtuse. Just nail the detail. That's where the devil lies.'

From where I sat, I read upside down as he wrote 'detail' and 'devil'.

He lifted his gaze, and his deep grey eyes smiled from behind a curtain of chestnut fringe: 'I'll research.'

I couldn't tell if he was humouring me, so I made one last pitch for attention to detail.

'Agatha Christie—queen of murder mystery—knew her poisons so well that a real murder was solved using her novel, *The Pale Horse*. It practically introduced the world to the lethal efficacy of thallium, and described the symptoms of thallium poisoning better than the medical journals. The very year the novel was published, 1961, the British serial killer known as the Teacup Poisoner began experimenting with it. Heck, just ten years ago a girl in Japan, an admirer of Teacup, killed her mother with thallium and blogged about it. You know you've hit the detail when your novel informs *real life*.'

Hiero snapped his folder shut. 'Life and art.'

'Art and life,' I replied, in what had become an in-joke.

Through my office window I saw evening had thickened to night. A hint of damp drifted through the old wrought-iron air vents, and with it the tick and croak of frogs.

I leaned back in my chair and let my eyes roam through my office. My gaze inevitably fell on the bookcase taking pride of place on the long wall. Its shelves bowed under the weight of classics.

Art. Art was going to kill me. They could write that on my headstone.

Hiero caught my glance. In a moment he was out of his seat, and at the shelves. As he scanned the spines, he murmured, 'Chandler, Lewis, Nabokov, Salinger, Tolstoy, Vonnegut …'

This was no book-of-the-month portfolio club set. These books were marked by life, picked from charity shops, garage sales, laundromats, each stained by the grit of life, creased by fingers uncaring or eager.

How I loved those books. How I hated those books.

'These guys are gods,' breathed Hiero.

Gods?

'Come on, Hiero. They're writers. Leave divinity to the surgeons.'

A curious smile lit his face when he turned toward me.

'No, I'm serious, Jack. *Gods*. Know why?'

I spread my arms, 'Explain the theology to me.'

'Who alone knows a man's thoughts in the last moment of his life, as a bullet tears his brain apart?'

Jesus. A sudden thought disturbed me. Hiero could be manic; was he suicidal? 'You're going to say "God"?' I said.

'And writers, Jack. Authors.' He sat again, hunched toward me, his shoulders trembling with contained energy. 'Only God and Hemingway could know that, at the very end, the Old Man dreamed of lions.'

'So you're a god?'

He smiled, spread his arms wide. 'Well, I'm writing a novel.'

Who was I kidding; I would put a thousand bucks on Hiero never finishing his novel. He had that mania that might never settle on anything in life.

'There's just one thing that destroys your theory,' I said. 'These authors, these gods of yours, Hiero: their creatures are fiction. Make-believe. They live in worlds built from dreams or nightmares. If anything, *false* gods.'

Night had taken the corridors when we said our goodbyes. I locked up my office in the pale green light of an emergency exit sign.

And slipped on the tiles. I crashed onto my hip and sent my briefcase careening into the darkness.

When I'd collected myself, I discovered what had caused my fall. I'd slipped on a leather folder. Loose paper had slewed from it across the tiles. I gathered them up, then held the folder up to the poor light.

Printed on one side of the folder in permanent marker was *Hieronymus E. Beck*. And below that, *Blood and Ink*

I'd slipped on the notes for Hiero's novel.

And my life would never be the same.

2

As I drove home that night, I struggled to drown the pity I felt for Hiero.

Back in the US, without my goading, he would probably forget about writing. He'd travelled halfway round the world for my tutelage, but hadn't bothered turning up to my lectures. Couldn't blame him on that; these days, half the kids stayed home and watched them online.

Besides, he lacked talent. *Real* talent. With his looks, he would have more chance in Hollywood. I convinced myself it was a good thing he had lost his notes. That even if I knew where he lived, I wouldn't return them.

But my conscience must have been uneasy. At my apartment, I ate a microwave dinner at my writing bureau, and examined his notes.

The folder held even less than I had first thought. Besides loose paper, there were five sets of stapled pages, each of two or three sheets, and all titled 'Research'. The cover page of each set appeared to be a typed template. Hiero had probably paid twenty dollars for a decrepit typewriter from a charity shop. Another Hemingway-wannabe.

I retrieved the topmost set and held it to the light to read. The first line of the template began 'How'. Next to that was written in curling script 'Asphyxiation'.

So I was holding a template for murder, and Hiero had begun with the pointy end of the stick, the means.

Below, written in the same curling script, were the words 'Where: Point Walter'.

Point Walter lay on the other side of the river, a spit of land surrounded by nature reserve. If I stood on tiptoes on my balcony, I could probably see the light on its jetty.

Next came 'When: 'Neath the Rising Sun' (and my author brain grimaced at the incorrect capitalisation).

Below that, the last item, 'Who: Female jogger. Redhead.' An ellipsis, then 'large-breasted'.

I gave him a tick for the hyphen, then laughed, thinking Hollywood and Hiero would get along fine.

A memory of my ex-wife killed the moment. I read on.

Below the cover page lay freehand notes. Hiero had made a study of methods for asphyxiation. Under 'Garrotting', he contrasted the effects of different kinds of rope and wire. The likely particulate trace evidence left by each, the texture of abrasion left upon skin, the chance of rupture, and the likelihood of crushing the windpipe cartilage. Wedged among the paragraphs were diagrams of the larynx, littered with details of angle and force, and calculations of the minimum required strength.

I adjusted my opinion of Hiero's career aptitudes. This kid needed to get into engineering. Safer in the current economic climate. Paid better too.

A figure at the bottom of the last sheet in the set drew my eye, because it appeared to have been photocopied and pasted in. It was a strikingly barbaric-looking device consisting of a bizarre knife that sprouted a second, curving blade, and a long cord knotted to a metal ring. The caption read '*Kyoketsu-shoge*'. Apparently Hiero's research had reached as far back as feudal Japan and the weaponry of ninjitsu.

Fighting heavy eyelids, I skimmed the rest of the notes. They seemed to form a sequence of five murders in all, with each marked with a number in the top right corner in black permanent marker. Some sheets were full of black type with sketches filling the margins, others had great blocks of white paper. Hiero's novel was dealing death in a variety of ways, some obvious (asphyxiation, poison, blunt-force trauma), and some nonsensical (choice, observation—I mean, *what*?). No more large-breasted redheads though.

I replaced the top sheet, and stared at it a moment.

How: Asphyxiation
Where: Point Walter
When: 'Neath the Rising Sun
Who: Female jogger. Redhead … large-breasted

He had been a busy boy. I suppose it should have been gratifying that he had taken my advice to research to heart.

Sleep hit me before I decided what I would do with the folder. I binned the remains of my dinner and climbed the steps to my bedroom. The bed felt empty that night, and I blamed Hiero's hormone-charged imagination.

Tomorrow I'd visit Bedshed. Stop sleeping in one half of a king-size bed.

3

Morning rose in glorious light, but I didn't make it to Bedshed.

A newspaper had been stuffed through my mail slot, even though I'd killed the subscription a week before.

I read it over breakfast. It was on page seven that I found the article about the assault.

The previous night the victim, described as being in her early twenties, had been jogging the path that winds around Point Walter, when a hooded man had leapt from the bushland adjoining it and wrestled her to the ground.

I didn't want to hear if she'd been successfully sexually assaulted. My gaze flicked forward by habit toward the next article.

But it caught on a word in italics: *kyoketsu-shoge*.

It came after the words 'knife' and 'cord', enclosed in parentheses, and was no doubt the late-night research of some bored intern, but there it was.

The attacker's intent had not been rape. He had meant to garrotte the woman. Murder her. With a *kyoketsu-shoge*.

My vision glazed for a moment, then refocused to read the rest of the article. With relief I read that she had 'fought her attacker off', escaping with minor lacerations to the throat—and, dangling from her neck, the weapon.

The *kyoketsu-shoge* was the sole reason the assault made news, and perhaps why it was crammed into the stop press.

A tearing sound briefly drowned my senses. It came from within, and I think it was the sound of my life peeling away from what the average person calls Reality.

When it subsided, I tried anxiously to stick it back down.

Hiero's dossier had said asphyxiation, sure. But how many assaults did the city of Perth host each year? Tons. Whole handfuls.

And assault by *museum artifact* …? Not so much.

It said female, too. So what? Weren't they all?

The article lacked a photo, so I couldn't check if the victim had red hair or big boobs.

And another vote for the Reality column: the attack had happened at evening, which was the obvious time to strangle someone. But the dossier said sunrise.

But it also said *kyoketsu-shoge*.

A relic of feudal Japan. Empire of the Rising Sun. The dossier didn't say sunrise. It said, 'Neath the Rising Sun.

Shit. (Peeling sound.)

I hurried to my writing bureau, where I'd left Hiero's dossier, hunched over like an old man, and pawed through the sheets for the set I wanted— the one with a large number one inked in the top corner.

When I found it and re-read the notes on asphyxiation, a ripple of relief rolled through me. No, it didn't say *kyoketsu-shoge*. It *mentioned* *kyoketsu-shoge*, among many, many alternatives. The stats were looking up again.

Come on home, Reality. The coffee's on.

I stuck her back down, but as fast as I did, a corner dog-eared up.

I remembered the graze I'd seen on Hiero's forehead the previous night. Sign of a struggle? He could have left Point Walter after dark and easily made my office by eight. In fact, he had been ten minutes late—ten minutes late when it was usually me who found him waiting, slumped against my door.

And what if this *woman* who was attacked at *Point Walter* with a *kyoketsu-shoge* had red hair and big tits?

'Murdoch Police Station,' said a voice. 'How can I help you?'

I pressed the phone receiver to my ear. My mind went blank.

'Hello?' said the receptionist.

'Hi. I—Do …' (Professor of literature, note.)

'Sir?' she said, and the sunshine dropped out of her voice. 'What is your name, and what do you want?'

'My name?' I said. My eyes darted around my study. 'I'd rather not say.'

There was a pause on the line. It may have been my imagination that heard a sudden hiss, as if it switched to speakerphone.

'Would you like to be transferred to the Crime Stoppers hotline, sir?'

'Crime Stoppers? Yes, yes!' What the hell was I saying?

There was a click, and the line swelled with a community announcement about opening hours and a hospital commissioning. Then it cut out mid-sentence.

'Crime Stoppers,' said another female voice.

'I'm calling about the assault last night, the girl. The *kyoketsu-shoge*. I …' *What?*

'Do you have information pertaining to the crime?' said the voice.

'Yes. No. It's information I want.'

'This is not a reporting service, sir. If you would like to—'

Then the mind-fart: 'The girl. Did she have red hair and large breasts?'

The receptionist said a word I didn't catch, then one I did, 'Sicko.' She hung up.

I laughed. It was an odd sound. Then I dialled emergency.

'Emergency services,' said a voice. 'Which service do you require: police, ambulance, or fire?'

Why weren't all the questions multiple choice?

'Police.'

The line cut over to a call tone, which was promptly picked up.

'Please describe the nature of your emergency.' A man's voice. Clipped tones.

'I need to know—'

'Is there an emergency, sir?'

'No. I—'

'Then I must inform you that two false calls have been logged originating from this number. If you persist, charges will be pressed. Do you understand?'

I hung up. Dropped the phone like a snake.

Then I walked circles in my study with a palm pressed to my forehead.

A policeman had just been rude to me. Me, who had never received so much as a speeding ticket.

I picked up the phone again and dialled international.

The call ping-ponged through the network, and rang for what seemed an age.

'Sparkes,' said my ex-wife.

'Kim,' I said.

'Shit, not today, Jack.'

'Good morning to you, too,' I said.

'It's not morning here, Jack. It's the afternoon. The morning finished hours ago, and I'm still trying to wash off the stink of faculty politics.'

'Play their game, Kim, and you stink their stink.' I couldn't help it.

'Oh!' she said, and the sarcasm came dripping out of the handset. 'I forgot I was talking to the man with the pristine arse. How's that novel coming, Jack?'

'How's Tracey?' I said.

'Always the segue,' she said, but the venom dried up. 'Tracey's on the east coast for two months. She's taking a holiday, visiting friends. There's a seminar by Robert McKee—some screenplay guru.'

'Screenplays? When did my daughter develop attention deficit?'

Kim laughed, and it made me smile till I remembered why I'd rung.

'Kim, be honest—'

'Always am.'

I told her about Hiero's notes and the assault.

She said, 'This Hiero, he's in your exchange group?'

'Sort of. What do you think?'

'What do you mean, what do I think? Attention deficit. That would make a nice screenplay. Your student could be played by Leonardo DiCaprio, and you could be Tom Cruise.'

'I'm serious.'

'So am I,' she said. 'Or maybe Tom Hanks.'

'You think I look like Tom Hanks?'

'Call me later, Jack. I feel like crap.'

She hung up.

4

I didn't sleep well over the weekend. Neither could I battle my insomnia with a book. And the newspaper boy seemed to have sorted himself out, as no more papers appeared.

When I got to my office Monday morning it felt like a month had passed. I was still holding my briefcase, with the key in the door lock, when a secretary collared me. Her name was Grace, and her eyes sparkled with gossip.

'Did you hear the news?'

'What news?' Why was I *smiling*?

'Rhianne Goldman was attacked last week. One of our students.'

'Rhianne?' I said, conscious of my lungs hauling air.

'On exchange from Santa Fe. Doing journalism.'

It leapt out of my mouth before I could shut the gate: 'Does Rhianne have red hair, big breasts?'

Grace's hand went to her own ample bosom and fluttered.

'I—' I said, racking my brains for words that would patch my reputation. Couldn't find any. Hang it. 'Well? Does she?'

'Yes,' she said. 'And, I suppose she is … quite well proportioned.'

'Big?' I said, and gestured for emphasis.

Her face froze for a second, eyes large. Then she shook her head and retreated down the corridor, her rubber-soled pumps squeaking on the tiles.

Escaping through my office door, I flung my briefcase down, and booted my computer. Within minutes I was scrolling through the university's student database looking for two records. One each for Hieronymus E. Beck and Rhianne Goldman.

The addresses listed were in adjacent riverside suburbs, and in striking distance of the assault. I scribbled both contact numbers in my diary.

But which to call first?

The cautious half of my brain thrust my hand toward the phone, and dialled Rhianne's number.

A male voice answered, 'Yes?'

'It's Jack Griffen. I wanted to speak to Rhianne.'

'Are you a reporter?'

'No, no—professor of literature. Rhianne is a student of mine. I wanted to see how she is.'

'Traumatised. Why don't you call again next week.'

'But it concerns her degree. It could impact her visa. I must speak with her. I'll be brief.'

There was silence, then the rumble of a receiver being put down.

A minute later a girl's voice said, 'Hello?'

'Rhianne, you don't know me. I'm a professor at UWA.'

'You're calling about my visa?' she said uncertainly.

'No. That was a lie, but please don't hang up.'

More silence, then, 'What do you want?'

'This will sound crazy, but I need to know if you recognised the person who attacked you.'

I heard rustling, and then a sniffle.

When Rhianne finally spoke, her speech sounded laboured. 'I can't talk now. I have to go—'

'Please don't hang up,' I said, louder than intended. 'Just tell me if you saw him. What did he look like?'

Just tell me he was five foot nothing, or weighed twenty stone, or had dark skin.

She hung up.

I replaced the receiver, leaned back on my chair, and raked my hands through my hair. I screwed my eyes up and watched the firework patterns wriggle in the dark. When I opened them again my gaze fell on the whiteboard mounted beside the door. Half of its surface was covered in a tangle of green marker, a mind map for my novel, which was in permanent gestation. The other half of the board contained a schedule of my contact hours for the semester just finished. Lectures and tutorials were blocked out of a grid representing the week.

The sight of that grid usually depressed me. It said *students*. It meant work. Tunnelling for coal in dark minds.

But today it prompted a different chain of thought. Students, always joking around. And Hiero, the biggest joker of all.

The realisation burst over me as if the sun had emerged from behind a cloud and filled my office with light.

It was all one big joke. A last pull of the professor's chain before Hiero left for home. And I'd swallowed it hook, line, and sinker.

A smile spread over my face, and my muscles relaxed in a wave from my neck down.

Definitely Hollywood.

Rhianne had to be in on it.

And the newspaper? said the cautious half of my brain. The *police*?

My office plunged back into gloom.

I wasn't thinking straight. With a glance at the portal in my door, I trundled the bottom drawer of my desk open, and retrieved a bottle of Johnnie Walker. I unscrewed its lid and took a nerve settler.

Before I replaced it, I held the bottle to my eye and, with a shock, noticed it was almost empty. The cleaner must have found it. It was the first bottle I'd put there, and that was less than a month ago.

I called the second number.

No answer. Hieronymus would be gone, home to San Francisco. I wanted to talk to his host family.

I looked up his record again in the student database and scribbled the address on a post-it note. While I was at it, I wrote down Rhianne's too.

A quarter of an hour later I was pressing the doorbell of Hiero's billet.

Someone was home. A family mover was parked in the drive, and its hatch was open.

Footsteps thumped on a wood floor and the door swung open. A girl of about ten years stared up at me, but before she could speak her mother appeared and shooed her away.

'Hello?' she said.

'Hi. Sorry to bother you. Did you know your car hatch is open?'

She glanced past me at the driveway and frowned. 'Ohhh,' she said, then shouted over her shoulder, 'Renae!'

She stepped past me onto the porch, and I followed her to the car. She tugged a bag of shopping from the trunk and slammed the hatch.

'Thanks,' she said.

'No problem. You must be a glutton for punishment—big family *and* an exchange student.'

Confusion wrinkled her brow. 'Sorry?'

'Hiero Beck, the American exchange student billeted here? He left Saturday?'

'I'm sorry,' she said. 'I don't know what you're talking about. Perhaps you have the wrong address?'

'Perhaps,' I said, and had a struggle keeping the smile on my face as I took my leave.

After that I brooded in my car for a long time, staring at the family mover parked in the driveway without seeing it. My fingers drummed on the steering wheel until calm stole over me.

I needed to take an axe to the root.

5

The front door of Rhianne's billet didn't have a doorbell. I rapped on it with my knuckles, and grimaced at the racket it made in the quiet street.

The door swung inward to reveal a gloomy entryway and a pervading silence. A man stepped out of the gloom and closed the door behind him.

'Can I help you?' he said, somehow making it a threat.

'My name is Jack Masters. I'm from immigration—' His expression tightened. 'Here to help,' I hastened to add. 'Rhianne's visa expires this week, but given the circumstances she will be allowed an extension. She just needs to sign.'

'You have the paperwork already?' he said, suspicious.

I yanked the leather folder from my briefcase, and held it up, back to front. Hiero's name taunted me from the reverse side.

The man disappeared back into the house, and I took it as an invitation to follow. From the entryway, a flight of stairs reached up from the gloom into a loft lit by high windows.

'She's up there,' the man said, jerking a thumb at the stairs. 'The doctor said she's still in shock. Don't be long.'

He vanished down the corridor, and I mounted the steps.

Rhianne lay curled up in bed. She made a pitiful lump beneath the covers. When I entered the room she sprang into the corner like a disturbed spider, bedclothes snarled around her slight frame, and somehow managed to shrink even further. Blister packs of medication lay on a bedside table, half-used.

I came to a halt by the bed under her wide-eyed gaze. Her red hair was collected up into a loose ponytail, and revealed an alabaster neck scored on either side with angry red welts. A speckle of dried blood ran in a line down each welt.

Reaching for my most soothing voice I said, 'I'm really sorry, but please, will you just look at this.' I held Hiero's folder toward her.

She continued to stare until I was sure her eyeballs would dry in their sockets. At last she blinked. The spell seemed to break, and she took the folder.

'What is it?' she said.

'It'll be easier if you just look.'

She laid it in her lap and, without remarking on what was printed on its cover, opened it.

A murmur of conversation floated up the stairwell as I watched her gaze zigzag over the first page, the one that foretold her assault in four brutal lines. I fancied I even saw her gaze dip to her bosom.

When she finished reading the top page, she flipped it over to read the next, then glanced up at me.

'What is this?'

I heard the front door *thunk* and footfalls in the corridor below.

'Never mind what it is. Do you know Hiero? Hieronymus Beck?'

She shook her head. 'Should I?'

'He's an American,' I said.

She frowned.

'Not *because* he's an American,' I said, exasperation leaking through my made-calm. 'He's a linguistics student on exchange at UWA.'

'I'm doing journalism,' she said.

On a table beside her bed were stacked books. Tilting my head to read their spines, I read aloud. '*Wuthering Heights*, *Lady Chatterley's Lover*, *Gatsby*, *Breakfast at Tiffany's*, and—good Lord, *Ash Wednesday*. T.S. Eliot is not a poet I can tempt even my students with. Been reading it long?'

'Long? I never stop,' she said matter-of-factly.

I heard the footfalls pause, then come clattering up the stairs. Fear tugged my guts.

'Look, did you see your attacker or not? I can get his photo from student services.'

She shook her head again. 'It was dark. He wore a hood.'

'Is that it?' I barked. 'How tall was he? Above six foot?'

She shrank away. 'I don't … He was—' Her eyelids drew together, and

I knew what she was going to say before she said it. 'About your height.'

Of course he was. Hiero was about my height.

The clatter on the stairway died as the same feet fell on the carpet at the stair's head. Two men I didn't know entered ahead of the man who had greeted me at the door. The newcomers were smiling in a way that struck my blood cold.

The older of the two men extended his hand, and I took it on reflex. We shook hands, and he said, 'Afternoon sir. I'm Detective Thomas, and this is Detective Palmer.' I gave the other man my right hand, which had turned into a dead fish.

'We'd like to have a chat with you,' said Thomas. He gestured to the doorway. I retrieved the folder from where it had fallen on the bedclothes, and walked out of the room, feeling four sets of eyes on my back.

Minutes later I was seated at a kitchen table, facing the detectives.

'Coffee?' said Thomas. 'You want some coffee?' he said to me, then to his partner, 'You want some coffee?'

I nodded just to be agreeable.

Palmer rose, switched on an electric kettle, and began poking into cupboards for cups and coffee.

'So, Mr Masters?' said Thomas.

'My name is Griffen, Jack Griffen,' I said. Lay it all out. This was good. Sanity was settling again on my shoulders like snowfall. The police station is where I should have gone in the first place.

A theatre scowl appeared on Thomas' brow. 'But the owner of the house says you introduced yourself as a Mr Masters from immigration.'

'I'm a professor at UWA, and—' I smiled. God it felt good to be having this out face to face. 'You need to see this.' I slid the folder toward him. 'I fear I know who assaulted Miss Goldman.'

Thomas' eyes didn't leave me as he reached for the folder, turned it right side up, and opened it. I made sure he was reading the right page, then sat back. The kettle was roaring like a jet, and I found myself salivating for the coffee.

Thomas muttered something, and a moment later my brain interpreted it. He'd said *kyoketsu-shoge*. He glanced at me. I answered him with a twitch of my eyebrows.

The kettle clicked off and its wail died as if it had been dropped from a cliff. The other detective poured three cups, and the aroma of coffee filled the small kitchen. He placed a mug on the table for each of us and sat.

Thomas slid the still-open folder in front of his partner.

'Mr Griffen, do you know why we log calls to all police services?'

I shook my head. I didn't, but I wanted to know. Little-known facts like that made great detail for a story.

'Because perpetrators of violent crimes—it should come as no surprise to a man of your intellect—are as thick as two bricks.' He sipped his coffee and grimaced. 'And twisted. Do you know how many rapists call us to see how big was the wrecking ball they put through some young lady's life?'

I didn't. And I didn't want to know anymore.

Sweat sprung out under my armpits, and trickled down the inside of my upper arms.

I jabbed a finger at the folder. 'I called because of that.'

Palmer closed it, raised his head, and began plucking at his lip with thumb and forefinger.

'Hmm,' said Thomas. He retrieved a notebook from his shirt pocket and a pen stowed in its spiral binding. 'Do you know Miss Goldman?'

'Well, yes—now.'

'Before today.'

'No.'

'Never set eyes on her?'

Was that a trick question?

'I can't *guarantee* I've never seen her. UWA has over twelve thousand students, and she's in the same faculty. But I don't remember having seen her before today.'

Thomas scribbled in his notebook.

'What were you doing last Friday evening, between nine and eleven?'

'I met with Hiero.' I stabbed a finger at the folder. 'That Hiero. Then went home.'

'And you live …?'

'Nedlands.'

'Full address, please.'

I gave it, and Thomas took forever to record it with his ponderous script.

'Anyone verify your whereabouts?'

Shit. Something else to blame Kim for.

Then another voice: *Nah-ah, Jack. The blame game goes back much farther than that, and you started it.*

'No,' I said, gulped coffee, and burned my throat.

'Okay, Mr Griffen. We'll leave you be for the moment. But please don't leave Perth.' He smiled the death-smile again.

6

Tuesday passed in a dream.

I gave my Orwell lecture by rote and left the theatre without taking questions.

Wednesday I hid in my office nursing a growing headache. Turns out the cause was the pressure of a thought that wanted out.

A fever woke me at 2.33 Thursday morning.

But it wasn't a fever. I'd twisted myself up in the bedclothes and sweated through a nightmare. This nightmare didn't linger like normal. Its power dispersed in an instant, was squeezed to the edges of my mind by the thought that had finally burst through: the other notes.

Hiero's folder held *five* sets of notes. One had been enacted. A failure, but not for want of trying. Four remained.

I hurried down the stairs to the ground floor of my apartment in the dark. I missed a step and felt a moment of terror when my torso lurched past my feet, before I clutched the balustrade and fought myself upright.

In my study, I found the pull-cord of the reading lamp by feel, and raked the folder to me. Thomas had slid it back to me with a condescending, 'You keep that safe for us.'

I opened it and hunted for the next set of notes in the sequence.

It wasn't hard to find. Each of the five précis had printed in the top right corner in black permanent marker a number. Perhaps the easy-index should have concerned me more. The sheet for asphyxiation sat on top of the pile. To 'Who: Female jogger. Redhead … large-breasted', I could now add: 'Rhianne Goldman'.

That is history. Move on, Jack.

Slipping Rhianne's sheet under the bottom of the pile, I was faced with the second note. It was the same template. I ran a finger down the margin of the topmost page, and stopped at 'How'. The next word was 'Poison'.

My mind flared with the memory of goading Hiero to nail the details, because that was where the devil lay.

'I'll research,' he'd said, and smirked at me from behind his fringe.

Below the word 'Poison' were notes on the word's origin. Hiero had underlined its roots in the Old French word for magic potion. And next to this he had listed a number of notable deaths by poison, concluding with Socrates drinking hemlock for the charge of 'introducing new deities'. Next to this, a smiley face blazed incongruously.

I scanned the page for the details, while telling myself this was all hypothesis. Loose conjecture that I could drop any time, no harm done. The door to my study could burst open, and the candid camera enter, and I'd laugh it all off.

For 'Where', Hiero had written: 'A bedroom a hundred feet above a sprawling, glittering mass of humanity.'

Great time to get poetic.

Then tagged on the end, almost as an afterthought, was 'Hong Kong'.

For 'When', he'd written: 'A celebration'.

My eyes flickered before I reached 'Who'. I had to fight the compulsion to look away, slip the paper beneath the others.

It said: 'Female, Asian'.

That narrowed it down to—what?—one billion? If I was to infer this female Asian had normal breasts, maybe that cut it down another—

I gave that calculation away.

A bedroom in a Hong Kong high-rise and a celebrating woman. It sounded like the setting line of a screenplay.

No, it's a prophecy, damn it. Wake up.

But the oracle has drunk too much of the mystic wine, part of me protested. What the hell could I do with Hong Kong, female, party?

Antarctica, penguin, standing around, was hardly worse.

And what kind of a celebration did you have in your bedroom?

I stared at the summary sheet. Same format, different girl.

How: Poison

Where: A bedroom a hundred feet above a sprawling, glittering mass of humanity. Hong Kong.

When: A celebration

Who: Female, Asian

The memory of Hiero's eyes struck me again. Their glint forced me to calm. I rehearsed a few facts. I was an intelligent man. I'd been told just that today by a policeman.

I recalled what I knew of Hiero, to recollect how the world looked to a student. I tried on his shoes, walked around in them a while. They didn't take me any place I wanted to go, but everywhere I went, I bumped into *other students*.

Rhianne was a student. An *exchange* student, like Hiero.

What were the chances?

Who cares. Again, it was an easy hypothesis to test and, if no good, discard.

From the back of my bureau I dragged my laptop, opened it, and waited while it booted. My fingers hung over the keypad, ready to enter my password, but it went straight through to the desktop.

I opened a web browser and hit the bookmark for the university staff portal. Soon I was peppering the student database with queries.

Students from Hong Kong? Many.

Exchange students from Hong Kong? A handful.

Studying humanities? Two.

And—thought the intelligent professor—exchange students from Hong Kong with a birthday in the next week or so? One.

I clicked on that student's profile.

Li Min gazed out at me, the skin around her eyes crinkled by her smile. Hair bobbed, and wearing the kind of chequered blouse that either meant she was a square, or conducting a subtle subversion. She was an Arts student, so probably the latter.

Her smile looked genuine, in any case.

Would she still be smiling on her birthday—in *two days*?

Crap.

I spun on my chair, and hauled myself back up the stairs to my bedroom. It felt empty during the day. Cavernous at night. Through a chink in the curtains I glimpsed channel markers winking red and green over the Swan River. The breeze streaming through the window smelt of frangipani.

I undressed, then redressed in track pants and t-shirt. I descended to the ground floor, and keyed the alarm to arm. The last thing I did before I bounded off across the lawn was to press the button on my Medline watch that told it I was going for a jog, and that it was okay to be in the Orange Zone for a while. Told it I was happy to walk at the precipice of death for a few minutes tonight in order to push away that unknown future time when my heart would throw me over the precipice without my say-so.

I should have stretched, would pay for it tomorrow. But I needed the rush of air around me, the thump of my feet on the tarmac. The smell of dew-wet grass.

I needed to think.

7

'Sorry, Mr—'

'Professor.' I corrected the woman behind the Cathay Pacific ticket counter.

'Sorry, Professor Griffen, the chances of getting on that flight are slim. The waitlist is already long.'

I thanked her and shuffled off the head of the queue.

I set my briefcase down on the floor and shrugged my shoulders in an attempt to stretch my neck. My body felt stiff from the base of my spine up. The buzz of the airport's eternal twilight filled my ears.

There were no seats on Flight CX170 from Perth to Hong Kong. The prophecy written on the sheet in my briefcase foretold the imminent murder of Li Min. But Fate had spoken again. The next flight with seats wouldn't get me there on time.

Can't argue with Fate.

Besides, Hiero wouldn't do it. Perth was one thing, and he can't have meant more than to scare Rhianne. She was a slim girl. If he'd meant murder, she'd be dead. So he'd done his research, and learned what mortal fear looks like, and how the garrotting cord feels in your palms as it pulls taut on young skin.

But Hong Kong? He was yanking my chain.

I wandered past a bar, and ran my eye over the bottles arrayed behind it. Perhaps a snifter would loosen my neck. An electronic billboard flashed an advertisement for a service that offered to turn your pet's remains into jewellery-grade diamond, and I wondered if I'd slipped into an episode of the *Twilight Zone*.

Then I remembered Li Min's voice on the phone. I'd called her number and reached an answering machine. The same smile I'd seen on her photo was in her voice, and I could *see* her speaking, recording the message, telling me, telling the world, she would be away until the next day. Her birthday.

But Hong Kong? It was unreachable.

Yet here I was at the airport. After one of the weirdest days of my life.

Phone calls. The day had been full of phone calls, and I hate phones.

I'd called Li Min's number, of course. When that failed, I checked the university record for her next of kin, an Aunty Mae. But Aunty Mae's line was disconnected. So I tried the property manager of the high-rise listed as Li's address. They put me through to a 'concierge' who sounded like he was in a call centre. He had great English, and said he'd take a message, and didn't say he'd file it in the rubbish bin. The lady at the embassy didn't lie: she said she would *not* take a message, as Li Min was not an Australian national.

I even tried Hong Kong police, but chickened out before it picked up. That's when I figured that Jack Griffen calling just about anybody was a non-event. More firepower was needed.

So I bit the bullet and called the Murdoch detectives. I got Thomas, who asked me if there was something I wanted to tell him. So I told him Li Min's life was in danger. That didn't seem to count.

By that stage it was late afternoon. My forehead was resting on the edge of my office desk, when I heard the *tap-tap* of high heels walking the corridor past my door. It was probably Grace grabbing dirty coffee cups that the resident slobs had left in the lunch room. The sound triggered a flash of inspiration: if one voice wasn't loud enough to be heard, maybe two would?

I dashed to my office door and threw it open in time to startle her. Cups rattled in her grasp as she jerked away from me. I'm not sure if it was my imagination, but her eyes had held a strange light ever since I'd gone on about Rhianne Goldman's breasts.

'Prof—'

'Grace.' Winning smile. 'I need a huge favour.'

Her gaze dipped, and she rearranged the skewed collection of cups gripped in her hands. Before she could demur, I went on.

'You know the assault. Rhianne Goldman?' Now she was leaning *toward* me. 'Don't ask me how I know, but I think another student is in danger.'

'Who?' she whispered.

'An exchange student from Hong Kong. A young woman.'

Ten minutes later, Grace had joined my lobby group of two. She seemed, in fact, to have been primed from birth to throw her formidable frame behind a scandal, any scandal. I sat on a desk opposite her, and listened to half of a conversation as she called Detective Thomas.

She used the words I'd coached her to use. She didn't mention my name. But I knew by the way her speech degenerated into monosyllables, and her glance kept darting at me, that my name had been mentioned. When she hung up, I had to press for an answer.

'He didn't buy it?' I said.

She shook her head, and began arranging piles of paper on her desk.

'Damn. Why not? What did he say?'

She still hadn't looked at me. 'He said that all necessary precautions—'

'He guessed I put you up to it, didn't he?'

A nod.

'Why the hell won't he believe me?' I rose, and paced around the empty desk. 'Would it really be that hard to check this girl's okay?'

Grace finally looked up. One of her hands crept across the desk toward me. Her knuckles were hidden beneath a chaos of costume jewellery.

'Professor ... Jack. He was very polite, but he said there was—' She halted. Then in a rush, 'A flag on your—on you.'

'A flag? What does that mean? What kind of flag?'

'An MH flag.'

I was completely baffled. 'A what?'

'A mental health flag. He said you have a "psych admission" on your record.'

'That's preposterous!' I stormed from her office.

Preposterous.

Only, it wasn't.

Back in my office I killed time researching how a Murdoch detective could have discovered I'd once been admitted to Graylands Hospital suffering nervous collapse, while the import of this trickled into my consciousness. Turns out the *My Health Records Act* of 2012 exposed digital records to police for 'the detection, investigation, and prosecution of criminal offences'. Learn something every day.

When I'd slapped the laptop shut, my fears had crystallised.

Li Min of Hong Kong was marked for murder.

I knew it.

But no one would believe me.

And the cherry on top: the police suspected I'd assaulted Rhianne Goldman.

Surprise lit the face of the woman at the Cathay Pacific desk when she looked up to see me again. She took a moment, evidently, to remember me, and what I wanted. She smiled tightly.

'I'm sorry,' she said, 'the waitlist hasn't shrunk any.'

'How about Business Class?' I said.

She shook her head.

I sighed. 'First?'

Now her eyes held a new light. She tapped at her keyboard and confirmed there was a seat.

'How much is that?' I said.

She told me.

I did the sums in my head. It was more than a month's pay, and my bank balance was already skimming, bouncing just above the mortgage line like a skipping stone. If I paid for this ticket, the stone might just bite on water and plunge into the silt …

'Okay,' I said. 'I'll take it.'

The last thing I did before boarding flight CX170 to Hong Kong was photocopy all of Hiero's notes, and post them to a nonsense address in Queensland, with a return address of Murdoch Police Station.

8

First Class was worth killing the mortgage.

I drank red wine before my entrée of Iberian Ham Crostini with Date and Ricotta, again before my mains of Porcini Mushroom Cannelloni, and again after my dessert of Hazelnut, Coffee and Muscovado Syrup Cake, to bed it all down. And to bed the wine down, a finger of Glenlivet Single Malt Scotch Whisky.

On the video screen, which folded out from beneath my lounge chair like a piece of the International Space Station, I watched the movie *Twelve Monkeys*, the one that proved to me that Bruce Willis can act. When the credits rolled I lay my seat back, closed my eyes, and strafed the radio channels. I found a Sibelius marathon and left the dial there. The music reminded me of our honeymoon. We had played CDs of classical music so loud the hotel management had called. Jean Sibelius had done it.

That was twenty-three years ago. Hong Kong.

That's what I was doing. That was my cover for this ridiculous flight. The story I could quickly own. It was a re-enactment ... spoiled only by the empty seat by my side.

Eventually I slept, and my dreams were full of Sibelius, and the voice of an announcer who became as God.

But I must have drifted too deep for the radio to reach me, because I later dreamed of a meeting with Hiero. It was odd because it was simply a memory, with only the slightest embellishment.

I remembered Hiero telling me he wanted to write a modern Gothic horror. He had written a short story to test the waters, and read it to me.

His story began with a woman returning home. She had left the house to shop for groceries, but returned with a large, square parcel that was wrapped in brown paper and tied with string. Oblivious to her husband's questions, she ushered him into their bedroom, laid the object down, and gestured for him to open it.

Playing along, he began to tear away the brown paper, when through a hole he saw an eye staring back at him. The eye looked human, but its whites were lurid yellow. The shock of that burning gaze upset his balance and he fell back from the object.

Impatient, his wife tore the remaining paper from the painting, lifted it onto a hook, and stood back to view it.

'Isn't it …' she said, but fell silent, lost in the image.

'What is it?' said the man, sufficiently recovered to appraise the painting in the whole.

'A painting,' she said.

'I can see that. But where did you get it? And why? And what on earth *is* it?'

'I bought it from a little old wisp of a man with a cart. He was parked out front of the mall this morning selling art. He said it is very old. I couldn't resist—it's so, so … *spiritual.*'

The man agreed it looked old. The oil paint was cracked and crazed, and the wood frame marred by numerous dents as if it had been repeatedly dropped.

The subject was a creature vaguely manlike. It stood in a grotto, surrounded by stunted trees so gnarled their crowns dug into the ground; and rocks that were pitted from wind and rain. Dull red scales covered the creature's frame, marred by knots and burls. From its head sprouted four horns like elephant tusks, yellowed by age, and trailing tatters of rotting velvet. They resembled a grotesque crown.

But despite the creature's nightmarish form, it was its gaze that froze the man's blood. The eyes seemed to burn with a light of their own.

'How much did it cost?' he said at last. It was all he could think to ask.

When his wife appeared not to have heard him, he repeated the question.

'Two thousand dollars,' she said.

Anger flushed his cheeks, but something about his wife's posture stopped his mouth. She stood erect, head canted to one side, gaze fixed on the painting.

The next morning, after she left for work, he took the painting down, wrapped it in a towel, and drove to the mall. There he hunted for a little old man with a cart of paintings, but found no sign of him. Worse, no one seemed to remember him.

He returned with the painting, but left it covered by the towel, stowed in the attic.

When his wife returned to find the painting gone, she flew into a rage. She stormed through the house until she found it and hung it again on the same hook.

That night as he lay beside his wife, listening for the rhythm of her breathing that would tell him she was asleep, and feeling the eyes of the creature staring at him unseen in the dark, he made a vow. When morning came he would talk to her. Reason with her that a thing so grotesque had no place in their house, let alone their bedroom. If she forced him to, he would *insist*.

He would take the painting down, drive to the dump, and watch it burn.

He knew better than to speak now, angry and afraid.

Vow made, he fell asleep. He fell asleep before his wife, something that had not happened since the first years of their marriage.

It was the smell that eventually alerted their neighbours, who in turn summoned the police. The man's decaying body was found in the same position in which he had lain down to sleep.

His wife was nowhere to be found, and became the prime suspect.

The second suspect was the artist, identity unknown, who had been commissioned to paint a scene of a grotesque monster, clasped in embrace with the dead man's wife.

A judder woke me to semi-darkness and the thrum of the Airbus A330's turbines. My ears popped with the rising air pressure. We were descending on Hong Kong.

The last image of that memory-dream to linger was of the creature staring at me past the wife's tresses.

The creature winked.

9

I have a confession: if a student gives me a story that mentions the multiverse, I fall into a little ritual. I curse, locate my bottle of Johnnie Walker, then work hard to find a reason to fail the piece.

The multiverse. You know the one. Hollywood caught a bad case of it a few years back—*Source Code, Mr. Nobody, Coherence, Everywhen*—and is still shaking the last of it off.

If you're not up on quantum theory, the idea of the multiverse comes from a particular interpretation of some seriously weird shit that happens when you play with photons—particles of light. As far back as 1803, scientists observed that if you fired a photon at two slits it seemed to do the impossible: pass through both. Fast-forward to today, and one of the mainstream explanations of this weirdness is that the photon only really passes through one slit in our universe—it just happens to create an entire other universe where all is the same except that in the new universe, the photon passes through the *other* slit.

(The other mainstream interpretation is the Copenhagen—famously poked at by Schrödinger's half-dead cat, or half-pregnant nun, I forget which—that states that until observed, the photon is not either-or but both-and. Which sounds just as daft to me.)

It's one of the rare things Hiero and I agree about: the multiverse—the idea that every time a choice is made, a whole other universe splits off in which the alternative is simultaneously chosen—is the death of choice.

On the bright side, if you're playing that carnival game where you pop ping-pong balls into the clown's mouth, you can rest assured there exists a universe where you walk away with the three-foot teddy bear.

10

I had planned to check into a hotel, then hit the streets to hunt down Li Min, but I settled for sticking my head under a tap in the men's toilets of Hong Kong's Chek Lap Kok airport. The dream of Hiero's Gothic horror had blown away any thought of pretending I was in Hong Kong to reminisce.

Plus I only had a few hours' buffer. Technically, her birthday began at midnight. I didn't want to learn the hard way of a pedantic streak in Hiero.

I would find Li Min, and, doing my best to look sane, warn her to be anywhere but her bedroom—or apartment—on her birthday. No more lies. They just sat around like unexploded ordnance.

The address I had copied from the student database was an apartment block in Sai Ying Pun. I withdrew cash from an automatic teller, then waited forever for my luggage to appear. Somehow it had ended up on the wrong carousel. I exited Arrivals, and merged with a throng of travellers surging toward the taxi rank.

There was no queue I could discern, and on any other day, I would have floated at the fringe of the crowd, too polite to push forward. But the adrenaline in my veins energised me. My height gave me a good view to kerbside. I picked my spot, and drove toward it, surging forward into the smallest gap, and standing firm when the shoves came back.

Soon I was seated in the back seat of a red taxi, steeping in the driver's Cantonese chatter, watching a million people I would never meet again rush past outside. The air was humid. The taxi's air-conditioner droned hard but added nothing but its noise to the cab's atmosphere.

The apartment block was one of five built to the same design. Each offered a grand view of the other, and not much else.

I got out, paid the driver, and was deciding whether to ask him to wait when he tore off with a howl of the engine.

Retrieving the slip of paper with Li Min's address from my pocket, I double-checked I was in the right place. Jade Gardens blazed in green lights, in English and hanzi. Each of the five towers was numbered; my stomach dipped as I realised that the address on the slip was not. I'd have to try each until I found the right one.

I began with number one. Its elevator shot me to the twenty-second floor in seconds, and I followed the signs to apartment fourteen. It was the last along the corridor. I knocked on the door, but no one answered. I would have to stake it out if I ran out of luck in the other towers. If I hit another vacant apartment, I had no idea what I would do.

Tower two saw me invited to dinner by a smiling couple and their three kids. I regretfully declined, but was thinking, what the hell, if I found Li, maybe I would return with a bottle of Merlot.

Tower three was an elderly couple.

Tower four's fourteenth floor was being pulled apart.

Tower five housed a German man who, when roused from bed, offered me some choice *Deutsch* and slammed the door in my face. I returned serve to the uncaring door with a few choice words of *Englische* and retreated to the lift.

By the time I returned to tower one, the readout on my Medline watch blazed iridescent orange at 10.33 pm. Next to the time a heart icon flashed with a pulse reading. I was pushing 130 bpm, and needed to calm down.

On the twenty-second floor, I found apartment fourteen again and knocked. Still no answer, so I planted my backside on the door and slid into a sitting position on the floor.

Time passed.

I soon learned to discern whether the lift at the end of the corridor was rising or falling based on the rumble of its passage. Only three times in the next half-hour did the lift speaker *ping* announcing an arrival.

It made me wonder how many occupants the building had.

Which suggested another thought.

I rose from the floor with crackling knees, and strode down the corridor to apartment fifteen, and rapped on its door.

A young Asian man answered. He wore a singlet and boxer briefs, and massive headphones hung from his neck.

'Do you know the occupant of apartment fourteen?' I said.

'Sure.'

'Know if she's in?'

I watched him trying to read me.

'Have you tried knocking?' he said.

'Yes. Is she out much, at night?'

His mouth tugged down at the corners. 'She keeps to herself.'

Thanking him, I returned to fourteen.

I tried the apartment on the opposite side of the corridor, but got no answer.

Slumping onto the floor again, I checked my watch: 10.57.

My thoughts drifted, only to be snagged on a memory of the dream I'd had that day on the plane. I remembered Hiero telling his Gothic short, and one detail leapt out at me.

It was the smell . . .

Feeling like a fool, I twisted around onto my knees until I could dip my face to the crack at the bottom of the door.

I sniffed—and got a nose full of dust that set off a sneezing fit. When it subsided I tried again with less gusto.

The faintest odour of chaos touched my nostrils. I sniffed again, straining to identify it. It could be curdling milk.

I sprang to my feet and returned to apartment fifteen. The guy didn't bother being polite this time, just grunted at me.

'Looks like a blown fuse in my car and I can't get the hatch open,' I said. 'Do you have a toolbox?'

He gave me a look like I had to be kidding.

I went down the apartments, rapping on doors, until finally, at apartment three, I found a middle-aged man who disappeared and returned with a steel toolbox. He yielded it in exchange for my driver's licence.

The box banged against my leg as I carted it back to apartment fourteen, straining to quiet its clanking contents.

A quick rummage through it yielded a twelve-inch flat-blade screwdriver. With a glance up and down the corridor, I set it to the doorjamb.

There I paused.

For a moment I felt like I was about to pop the safety seal on Life.

Then I squeezed on the lever until, with a sharp crack, the door jumped backward. I eased through the gap, and shut the door.

Turning, fear froze me. A child's terror I thought I'd conquered long ago. Of what the dark hides.

Worse. This was someone else's darkness.

11

The only light in the apartment came from outside, where the corner of a venetian blind had caught on an empty vase.

Gingerly I crossed the room, fumbled for the blind's dongle, and twitched open its louvres. Hong Kong light pollution leaked in, and my eyes adjusted.

The room comprised a kitchenette, dining area, and lounge. Between a small, circular dining table, a two-seater couch, and a couple of bookcases, there wasn't a lot of room left.

I stuck my head over the kitchenette's sink and sniffed at the dishes piled in it. Two wine glasses sat on the draining board. Lumps of a whitish substance sat in the bottom of the sink amid a tangle of chicken bones. They might account for the smell.

Two doors were set in the wall opposite the kitchenette. Bedroom and bathroom, I guessed. I crossed the room, and chose one.

Turns out I chose the bedroom.

The bedroom was darker than the living room, but even so, I couldn't miss it. Hanging over the edge of the bed, angled to catch the scant light coming from behind me, was a slender leg.

I swept a hand down the inside of the wall and caught the light switch. Dazzling light blazed over the room, and burnt the scene into my memory.

Li Min lay on top of the covers, naked, one leg crooked over the side of the bed, arms folded up over her head. She wasn't smiling any more.

I moved to her side, and my hands reached out mechanically. Her skin was cold to the touch. With two fingers I felt for a pulse at her throat, but it was as still as everything else in the apartment. Dead.

I retraced my steps into the living room, and for a moment wondered vaguely where the phone might be, with the notion of calling for an ambulance.

The next thing I knew I was hunched over in a dark space that smelt of tile cleaner—the toilet. I don't remember how I got there. My guts surged again and again, like an animal trapped in my rib cage. My mouth gaped involuntarily. I don't know how long I squatted there, but nothing came out of my mouth but a trickle of spit.

When the vomit-reflex finally let go, I collapsed onto the floor, my trunk wrung out and aching. And only then did great sobs tear their way out of my throat. Whole-body sobs. A child's sobs.

After that, I sat for a time in darkness on the toilet floor, and listened to the echo of my breathing.

Returning to the bedroom, I forced myself to look at Li Min. I had never seen a dead body before, except once, at the funeral of a great-aunt, although I couldn't be sure I hadn't constructed that memory from overheard conversation.

Li Min looked like a discarded object. Unable to bear the sight, I cupped a hand under her leg that hung over the side of the bed, and gently lifted it and arranged it next to the other. It moved easily. In her wardrobe I found a dressing gown, and draped that over her. Now, she could almost be sleeping.

My senses played tricks on me and I fancied I could smell Hiero's aftershave in the air.

All this time I had to fight the urge to sit down again. My eyes wouldn't stop blurring. But the thought that he had stood in this same room only hours before steeled my nerves.

I surveyed the room and tried to piece together the last moments of Li Min's life.

A bedside chest of drawers held a lamp with a rice-paper shade, patterned with flowers and bees. Beneath clustered a zoo of stuffed animals around a digital alarm clock and a box of tissues. Lying in the scant space left was a shallow dish, still glistening with a trace of moisture, and a hypodermic needle, the kind I had seen in the dirt beneath the cisterns of public toilets.

So Hiero's 'poison' had been heroin? Heroin in a massive, killing dose.

I hunted through the drawers. The top two were filled with underwear, socks, and handkerchiefs. The bottom drawer held only one item, a pink journal. I retrieved it, but found it secured by a tiny padlock. On the floor at the base of the drawers lay a condom wrapper, torn nearly through.

A sharp rapping sound startled me, but not from fear. Anger was fast burning that off. Someone was knocking on the outer door. The light coming from the living room swelled.

I thrust the journal down the front of my shirt, and with a final glance at Li Min's still body, strode from the bedroom.

The outer door was half open, and two faces poked through the gap, silhouetted by the corridor light.

I hefted the toolbox, pulled the door open, and brushed past them.

'Blocked toilet,' I said without stopping.

They were a little couple with wizened faces. The man chattered at my back, but I didn't stop. At apartment three I exchanged the toolbox for my driver's licence, and if the owner thought anything strange, he wasn't saying.

I had to walk a long way before I could hail a taxi, but was glad to be moving. The last thing I wanted to do then was sit alone.

I gave the driver the name of the only hotel I knew in Hong Kong. The one Kim and I had stayed in years before on our honeymoon.

The hotel was expensive, and the taxi had taken the last of my cash. My second mistake in Hong Kong was to use my credit card to secure the room. The first had been to secure a toolbox with my driver's licence.

12

True crime is a genre of non-fiction. It's an odd name. Libraries don't have shelves for true architecture or true history. I guess it must be because there is a market for it, and people devour true crime in the same way they devour thrillers and period romance.

Hiero confessed to me one time that he read true crime from the age of eleven. *Disco Bloodbath*, Ellroy's *My Dark Places*, *The Stranger Beside Me*, everything on *Time*'s top twenty, and anything else he could get his hands on. Everything his father brought home. Even the autobiography of Viennese serial killer Jack Unterweger, which was written in prison.

I say 'confessed' but Hiero didn't think of it as a confession.

He said that of them all, Truman Capote's genre-defining *In Cold Blood* was his favourite—a non-fiction novel about the murder of a farming family in lonely Kansas committed by two ex-convicts. More than any other, he said, its message went beyond murder. It was about free will and destiny; the choice of one murderer, and the DNA of the other. That's why it was a classic.

The book's success didn't do Truman Capote much good. His obsession with the case plunged him into depression. He fell into a bottle and never emerged. Never wrote another full-length novel, and died of liver disease compounded by a cocktail of drugs, alone, nineteen years after the murderers swung from a Kansas State Penitentiary gibbet.

And this was what Hiero was reading at age eleven.

13

Barely an hour.

That's how long it took the police to track me down to my Hong Kong hotel room.

My guess is the nosey couple had found Li Min's body and called it in. The police had canvassed the corridor and obtained my details from the man with the toolbox. It isn't hard to copy down a driver's licence. A search for my name in the hotel registry database would have quickly yielded my hotel.

On reaching my room, I had tossed my briefcase on the bed, and taken a shower. I'm not normally a long showerer, but when I towelled off, the clock by the bed told me I'd been in there for almost half an hour.

I put my trousers back on, found a bottle of bourbon from the minibar, and took it out onto the balcony. From the fifth floor I was close enough to see the police car arrive, and its officers stride purposefully into the lobby. A minute later the phone rang. I answered. It was the concierge, checking that everything was to my satisfaction.

Checking that I was *in*.

The cops were coming for me.

For a moment I contemplated waiting for them to arrive. My anger seemed to have burned itself out, and now I simply felt sick. The urge to wait for the police was strong. They were the good guys. I was a good guy.

But then I remembered Detectives Thomas and Palmer of Murdoch Police Station. I remembered the death smile. You didn't give the good guy the death smile.

I threw a shirt on—no time for the tie, which smelt of vomit in any case. I picked up my shoes, socks, and briefcase, and slipped out the door and along the corridor toward the fire stairs.

Bounding down the stairs on bare feet, I had reached the third-floor landing when I heard footsteps rising up the stairwell, and the measured breathing of a fit man. I ducked into the corridor, shut the door, and pressed my ear to it.

My wrist buzzed once, and I realised my Medline was bleeping at me. The adrenaline of my flight had pushed my heart rate into the red zone. I wrapped my hand over the watch to mute it, and tried to think calming thoughts.

The *clap-clop* of standard-issue Gore-Tex leather combat boots rose, until they sounded from the other side of the door, then began to die away.

I lifted my hand from the watch. My heart rate was dropping back into the orange zone. I eased the fire door open, and with a glance up the stairwell, padded downward on my bare feet. I didn't want to die. I also didn't want to burst from the stairwell into the lobby looking like a fugitive.

At the ground floor, I paused to put my shoes on, took a breath and squared my shoulders, then entered the lobby.

Through the glass revolving door that gave onto the street, I could see a tour bus parked with its freight hatches thrown open. It had evidently disgorged its passengers into the lobby. The buzz of voices and clatter of luggage on tiles filled the air.

I set my face toward the revolving door and headed for it, my back prickling with imagined glances. I hoped there wasn't a cop stationed on the street.

There wasn't. I had escaped.

I walked till my feet began to ache, stopping only at an automatic teller to drain my savings accounts dry. (It held more cash than I remembered— my maths was off or perhaps a forgotten annuity had dropped?) I now had almost nine thousand Hong Kong dollars in my wallet, and after that it was the credit card, and a big fat blip on the radar every time I charged it.

From a street vendor I got a greasy skewer of fish curry balls, and broke a hundred dollar note. When I finally found a public phone with an enclosed booth, I entered and hunched over the machine to take the weight off my feet.

I picked up the receiver, fed coins into its slot, and dialled Australia.

'Murdoch Police Station. How may I help?'

'I want to speak to Detective Thomas,' I said. Then added, 'Tell him it's Jack Griffen,' thinking that ought to shift him off his donut.

Tinny holding music, then a gruff voice. 'Thomas here, Mr Griffen.'

'How's the investigation going, Detective Thomas?' There was a tremor in my voice.

'So-so,' he said, as if I'd disturbed him as much as rain would a rock. 'We have one person of interest who doesn't follow instructions too well.'

'I guess you're talking about me,' I said.

'Uh-huh. Want to tell me about it?'

'I'm in Hong Kong.'

That put a ripple through his calm.

'Then if you want to avoid a world of trouble, you'd better get your arse back to Perth.'

'He's done the next one.'

'Who's done what?' he said irritably.

'Detective Thomas of the Murdoch Police Station, I've called you to inform you that Hieronymus Beck has assaulted another girl. The next one on his list. And this time he succeeded. She is no longer alive.'

Thomas was silent.

'You do remember the list I showed you four days ago?' I pressed. 'Now do you believe me?'

There was a longer pause, then he said, 'Okay, but the best place in the world for you right now is here, so—'

'*Okay*?' I shouted. 'Li Min. Her name was Li Min. And now she's *dead*.'

I hung up.

The digital readout on the phone said I had $5.60 credit left. I dialled the US, California.

A sweet voice spoke from the receiver, and echoed in my head: 'Hello?'

'Tracey, honey, it's Dad, I just—'

A giggle interrupted me, then, 'Just kidding. You got the machine. Leave a message at the …' *Beep*.

Where was she? It was early morning in San Francisco, and Tracey had never been an early riser.

Then I remembered. She was in New York, attending a seminar by some screen guru. Damn.

I hung the receiver up, and waited without much hope for it to return my remaining credit. It didn't.

From the safety of the booth I scanned the street for uniformed cops. Nothing. Across the street a damaged neon sign advertised an internet café. Exiting the booth, I crossed the street, and descended steps that hadn't been cleaned in a long time. I bought a watery coffee and an hour's credit, and wedged myself into a corner seat in front of a terminal. The air was pungent with sweat and takeaway food.

I must've been the oldest patron by twenty years. Placing my briefcase on the desk by the terminal, I hunkered down behind it.

Behind closed eyes, my thoughts eddied and wouldn't settle. Li Min's face kept bobbing to the surface, and then came the painting of the devil creature and its yellow eyes. I felt the cold shower water that had made me shiver, and remembered how my eyes had stung when I'd cried again. I don't know if the tears were for the girl or me. Probably me. I didn't know her from a bar of soap.

But hardly anyone has seen her the way you have…

The part of my brain that I would have until then called cautious kept jabbing me with the assertion that the police hadn't been looking for *me*.

But beneath it, a harder voice told it to shut up. Start working on a way out of this hell.

I knuckled my eyes, and opened them. A quick scan of the room confirmed no one was looking at me. Okay.

My first task was to gauge Hiero's next move. I had failed at that once already, so I decided to take my own advice. I would research.

From my briefcase I retrieved Li Min's journal. The cover was extremely pink. I shot an embarrassed glance about the room, but no one seemed to be paying me any attention.

The journal's lock was sturdier than the usual bonbon treat securing a girl's journal (a guess based on a sample of one: my daughter's). But the clasp it held was weaker than a tin can. It tore away easily, and I folded the journal's cover back.

The first page was covered in a neat, small script. The date at the top left of the page indicated the first of January. Li Min was a journal keeper. I flipped forward till the writing abruptly disappeared and I hit blank pages, then backtracked to her last entries, looking for what exactly, I wasn't sure.

As I read, the dead girl's voice spoke in my mind. And her favourite word was Hieronymus. Never Hiero. Always Hieronymus. It was an infatuation, complete and utter. I skipped back through the year to find where the infection had begun, and found her first glowing tribute to the ebullient American with the brown hair and deep grey—almost alien—eyes and the chivalrous manner. As I flicked forward, the voice told me of group dates to the movies and karaoke, coffee with friends, and, ultimately, dinner alone. They read heavy books together on blankets by the river, and she learned of the novel he dreamed to write. She believed in the dream.

Now her journal entries grew terse. The end of semester closed in, and she feared their parting would be the end of the relationship.

She wrote nothing in the final week of semester, and her journal ended with one last abrupt entry. It had been written only yesterday. It said: 'Tonight we celebrate our love'. 'Love' was followed not by a full stop, but an absurd winking emoticon.

Following that was the last phrase Li Min wrote in her journal, perhaps the last she ever wrote: 'Cometh the hour, cometh MC Griffen.'

14

It took a moment for the bomb to drop.

Griffen?

I scanned the last journal entry again. Obviously I had misread.

But no. There on the page, in stubborn ink: Cometh the hour, cometh MC Griffen.

Griffen?

The girl I didn't know knew me. The *dead* girl, the hard-liner in my head added.

And why *MC* Griffen? Of what Ceremony was I supposedly Master, pray tell, dead girl? Your celebration of love?

What the hell was *I* doing in *Li Min*'s journal entry for the day she died?

I clapped the journal shut and threw it back into my briefcase, and withdrew, instead, Hiero's folder.

I wet the end of a finger and flicked through his notes, past the injured girl, past the dead, to Number Three. The action was comforting; the autopilot of marking a term paper. Perhaps I was still in shock. I withdrew it and extracted the key parameters.

How: Blunt-force trauma
Where: Underway
When: TBD
Who: Chälky

He had dropped the poetry, which was helpful, but the information was scant. It read like a placeholder. 'Blunt-force trauma' was clear enough, but 'Underway'? What did that mean? Would the murder take place in a subway?

And for 'When', he hadn't even bothered with a cryptic clue this time. 'TBD'?

The name, Chalky, wasn't familiar. It sounded like a nickname. Assuming Hiero was targeting exchange students, would it be enough to determine which one was next in his sights?

I pulled the computer keyboard over, and with its sticky keys entered the code for my hour's credit. Soon I was looking at the familiar login screen for the university student database. I entered my credentials and fidgeted while thousands of miles away a computer tucked into a closet on the university decided whether to trust me.

The seconds mounted till at last it replied: *Forbidden*. My access had been terminated.

Which was either an error—possible—or meant the police had contacted the university. And the only reason I could imagine for them to do that was that they suspected I was on the loose and stalking students.

Ignoring the part of me that said, 'Bugger them—forget about it and let them find out the hard way who is stalking students,' I rubbed my face with both palms and tried to think of Plan … which plan was I up to now? Let's call it Plan F.

The professor was fumbling over Plan F, and Hiero, the alpha male, was still cruising on the alpha plan.

Think, man.

A roar filled the dank room. A young gamer threw up his hands and belched triumphantly. A minute hand on a clock on the wall crept towards the hour.

My screen was still telling me politely but forcefully that I was *Verboten*, when I noticed the fine print beneath the message, the essence of which was that in the event I thought the response mistaken, I should contact the administrator.

Plan F grew legs. I would contact the administrator. One *particular* administrator, to be precise.

I closed the database screen and logged into Skype. Within the program, in a pane on the left, lay a list of my contacts. Beside each contact a coloured dot indicated if they were logged into Skype. Scanning the names through a smear on the screen I found the one I wanted, Matthew Price. His dot was a happy green. He was online, like always. Matt would be first in line for surgically implanted net connections when they arrived.

He was a click away. He was also an administrator of the university computer systems. Matt Price was my ticket back into the database.

He also happened to be my daughter's ex-boyfriend. And in this case, that was good. Theirs had been an amicable parting, and I had always had time for him. I hoped it would be enough now.

I initiated a chat session: 'Matt. Can you talk?'

A full three seconds later his reply bobbed onto my screen: 'Sort of. In the thick of a rollout … what's up?'

'I need you to run a query on the student database.'

'Can't you?'

'No. I can't login.' *Please don't ask me why.*

'OK. Send me the details. I'll run it tonight.'

'It's urgent. I need it yesterday.'

A pause.

'Send it through.'

'I want a student with …' What? I racked my brain for where to start. 'A name like "chalk".'

Another pause.

'Okaaay. What sort of *like*? Looks like chalk, sounds like chalk, hobbies include collecting chalk?'

'Whatever you've got,' I said.

A full minute passed, while I watched the cursor pulsing on the screen. Then his reply came.

'Not much there. Best I got is Ryan Faulk.'

'Is he an exchange student? Sorry, meant to say limit the search to exchange students.'

'Nope.'

Damn.

I snatched up Hiero's third sheet and ran my eye over it again.

That's when I noticed the 'a' in chalky had an umlaut. Faint, but there.

I typed: 'Okay. Forget chalk. Just give me students from Germanic countries.'

While I waited I opened a web browser, and searched maps for 'Underway'. It gave me the visual equivalent of a shrug, so I tried splitting the search term into 'Under way'. That retrieved three results, one in the US, and two in the UK.

Perhaps, if the target were German, I needed to translate it first? I opened another browser tab and entered Underway into a translator. The translation appeared: *unterwegs*.

That word tickled the back of my brain, but I had no idea why.

I poked around with it, using my limited German. Apparently it could mean on the way, on the road. Even on the run. Was Hiero going to murder on the run?

Two minutes passed this time before Matt responded, and then a list spewed onto my screen. It had to be twenty names long or more. This was getting me nowhere. Maybe the umlaut was just fly crap.

My mind returned to the murder template's 'When'. The first sheet had a time, albeit cryptic—''Neath the Rising Sun'. The second was simply vague: 'A celebration'. But this sheet had no time at all. Nothing but 'TBD'—To Be Decided. Big help.

Did I need to think more lateral? Maybe TBD stood for something else. I squeezed my mind sideways. Maybe it was an abbreviation for a time period, a celebration, a season …

I dragged my Skype connection with Matthew to one side, opened yet another browser tab, and searched for definitions of TBD.

The first result was something called TBD Fest. My pulse quickened. Clicking around the site I discovered that TBD Fest was 'a multi-day festival that embraces creativity through music, art, design, food, and ideas.'

Perfect.

My mind filled with a vision of students thronging a stage, surging half-seen to the music, and prowling at its edges in the near-dark, Hiero.

But after my initial excitement I saw that the festival had just been held in Sacramento, US, not Somewhere, Europe.

Returning to the results of my search I discovered that TBD might be a record label, a restaurant, an organic food importer, or an accountancy firm. It could mean To Be Delayed, To Be Deleted, To Be Discontinued.

Equally well it might stand for Tick-borne Disease, Tibetan Book of the Dead, or Triazabicyclodecene (good for all your Horner-Wadsworth-Emmons reactions needs).

It could signify The Best Deceptions.

In short it could mean just about anything.

It could even mean Tipsy Borderline Drunk, which was becoming more appealing with every minute I sat in the internet café.

It took a memory of Li Min's forever stilled body to snap me out of my self-pity.

Only then did I gain the presence of mind to step back. Perhaps I was being *too* lateral. Hiero's second sheet, the one foretelling Li Min's murder, had been figurative, slantwise. But the first sheet, detailing the attempted murder of Rhianne Goldman had been mostly straight down the line.

I activated Skype again and typed another message: 'Give me the cities of all exchange students that did humanities last semester.' Li Min had returned to her home city at the end of semester. Perhaps Chalky, whoever he or she was, would too?

Scant seconds elapsed before another list rolled up my screen. It included many exchange students from Western Europe. Two girls and a guy from Strasbourg, which was French but might as well be German. Another girl from Copenhagen.

I scanned the cities listed there, until my gaze struck one: Vienna, Austria.

Vienna. Now I remembered why *unterwegs* had made my brain itch. Johann 'Jack' Unterweger. Bestselling Viennese author, TV host … serial killer.

The same Jack Unterweger that had been on Hiero's prepubescent reading list.

A chill stole over my body. What exactly was Hiero doing?

Not wanting the answer, I asked, 'Which student lives in Vienna?'

'Annika Kreider,' came the reply.

Annika Kreider. The name caused a flash of recall. Didn't she take my comparative literature course? A tall, blonde girl with serious eyes. She had come to me to discuss a project proposal—a taxonomy of narrative forms in early twentieth century Prussian literature. It had sounded deadly dull.

On a hunch I searched for that name and 'chalk', and was immediately rewarded: Kreider, derived from *kreide*, the German word for chalk.

Chalky. I'd found my man. Woman.

Jack Unterweger had killed at least twelve women over a span of seventeen years. Worse, he'd been convicted of the first murder, jailed, released, become a celebrity, and 'helped' police attempt to solve murders he himself had committed after his release from prison. All women. All strangled with their own brassieres.

Hiero was gunning for females. I could add that to the next search.

Next? For a moment I'd begun to think I was playing a game.

I asked for her phone number in Vienna, but Matt could only find an address. I copied that down, and said, 'Thanks, Matt. Hope you get your rollout done.'

'No probs, Professor,' he replied. 'Glad to help.'

Professor? He never called me professor. Matt's rollout mustn't have been going so smoothly.

The last thing I did before logging off was to send Kim an email. They say communication is vital to marriage. A degree in literature doesn't help any. My email simply said: 'I'm in the shit.'

15

I crept up from the internet café and onto a street flowing with nightclubbers, and an hour later, arrived outside a hotel that had metal grilles over its windows.

From the number of barely dressed women that approached me on the street, I gathered the hotel charged by the hour. The receptionist took my cash and my name, Steve McQueen (mental note to come up with a fake name beforehand next time), and didn't ask for ID.

When I stumped up the stairs and found my room, a cleaner's cart was parked in the corridor outside. Inside I found a Filipino lady talking into a phone and jouncing a pillow from its cover with one arm. She glanced at me without stalling her conversation, pulled a fresh pillow cover onto the pillow with the phone pinched in the crook of her neck, and exited the room into the corridor, tugging the door shut behind her.

It wasn't clear whether she had actually finished cleaning the room. I took a shower and found a wreath of hair clinging to the drain, but perhaps that was a feature. Like the paper sash they leave over toilets.

When I exited the bathroom, wrapped in a towel, I laid another towel on the bed. The bed had a spread on it, but its pattern was the kind that masks dirt and stains. The kind that can get away with being washed once a year.

From the bedside table I pulled the telephone and a slab-like phone book. Pages had been torn from it in many places, maybe for a phone number, maybe for a handkerchief, maybe for a lot of reasons. I flipped through it with only a vague notion of what I was looking for.

A lot of flipping later, I stumbled onto my first pawnshop. It was called Happy Pawn.

I'd researched the dark side of pawnshops in Thailand and Taiwan for my novel, and hoped it would apply to Hong Kong. As my fingers punched the phone buttons, I couldn't suppress a shiver of excitement to be calling one up now.

When the call connected, I got a barrage of Cantonese.

I said, 'English?' and the party hung up. Placing a finger under the next pawnshop, I dialled again, with the same result. The third call reached an answering machine. Its message was in English, and was telling me about a number of businesses, including a pawnshop, when the message cut out and a dry voice said, 'Huh?'

'Is this the Sing Ping pawn shop?'

'Huh,' said the voice, using the term now in the affirmative.

'I was looking to purchase an item, and wanted to know—'

'Huh,' said the voice again, the word now meaning, 'Hurry the hell up and tell me what you want.'

'I wanted to buy a ...' I found I had to cross a threshold to finish the sentence, like a hiccup that wanted out. 'Passport,' I finished.

'Uh-huh,' said the voice.

Progress.

'What kind?' it continued.

'Australian,' I said.

'New or doctor.'

I gathered he meant an entirely new passport or an alteration to an existing one.

'I have a passport, but need to alter the details, the name and number.'

'Doctor, uh-huh. Chip?'

'What?'

'It chipped?'

How could a paper booklet be *chipped*? I had no idea what Mr Huh was on about.

'I don't know. How do I tell?'

'Feel cover. Is it fat or thin?'

I lugged my briefcase onto the bed beside me and retrieved my passport. I flipped open its blue cover and pressed it between my fingers.

'Thin, I think,' I said.

'Ha-huh,' said the voice. 'Good. Easy. Cost seventeen nine, nine, nine. Bargain.'

Eighteen *thousand*!

'Look, I've only got nine grand—*nine* oh, oh, oh—and I need half of that to buy a plane ticket.'

A pause.

'Okay, I do you budget.'

I had no idea what a budget passport was, but I said okay. He asked me if I wanted to courier it over and back, but I said I'd come—I had no way of guaranteeing I ever saw my passport again. He gave me directions and hung up.

The pawnshop was nothing like what I'd imagined, and neither was the man to whom I'd spoken. His shop, which was in actual fact for electronic appliances—stereos, camcorders, laptops—was well-lit and polished, glass and chrome, on the third level of a shopping mall. The man himself was clean-cut in a grey suit. He wore a red bow tie, and gold cufflinks gleamed beneath his suit sleeve. A wisp of grey hair floated above the dome of his head, a failed comb-over. When I arrived, he was speaking to customers browsing in the shop, which was how I recognised him.

Two anxious minutes later, the customers left, and I sidled up to the counter and whispered, 'Passport?'

He said, 'Audio?' and walked me through to a booth that formed an alcove in the store for listening to headphones. He gestured toward a seat and, as I sat, took the passport I held out to him. He disappeared into a back room, and without missing a beat reappeared a moment later to talk to other customers.

Sing Ping Electronics was utterly unlike the image of passport-forging pawnshops I'd formed from researching the black market for my novel. Maybe it was just Hong Kong.

To look the part, I clasped a set of noise-cancelling headphones over my ears and ramped the volume up on the attached device. Its buttons were no bigger than pimples, the whole device swallowed in the grip of an anti-theft vice.

An hour later, while crooning, trance-inducing vocals told me I couldn't outrun some guy's bullet, I was getting restless. I crossed and recrossed my legs, and my gaze kept hunting for the store owner, looking for a sign that my passport was done.

He floated through the room ignoring me, impeccably dressed, unflappably smiling.

By coming here I had thought I would be able to safeguard my passport. But what if it simply disappeared? I wasn't about to go to the police.

As if on cue, a pair of police officers strolled past the shopfront. My eyes were drawn to the steel bulk of the gun holstered on the nearest officer's hip. If it was standard issue, it was probably a Smith & Wesson Model 10, a six-shot, double-action revolver.

Guns have always fascinated me in the same way snakes do, and I had researched them for my novel in unwarranted depth.

They come in so many varieties, but all boil down to one simple, efficient mechanism. The hammer strikes a combustive powder, which explodes in a pressure wave that is channelled along a (possibly rifled) tunnel to fling a small, dense object or objects through the air and into flesh, which is crushed and torn by the impact.

Typically, blood leaks out of the target, taking with it the magic that turns the universe's most complex arrangement of atoms into pig chow.

A crude mechanism. But like the combustion engine, wrapped up in shining steel it seems modern, even elegant.

I realised with a start that I had been staring at the gun. When I glanced up, I found the officer's eyes on me. I swivelled on my chair and attempted to dig the music.

Forty-five minutes later I felt a tap on my shoulder. I turned to be greeted by the benevolent gaze of the pawnshop owner. In his hand was a parcel, which he gave to me. When I had counted out the money—and he had double-checked my counting—he said, 'Thank you, sir. Shop here again.' He turned away, paused, and turned back to me long enough to say, 'Dress down a little,' and gave me a wink.

I *am* dressed down, I thought. I'm not wearing a tie.

In a toilet cubicle around the corner from the shop I tore open the package—and breathed a sigh of relief when inside it I found my passport. Well, *a* passport. It no longer claimed to be the passport of Jonathan Donald Griffen. The photo was still me, but the name alongside it said Trevor Scott Williams. The number had been altered too, and inside I found a rash of immigration stamps for Hong Kong and cities scattered throughout Southeast Asia that hadn't been there before. Trevor was younger than me by four years (mental note to put a spring in my step). Clipped to the passport, a barely legible note said, 'Expat in Hong Kong'.

Back at the hotel I stayed long enough to cut my hair with a beard trimmer I'd picked up from a convenience store near the hotel. When I was done I bowed my head toward the mirror and strained my eyes to check the job. The shave had revealed a white crescent of scar tissue carved into the side of my skull. A memory of the fall that had caused it flashed through my mind—a dive into deep snow and the numbing strike of a ski blade. And Kim's voice, 'Jack, are you—'

I shook it off.

My cheeks were disappearing beneath a thick, salt-and-pepper stubble, and I touched the trimmer to it before deciding to leave it.

In a bag on the bed lay a few other items I had procured with my precious cash. A t-shirt, blue jeans, joggers. I stripped off my shirt and trousers and dressed in the new clothes. When I looked again into the mirror I saw the image of a man attempting to cling to a childhood long faded. Fine.

I tilted my chin up and stared the man down. That man wasn't just any guy; he was a gypsy poet. A rambler, a collector of experiences, one whose senses were flung wide open to any morsel of life that might happen to fall within his reach.

For a moment, an urge took me, stronger than the desire to reach Annika Kreider before Hiero. I wanted to *write*. I felt it deep as my bones. The upswell of the Muse missing for so long. I knew without a shadow of a doubt that if I could sit at my laptop, or over a notebook, I could knit the sentences that would diagnose my life.

Strange, that I picked that moment to finally come clean on the reason for the embryo of a novel I had brooded over so long: it was not to stake claim to professional kudos, or even for the creative joy. I wanted to write—*needed* to write—to work out how the hell my life had run off the tracks, and parted company with the two people in seven billion I cherished most of all.

16

It is physically impossible to make yourself not be nervous. To be aware you are nervous causes nerves.

This realisation came to me at the airport as I was striding toward the metal detector standing between me and my departure lounge. Sweat sprang out on my forehead, and tickled me behind the ears.

What if the police had circulated my photo? What if the passport alterations were obvious? I had no way to tell they weren't. What if my face tugged three ways when I tried to lie to immigration?

By chance I caught my own reflection in a mirror before I joined the end of the queue for the metal detector. My scalp was freshly shorn, my face grizzly, my clothes downplayed, but hanging at the end of my arm was something that jarred with everything else: my briefcase.

Without breaking stride, I veered into a bathroom as if that had been my intent all along.

I placed my briefcase on a bench, snapped its catches back, and opened it. Its contents were a mess of the paraphernalia of a professional academic. I retrieved the remaining papers from Hiero's leather folder, and stowed them in a jeans pocket. Then I pawed through the papers piled in the base of the briefcase—a couple of bad essays I hadn't returned to their authors because I'd written expletives in the margins, a journal paper on yet another interpretation of *Beowulf*, a form letter from the university extolling its new workload management system, and a parking ticket I'd fought hard to have waived. I dug through the litter and back through time until I reached the faux-leather bottom and saw the stain left by a banana that had once, long ago, lain there forgotten for weeks.

Why did I never clean this crap out?

I gathered it up and dumped it into a bin.

Tucked into pouches and pockets on the inside of the briefcase lid were smaller items—pens, a thumbdrive, a photo of Kim and Tracey, conference name badges, and a tangle of rubber bands that were beginning to crack with age. I took the thumbdrive, photo, and the Sheaffer pen engraved with my name, a gift from the university for fifteen years of mind-strain. The rest I tossed into the bin.

The inside of the briefcase was bare now, but for the lint collected in its corners and creases, and a pack of business cards held together by a bulldog clip. I picked up the cards and squeezed the clip jaws open.

I flipped through the cards. There were mementos from GPs, physicians, sleep specialists, dieticians, endocrinologists, cardiologists—this set I called the *Meds*. Then came the psychologists and a psychiatrist (who tried to convince me I was thinking my heart into a terminal velocity)—this set I called the *Heads*. I had a more productive conversation with the acupuncturist. He at least recognised I was the nail that had been hit with a variety of hammers, and made me a cup of tea. He, together with a herbalist and a naturopath, made up the last set—the *Teds* (most lovable and cuddly) and rounded out the deck. The Joker was an engineering consultant, a friend, with whom I'd worked to build the—at the time—cutting-edge application of tech that was my Medline. There were better devices on the market now, but that was mine. I'd helped design it. I knew what was in it.

If the paper in the base of the briefcase was the sedimentary record of my working life, this pack of cards was the same for my dance with the medical fraternity.

I had swung down the line from one partner to the next, and finally fallen off the procession with this diagnosis: idiopathic postural orthostatic tachycardia syndrome.

Idiopathic from the Greek, *idios*, meaning 'one's own' and *pathos*, meaning 'suffering'. That is, your own unique brand of pain.

Sorry, Mr Griffen, but we don't know why your heart sometimes stops beating when it stays too long above 160 beats per minute. Best to live *calm*, eh?

To my mind, that *idiopathic* resembles *idiot* is no accident.

Idiopathic attached to any diagnosis is its doom. It means the sample space for your disease is one. You're it. And medical science doesn't do ones. Clinical studies, and the drug companies that fund them, most definitely don't do ones, unless the one is followed by billion.

So the diagnosis is your polite instruction to leave the party. No more dancing for you. A part of your biology, or psychology, or pathology, or some other -ology, is irreparably, mystifyingly screwed. Get over it, and get on with whatever life it leaves you. And be aware that unpaid bills will be handed over to our debt collection agency. Have a nice day.

I never sank so low as to get an aura-photo, but what's the bet even that would have come back green with purple polka dots?

I pressed the cards together, re-clipped them, held them over the bin, and hesitated.

That pack of cards had become part of me. Every one a joker, really. I knew it was a sick kind of nostalgia to hold on to them.

But I put the pack in my pocket.

With a final look at my forlorn briefcase, I exited the restroom.

Striding again toward the queue I felt naked.

When I stepped beneath the detector, it shrieked at me. I ignored the attendant's instruction to try again, and instead walked over to her, pointing at where I imagined my failed pacemaker lay.

Knowing my body was going to fail every metal detection test was strangely soothing. I felt no tension waiting to see if it would go off. It always did.

She called over a male officer, who frisked me, and gave me the okay.

At immigration, I lied like a pro, and the officer stamped my passport with a smile and told me to have a nice flight.

As I joined the flow of travellers heading for the departure gates, it occurred to me why it had been so easy: barring the odds and ends in my pockets, and the chunk of silicon near my heart, almost nothing remained of Jack Griffen. I had even left my name behind.

17

Thirty-thousand feet in the night sky above the sands of the ancient Persian Empire, modern-day Iraq, I had finally found calm.

A calm that was broken minutes later, at 6.39 am Hong Kong time.

Transit at Dubai to the Vienna leg had passed in a blur. My heart had been beating at a leisurely 80 bpm. Seated in Cattle Class of the Emirates Airlines Airbus A380, my decisions were limited to whether I would have the satay chicken with rice or the beef and vegetables, and when precisely to empty my bladder of its beer ballast. Until the plane landed, I was in Fate's iron grip.

After the cabin lights dimmed, I switched on my personal light and pulled out my fifteen-year pen and a notebook I had bought at the airport. I doodled in its margins and began turning over in my mind the plot of my novel.

The small video screen embedded in the chair in front of me was a distracting glare, and it was while navigating its menus to kill the screen that I discovered I could access the internet.

With a moment's hesitation, I called up my email.

My inbox was full of stale letters, but for three new messages, marked in bold. Two were spam. The third was from Matthew Price, the university systems administrator.

I opened it and read the following message:

> Jack,
> I looked into your login problem. Not sure what's going on there, but—get this—your account was hacked a couple of weeks back. I don't know what the hacker got, but I traced the attack origin to a cloud server on the west coast of the US.
> I hope you don't mind, but I returned fire and hacked the

server. Turns out it's currently registered to a H. Beck. Does that name mean anything to you? I poked through the server's file system and found the only active branch of the tree besides security patches (hah!) is a Wordpress blog. I'll paste the address below. It's private, but I dug the admin password out: ConRadsh3art. Doesn't make any sense to me, but maybe you'll have more luck.

Sorry to disturb you. The attacker is probably just some script-kiddy who got hold of a hacking library, but better to be safe …
Cheers, Matt.

My heart was no longer beating at 80 bpm.

I quit the email and entered the blog address Matt had sent me into a web browser. After an agonisingly slow load time, a title blazed on the screen, bright in the dim cabin: *Blood and Ink* by Hieronymus Beck.

My eyes flicked to the title of the first blog post: Chapter 1.

Below it, a few short paragraphs. Reading them, the hairs on my neck stood up.

My thigh muscles clench and unclench. Much longer and they will begin to cramp. The smell of crushed sedge rises from beneath my feet, as my ears strain for her footfall. It's nearly 7.36 pm, and she keeps time like the Japanese Metro. Not much longer now.

I hear the *rap-rap* of runners on asphalt. A quick glance confirms, even in the darkness, the telltale pink light of her Bluetooth headphones bobbing along the path. In my right hand, the heavy wooden handle of the *kyoketsu-shoge*; in my left, the coarse braid of its cord, two feet of length. My entire body clenches, ready to spring. Three … two … one …

I burst from the bushes as she passes—and the *shoge*'s ring snags on a branch, whips me around. We collide and go down in a tangle of limbs. She writhes under me, and I start giggling, because we must look like kids having a fight. She bows her back to throw me, lifting her head clear of the ground, and I loop the cord around her neck. It pulls taut on her skin and I cross fists to tighten the choke—when she crunches her knee into my groin.

The stars fall from the sky. I barely notice the *shoge*'s handle clock my forehead as she springs up, with it still wrapped around her neck. I hear her sprint away—*RAP-Rap-Rap-rap-rap*—much faster now and fading.

But, *God*, I don't care. My entire body is a crushed nerve. And still I can hear myself giggling.

My hand went to Hiero's novel notes stowed in my back pocket. I wriggled in the seat until I could extract them. I placed the folded-up wad on the tray table, unfolded it, and smoothed the paper flat.

The topmost sheet described the (attempted) murder of Rhianne Goldman. The title of the page was Case Notes #1 for *Blood and Ink*, by Hieronymus Beck. Scanning down the creased paper, my gaze snagged on the word *kyoketsu-shoge*. I couldn't believe it. Hiero had blogged his failed attempt to murder Rhianne Goldman.

With clumsy fingers I peeled the top sheet away, and slipped it beneath the stack. The sheet revealed was titled, Case Notes #2. I knew every word on the page without reading it.

My gaze flicked back to the slow-motion-car-crash of Hiero's blog. I scrolled down, whipping past blocks of text, more blog entries. Words jumped off the screen, and I sketched his movements piecemeal. A scramble to get to my office after the abortive assault. A midnight wander through Nedlands. More placenames from the university campus, which Hiero had apparently haunted before flying to Hong Kong. I scrolled until I found the date I wanted, yesterday's. Below its title, 'Chapter 8', was another handful of paragraphs.

Deed done. The heroin flooding Li Min's system has shut down her heart.

Some girls look good with short hair. Li Min looks good dead.

I don't mean to be cruel. It's true. A quiet has settled over her fragile body, now that her anxious spirit has set sail on eternal waters. Her skin is smooth to the touch and already cooling. With a finger, I travel over it, across her flanks, which are covered in almost microscopic down—find a small birthmark on her inner thigh I hadn't noticed before. Got to slow down, lover boy.

An idea occurs to me. I grasp her wrists and lift her arms, which have come to rest at awkward angles. I move them above her head, and bow them into a heart shape.

Ah, true love.

Then I'm laughing. What a prick.

I tweak her nose, and begin the mop up.

Condom. My underwear—third wear, turn them inside out. (Shit, I wouldn't be surprised if the washing machine spits these guys out.) *Her* underwear, just to be safe. Wipe off the lamp switch, drawer handles and top, door handle. In the living room, let's see. Did I touch the kitchen taps? Rinse some dishes? Doesn't sound like me. Do 'em anyway. Wine glass, the one without the lipstick. Glossy magazine. Pretending to be interested in wood-turning—those were hard yards, but worth it. Light switch and done. Need to hurry now. The MC is coming.

'Night, honey,' I say into the quiet apartment, and exit stage left.

I finished reading the entry and lay back in my seat. My skin prickled with heat all over my body, and my temples were throbbing. I flicked my wrist to see the Medline's display—in the orange, okay.

I blinked and read the blog post again. Still couldn't believe it. Not only had Hiero recorded how he tried to murder Rhianne Goldman, he had recorded how he actually murdered Li Min and put it on the *internet*. Sure, the blog was private. But it would only take the click of a button to publish it to the world.

And again there was that reference to MC, just like the one I had found in Li Min's journal. She had written it in anticipation of Hiero's arrival. But she had written MC Griffen.

What did it mean? It made no sense.

I shut my eyes, but behind my lids blazed an image brighter than the screen—the memory of Li Min's lifeless body, which shock had seared onto my brain. I tried to push it away, but it didn't budge. I had to open my eyes.

My thoughts swam for minutes until I gathered the strength to close Hiero's blog. I switched back to my email and wrote a message to Kim.

Kim—still in the shit.

You have to see this, and then, please, forward it to the Murdoch police, with the subject, Re: Jack Griffen and Rhianne Goldman.

Go to the URL I'll paste below. It's a blog of the little psycho recording what he is doing. It's there in black and white, an account of how he murdered a girl in a Hong Kong apartment.

The blog is private, but you can enter it with user 'admin' and password 'ConRadsh3art'.

Now do you think I have attention deficit?

Message sent, I switched off the screen and put away Hiero's notes and my notebook. The urge to write had evaporated. I pressed the call button, and when a hostess arrived I asked for the stiffest drink they stocked, wondering at what point they would refuse to serve alcohol.

Turns out to be the fifth drink.

18

Dear Professor Griffen

My name is Hieronymus Beck. I'm writing to petition you to accept me as a graduate student in your Modern Literature program for the first semester of 2015.

Wait! Hear me out! I'm already accepted in the Linguistics grad program, and am all paid up (sorry, it's cheaper than your class). I wouldn't add any admin load, so I guess I'm just asking for the permission to sit at your feet.

Jokes aside, I've attached a resume. But you're probably more interested in what makes me tick, right?

It was my father who taught me to love Story. Joy, according to him, is either a swift clean bowel movement, or a good book. Sometimes both at the same time.

My mother doesn't care much for fiction. Can't understand why anyone would waste time with reading made-up stuff. She says if fewer people escaped from real life, real life would be a heck of a lot better.

But me? Story is life.

I haven't met you in the flesh, but I feel like I know you. I've read every one of your short stories I could get my hands on—'Full Metal Jacket Potato' is sheer genius!—and I suspect we're kindred spirits.

Kind regards, and breathless with hope,

Hieronymus Beck.

19

My ears popped.

We were dropping through dense cloud toward Vienna.

The PA had announced that the entertainment services would shortly be switched off. I wasn't sure if that included the internet in Economy, but I hastened to check my email just in case.

There was one new email, from Kim.

> Jack, now I'm starting to worry, goddamn you.
>
> If it were only ADD, I could live with that. Did you break your crown again, Jack? Get on the bottle?
>
> I checked the URL you sent me. Yes, it exists, but no, the password you sent me doesn't open it.
>
> Look, I'm sorry. I just read what I wrote. I'm concerned. Where are you, anyway?

I had to suppress the urge to swear. I opened another browser tab, entered the address of Hiero's blog, and typed the password, ConRadsh3art.

And in response I got an Access Forbidden.

I switched back to my email and typed a message to IT Matt. He got the password once, he could get it again.

But before I could hit send, the browser died. The screen switched to a world map, showing a little plane icon closing in on Vienna. In-flight entertainment, including internet access, had been shut down.

No suppressing the swearing this time.

We had landed, and I was still stewing on the failed password when immigration loomed, and a new fear spiked my belly. I'd had hours on the plane to concoct my story—make that, Trevor Williams' story—and had done nothing. I was walking up cold to a guy in uniform trained to spot nervous liars.

I joined the end of the line, which was moving at a snail's pace. When I reached its head, the officer greeted me in a heavy Teutonic accent.

'Good morning, sir.'

I looked into his eyes and saw his X-ray gaze. Might as well throw my hands up and yell, 'Sanctuary!'

'Mmm,' I managed, and deposited my passport onto the counter.

With a smile, he flicked it open.

My mind raced. Was it more suspicious to watch him or not, or a mix of both? Maybe that was *precisely* what they looked for. My scalp tingled with the sensation that means you're going to sweat.

Don't think about it. Don't think about it.

Wasn't that Sibelius good? Better with a drink. I could use a drink.

'You've had a haircut, sir,' he said, looking at his screen with a smile and tapping at his keyboard with deliberation.

Haircut! *You idiot.* Was that suspicious?

I just smiled and ran a hand over my scalp, not trusting myself to speak.

'And what is the purpose of your visit to *Vien*, Mr Williams?'

Purpose?

'Visiting friends,' I said.

'Without luggage?' he said, a slight crease forming over his brow, still not looking at me.

'Good friends,' I said with a breathy laugh.

'You like Mozart?' he said. 'We have a little statue to Mozart.'

'I like Mozart.' Love *Sibelius.*

He tapped some more at the keyboard, gaze still inscrutable.

Then: 'I hate Mozart.'

—Bang!

He stamped the passport. I nearly wet my pants.

'Have a good stay in our city, Mr Williams,' he said, and nodded to the next person in line.

Just like that I was through.

I had gone ten paces when another officer came alongside me and said, 'Would you please step this way, Mr Williams.'

And so I discovered that what Mr Huh of Hong Kong's Sing Ping pawnshop meant when he said 'budget passport' was that the man I was pretending to be had flags on his passport. He had been caught travelling with small amounts of marijuana that he claimed were medicinal, but which were obviously to be sold to make a little extra holiday money.

The result of this was a strip search.

They got two-thirds the way through before my Medline went into the red zone, and when I told them that if I didn't calm down, they would soon be frisking my corpse, I guess they figured they had scared Mr Williams enough and didn't want a lawsuit on their hands.

No mention was made of the name Jack Griffen inscribed on my fifteen-year pen. I guess they thought Mr Williams was a petty thief as well as small-time drug trafficker.

I cleared customs with a curious sense of relief and the smell of latex on my skin.

20

The first thing I did on the other side of Viennese customs was to stop at one of the airport's currency exchange counters and convert my Hong Kong dollars into Euros.

The next was to locate a free internet terminal.

In my search I passed huge rain-streaked windows through which taxi headlights glowed. The blurred forms of travellers threw shadows across the glass. With a shiver, I realised that out there, somewhere, Hiero was probably already prowling.

I emailed Matt for the password to get back into Hiero's blog, and looked up directions to the address I had for Annika Kreider, Chalky. The address wasn't near a subway station, so too far to walk. Speed was of the essence, and anyway, a rain squall had engulfed the city. The sight of it made me spend precious minutes and precious Euros on the cheapest overcoat and hat that Hugo Boss stocked. I shrugged the coat on as I stepped outside, but the cold still took my breath away. I hailed a cab, a brown Mercedes, and gave the driver the address.

The apartment was in a tenement row beyond the ring road, in the new city which looker older than the old. The kind of place where a man had kept his daughter locked in the basement for twenty-four years. I asked the driver to wait (thinking more and more of accruing witnesses to my *not* murdering) and ran up the short flight of steps and into a cool lobby. I found a buzzer for apartment 27 and pressed it.

There was no reply, so I pressed it again.

When I was still dripping on the foyer tiles a minute later, I ran a hand across the buzzers. Voices came through the speaker like scattershot, and the door clunked open.

The building had no elevator, being only three floors high. I raced up the stairs, then along the second-floor corridor till I came to apartment 27.

I put my ear to the door and listened. I couldn't be sure, but thought I heard the muted throb of a television. I knocked long and loud.

At last, I heard a shuffling tread approach the door. It opened to reveal a woman with greying hair caught up in curlers, and a vast bosom restrained by a faded nightgown.

'*Was*?' she said through a frown. Behind her, German voices droned in the universal language of soap opera.

'I wanted—do you speak English?' I said.

The frown deepened. The door began to close.

'Wait,' I said, and placed a palm firmly in its path. 'I'm looking for Annika Kreider. It's very urgent.'

She stopped pushing the door, and the frown eased.

'Annika?' she said.

'Yes, yes.'

The old lady disappeared, leaving the door ajar. She returned and thrust a slip of paper at me. I read it, and to my dismay saw it was a forwarding address. As I turned to leave, she said, 'You are the second today.'

'I'm sorry?'

'An American,' was all she said, and shut the door.

The cold on the street was bracing after the stuffy building. The taxi driver had the engine running to keep warm, and a plume of exhaust was boiling from the rear of the car.

I slid onto the back seat and handed him the new address. He grunted, put away his newspaper, and drove.

I watched the cab fee readout rise, all the while thinking of my dwindling cash, which had already taken a hit when I converted my Hong Kong dollars to Euros at the airport.

The new address was within the old city, and frustratingly close to where we had passed not half an hour before. I again asked the driver to wait. He nodded, but demanded payment. I counted the cash into his outstretched hand, leapt onto the pavement and hurried to the door of a slim townhouse of five storeys. Inside, I found the glass lobby door unlocked. I took the elevator to the fourth floor, muscles tense, and was soon rapping on the door of apartment 4c.

The door swung inward under the blows of its own accord. I ran my fingers along the doorjamb and felt the sharp pain of a splinter. Someone had forced the lock.

I shoved the door back onto its hinges and entered.

Another quiet living room. Bars of muted winter light sheared the gloom in places, and revealed a clutter of tall leather couches and armchairs. Standing over them were pedestal lamps and dark bookcases, crammed together with barely enough space to manoeuvre. Beyond lay a kitchenette beneath a large, curtained window. Dark doorways gaped left and right—I thought of what I'd found in the bedroom in Hong Kong.

But to get to either, I would first have to wade through the wreckage. Every bookshelf had been emptied, its books flung down. Vases and picture frames from a mantel had been swept into a heap, and I saw at least three paintings or prints that had been torn from their hooks and smashed on the coffee table.

I was looking at a thorough ransacking.

Or something meant to look like one.

I picked my way through the debris, hearing a crunch and tinkle under my feet more than once, and toward the left doorway. It led to a small bathroom. The mirrored door of the vanity cabinet hung at an angle from one hinge, and its contents had been smashed and spread across the tiles.

I returned to the living room, and tiptoed to the other doorway. It led to the bedroom, which had also been turned upside down, but was mercifully empty of bodies.

Back in the living room I swept a pile of magazines from the couch and sat, sucking on the finger that ached dully at the splinter site. Dust motes drifted in the glancing light.

The taxi was waiting, the fare rising by the minute, but I needed to sit and clear my head.

Annika Kreider was home fresh from university. It was reasonable to guess she hadn't found a job yet and slipped into a daytime routine. Had Hiero expected to find her here, and flown into a rage when he found the apartment empty?

On the wall, a great glass-fronted clock chimed the hour—ten chimes—then fell silent. But the second hand kept winding around. Tick, tick ... all the way to the heat death of the universe, and the end of all clocks.

How many murders before we got there? One less if I got my backside into gear.

'What are the chances this break-in is a coincidence?' I said.

—And was surprised when a voice like my own answered.

'Possible, but you'd be a fool to believe it.'

It *was* my voice.

No, it was my daughter's voice. It was Tracey's.

It was both. My voice in the still air of that wrecked apartment; and hers in the vault of my mind.

Okaaay.

It seemed my novel wanted out in any way it could, and if that meant hijacking real life, then so be it.

It had taken Kim and Tracey to leave my life for me to realise how much I talked to myself. My next thought was that perhaps I was finally going mad. The concoction of drugs I'd tried over the years to heal my idio-*pathetic* heart had finally congealed into a mutant mess that was eating me away from the inside.

Then I remembered that a young girl's life was hanging by a thread.

So I decided to play along. What did I have to lose, except my mind?

'This has to be Hiero's doing,' I replied.

'But why?' said Tracey with my voice. 'He didn't trash Li Min's apartment. He just ...'

I looked the room over, still rooted to the couch. It was every person's nightmare, wasn't it? To return home to find that a stranger had been in your house, in your space—the space in which you lived so much of your life. Had touched your things with their fingers. Leered at your photos. Tracked mud over your memories.

Break-ins. Police statistics listed them in the category Crime Against Property. They should be listed under Crime Against Person, Grievous Spiritual Harm.

'He wanted to scare Annika,' I said.

An image of Tracey leapt from my mind and into that room. She turned her green eyes toward me. She had freckles again. (Why did I give her childhood freckles?)

She shook her head. 'It's wrong. Hiero doesn't scare. He charms.'

'Then maybe there is something here he wanted.'

I carefully retraced my steps through the wreckage, while in my mind's eye, Tracey probed among the fallen books. I felt glad for the company.

I lingered, looking for a pattern, a detail at odds with the chaos of destruction.

But nothing jarred. If it had hung, it had been torn down; if it could be moved, it had been flung. The only exceptions were the largest breakables, vases, a mirror, a porcelain lion. They had not been smashed.

I touched a large vase of modern design.

'Why isn't this on the floor in pieces?'

'Noise?' suggested Tracey.

Noise? I looked again at the vase and realised it would have been impossible to break without making a tremendous racket. Looked at from that perspective, every broken item in the room was small—small enough to crush beneath, say, a muffling couch cushion. The destruction appeared too controlled to be the result of a temper tantrum.

I winked at Tracey. 'Clever girl,' and wondered if that was a kind of arrogance.

My mind now primed to think of sound, I noticed, tucked into a corner of the bookcase, a sleek silver stereo that had also avoided destruction. Its speakers put out a faint hum and I turned the volume a notch down to prompt an electronic readout. Crisp green digits indicated it was set very high.

Maybe Hiero had broken in, turned the stereo up high for cover, then carefully, methodically, smashed every one of Annika Kreider's belongings that could safely be destroyed without raising the alarm.

Wonderful. But why?

Snaking through the wreckage at my feet was a cord. Lifting it with a finger, I traced it to where the telephone lay smothered beneath books.

'You sure you want to do that?' said Tracey. Her heart-shaped face held a wry grin. I decided I would handle it from here. She disappeared and I was alone.

I scooped the phone from the floor and tapped the hook till I got a dial tone. Then I called international, Australia, and the directory by heart. I asked for Price, suburb of Subiaco. The female voice said she had found the number, and would I like to be put through.

I said yes, and waited.

It was late afternoon in Perth, Australia. Fifty-fifty Matt was in bed after an all-nighter. Too bad for him.

While I waited I thought about the long shot I was trying. It had taken Hiero less than a day to write up the murder of Li Min, judging by the timestamp on his blog post. What if he was even now blogging his actions? If I could find Hiero before he got to Annika, and forestall him, I wouldn't even need to find her.

A voice came on the line, male. I began to speak, then realised it was not Matt's voice. It was his father's. And this was an answering machine.

I waited for the beep, and said, 'Matt, it's me, Jack. I need you to get me the password to that blog again. The one you gave me stopped working. Please hurry. This is urgent.' I paused. 'Deadly urgent.'

I emerged from the townhouse into the heart of Vienna to discover the taxi gone, lured away by a better fare.

It was cold. Sunlight glittered on runnels of rainwater racing along the footpath. I jammed my hands in my pockets, hunched my shoulders and walked just to be moving. Shopfronts came and went, venting warm air across my path, each burst full of the aromas of perfume, or pastries, or frying meat. I turned a corner, and then another, and a great plaza opened before me. At its centre, standing massive and solid, was a building large as a fairytale keep. A sign told me it was in fact the Cathedral of Saint Stephen, which had stood on that spot for 900 years—battered by the passions of war, and the steady gnawing of the elements, but erect still. Knots of tourists were scattered across the plaza, taking photos, or craning their necks to take in the cathedral's bulk.

In another life I would have joined the gawkers. But from the corner of my eye, I spied an internet café. I hurried toward it, with the rueful acknowledgement that the internet was fast becoming my chief vice. I had been surrounded by strangers now for seventy-two hours straight (barring hallucinations) and was hankering for friends. Hell, acquaintances would do.

Inside the warm café, I began drafting an email to Kim—an argument really, for my sanity—when a message arrived in my inbox.

It was from Matt Price.

I stuck the message for Kim into the drafts folder and brought up Matt's. Had he got my voice message already? He made no mention of it. It appeared we had crossed wires. He said,

Jack.

You're right, the password has been changed.

I checked back on the server for evidence my own hack had been spotted. That looks okay, but I realised the password I gave you would have expired an hour at most after I gave it to you. Whoever set up that server is some tight-arse. A cron job randomly cycles the password every hour and texts it to a phone number. It would be a great system, *if* he'd locked the server down properly. >-)

I've set up my own silent service to copy the password to your email account, so you can login to the blog any time. Hope that's okay.

Later, Matt.

No sooner had I closed Matt's message, than another appeared. I opened it and found a single alphanumeric word: p3QUod4u. I called up Hiero's blog and entered the password, hunt-and-peck on the keyboard. The screen filled with the latest entry. I was in.

More than that. My long shot had struck.

Then I began to read and my heart sank, suddenly a deadweight in my chest.

Cathartic.

That's the word. It was tremendously *cathartic* to rip Chalky's apartment to shreds. To grasp every item—no matter the item—and hurl it down. She was such a prissy person. Perhaps I should have let her live long enough to see the mess. The sight of it might have killed her.

Ah well, can't unwind the past. The person formally known as Annika Kreider is now one hundred and forty pounds of ground meat. Witness the amazing transformation, from life and warmth and voice, to inertness, a cluster of ruptured organs, food for microbes.

And the alchemy that turns this gold of life into the lead of death? A simple shove. But it has to be the *right* shove at the right time.

And how had I, the magician, learned the secret of invoking this correct shove? From the train timetables I found in Chalky's apartment.

—*Train timetables*? Of course. Hiero had broken into Annika's apartment to learn everything he could about her movements. He'd ransacked the place to sow confusion. Heavy with foreboding, I read on.

Yes, Chalky is prissy. And very orderly, bordering on obsessive. Always first to class, with her notepad and pens arranged on her desk with millimetre precision.

I found her stash of timetables, neatly marked with her travel plans in colour-coded, ruled highlights. From them I learned which train line and station she would be using today.

But I don't think she intended to *catch* the train in the manner she actually did. I found her poised on the lip of Platform 5, almost inviting destruction. It was the essence of simplicity to nudge her in the small of the back as the train approached. Her flight through the air was reminiscent of Piggy's in *Lord of the Flies*. Even to the shattered spectacles. So too was the way her body crumpled on impact. (Air Control: *Achtung, junge Dame!* You are not cleared for flight!)

But the very next paragraph confused me. It began:

But I think she intended to catch the train, not the platform.

I blinked, started again, and read the whole paragraph. And my heart flared with hope.

But I think she intended to catch the train, not the platform. She paused to survey the platform below, which was thick with moiling passengers. Her train had already arrived, and she hurried toward the stair, handbag jouncing against her hip.

Helpful guy that I am, I gave her a hand reaching the platform. Straight over the edge of the railing, and thirty death-dealing

feet to the concrete. Her flight through the air was reminiscent
of Piggy's [PASTE]

Hiero had just described how he murdered Annika.

The very next line, he began again, describing the same murder. *Almost.*
The details were different. My hope lived in the space between.

I sat back and frantically tried to corral my thoughts. Hiero's latest
blog entry described him murdering Annika—*twice*. First by shoving
her in front of a train. And then again by pushing her over the edge of a
concourse. Both 'blunt-force trauma'.

Two murders. But only one could be true.

Or neither.

This blog entry felt fresh, as if I'd caught Hiero mid-edit. And if it
described two ways he *might* murder Annika, two contingencies, it would
mean she still lived. For the moment.

The idea was electric. I gathered my things and leapt out of my chair.

On the street I collared an elderly man in a long coat.

'Vienna Hauptbahnhof. Do you know it?'

'But, of course,' he said and pointed at his feet.

I doubted very much I was standing on the rail hub of a major European
city, and my scepticism must have shown.

'Thirty metres down,' he said, 'and then five minutes by U-Bahn.'

I tore off in the direction indicated. If I had to pitch a tent and stake out
the station for the rest of the week, I would. I only hoped I didn't arrive to
find an ambulance, and police, and, well ... chalk.

21

My first miscalculation was that Vienna Hauptbahnhof was impossibly huge.

I knew it would be big, but when I asked my mind for an image of a railway station it handed me the familiar picture of one of Perth's provincial patches of concrete. Not the sprawling, multi-level hub of a European city.

This would be haystacks and needles unless I could narrow my search. Then I remembered Hiero's blog post. He hadn't just said Vienna Hauptbahnhof, he had recorded the platform. I found a digital information board and looked up Platform 5.

As I wove through the dense crowd I tried to think calm thoughts. I would find Annika. She would be surprised to see me. Then I would tell her how close she had come to death. And she would believe me.

But on reaching the platform, I found no sign of her. Or him. There was no train at the platform, so I went back and forth along the lip of the platform scanning the waiting commuters, until the weight of curious stares forced me to stop.

Escalators connected every platform to the concourse above, covering a ten-metre drop. Far enough to kill, barring a miracle. A drunk might fall that far and live, something to do with relaxed muscles. I prayed that Annika was plastered.

Farther down the platform, an elevator rose in a transparent shaft. It was a third contingency Hiero didn't seem to have covered. If Annika rode the elevator to reach the platform when the train had already arrived, then he wouldn't have the opportunity to push her in front of it *or* off the concourse. In that case, she and I could board the train together, where she would be a captive audience, and would have no choice but to hear me out.

But then again, what were the chances she would take the elevator if the train were already at the platform? Half of not much. She would choose the stairs.

And Hiero would give her that helping hand.

I swore, and had begun pacing again when I heard a scream.

The scream was abruptly drowned by a metallic screeching that tore the air and made the concrete rumble. My head twisted round in the direction of the noise. It had not come from this platform.

The mechanical screech juddered on until it finally gave out with an absurd squeak. Utter silence filled the station.

I ran towards the platform, dodging through a crowd that was flowing as if by gravity to the source of the noise.

A train was pulled up with its gleaming nose two-thirds the way along the platform. Through its windows I could see passengers sprawled over each other, their faces a mixture of embarrassed smiles and wide-eyed shock. In front of me, a wall of commuters obscured the track. A woman in a heavy coat had fainted. A man pointed at something in the far gutter. A teenager in bright blue jacket raised a mobile phone and its flash burst over the front of the train; a man turned and slapped the phone from his hand, and it clattered on the concrete.

I strained onto my tiptoes to see to the platform's edge as cries of *Hilfe*! and *Ambulanz*! rose. A minute ticked by, and another, and I could neither get to the platform edge, nor see Hiero.

A flicker of motion in the corner of my eye drew my attention, and I noticed a figure climbing the stairs to the concourse. Maybe I noticed him because he was the only person not running or standing. He reached the head of the stairs, and turned away from me. He wore a long coat with the collar pulled up and a shapeless felt hat. He broke into a loping jog with the ease of an athlete or an egotist.

Who walked calmly away from—?

My feet moved before I could complete the thought. And I was after him, my shoes slapping on the concrete. I bounded up the escalator, two and three steps at a time.

It was only as I reached the top and raced after him that I heard angry cries of *Polizei*! rise from below. A quick glance over my shoulder caught a sea of faces looking back up at me. I saw an index finger that had been thrust at the dark below the platform's edge pointed at me.

A foreboding crystallised around my heart. The man fleeing the concourse wore the same bland autumn gear as me. The cheap coat and hat I had purchased at the airport that had seemed to offer a veil of anonymity now marked me a potential murderer.

I pounded after the escaping figure, along a walkway, up another escalator, and out onto a mall, but couldn't close the gap between us. We had gone barely a hundred metres before my Medline began beeping angrily at me.

For a moment I drove myself harder. I would catch him, and if my heart exploded in the process, too bad. I would pin him to the ground with my corpse.

But I turned a corner that led onto the street, and he was gone. I scanned left and right, hunched over, hands on knees, but saw no sign of him. He had escaped.

The street was thick with taxis. I hailed one and slumped onto its back seat, gulping air. It took me a moment to recover my breath enough to speak. I gave the driver the first address that popped into my head— Annika Kreider's—and only later feigned a change of mind, and asked the driver to take me to an out-of-the-way hotel.

When I had checked into the hotel, I used the internet terminal in the lounge to log into Hiero's blog. Sure enough, he had already updated the latest entry. It now read:

> However, I don't think she intended to *catch* the train in the manner she actually did. We had a 'surprise' meeting. We chatted. I convinced her to ditch her plans and come with me to the *Tiergarten*. (I love German!) I walked her to the edge of the platform as 'our' train approached, and whispered in her ear that I was going to show her something most people never see.
>
> It was then I noticed my shadow closing in. He'd made up time. Caused me to rush.
>
> I shoved Annika in the small of the back with one arm, and feigned to save her with the other. Didn't quite get the leverage I'd wanted, but still, her flight through the air was reminiscent of

Piggy's in *Lord of the Flies*. Even to the shattered spectacles. So too was the way her body crumpled on impact. The look on her face at the end as she corkscrewed right way up was priceless.

I glanced up from the terminal. The lounge was empty but for a family seated on a couch. The son stared fixedly at a handheld game console, while the mother brushed out her daughter's hair, tutting to her husband in Russian. All was well in their world.

I spent the rest of the night mentally drafting my surrender. Time to put down the dice. Hiero was not just evil. He was insane.

22

I woke the next morning to the smell of whisky, and a head packed with sawdust.

'You really slipped in the shit this time,' said Tracey from the gloom, seated in the room's only chair. My favourite hallucination had returned. Except she would never have said 'shit'. I berated myself for the off-character dialogue.

I opened the curtains a crack, rode a wave of nausea, and in the pale light counted the minibar bottles scattered across the floor. Apparently it was all of them. A fumbling search through my wallet revealed barely enough cash to pay for the bar, let alone the room.

A residue of bourbon glimmered in the bottom of a bottle, so I tipped it above my mouth and let the dregs dribble into my throat. I was my own physician, and I had prescribed a dose of hair of the dog.

At last I tried my voice, which came out in a croak: 'How was I to know he would switch train lines?' With the back of my hand I wiped away angry tears.

Tracey watched in silence.

She watched me sniff up the last tear, and rake my hands over my prickly scalp. She said, 'He's making up the rules as he goes along, Dad,' and for a moment I felt like the child. 'Edit, cut, paste. Whatever fits his fancy.'

In a sudden pique I said, 'I'll kill him.'

Tracey's smile was mixed with pity. 'No you won't.'

Pity from my own daughter. I wasn't going to take that. I gripped the hallucination in my mind and extinguished it.

In the closet-sized bathroom I dashed water on my face and rubbed my cheeks. They were rough with stubble, but shaving was the second-last thing I wanted to do right then.

The last thing I wanted to do was get on the telephone, but I might as well charge the call to the room. In for a dime, in for a dollar.

I checked the hotel booklet for the international extension, put the phone on speaker, and dialled. My head lay heavy in my hands as I listened to the faint hiss and the ping-pong of my call racing around the globe.

A call tone, finally. Four pulses before it picked up.

'Hello?' said a voice.

'Matt.' *At last.* 'You need to give the police the passwords—'

'Mr Griffen?'

'Yeah,' I said. 'Did you hear me? You need—'

'I got your message,' he said.

'Well, never mind that. You got there ahead of me. The passwords are working, but I need you to give them to the police so they can access the blog, too.'

Silence.

'Mr Griffen …'

There it was again. *Mr Griffen*? What the hell was wrong with the kid.

'I got your message,' he repeated, 'but I have no idea what you're talking about. And—'

'What do you mean—'

'—the police have been here.'

'Wait. Wait. Back up.' My head snapped up. 'What do you mean you have no idea what I'm talking about? The passwords for Hiero's blog. Remember? They cycle. You cracked his server.'

'Mr Griffen'—*Arrgh!*—'those things you said I did, I didn't do. I haven't spoken to you since … it must be last holidays.'

Heat flushed my cheeks, but my gut was growing cold.

'I know we haven't spoken,' I said, voice rising. 'I tried to call you. We *Skyped*, text chat, last week.'

'No, we didn't. I was away last week, at beach camp. Digital detox. I haven't Skyped anyone in weeks.'

'Shit …' I sighed.

I must've been silent a long time, because Matt said, 'Mr Griffen? Are you there? What's going on?'

'I don't know. I thought I'd just stepped in shit, but it seems I've been flushed down the toilet.' I lowered the receiver, then raised it once more. 'Whatever they say about me, Matt. It's not true. Don't believe it.'

And with those sage words I hung up.

I sat there in silence and tried to make the world stop spinning. The hard-arse in my head reeled off the score: I was (mostly) alone in a hotel room on the other side of the world, in an unfamiliar city filled with people speaking an unfamiliar language. I was broke, and suspected of at least one, possibly two, murders. I was doomed with the foreknowledge of another murder about to happen, and my one window into the mind of the killer, which had seemed too good to be true, *was* in fact too good to be true.

The blog was a honey pot and I was Winnie-the-Pooh.

Hiero had somehow intercepted my attempt to communicate with Matt. Had impersonated him and set me up to read his blog.

But why?

Quickly I packed my meagre belongings and descended to the lobby. I stashed Li Min's journal next to Hiero's notes in my coat pocket in an attempt to not look like I was skipping out on my bill.

Before I left, I checked the blog again. The latest entry held me with that same car-crash-can't-look-away feeling:

> On to the next adventure. By train, this time, I think. The 08:52 from the Hauptbahnhof on through a cavalcade of German cities, the names of which put me in mind of B-grade World War II movies. Destination: Gare de l'Est, Gay *Paree*!
>
> Not the *Orient Express*, but the same romantic sense of the European journey. Wintering trees and cigarettes and cocktails in the dining cart. Then chunnelling on to London.

And there it was. Hiero's rampage rolled on again like a locomotive. And now it was almost certain he knew I was reading this account of his exploits.

Well, I was getting on that train.

From a boutique telecom store I bought a prepaid phone, and loaded every last cent onto it. I called the Murdoch Police Station from memory and asked for Thomas. My call was dispatched and seconds later a very alert Thomas spoke.

'Tell me you're on your way home, Griffen.'

'No, I'm on my way to do your job. He's killed again, you know. Vienna. Hauptbahnhof station. Yesterday, right in front of me. I'm not going to let him do it again.'

'What you nee—'

I hung up.

Barely thirty seconds later the phone buzzed. No caller ID, but it had to be Thomas. I turned the phone off. Let him stew.

23

I swung the new suitcase onto the luggage shelf above my seat, even as the train filled with the hiss of automatic doors closing. I'd bought the suitcase at Aldi before cashing out on the phone, together with socks, jocks, a pair of jeans, a couple of shirts, and a windcheater. I was learning. A suitcase made me look less like a witless desperado. A little less.

I'd been the last to board, as I'd hung back, looking to catch a glimpse of Hiero. His latest blog entry, accessed on my phone, hadn't been edited. It still stated his intention to head for London by train—*this* train.

He was on here somewhere, and I meant to find him.

The fact that I knew he knew I was on the train probably should have disturbed me more than it did. That it didn't, I put down to the idea he imagined we were somehow chummy. I, the master, watching him, the apprentice, with a paternal eye as we travelled this adventure of discovery.

Well, if that was his idea, he was only about as wrong as any human can be. He'd find out how wrong when I caught him on the train and buckled his face with my supremely unpaternal fist.

The train bucked and swayed over a junction then picked up speed. Vienna began to sweep by outside and soon we were rising and falling gently past mist-shrouded fields.

From my pocket I retrieved my wallet. The tip of my train ticket poked from its fold. I slipped it out and checked my name again: Dieter Schleicher.

Herr Schleicher. Nice to meet you. Pity my German didn't get beyond, *Wo ist mein Hundefutter? Im Kuhlschrank.* (Where is my dog food? In the refrigerator.)

Don't ask.

I hoped the real Dieter had a nice time of his extended stay in Vienna. He'd seemed like a nice enough chap, to judge from the back of his head as it faced a urinal. From him I'd borrowed a ticket, and found an unexpected boon: a twenty euro note slipped behind it. When this was all over I'd find Dieter, pay him back, reminisce about dog food.

The train clattered over switches at St Pölten, the point on the map at which I had decided I would tour the second-class carriages. Hiero hadn't mentioned if he was riding first or second (or freight). I took a deep breath and flicked my wrist out to check my Medline. Pulse at 63 bpm. Plenty of margin to work in.

I exited the compartment into the thin corridor running the length of the carriage. Dieter Schleicher's seat was two-thirds the way toward the first-class carriages. I decided to head towards the rear of the train as far as the freight carriages.

I'm not an actor, but I can emote 'needs to pee' and I did so now. Through the squat glass portal of the next compartment I saw a family of three. The father was plunged in a newspaper, the mother picking through an open suitcase. The kid was standing at an angle, and was either hungry or also needed to pee.

The ticket inspector caught me then. He was a rotund man, singularly unsuited to the thin corridor. There was no way I could squeeze past without retreating to my compartment. Or maybe that was the point. Maybe advertisements for ticket inspectors specified fat guys.

'Ticket please,' he said. Clearly he thought I looked English.

Without a word I handed him my ticket, while behind him rain began to speckle the window.

He scanned the ticket briefly, clamped it in a metal punch, and handed it back.

'*Vergessen Sie nicht, in München umzusteigen,*' he said and dipped his head. '*Gute Reise.*'

'*Danke,*' I said. It was either that or the dog food line.

I ducked back into my compartment, and waited until he passed. He left a smell like Old Spice wafting in the corridor.

As I padded back along the corridor, I paused at each compartment just long enough to see its occupants. Every glance came with a little burn in my guts, and a quickening of my breath. My breathing slowed again each time I didn't find Hiero, but never quite to what it had been before

I looked. By the time I got to the last second-class compartment, I was sucking air like a marathon runner on the home straight.

I glanced into the compartment and found only a man and a woman, seated with their faces locked together in mortal combat. The man had long hair and the woman short. On the opposite seat sat a battered guitar case covered in stickers.

Unless Hiero was stowing away in the guitar case, he wasn't travelling second class.

I returned to my compartment and sat, waiting for my pulse to drop back to its normal 56 bpm. Outside an unrelenting drizzle rendered everything an endless grey, broken by the occasional burst of orange and yellow autumn colours. On a far-off road, silent toy cars matched our speed.

My stomach growled. I hadn't eaten since—when? Last evening, if you count a packet of hotel crisps. My stomach didn't seem to want to count them.

My hand was reaching for the door that led to first class when my phone buzzed. Hesitating, I retrieved it. On its screen was printed: *1 new message(s). See message.* I thumbed the invitation.

It was an email from g_w@dpsos.com. No subject. The message body was a single word:

Cold.

I glanced out the window at the spray churning away in the train's slipstream. Yeah, it was cold. So?

I passed through the door and into the gangway between carriages, to be assaulted by a rush of wind and the train's clatter. The noise was leaking though a tear in the accordioned wall.

At the opposite side of the gangway, a mere five feet, I opened the door into a first-class carriage. As I did so, the phone in my hand vibrated. Another message notification. Same sender. Still no subject. Again one word:

Colder.

Understanding broke through in an instant. Whoever g_w@dpsos.com was, they were playing a game with me, the children's game of hot and cold. They were telling me my hunt was taking me away from my prey. I was getting colder. I swung around, re-entered the gangway, and hurried out the other side, back into the second-class carriage.

Again the phone buzzed. One word:

Warm.

I stalked down the corridor, glancing again into the compartments. I had passed three when another message arrived:

Warmer.

A voice blared in my ear. Wincing I looked up to see I was standing right beneath a speaker. I covered my ears, but still heard it speaking German. Then a pause, and it spoke a much slower English. I uncovered my ears in time to hear: '—wishing you a good morning. This train will be stopping in two minutes at Linz and then travelling express to Salzburg. Those passengers making connections for Prague should disembark at Linz, and I wish you a pleasant onward journey.'

I hurried to the next compartment, and put my face up to the window, no longer caring if the occupants noticed me. The couple inside were bent over books, one on each seat. They didn't move a muscle.

I stepped toward the next compartment. My phone buzzed:

Warmer.

My breath steamed onto the cool glass of the next compartment. Inside were four chattering, grey-haired ladies. One paused to shoot me the hairy eyeball. I moved on.

Buzz: Hot!

The next compartment was a young man in a Yankees cap absorbed by a laptop's screen. Move.

Buzz: Hotter.

Empty cabin.

Buzz: HOTTER.

There were only two compartments left. I threw myself against the glass of the first—HOTTER! But it only held the young family. In the second and last, the mortal combat couple now lay dozing on each other.

That was all of the compartments. No Hiero.

I stepped back against the corridor window, breath coming hard. From far off came the faint sound of my Medline warming up.

My phone buzzed once more.

I glanced at it and thumbed the message up:

FCUKING MOLT3N!! 8-X

What? We must be playing a different game.

I tilted my head back to rest on the glass, and felt the tracks thrum through my skull. A mixture of weariness and anxiety and frustration overwhelmed me.

And then I realised I had not covered all the doors. There was one I had not checked. At the very end of the carriage, jammed at the head of the freight cars, was a toilet.

I slipped the phone into my pocket and padded to the toilet door.

There was no mistaking it now. My Medline was screaming at me to stop, sit down, chill out. Pass out.

Bugger that.

It didn't matter if I burst in on Hiero and smashed his face in, or went into cardiac arrest. Both would bring the train's cops. That's all I wanted.

The toilet doorknob displayed a little red tab.

I took a step back, lowered my shoulder, and threw myself at it. On impact, pain flared along my arm, and the door smashed open onto its hinges.

Momentum carried me into the tiny space. My head crunched on a mirror and I fell, sprawled with one leg hooked over the toilet seat, and an elbow in the sink. I felt a moment's fascination that the mirror had cracked in a cobweb pattern, before the disappointment hit me.

It was empty.

Then an alarm filled the air and the shriek of metal on metal, and I was thrown forwards. The floor juddered, and deceleration pinned me to the wall until finally the train jerked to a halt and let go.

There was a hiss of air as the exit nearest the toilet opened and a chill breeze carried a spatter of rain into the corridor.

And then silence.

A voice blared again over the speakers. It spoke German, some *nicht verlassen*-ing, but I didn't need a translation to know it was harried and probably pissed. The speaker clicked off, and an excited chatter filled the silence.

My mind finally caught up to events. Someone had pushed the emergency brake.

I gathered myself up off the floor and hurried back into the corridor, which was filling with confused passengers. Standing on tiptoes for vantage I scanned the corridor, but saw no sign of Hiero. With the doors open he could have easily slipped away.

The train had halted a few hundred metres shy of the platform, but just beyond the open exit, on the far side of the shiny concrete barrier, lay a multistorey parking lot, and a thousand holes for a man to disappear quick as water into a sponge.

I couldn't believe it. I'd been so close.

I returned to the toilet and examined the door lock. The lock pin had been bent, and stuck to the inside by a piece of chewing gum, which had held the door shut.

I looked at myself in the mirror. My face was dissected by the fracture lines.

Played for the fool again.

My only consolation was that no one had died this time. I couldn't say no*thing* had died. My self-respect had flatlined.

24

Call it post-traumatic stress syndrome. Call it deadly lassitude. Whatever it was, it kept my rear end stuck to the seat in my compartment. What was I going to do in Linz? Rush around asking if anyone had seen a guy jump from the train, and if so, where he might have gone?

I was hungry, but it was warm again in here. Cold out there.

So I sat.

The train wound up speed for the minute it took to arrive at the station, and then slowed to a halt. When it had disembarked its transferring passengers, it wound up again for the long haul to Munich.

And through all that I sat.

I bought a sandwich from a man for five euros and chewed without tasting it.

When I had finished, I retrieved my phone from my pocket and placed it on the fold-down table beneath the window. The last message from g_w still shone on its screen.

FCUKING MOLT3N!! 8-X, it said.

FCUKING MORON!! 8-X, is what it should have said.

'Why do you keep talking yourself down like that?'

I glanced up and found Tracey seated opposite me. On the nape of her neck the pale sunlight illumined a tiny scar in the shape of a butterfly.

I was going crazy, but at least I had company.

'Because I let two girls die,' I said bluntly. 'Probably three now.' I had decided the best remedy for the guilt building inside was to be honest. To only speak the truth—the raw, bleeding truth.

'No you didn't, Dad.'

'Yes, I did,' I said, thinking it must be hard for her to hear, before remembering she was only a mental projection. Mental projection, yeah.

That sounded saner than psychotic delusion. 'If I'd only moved quicker when I saw the newspaper article about Hiero's first assault. Or if I'd spoken different words to the detectives. Or gotten to Hong Kong sooner ...'

She shook her head.

'No, Dad. No one could have done more. You just like to beat yourself up. You've always done it.' She paused, and gave me what I knew to be her version of a significant glance. 'Well, not always ...'

That was true. She had me there.

'Since when did you get so wise?' I said, raising the ghost of a smile.

'I found God, remember?'

'Ah, yes,' I said, remembering the day Kim had told me on the phone. 'Your mother said, "Tracey's found God." I replied, "On Berkeley campus? Which faculty, Medicine?"'

'Typically smartarse, Jack Griffen,' Tracey said. 'That hasn't changed.'

I laughed, despite myself. 'I can't help it. All day I'm reading Palahniuk and Bazell. Edgy, irreverent wisecracks are what pass for literature these days.'

'We got off the point,' she said, watching the Austrian Alps flow by outside, face aflame with the rising sun. She still had the freckles.

'We had a point?' I said.

'Sure. The point in your life when you wriggled under a blanket of guilt,' she said. 'And never came out.'

I mused, 'The point.'

She was gone.

I knew the point. It was a day, nine years ago. A day when a seed was planted that grew into a tree that continued to bear bitter fruit. A day that had put me in Graylands Hospital, and given me a mental health flag—the same flag that in the eyes of Perth detectives made me a liar and a murderer.

Without wanting to, I remembered that day. I had a theory that if ever I succumbed to Alzheimer's, this memory would be the last to go, the last to be eaten by my malfunctioning grey matter. It would be the last morsel of Jack Griffen—alive and condemning to the very end.

The day began like any other. Awake at 6.30. Breakfast of scrambled eggs, plenty of pepper, plenty of milk, and sourdough toast, on the balcony with the paper. I read the comics, the weather, and the sport, in that order, and usually only turned to the first pages if I was feeling particularly fortified. The paper was the only affected part of my morning routine—literature professors are meant to be redolent of the old world, but I drew the line at a pipe.

By 7.15 I was treading the riverside path to the university in my leather brogues, watching the early-morning sun glint on the Swan River, hearing the hum of the distant freeway. I didn't wear a watch in those days, and the Medline had yet to enter my life. If I was lecturing that day, and it was a new one, I'd turn the logic of the argument over in my head. If not, I might toy with the outline for a short story—maybe a little tester for a new genre. If my mood was sour, I might recall the latest rejection letter for my thesis novel, and pick apart its grammar.

The special day was a 'short story' day. I'd had an idea for meshing star-faring science fiction with the 'avenging prince returns' of Monte Cristo. The sense of possibility at the beginning of a story is delicious. Ideas were still percolating through my mind when I got to my office. I had barely laid my briefcase down when the phone rang.

The moment I heard Kim's voice I knew she had cataclysmic news.

Kim has always been collected. If she was wrathful, it was a measured wrath. If joyful, a rounded joy.

But that day she spoke in fragments with long pauses between.

She was talking about Tracey, our daughter. The last time I had seen Tracey, two days prior, bustling out the door with her bag for music camp, she had been her typical twelve-year-old self. A roaming one-girl flash theatre of tragicomedic musical; a tangle of summer-tanned limbs, freckles and smiles, and hugs that let you smell the sea in her hair; a body connected to the ground rail of the earth.

But the girl I found stretched on a bed at Princess Margaret Hospital seventeen minutes after Kim hung up barely looked human.

She lay in the intensive care unit, pale and inert. Sensor wires snaked over her body, and IV drips were plumbed into both wrists. Her eyes were closed above an oxygen mask. Kim sat beside her, one hand holding Tracey's limp wrist. Only Kim's frantic eyes marked her as not just an extension of the body on the bed. Her face was pale, too, and lacking make-up.

That became the first of the ten most torturous days of my life. I watched as Tracey vomited, fainted, groaned, and made confused utterances, and Kim went with her every spasm in vicarious torment. I watched as her forearms became spotted with a junkie's train tracks as her cannulas were constantly moved when her veins collapsed. When she was conscious enough to joke, she said they were curing her with acupuncture.

I watched. I went home to shower—somehow never quite washing away the sweat stink of that first day's mad dash, or shrugging off the buzzing sound that seemed to be in my ears and eyes. I put food in my mouth, chewed and swallowed. And I thought.

If my life was a two-hundred-ton locomotive cruising the line, Kim's call had been the rail spike laid on that line by fate. Isn't it scandalous that half an ounce of steel can derail and send lancing, tumbling, careening over the blue metal, a two-hundred-ton piece of clockwork perfection?

The rail spike in this case had a name: meningococcal septicaemia.

It is caused by the proliferation of a little buttocks-shaped bacteria a micrometre wide, *Neisseria meningitidis*, that lives up the noses of one in ten adults. Once in the blood stream, the bacteria population explodes, causing widespread vascular damage, haemorrhaging, thromboses, cell death, and the telltale non-blanching rash. If not treated, within hours it can lead to multiple organ failure, permanent disability or death.

That's the clinical explanation of the disease. The mechanism of the microscopic war that ravages the body, which can leave a person stone dead in hours.

But the cause, the reason why? Why Tracey, why my daughter? Why now? No one could tell me. No one knew.

Ten days later Tracey emerged from under the wires and tubes, fully restored to health. The only physical legacy of her ordeal, courtesy of a skin graft, was a small scar on the nape of her neck in the shape of a butterfly. Some people paid for tattoos, so Tracey thought she got a good deal. The butterfly's symbolism of emergence occurred to my writer's sensibility.

Kim came out of that time, pausing only to pick up the pieces of herself, and entered life again.

I came out of those ten days a different man. Though I didn't know it then.

25

Hours after my imaginary conversation with Tracey, I was staring through the window at the passing sights of Paris as we approached Gare de l'Est.

Paris.

It hung before me this evening, 'the vast bright Babylon, like some huge iridescent object, a jewel brilliant and hard, in which parts were not to be discriminated nor differences comfortably marked. It twinkled and trembled and melted together, and what seemed all surface one moment seemed all depth the next.'

Well, that was Paris according to Henry James in *The Ambassadors*.

I don't think James was describing Paris crawl by on the other side of a window smeared with greasy handprints, hard-pressed by a gnawing hunger and suffocating in a cloud of guilt.

I was feeling about as low as you can go, when my phone buzzed.

Without hesitation, I retrieved it and picked up the call. I wanted company, even if the company told me I was in big trouble.

'Thomas,' I said.

'No, Mr Griffen. This is DCS Collins of the Metropolitan Police, London. I've been talking to our Interpol liaison.'

Interpol.

'Nope,' I said to myself. 'I can go lower.'

'I'm sorry?' said Collins.

'Nothing,' I said. 'What can I do you for, Mr Collins?' *Cup of sugar? Dogsit? Signed confession?*

'Mr Griffen, Detective Thomas of Perth, Australia, initiated contact with Interpol. We need to talk to you. In person.'

His voice sent a thrill of hope through me. It sounded reasonable. In control. Calm, but serious.

'I'm listening.'

'It's concerning Hieronymus Beck. Detective Thomas shared your information with us and we believe he means to murder again.'

Again!

'What information?' I said. 'And can you be precise about what you think Beck has done?'

'I'm sure I don't need to tell you, Mr Griffen, but we suspect Mr Beck committed assault in Perth, murder in Hong Kong, and attempted murder in Vienna. We need—'

'Wait a minute. *Attempted* murder?'

'The victim, Miss Kreider, was admitted to hospital and remains in a critical condition. For now, it is attempted murder.'

'Thank God for that,' I breathed. 'Tell me what to do.'

'You're bound for London, correct? I have your itinerary as arriving in Paris late tonight, Gare du Nord, departing tomorrow morning on the nine-thirteen am Eurostar.'

By 'itinerary' I guess he meant Hiero's blog. But it was Gare de l'Est I could see through the windows, not Gare du Nord. And London? Who said anything about London? My intention was to find a bottle in Paris to drown in. Collins' certainty was a slap in the face.

Suddenly alert, I swallowed the correction. A memory of my Skype contact with a fake Matthew Price sprang to mind. 'Wait. How do I know you are who you say you are?'

'Call Detective Thomas. He will confirm my identity.'

'I will.' I hesitated. 'And yes, I'll be there,' thinking it would be easy to call back with the truth if Collins checked out.

'Meet you at the station,' he said and hung up.

The phone's active-call icon had barely vanished before I dialled Thomas. 'Griffen,' he said.

'I got a call from a Collins working for London Police. Is he for real?'

'You mean is he a real cop or a pen-pusher?'

Thomas sounded ticked off, but he'd answered my question.

'Whatever,' I said. 'No offence, but we're finally getting where we should have been a week ago. Which is great, except we're down a girl on where we should be.'

'One and not two, eh, Griffen?' said Thomas, and there was an odd, grim satisfaction in his voice. 'Bet that pissed you off.'

'What are you talking about?'

'The girl in Vienna. Pushed her in front of a train, but you didn't get her square on, did you? Looks like she's got an even chance of pulling through.' He sounded gleeful. 'No pretending you didn't know this one, Griffen. She was in your class. You interviewed her for a project barely a month ago.'

I couldn't believe it. The idiot still thought I was the one doing the murdering.

My mind made a dozen false starts on putting Thomas in his place, before I settled for: 'Whatever. I'll be playing with the grown-ups from now on. They believe me.'

'They haven't *seen* you,' he spat.

Looked like I'd finally gotten under the detective's implacable calm.

He went on at full-tilt rant. 'To think the government pays to grow psychos like you. You sit there in your little offices divorced from real life and read all that wanky crap written by other men in little offices and your brains rot and life becomes a game.'

I said, 'I'm hanging up n—'

But Thomas barrelled on: 'I mean, what the hell do you want with her hair?'

Pure confusion made me answer.

'What?'

'Her hair. You snuck in to the hospital after you nearly killed her and took a lock of her hair. What's the matter? Did you grow a conscience at the sight of her with her chest caved in and her face a mess? Couldn't bear to finish the job, so you took a trophy?'

What the hell?

'I'm gunna hang up,' I said. 'But do me a favour—No: Do *yourself* a favour, and check if Li Min from Hong Kong has all her hair.'

I hung up.

Everything Thomas had said swirled through my mind. I was losing track of it all. No way seemed up anymore. Hair? I tried to remember Li Min. Had her hair looked odd? But I hadn't really looked. I'd touched her just the once, to arrange one leg by the other. The integrity of her haircut hadn't been front and centre.

I began to call up Collins' number to fix my arrival time, when I heard again the note of grim satisfaction in Thomas' voice. For all his froth, he sounded like he was speaking to a man who was about to get his.

I removed my finger from the phone. The cautious guy in my head nodded his approval.

Something was still jabbing me in the brain. Collins had got my timetable wrong, but he'd known I was on a train from Vienna to Paris, and assumed I was heading to London.

And then I guessed the answer.

I pulled up Hiero's blog on my phone, and entered the password that fake Matt's service was still spitting into my inbox every hour.

There was a new entry. This one included details of the connection at Paris. But Collins had made the mistake of thinking the blog was describing my journey.

It read:

> I disembarked onto a platform at Gare du Nord.
>
> The first proper whiff of Paris I got was urine. Someone had peed on a newspaper kiosk. I guess it was an editorial. My knee joints felt rusted in place, but I needed a piss myself.
>
> Tugging my suitcase off the platform, I found the restroom, and uncorked my bladder. At the sink I splashed water on my face and ran my wet fingers over my scalp. Its prickliness still surprised me.
>
> The passage to Paris had put blue bags under my eyes—the shock of the chase, then the boredom of the journey. Mountains lose their romance after a while, even European mountains.

So Hiero had also shaved his head. Useful to know, unless now he knew I was reading the blog, he had begun to seed it with misinformation.

Curious to know what account Hiero had made of his flight from the train, I scrolled down to the previous entry. And there my swirling thoughts were tossed over Niagara Falls.

As I'd thought, the blog entry described the first stage of the journey from Vienna. But it was the way it was said that stunned me. This part in particular:

> My phone buzzed. I pulled it out and retrieved the message.
>
> It said: Cold. The little shit was taunting me. He'd tracked me down, and boarded my train, and now he was taunting me.

So *that's* where Collins had got the idea Hiero's blog was describing not his journey but mine.

All along I had assumed Hiero was recording his own exploits. Saving them up to enjoy later. But, no. The blog was just another part of the set-up. It was brilliant. I'd even pointed the police at it, just like a real, egomaniacal psycho.

I quickly flicked back through the previous entries I had already read. With growing dread, I found every one—*every* one—read just fine if you imagined the narrator was me. Read better, in fact. I came to the entry that described the murder of Li Min, and remembered her journal. The very last line, what did it say?

> Cometh the hour, cometh MC Griffen.

I had puzzled over what that meant. What did she mean by using my name? I had assumed that MC stood for Master of Ceremonies, and wondered what ceremony I was supposed to be facilitating. But now reading it with my fresh perspective, I remembered there is another term for which MC is a well-worn abbreviation. One that, given my line of work, should have occurred to me first.

It is Main Character.

A sudden fear gripped me. Li Min had put my name in her journal—I guessed at Hiero's prompting. Had she also spoken to friends? Made other notes I wasn't aware of?

All at once my train compartment became a cell. A trap that had snapped shut around me. Claustrophobia surged through me. They could park the train in a tunnel, lock the doors, and throw away the key.

Darkness smothered my mind.

And then a chink of light pierced the darkness.

Collins' voice came back to me—*he means to murder again.* He believed me, didn't he? He was a London copper. Worldly-wise, hard-bitten, intelligent. He would know this was a set-up. It would stink a mile away to a guy who must've seen his share of fugitive psychos and intercontinental sewage.

There was no reason for Collins to believe my/Hiero's blog wasn't pure fiction woven around the brute facts of Li Min's murder and Annika Kreider's assault. So he'd gone fishing, maybe, called me. Told me to come in from the cold. Well, my train would be pulling into the station in minutes. But I'd have to shelve the idea of a cheap hotel and a hot shower. I had minutes to leg it up the road to the Eurostar terminus.

Because I would go on to London, as Hiero's blog foretold. But I wasn't sticking around till tomorrow morning to be arrested. I was going tonight.

26

I sat in a café on the ground level of St Pancras Station, London, and watched policemen jog back and forth on the first level.

From my vantage point at a window I could see the tall black helmets of uniformed bobbies, as well as men who had to be plain-clothes officers. Near the head of the stairs that connected the ground floor to the Eurostar platforms six metres above, beneath the station's famous statue of a reunited couple, was a solid figure in a suit, hands sunk in pockets, conducting a war council. I wondered if I was looking at Superintendent Collins.

I drank coffee and let my gaze wander the length and breadth of the network of girders arching above like the ribs of a colossal beast. The roof span had been the largest in the world in its day. But that day was more than a century ago. I turned my thoughts back to the present.

So: it had been a sting, after all. A sting that would have stung if it hadn't been for Hiero's ever-so-subtle deception about which train I'd taken. I would have been the fly in the web. Not the grasshopper sipping adequate Arabica.

As it was, part of my mind was screaming for me to get the hell out of there. But for the moment, the right side of my brain—the poet, the novelist—held sway. I drank more coffee.

To my right, an old-timer choked on his coffee and spluttered. I grimaced, annoyed by old age as much as this man's clumsiness, before a more worthy impulse took me; I leaned over and offered him a serviette.

He nodded thanks, took the napkin, and tried to speak, before another gale of coughing overcame him.

I returned my gaze to the theatre above me. A failed sting (*so far*, said left-brain). It was fascinating.

The uniformed cops reminded me of ants who had lost their line. One minute fast, strong, determined, the next a milling start-stop. The men in charge appeared to have come unplugged. Maybe this was a career-wrecking sting.

But not Collins—if that's who it was. He just looked pissed. And was still giving orders.

Maybe it was time to leave.

A quick glance into my cup told me it held three, maybe four gulps. I decided I would finish it, slowly. Then rise, exit the café, and mix with the passengers thronging the stairs, the exits to the tube, King's Cross. Somewhere.

'*Danke.*'

I turned to find the old man's rheumy eyes on me, and his scarecrow arm upraised. His hand held a brownish lump. My mind made a couple of false starts at recognising what he held, before realising it was the (now used) serviette I had given him.

He nodded thanks, dumped it on his saucer, and then said the thing that froze me: 'They are looking for you, *ja?*'

All I could do was stare at him, my face feeling like an amputated limb.

He smiled and patted my arm with his scarecrow's hand.

'I will not tell,' he said, smiled, and tapped his forehead. And now it was his turn to gaze up at the unravelling sting. My voice would still not engage gears. He went on: 'I have seen too many uniformed men begin … bad things this way.'

He drew back his sleeve to reveal a forearm thin as a stick. Beneath the wrinkles of its skin lay the faded ink of a tattoo, a number.

(A fleeting memory of my seven-year-old self asserting to Mrs Arnott that concentration camps were places where one was made to concentrate.)

His eyes, the palest blue, whites shot with veins, peered into me, and for a moment I fancied I could see his memories playing on their surface.

Bad things, indeed.

He patted me once more with a hand that now seemed like worked iron. 'And you don't seem like a bad man.' He paused, looking me over again. 'But you should go.'

I left without another word. I hoped he understood that if I'd been able to, I would have thanked him. For his silence, and much more for his words.

Until then, hunkered down in the café, looking out on the failed sting, had felt so cool. So it came as a shock the way my body reacted to stepping out onto the concourse. My back prickled with imagined stares as I turned toward an exit to the tube.

The exit couldn't have been more than fifty metres away, but it telescoped in my vision and the distance suddenly seemed a kilometre. I became conscious again of the way I was walking. My legs had forgotten forty years of instinctual memory, and had to be told what to do—lift, extend, drop, push, lift …

And my arms. What good were these articulated tubes of bone and flesh attached to my shoulders—good for nothing but dangling weirdly and giving me away was all. They added to the mental burden exacted by this dance called 'walking' that I was having to spontaneously choreograph.

Halfway to the exit I stole a glance at the railing above me. The dance faltered—one of the plain-clothes cops was staring back at me. No. Not staring. His gaze swept on, across the crowd flowing with me.

Fixing my eyes ahead, I marched for the exit, fearing at any moment a tap on the shoulder. That gentle touch that would undo my world.

But no touch came. I was jostled at the exit, where the bottleneck forced commuters together. A middle-aged woman with a bright pink suitcase, and brighter pink lipstick, forced herself past me. She smelled of sweat and cheap perfume.

And then we were through. Turning to look over my shoulder, I saw the concourse and platforms rise up and out of sight as I descended the stairs.

At the bottom of the stairs I found a cavern filled with the rumble of trains near and far. Hanging from a stretch of tiled wall was a restroom sign, and I made for it.

The restroom was laid out in an L of off-white tile. Sinks and urinals lined the straight, and round the corner was a row of cubicles. Opposite the cubicles stood a single sink. Ignoring the yellow grime covering it, I rested my forearms on its lip. All the nervous tension left me in a moment, and I collapsed forward like a marionette with cut strings. I remained like that for a full minute, head hanging above the sink's drain, heavy eyes mapping the mottled stain of black mould around the drain, indulging in sink-related nostalgia—teeth brushing, one of my fondest memories from another life. A normal life.

When I raised my head to look into the mirror, I didn't recognise the man staring back at me. My flight—the hunt—was etching lines in my face. Dark smudges ringed my eyes, and my skin looked papery.

Something was going to have to give. That something was probably me.

The roar of a flushing toilet filled the confined space, startling me. In the mirror I saw the cubicle door behind me open, and a man emerge. He filled what was left of the mirror's surface. Our gazes locked, and in the same moment his lit with recognition, and I realised his uniform marked him a cop. His expression twisted with fear and ... hunger?

A split second later, all was motion.

His image tilted from view; I rose from my elbows and spun.

A thunderous roar filled the air, pressing my eardrums. The sheer intensity of sound stunned me.

We froze, staring at each other, while pieces of glass fell like diamonds onto the tiles.

A heartbeat passed. Another. Thought returned. This was no cop, couldn't be. He was a kid. Barely needed to shave. But—No. He had to be a cop. The uniform, the gun. The *gun*.

It sat in his grip, its weight dragging his outstretched arm floorward. A tremor shook his arm. His gaze was fixed on the gun. His arm began to shake more wildly.

That's when I did the dumbest thing I've ever done. I reached out and took the gun, simply tugged it from his shaking fingers. It slipped free without resistance.

Then it was my turn to stare at it. A Glock 17, twenty-two ounces, but heavier than I'd imagined. The faint acrid smell of propellant wafted from it. Beside me, the shattered mirror bore mute testimony to the gun's killing potential. Shards had come away from the tight, black entry hole; beneath the surrounding glass a rough circle had puckered the plaster, a rebounding concussive pressure wave.

As if to convince myself the two were related—gun and impact crater—I touched the still-warm barrel, then fingered the hole. Then with the same finger, I tapped my chest, above my heart.

Yeah. *That* would have done it. That 'something' might have made me give.

I looked into the eyes of the cop, and felt pressure in the pit of my belly, like an uncoiling snake, and knew a moment of potent rage.

It was only then I realised we were still alone. Trains rumbled and shrieked outside. From round the corner came the splattering sound of a leaking urinal, but no footsteps, no voices.

A flicker of movement in a mirror-shard caught my eye. I looked up in time to dodge a punch he threw, but it caught me a glancing blow to the jaw. My teeth squeaked as they ground under the blow.

Rage coursed through me. I swung the gun in an arc. Its handle clipped him across the bridge of his nose. A stream of blood erupted from one nostril and dove for the floor faster than gravity demanded.

The sight of that blood, glistening red, stark against the tiles, chilled my rage. Numbness washed through me. I became a spectator of my self.

I reversed my grip on the gun, so the barrel now pointed at his chest.

'In there,' I hissed, prodding him back into the cubicle. His regulation black leather shoes slipped in his own blood and he fell-sat onto the toilet.

I jabbed the gun at him, made him look at me. At it.

'You stay there.'

I looked him over.

'Give me your radio.'

He took an eternity to unbuckle the radio unit and hand it to me. I dropped it between his legs. It made a *plop* in the bowl.

'Do you have a watch?'

He nodded, tears budding in his eyes.

'You move before half an hour is up, and I'll—' I jabbed the gun at him. 'Okay?'

He nodded still more vigorously.

Stepping back, I took a last look at my handiwork: a terrified kid in well-pressed trousers, cupping blood in his hands, with tears in his eyes.

'Thirty minutes,' I said, and pulled the door shut.

I paused in front of the broken mirror long enough to pull my handkerchief from a pocket and wipe the drops of blood from my face.

The numbing sensation was sloughing away as I strode from the restroom. In its wake came the after-effects of shock and an urge to vomit. When I emerged onto the platform, fearing the telltale bulge of the gun now stashed in my pocket, it was still thronged with passengers.

A tremor shook the platform, and the whistling of churned air filled my ears, heralding the arrival of a train. It emerged from the black tunnel mouth like a god of the underworld.

It screeched to a halt and opened its doors. Without hesitation I joined the current of bodies flowing into the nearest doorway, fearing with every bump and jostle to hear a cry—'He's got a gun!'

But no cry came.

The doors hissed shut, and acceleration tugged me sideways. The view of St Pancras Station was swallowed by the tunnel wall.

Pancras. Funny name. Lacking only a vowel to be Pancreas.

I was exiting the pancreas. What did that make me? Jack, the digestive enzyme; Insulin Griffen.

27

'The name is Marten. M-A-R-T-E-N. Inspector Marten Lacroix.'

On any normal day Detective Chief Inspector Marten Lacroix would have waited patiently for the party on the other end of the line to understand.

But today was not a normal day. Today she was hunting a psycho called Jack Griffen.

'Marten. As in the weasel. As in Dr Martens boots. As in—' She gritted her teeth. 'The man's name "Marten".'

A man's name. Yet another gift from her dysfunctional parents.

They had never agreed about anything, so why start with their daughter's name? Her father had insisted on French-république-stock Marianne. Her mother was fixed on pride-of-the-Bronx Tenisha. So rather than someone play the grown-up and concede, say, Marianne Tenisha, they coined 'Marten'.

Pity it had been coined centuries prior and taken since by countless baby *boys*. Would it have killed them to buy a vowel? Just another 'e'?

Static crackled from the handset pressed to her ear. Finally—a cough. Progress. Then, 'Ah, yes. Marten Lacroix. I have you now. What can I do for you, Mrs—'

'I need information about Jack Griffen.'

'What kind of information.' Businesslike, now.

'Whatever the Australians gave you. The Chinese. Vienna. Everything.'

Marten heard rustling on the other end of the line.

'Yes, here it is. Fresh off the press, the profile—'

'No, I don't want your profile,' she said. 'I want the *information*.'

She was tempted to add, 'Because I'll do the profiling, and it'll be right.'

Right? No, too much. But it would be *better*… That was the profiler's promise. A nudge that made the stranger-rape bogeyman human.

With a start, Marten realised the voice had spoken. She said, 'I beg your pardon?'

'I said, I'll need authorisation.'

'Faxing it now,' and she hung up.

It had taken years of hard work to be able to say that, but it had been worth it. Woman of colour, five years a young cadet, selected for one of the few international placements in the FBI program, top of her class, and an extended collaboration in the US. Then, The Fall, and back to the UK, and a grind to lose the stigma of a quasi-dishonourable discharge.

That was all finally in that faraway land, The Past, and by God the air was better here.

Within minutes the fax machine on her desk began to hum and the receiving light blinked orange.

Faxes. So seventies. So Interpol.

Still, it got the job done. Page upon page of raw material on Jack Griffen. And if she relished the challenge, she had a right to it. Inspector Marten Lacroix was not Sherlock Holmes to turn to cocaine in a fit of boredom, but the past months of gang violence and psychosis-driven murder had reminded her starkly of the sacrifices she had made to leave the continental drift of departmental promotion to specialise in profiling.

Too many *CSI* episodes. Too many Ruth Rendell novels.

But then she lifted the first sheet hot from the fax and her eyes lit with the challenge.

'Jack Griffen: Divorced. One daughter, living in the US with her mother. Born and raised in Perth, Australia, Bachelor of Arts (Hons) from the University of Western Australia, then a PhD from the same, and finally, without so much as moving down the road, a professorship in Literature in the Faculty of Arts.' An intellectual. So often a factor.

Earning a reasonable wage, but riding the line on a mortgage in an expensive neighbourhood, probably a legacy of the divorce. Perhaps Griffen's wage was draining down a secret hole?

But no police record. The nearest thing to a black mark was a parking infringement from the council on which the university was situated, waived on appeal.

Preliminary interviews with Griffen's acquaintances were summarised below. Garbage mostly, to Marten's mind. Pleasant, polite, quiet.

Emails and net activity awaited a warrant and subpoena to the university IT department, and Griffen's internet service provider.

All in all, not much to go on. But Marten could wait. The picture would fill out.

It was then that Marten noticed a small stack of cards of assorted size and colour that had been left on her desk. The cards were held together by a rubber band, and a post-it note was stuck to the top. Marten peeled it off and read, 'Marten: dropped by Griffen at St Pancras during aborted arrest.' The note was penned in felt marker in her supervisor's unmistakable hand. Marten raised her eyes to the ceiling; so much for chain of evidence.

The rubber band came off easily, and splaying the cards, Marten saw that they appeared to be business cards for practitioners of a bewildering variety of medicine: doctors, specialists, eastern medicine…

The oddest thing was not so much that Jack Griffen (she assumed) had need of such a wide range of medical expertise, but that he'd kept the cards.

Am I dealing with a massive hypochondriac? That was an intriguing thought. Hypochondria had been a notable feature of high-profile serial killer cases. John Wayne Gacy; John Christie; Richard Chase, the Vampire of Sacramento.

On closer examination, she found scribbled in the top right corner of each card a weird doodle. Simple, line-drawn icons that Marten couldn't interpret, but shuffling them back and forward, a pattern emerged.

Those cards for practitioners focusing on mental health—psychologists, psychiatrists—all had one icon; those focusing on physical health another; and the leftovers, those practitioners of likely-not-rebatable therapies, yet another.

The icons were evidence of an odd obsession.

Or an odd sense of humour.

Only one card lacked an icon, a card for the ETN Engineering Consultancy. Flipping this over, Marten found printed on the reverse three words: Idiopathic Takotsubo cardiomyopathy. Only 'idiopathic' was clear; the remainder had been struck through.

Marten looked up Takotsubo cardiomyopathy. Takotsubo, so-called for the 'octopus trap' shape it gave to the left ventricle of the heart, could be brought on by bereavement, illness, worry, or even, apparently, a happy event such as a wedding (Marten felt a frisson race through her limbs). It was also known as broken-heart syndrome.

Okay.

But those words had been crossed out. Only 'idiopathic' remained clear.

She had to look that one up too. It meant: unknown origin; without apparent cause.

Did Jack Griffen have—or imagine he had—a mysterious medical ailment? *Le malade imaginaire* was a hot-button topic of her father's, and about the only complaint he ever voiced about the 'pill-popping hypochondriacs' of his birth country.

Part of Marten desperately hoped Jack Griffen was fixated on his mortality.

Because if so, perhaps she had discovered a foundation.

Immediately below the words was a doodle Marten could interpret. A skull and crossbones.

Marten spoke her thoughts aloud, 'Death wish, then. A death with meaning …'

'Happy to oblige,' said a voice, and Marten turned to see Collins standing behind her. 'How do you want to go?'

'You're the one with the death wish, sneaking up on me like that. So, where did your lads lose our guest?'

Collins grimaced, acknowledged the blame. 'Somewhere in Greater London. His phone pinged a couple of towers, nothing useful. He must be cycling it. But he slipped the net at St Pancras.' He paused before adding, 'A junior let Griffen take his firearm.'

'He's *armed*?'

A nod.

That didn't fit with the profile already forming in Marten's mind. Griffen didn't sound like a gun-toter. Violent, obviously. But nothing so clinical and ordinary.

'I won't ask why you went armed to catch a bookworm.'

'Do you want to talk to the officer or not?'

'I'm a married woman, guv.'

He grimaced. 'That was an olive branch, not a come-on, Lacroix. You're the one needs profiling.'

'Let me see the kid.'

'Why the hell did you take a child to this sting?' Marten said, eyeing the young officer through the one-way glass. She could see the sheen of sweat on his jaw. There were no wrinkles around the eyes sitting above the sticky plaster covering his nose.

'Griffen was on the wrong train, came the night before. Officer Trent,' Collins jerked a thumb at the young man, 'wasn't even supposed to make it to the show.'

Marten followed Collins into the interview room.

'Sir,' said Trent, standing to attention.

'Sit down,' said Collins. 'You're not in trouble. DCI Lacroix here,' he nodded at Marten, 'wants to ask you a few questions about this morning.'

She extended her hand and a standard-issue comforting smile. 'You can call me Marten.'

Trent blinked.

Marten sighed. 'Shit, Trent. Actually, I don't care what you call me. I do care what you can tell me about Jack Griffen.'

A strange light came into Trent's eyes. 'The Intercontinental Killer?'

Marten glanced at Collins resignedly. 'The Intercontinental Killer? Which rag coined that—no, don't tell me. *The Sun*?'

'*Guardian.*'

Figured. She gave her attention back to Trent.

'Just tell me what happened.'

Trent flinched, and seemed to reach for a cigarette that wasn't there before replying. 'He tried to kill me.'

Marten fished a notebook from her jacket. 'What makes you say that?'

'What else does a guy mean when he points a gun at you and pulls the trigger?'

Marten frowned. 'Jack Griffen tried to shoot you?' She glanced at Collins, who shrugged in response.

'Yes, ma'am.'

'You remember when I said you could call me what you like?'

'Yes, ma'am.'

'Don't call me "ma'am".'

'Yes, m—' He fell silent.

'Alright, Trent,' she said, and settled back into her chair. 'Just describe what happened. Everything you can remember.'

'I'll try,' he said, with the first sign of a smile.

She studied Trent's face, the tilt of his head. He was trying for offhandedness. She had seen it before. One of the mind's defences against new and deep trauma. She would have to work past it to extract the information she needed, but it was better than the usual bravado.

Trent continued. 'I heard footsteps before I finished on the loo. I heard him—well, I didn't know it was him yet. I heard the steps stop outside my cubicle. Didn't hear the taps run, maybe that's why I thought it a bit odd.'

Retrospective detective, thought Marten. Seen that before, too.

'You flushed,' she said, 'and stepped out of the cubicle with the intention of washing your hands.'

Trent smirked. 'Always.'

'And what was Griffen doing when you emerged?'

'Just kind of leaning over the sink. His head was down, like he was crying. He looked up into the mirror when he heard me.'

'Then what.'

'Well, I don't know. I guess he went psycho.'

Marten noticed Trent sit forward, tense.

'He swung a punch, missed. But it was a feint. He dove for my gun—'

Collins butted in. 'Why wasn't your piece secured?'

'It was, sir! But he was fast, and I couldn't believe it. I guess I was, well, surprised, to be honest, sir.'

'Now Griffen has your gun,' said Marten. 'What happened next?'

Trent sat up straighter. 'We grappled. No way I was letting him point my own gun at me. But he swung his elbow, broke my nose. I lost touch, and next thing I know …' His voice trailed away, and his gaze abstracted.

'Next thing I know there was a gunshot and I thought, "That's me done."'

Silence fell, seconds were parcelled out by a wall clock.

'If you hear it,' said Collins, 'it missed.'

Trent inspected his fingernails and gave the briefest nod.

'What then, he ran away?' said Marten.

'Not straightaway. He pushed me into the cubicle, told me to sit, dropped my radio in the loo. Told me if I came out he'd blow my brains out.'

'Why didn't he just shoot you?'

Trent shrugged and went back to the fingernail.

'But he has your gun,' said Marten. Her eyes ran over the shirt-enshrouded torso of this twenty-something, and she remembered the profile she'd received on Jack Griffen didn't include a recent photo. But he was an academic, probably not Mr Universe. And he had disarmed this pride of the force?

'We searched the station,' said Collins. 'No sign of it. But we found the cards I left on your desk. Looks like he dropped them in his flight.'

Marten rose, and turned to leave. At the door she paused. 'And through all of that, the only thing Griffen said was, "Stay or I'll blow your brains out"?'

Trent considered for a moment. 'No. There was something else.'

'Yes?'

'He said something about liking incest.'

Silence.

'Officer?' said Collins.

'Honest, guv. "I like incest", or "I'll act incest".'

'What?—wait,' said Marten. 'You sure it wasn't *alea iacta est*?'

'Might've been,' grunted Trent, with a glance that said he was no longer sure who or what he was looking at.

Collins quirked an eyebrow. 'Marten?'

'Benjamin and I had one date last year, alright?'

'A date,' said Collins, voice level.

'A movie. *Rage*, with Nicholas Cage,' she said a little defensively. 'His daughter says it. *Alea iacta est*. It means "the die is cast".' Julius Caesar said it on crossing the Rubicon into Italy with his army, an act punishable by execution unless he conquered.'

Marten turned to Trent. 'Any idea what he meant?'

'Nope.'

That made two of them.

28

St Pancras, Saint of the Pancreas, was far behind me.

I travelled in a daze for an hour that seemed a handful of connected moments. I switched trains again and again, guided by a vague intuition— watching the buildings and streets thin imperceptibly—moving gradually, chaotically away from the heart of London, from St Pancras, from the kicked-anthill of a failed sting, and from the memory of a kid in cop's clothes seated in a toilet cubicle, sniffing up snot and blood, and from that moment.

That moment. The moment I read the word *kyoketsu-shoge* and my life dog-eared so far from Reality it came unstuck completely.

When at last I got off the train and descended from the platform, it was the glimpse of a park that drew me. Even seen through the scratched surface of the carriage window, something about the trees, heavy with leaf, and the unkempt grass, and the benches strewn across it said *haven*.

The train doors hissed open, and I stepped onto the platform along with a couple of teenagers wearing backpacks. They reminded me I'd left my new suitcase on the Eurostar. My wealth had shrunk again, to the clothes I wore, a cheap phone, and the wad of Hiero's notes. And, now jammed awkwardly beneath my windcheater, one Glock.

The doors hissed shut behind me and the train rumbled away.

The part of the station sign that hadn't been obscured by graffiti said 'Broadway'. Where the hell was that?

England.

I was deeply lost.

But standing was suspicious. Autopilot engaged. My legs shunted me toward the station exit. I had been planning only moments ahead for so long I was spent. Seconds later the autopilot disengaged. A ticket barrier barred the exit. It wasn't until I leaned on the metal bar, tried shoving it with my hip, that I understood this might be bad.

A uniformed man was sitting in a little office with a view of the barrier. His head bobbed above the lintel of the office window, and he glanced at me benignly. His presence rang distant alarm bells. Meanwhile I was still trying to comprehend why the gate was refusing my every attempt to move it.

My gaze had finally travelled to the metal box from which the gate protruded, and the slot in its face, when yet another rock went *splut* into the mire of my mind: a ringing noise.

My ears were still ringing from the gunshot, that was it.

No. The sound came from outside my head.

I stopped pushing on the gate and stood straight, while my brain informed me as an aside that what had prevented me from exiting was the ticket expected by the machine. A ticket I didn't possess.

The face of the man in the office rose, a faint frown now creasing his brow.

And finally, finally, I located the source of the noise. My phone was vibrating with a call.

It buzzed like an angry hornet in my pocket, a voice from another world.

The man was rising from his seat by the time I retrieved the phone.

My first thought was that Collins had tracked my jittery flight through the rail network. That any moment cars would screech to a halt outside the station and disgorge angry cops.

The train officer, standing observing from the door of his office, became in my mind's eye their messenger, harbinger, vanguard.

But the call had no caller ID.

I poked the pick-up button, and put the phone to my ear.

For a moment I thought I had missed the call. Then a voice spoke.

'Jack,' it said. 'How's it hanging?'

'By a thread,' I said.

I didn't recognise the voice at first. Not in the normal way. But the smothering intensity of emotions that engulfed me—fear, sorrow, anger, above all anger—told me whose voice it was.

'Hanging by a thread, Jack?' Hiero chuckled. 'Tatty cliché from the lit professor? I'll let it slide. You've had a rough week.'

From the corner of my eye, I saw the train officer move. He walked toward me. He would catch me, on this station in Greater London, while Hiero listened. I was going to jail—starting right here, right now. And Hiero had the next best thing to a front-row seat. Hiero, the one who had put me here.

Triggered by a deep self-defence response, my free hand patted my jeans, then fished in its pockets for a ticket I didn't possess.

'Professor? Still there?'

'I'm here,' I whispered, gaze fixed on the machine slot that wanted a ticket. The train officer was an approaching dark blob in my peripheral vision, accompanied by the jangle of his keychain.

'You have no *idea* how hard it has been, the wait. We can finally talk.'

A gravelly voice intruded. 'Do you need assistance?' The train officer had reached my side.

Assistance? The question was so absurd I nearly giggled.

'Jack?' Hiero's voice sounded tinny as I took the phone away from my ear, and made a show of patting my pockets again.

'Your ticket, sir?' the officer said, and the welcome light in his gaze dimmed.

'Jack?' Hiero's far-off whine grew louder. I planted my thumb over the speaker holes.

I felt in my back pocket for the bulge of my wallet, and retrieved it. What I meant to do with it I can only guess. Bribe the man in Euros? Jack Griffen had never bribed a man in his life. This was now the thread my life hung by.

I flipped my wallet open, and was riffling through it for paper money when the thick-skinned, liver-spotted hand of the officer settled over mine. He patted it once, then seized the corner of a card poking from the wallet flap. He drew it out, and I recognised it as the ticket I had stolen from Dieter Schleicher while he emptied his bladder in the Vienna Hauptbahnhof, the ticket that had taken me from Paris to London on the Eurostar.

He held it at arms-length and squinted. 'Swiss?' he said.

'*Nein,*' I replied.

'Ah,' he said, and a smile wrinkled the skin around his eyes. 'Germans don't like to make mistakes, do they. But this is a through ticket.' He lay a stumpy finger on an indecipherable smudge.

With a practised arm, he slotted the ticket into the metal box, and I nearly fell as it flipped forward, and spat me out of the station.

'Have a nice day, Mr Schleicher,' he said, and returned to his office accompanied by the jangle of his keychain.

'*Danke*.'

A short flight of steps, across the parking lot, and I came to the roadside. Beginning at the far kerb was a path that led to the park that had beckoned to me from the train. With a glance each way, I crossed.

The phone was heavy in my hand as I walked. I drew a deep, steadying breath, and brought it up to my ear.

'Jack!' Hiero shouted.

'I'm here,' I said. 'Ticket trouble.'

A pause. 'Okay, I guess—'

'You're sick, you know.'

'Oh, come on. More two-dollar words.'

'No, I mean it. You're sick in the head.' With an effort, I calmed my voice. It occurred to me that this might be my one chance to halt this juggernaut. Make this nut-job see sense. 'You need to see a doctor. Is researching this novel really worth *lives*?'

'Researching?' he said, incredulous. 'Wait—wait. You think this is just about *researching*?' He laughed. 'Haven't you got it yet?'

He paused and in that scintilla my mind closed around a truth I already knew.

'My novel, Jack: you're living it.' He whooped in delight. His voice, when he spoke again, was ecstatic. 'Jack, I'm not researching my novel anymore. Haven't been for weeks. I'm *writing* it. Now. "Life is a text", and I was born with this text in me.'

'Postmodern bullshit,' I said. 'Authority-creep. Lit majors wanting high priesthood over all of life.' Although, if I remembered right, that conceit came from Barthes, 'The Death of the Author'. I could go along with that right now.

'No, no!' said Hiero, urgent, sincere. 'It's true. If there was ever a doubt, this is the experiment that proves the theory.'

I reached a park bench resting in the shade of a solitary oak whose branches were still heavy with leaves, showing touches of yellow. I sank onto the bench's cool metal and cradled my head in one hand. It was beginning to throb.

Hiero changed tack: 'You stole Li Min's journal.'

The words tore through me like a bolt—how did he know that?

He said, 'Didn't you ever wonder what MC Griffen meant?'

I had. And I had discovered its meaning. But I let him say it: 'Main Character.'

'So I'm writing your story?'

'Professor,' said Hiero in a patrician tone, 'characters don't write their own stories.'

My pulse throbbed in my neck once, twice. Then the enormity of Hiero's crime crashed over me.

'You're the *author*,' I whispered. The realisation that Hiero was writing his story with my life, had robbed me of agency, brought home the horror of Li Min's murder more than the sight of her cold body had. He had stolen her entire future.

'Got it in one.'

'But, Hiero—' I found tears in my eyes. 'You murdered a girl. Her life for … for a story?'

'Why are you shocked? Great art requires great sacrifice. History is replete with art bought with blood. Wasn't Van Gogh's *Starry Night* worth the price of an ear?'

'Van Gogh was insane. And, besides, he mutilated himself.'

'Fah. My point is the currency: immortal art costs mortal blood.' He paused. 'I confess there are perks. Li Min might have been a virgin, but she was a tiger in bed. So overwhelming I nearly left it too late. Three hundred mils of intravenous heroin at ten in the morning, while you were winging your way to Hong Kong. Would've been an interesting scene if you'd caught me rushing out of her apartment with my pants around my ankles. If the story had climaxed there, it would have made my novel more of a novella.'

I wiped snot from my nose and sat up straighter.

'I will stop you.'

'No, you won't, Jack. You're going to try, try again, to prevent another person from dying. And fail again.' His voice brightened. 'But hang in there. You'll get your chance.'

'I'll just stop, then. Right here.'

'As much as that would suck, Jack—I mean, I'd have some serious rewriting to do—I won't stop. And I think you know it. History would label you the guy who could've made a difference, but opted instead to sulk.'

'You bastard—'

'Shut up and listen. I'll say this once. I've had to move the next one up a bit.'

'Next one?' I said dumbly.

'Consult the usual sources,' he said, 'but do it quick. I'm on recon now. I'll give her, oh, let's say forty-eight hours. And, Jack, that's being generous. She's really …' He paused. 'Not my type.'

It dawned on me. Hiero was looking at her right now.

'Bye, Jack. And take care. Remember, the clock's ticking.'

'Please—'

'Oh, and, Jack: bring your A-game. This one's closer to home.'

29

'Kim here.'

'Mrs Griffen?' said Marten.

'Griffen?' came the reply, and Marten listened closely for the next words. What did this woman think of the man who had been her husband, shared her bed for fifteen years?

'Your info is dated by—Who am I talking to?'

Marten wasn't sure what emotion she heard in the voice of Jack Griffen's ex-wife.

'DCI Marten Lacroix of the Homicide and Major Crime Command, Metropolitan Police.'

The silence on the line was easier to read. Marten spoke into it. 'When was the last time you heard from your ex-husband, Mrs Griffen?'

'It's Sparkes, and about ten seconds ago.'

Marten rushed on. 'Did he say where he was calling from?'

'No, and I wouldn't tell you if he had, Inspector Lacroix.'

'I must warn you, there are severe penalties for obs—'

'Save your breath, Marten. I'm not an idiot.'

Change of tack required. 'Aren't you concerned for Jack?'

'Of course I'm concerned.'

'Then won't you help me?'

'Help you *what*?'

(Put the psycho behind bars.)

'Help *him*,' said Marten.

'What sort of help do you think Jack needs?'

I'm supposed to be asking the questions, lady.

'He's clearly—'

'There is nothing clear about Jack's situation.' Marten heard a sigh, a sign perhaps that she might finally have a foot in the door.

'What do you mean?'

'This Hiero …'

Ah. 'Hiero.'

'What has Jack told you about … Hiero?'

'His name is Hieronymus Beck. An exchange student, one that Jack took a special interest in.'

'You do realise,' said Marten, unable to keep a smile creeping onto her face, 'that the faculty has no record of an H. Beck. That doesn't bother you?'

'Bother me? Ms Lacroix, are you a married woman?'

'Yes ma'am. Seven years of bliss.'

'Wonderful. And clearly you have an imagination, so try picturing this: You have a child—'

'I don't have to pretend about that. My boy is almost five.' Marten's mind flitted to David wearing his Cookie Monster backpack, which was larger than him. Had Ben remembered he couldn't pack nuts in David's play lunch?

'Excellent. Now pretend with me that you travel home today to find—God forbid—your son sprawled in the hallway of your home. Unresponsive. Breath shallow. Temperature spiking.'

'Kim—'

'No. Stick with me, Marten. The bomb that has flattened your son, and may take his life, is called meningococcal septicemia.'

An image flashed through Marten's mind, of David collapsed on the hallway parquetry, like a disregarded toy.

'They tell you he's not dead but, Marten, to your mother's eye, he sure looks dead. And the experience puts you through the wringer, but—after tears and worry and prayers—he makes it. The sun shines again …'

'But?' Marten couldn't help it, she was hanging on Kim's words now.

'Then you discover that your child's illness was the *decoy*. Fate threw that to divert your attention from her true mischief.'

Marten's gaze fell again to the framed photo sitting on her desk. She was already seeing afresh the face of her husband, Ben, as Kim went on.

'Jack was falling apart—from the inside out. The façade stayed in place till the end, until that's all there was.'

Marten wanted to press: 'What happened?' but something in Kim's tone told her she was done. Whatever urge had led her to spill her guts to a total stranger had passed.

'You asked me if it bothered me,' Kim said. 'What bothers me is to talk with a man that looks like my Jack, sounds like him—but ... isn't. Everything about Jack bothers me.'

'But you still take his calls.'

The phone speaker pulsed in Marten's ear. Another call.

'I have to go. Thanks for speaking to me. And *please*—if you have any info about Jack that might help me find him. It could save his life.'

'Jack's not a liar, Marten. That much I still know.'

Maybe he believes his own bullshit, thought Marten, but held her tongue and hung up.

30

Melodrama.

If you're like me, the word makes you think of overacting and sickly sweet soap opera.

Hiero and I once argued over the true meaning of melodrama. In a lecture I'd given my definition: a story with a who, a where, and a how, but lacking a why.

Without a *why* to bind them together, you just had a bunch of people doing a bunch of stuff. That wasn't story; that was life.

Melodrama was a horse chase into a blind canyon, and a Mexican stand-off, while the damsel watches on with a handkerchief clutched to her face. Drama would give the damsel a Colt Peacemaker stashed in her skirt, and a grudge stretching back years that kicked off the whole love triangle.

Hiero said that was crap, that my version was simply melodrama with more moving parts. He said melodrama was anything that didn't make your soul bleed.

31

'He said "Closer to home", Kim. I mean—what the hell does that mean?'

'Calm down, Jack.'

'You say that like I have a choice.'

'Okay, okay. But you're scaring me.'

'Good.'

There was silence, and I thought she was going to hang up.

'Someone called.'

My grip on the handset tightened.

'Who? Him?'

'No. A detective. From London. Marten something. Marten Lacroix.'

'What did he want?'

'*She* asked questions about you.'

'Like what?'

'If you'd contacted me, and … other questions.'

It wasn't like Kim to be vague.

'What—' The call cut-off warning beep interrupted me, telling me I had a minute left. Damn public phones. One step above carrier pigeons, and without the personality.

As much as I burned to know what questions this Marten had fired at Kim, time forced me back to the pressing issue: '"Closer to home". What could he mean?'

'Well, where's home, Jack?' Her question brought me up short.

'Home?'

Beep-beep. Thirty seconds.

'Jack?'

'I have to go. He's going to kill, and I'm all that stands in his way.' I waited for Kim to laugh at my melodrama. When she didn't, I felt a spike of fear.

Rushing now, she said: 'Go to the police. You have to. Please. For me.'

For me. I couldn't remember the last time Kim had said that.

'I can't. They don't believe me. I'm it. Time to put my jocks over my jeans.'

'Jack—'

'Bye, Kim. You probably won't hear from me, for a while anyway. I dropped my last euro on'—I nearly said *you*—'this call.'

'What will you do?' She sounded horrified, before the precision machinery of British Telecom cut her off.

'That,' I said, as I gazed through the grimed glass of the phone booth at shoppers wandering about the plaza, 'is the question.'

32

If you want to see how someone's mind works, observe the connections they make. The little switches in speech that seem like non sequiturs, but closer scrutiny reveals to be brain tells.

The night Hiero burst into my office proclaiming, 'The gods are hard to handle,' brandishing a scalping knife, was not the first time I had seen that knife.

He told me its story. Indeed, he called it a 'storied knife'.

It was a gift from his father, who had obtained it from a cop in LA. The knife, he said, had been used in a real-life scalping in an old case. The cop had purloined it from the evidence lock-up, and sold it to Hiero's father for ten bucks.

Hiero scratched at rust caking the etching on the blade, wondering aloud if the blood had been spilled on the streets of LA, or the plains of the Wild West.

I said, 'Sure he didn't get it throwing darts at balloons?' The knife looked like a carnival prize to me.

Hiero grunted. 'This from the man who thinks Batman didn't kill the Joker.'

It was a reference to the famous graphic novel, *The Killing Joke*, which pits Batman against his nemesis, the Joker. I thought (silly me) the connection that prompted Hiero's comment was the final setting of *The Killing Joke*, an amusement park.

If I'd paid closer attention, I might have noticed a much more disturbing connection. That between hero and villain.

33

I sat clutching my head in my hands, peering through the gaps between my fingers at the Bible slotted into the pew in front of me.

What I felt was shame, I decided. The sensation was new. It was like meeting an identical twin with poor hygiene and no concept of personal space.

I closed my eyes, and watched memories of the morning parade past. After calling Kim, I'd exited the phone booth, crossed the road and sat at the mouth of an arcade where the foot traffic was heaviest.

Next came the face of the lady. She wasn't the first person I'd asked for money, but she was the first who had spoken to me. If you can call a thorough telling-off speaking.

She had looked me in the eye through her bifocals, as we stood there on the footpath by the intersection. Her words had been calm, her manner lucid—no expletives, no heat—and she had told me in her matronly tones that I was a worthless reprobate, subsisting on the ill-placed kindness of my betters, and staining the streets with my very presence.

After that, I'd pilfered a pair of pharmacy sunglasses with mirrored lenses so no one could look into my soul again, while I scrutinised everyone who passed from head to toe, and picked my targets.

There had been more like that old woman, though none so eloquent. Many refused even that one-way eye contact. Some swore, and walked through me; and occasionally, someone dropped fifty pence into my outstretched palm.

I sat up and dug my wallet from my jeans pocket. I tipped the coin purse upside down and counted the fruit of my morning's depredations: six pounds, twenty pence, and a lollipop.

It wasn't fair. I should have been angry—I should have put that old bag in her place. I should have said: 'I am Professor Jack Griffen, and I am selling my pride to save a girl's life.'

But I couldn't. I couldn't even muster anger. Instead, I had felt shame.

Some part of me—some part truer, deeper?—asserted that shame not anger was the right response. Whoever that pontificating prat was deep inside me, I wanted to haul him into the rainbow haze of the stained-glass-filtered light and slap him.

A microphone squawked with feedback. At the front of the sanctuary, a young man began talking about an upcoming camp, before he was interrupted by a lady sitting in the pew in front of me.

'Offering,' she said.

'Oh,' said the man at the microphone. 'Pass the offering bags around. Today's collection is for Im Jai House orphanage in Thailand. If you're a guest with us—' Did he glance at me? '—please be our guest and let the bags pass.'

From the corner of my eye I watched the offering bag snake its way toward me from the front pew.

In my palm, the six pounds, twenty pence sat heavy. The lollipop had somehow found its way into my mouth.

The bag arrived at my pew. A man standing in the aisle helped it round the corner, and stretched to pass it to me.

'The bag' turned out to be a beanie. The touch of its coarse wool triggered a memory of a ski holiday with Kim and Tracey. Funny, Tracey had spent more time hunting two-dollar coins revealed by the late thaw than skiing. The thought made me smile.

This beanie sagged to a point with coins already placed in it.

I curled my hand around the last money I had in the world—save the credit on my phone—and plunged it to the bottom of the beanie.

I opened my hand. And my fingertips brushed paper money.

Its touch was an electric shock.

My hand closed around the bills.

With a glance along the pew to my right, I withdrew my hand, and passed the beanie to a boy sitting a couple of spaces over. He took the bag, but he stared at me.

I tried to smile. Failed.

Ignoring him, I faced front again and tried to count by feel the paper bills hidden in my grip.

It was an impossible task, but I enjoyed the satisfyingly thick wad of notes and dreamed that it was at least a couple of hundred pounds. Enough for a bed, and a bite, and a train ticket to … somewhere.

Such a mundane wish. Sleep, food, transit. Hiero had pushed me into a fugitive thriller. Maybe I needed to switch genres. Superman never had to worry about having clean underpants. Or maybe a hard-boiled detective story—something from the Golden Age of detective fiction, the twenties and thirties. I could be Hammett's Sam Spade; or better—Chandler's Philip Marlowe. Chandler was the lyrical writer.

'Down these mean streets a man must go who is not himself mean, who is neither tarnished nor afraid. He is the hero; he is everything … He must be the best man in his world, and a good enough man for any world.'

But Marlowe was forever getting *sapped*—hard-boiled speak for getting hit on the head. I didn't want to get sapped.

There was something else that didn't fit with Marlowe. I couldn't remember him stealing from anyone who didn't deserve it. My gaze flickered to the front of the sanctuary, where a couple of musicians had shuffled onto seats. A song was in the offing.

I had stolen from these people for one reason, and one reason only: they were the biggest suckers.

Earlier that morning, as I had been plying the street corner, I had felt a creeping sense of looking-for-suckers and been appalled by it. Homing in on the kind, the weak. Men and women dressed well, with smiles sitting beneath eyes with a touch of guilt at their own success.

My jaded spirit had made me aware that there weren't enough suckers on the street (or, at least, I couldn't spot them); serendipity had put me across a park from a church.

Profiling people for those most easily parted with their money was an alien thought to me, but it had crystallised alarmingly fast in the face of need. Pragmatism had trumped morality in the time it took to cross the street and walk half a block.

The singing began, my cue to leave. Act the embarrassed guy in the wrong church.

It wasn't until I had made the foot of the steps outside that I heard a voice. 'Sir? Excuse me, sir?'

I had determined to keep walking, when it said, 'You left these.'

I turned, and saw a man.

It took me a moment to interpret the question in his eyes and the tentativeness in his step. He moved like one approaching a wild animal that might scare and bolt.

'You left these,' he said, holding up the sunglasses I had stolen from a pharmacy rack.

'Thanks,' I said, and took them from his extended hand, 'although, maybe these belong in a church.' (Didn't you lay bad things on an altar?) It was meant to be a joke, but the guy had no idea what I was talking about.

I turned to leave.

'I couldn't help noticing you also *took* something.'

'Sorry?' and I recognised this was the man who had been standing in the aisle helping the money-beanie cross the gaps.

'The offering,' he continued. 'You made a withdrawal.'

A withdrawal. One way to put it.

I knew without speaking that my face would refuse to play along with a lie. The man took my silence as an opportunity to continue.

'I don't know what your story is—I mean,' his gesture took in all of me, 'you don't look like you're starving. Maybe it's drugs—'

'It's not drugs.'

'Okay. Just tell me how much you took.'

I glanced dumbly at my jeans pocket.

'I don't know.' I dug a hand into the pocket to retrieve the stolen money, but the man held up a forestalling hand.

'Leave it. I'll take a guess.'

'A guess? What are you talking about?'

'I'll make it up. Just …' and he handed me a ten-pound note. 'Here, take the candlesticks too.' He joked to cover his awkwardness. The execrable attempt at a French accent, and mention of candlesticks made it a reference to *Les Misérables*.

That made him the forgiving bishop. Jean Valjean was going on my next passport.

'It's not drugs,' I repeated. 'It's … hang it. A woman is going to die if I don't get to her first.'

Scepticism fought with some other emotion on his face until he stretched out his hand.

I shook it.

'John,' he said.

'Jack,' I said. Then: 'You're the biggest sucker I met today.'

With a wry smile, he turned and disappeared back into the church, the sound of singing voices swelling and fading as the door closed.

34

So, you need to know about *The Killing Joke*.

Released in 1988, the graphic novel, written by Alan Moore (of Watchmen fame) and illustrated by Brian Bolland, is the definitive origin story for the Joker. Critics loved it, gave it an Eisner and a Best Writer for Moore.

Told in flashback, *The Killing Joke* paints the Joker as an average man who had one bad day—the loss of his pregnant wife and accidental disfigurement—that sent him insane.

In present day, he embarks on a spree to prove a point to Batman: he wounds Barbara Gordon, leaving her paralysed, and kidnaps her father, Commissioner Gordon. He imprisons Gordon in a failing amusement park and tortures him to prove that all it takes for *any* man to go insane is one bad day.

When Batman finally catches up with the Joker in a funhouse, he gives the lie to the Joker's assertion. Gordon is unbroken, and Batman will bring the Joker in by the book.

The Killing Joke was shocking for a couple of reasons. The appalling injury to Barbara Gordon, and the Joker's use of naked photos of the injured woman in an attempt to break her father's mind are disturbing. But the part that spawned decades of debate among the fans is its ambiguous ending.

Picture it. Batman runs the Joker down, and offers him help to recover, fearing their enmity will one day be the death of one of them. But the Joker declines. He tells the joke of two inmates who attempt to escape from a lunatic asylum. The first jumps across the narrow gap separating two buildings, turns to the other, and offers to shine his torch across the gap so the other can walk across the beam of light. But the second inmate replies, 'What do you think I am, crazy? You'd turn it off when I was halfway across!'

The last page has Batman and the Joker chuckling at the joke as the police arrive. Over the silhouettes of the two foes, their laughter and the whine of approaching police sirens twine until silence falls. Framed are their feet, facing each other across a rain-spattered beam of light cast by the police car.

And then the feet are gone.

And then the light.

Thousands of diehard fans assert that Batman has done what he said he would. Arrested the Joker, as Gordon commanded, and returned him to Arkham Asylum.

Thousands more will assert that Batman finally broke; strangled the Joker, thus proving his point: it just takes one bad day ...

Hiero and I argued about this, too. Guess who thought Batman killed the Joker?

35

One hundred and forty-four pounds, it turned out to be, including the ten pounds given to me. With it I had checked into a cheap B & B, whose registry now said it was hosting a Mr A.A. Milne. I had decided for false names to start working through my favourite authors, and the author of Winnie-the-Pooh seemed altogether appropriate for the B & B's cottage decor.

And if you think checking in with a patently famous name (again) was a dumb idea, maybe that tells you something about my mental trajectory. I wasn't just on a quest any more. I was on a *righteous* quest. God had my back. After all, the churchman had smiled at me.

I had a day to understand and then thwart Hiero's next murder plan. With the money I had set up a war bunker, a think tank. I couldn't concentrate in a hostel (I also couldn't call Kim with privacy). In addition to my bed, I had a ham, cheese and salad dagwood and a Coke. I'd washed my clothes with soap in the sink, and I sat naked on the bed while they drip-dried in the shower. I had loaded more credit onto my phone, and had thirty pounds to spare for a train as far as ...

There was the rub.

If this was chess, we were approaching the endgame. I had to stop it here, on the soil of Mother England. I had to stop *him* here.

But I had no idea where *here* was.

I took the crumpled wad of Hiero's notes, and smoothed out the sheet for the next murder.

My index finger followed my gaze. Perhaps I was hoping it would catch on a word, a detail I had missed. Maybe there were other clues latent in the surface of the paper that I had yet to find: braille characters subtly pimpling the paper, or invisible ink that might be revealed by the oil on my finger?

But I found nothing new. I was left with the cryptic clues I had already tried and failed to decipher many times.

How: Observation
Where: Sidewise
When: Too late
Who: An old friend

Pausing to munch crisp lettuce, and wash it down with Coke, I began again.

Death by 'Observation'?

What the hell did that mean? Hiero had form for twisted meanings. His first victim had been the closest to a straight-up description: attempted asphyxiation by garrotting. Following Rhianne Goldman, Li Min had died of poisoning, an overdose of heroin. And Annika Kreider, Chalky—was she still alive?—had been pushed in front of a train, and Hiero had called it 'blunt-force trauma'.

Death by 'Observation'. No idea. It didn't matter yet.

'Where: Sidewise?'

'Sidewise in Time' was the title of a seminal science fiction story from the 1930s. In it pieces of the US begin transforming into their counterparts from alternate timelines—Roman legions from a Roman Empire that never fell appear on the outskirts of St Louis; Viking longboats raid a seaport in Massachusetts; the flag of the Russian Tsar flies over San Francisco.

(Hiero had thought the very existence of such a story in the 1930s proved the author was from an alternate reality. I think he was joking.)

As a description of a location it was about as unhelpful as it was possible to be. It effectively allowed any place from the infinitude of the multiverse.

As for time, 'Too late' was hardly encouraging.

But Hiero had given me a deadline: forty-eight hours. Something told me I could hold him to it. He had so far stuck to his own rules from a twisted sense of fairness. I had to count on him doing it again.

That left victim, the key piece of information. An old friend?

A mental tally of old friends and acquaintances in the UK came to, what, three? A school friend who had married a lass from Ireland—last contact maybe an email to wish him a happy birthday three or four years ago.

A second cousin of Kim's who had spent two years as an itinerant plumber in Australia, using our sleep-out as a home base. Again, I hadn't spoken with him since Kim left. And a colleague, Brian Skeet, with whom I'd co-authored a number of papers—one of which made it into *New Literary History*—now working for the British Library. The last correspondence I'd had with him was a tiny gloat for a mention we received in the *New Yorker*, maybe a year ago.

A disturbing thought: if Hiero meant an old friend of mine, which he had to, given he was setting me up, how long had he been at this? Planning such an elaborate frame? And why me?

And how old was old? Which friends could I rule out? There I hit upon a depressing truth: *all* of my friends were old friends, those that had stuck around. I hadn't invested in friendship for a long time. Not since Tracey's sickness.

Of those that still called me friend, were any holidaying in the UK?

This was infuriating.

Below the main items was a stream-of-consciousness of additional notes. Scanning it for the hundredth time, I strained to fish a useful morsel of information from it. One section looked like a limerick written by someone rhyme and metre blind.

> Said Professor Spratt With A Smile
> I'll Be In The Box With A Vial.
> With The Poison I'll Be
> Quantum Tangled You See,
> Thus Alive And Dead Both All The While.[1]

What I'd taken for a smudge turned out on closer inspection to be a tiny digit. The academic in me was immediately put in mind of a footnote. Of course, there was no footnote, but I wondered if perhaps Hiero had copied the text from an online source, and the footnote index had tagged along without him noticing. It also made me suspect my first impression, that each of these précis was typewritten.

But if copied, copied from where?

Fetching my phone from the bedside table, I entered the code for the hotel wi-fi, then made a search for the first line of the limerick.

The first few results seemed to be about a heart transplant patient thirty years on. Heart transplant didn't seem relevant. So I tried searching for the second line: I'll Be In The Box With A Vial.

Bingo.

I found the original at a physics nerd site. Hiero had only changed the first line of the limerick, and only one change at that. He had substituted 'Professor Spratt' for 'Schrödinger's Cat'.

Then it hit me. I was an idiot. Hiero and I had *talked* about this. Well, we'd talked about the many-worlds interpretation of quantum mechanics, which claims that every time a quantum event is observed, any time a choice is made, the whole universe splits in two. Say the choice is what you will eat for breakfast one morning. According to many-worlds, in one universe you sit down to a plate of bacon and eggs; and in another, *entirely separate,* universe you sit down to a plate of kippers. For once Hiero and I had agreed, that if this understanding of reality were true, it was the death of choice.

On making this connection, I couldn't keep a smirk from my face. Hiero, the little shit, had seeded this beautifully. I should have known the first time I laid eyes on this sheet that it was peculiar—an anomaly among the murder sheets. But the fear and rush had swamped my mind, prevented me from peering below the surface, and seeing what was hidden in plain sight.

Hiero hadn't cheated. He had known I possessed what I would need to decode his message.

Now that I did see it, it was embarrassingly obvious: it was, to paraphrase Aristotle, inevitable in retrospect.

I had to work backwards to Schrödinger's Cat.

Fuzzy memories of my college days tickled the back of my mind, physics lectures at eight in the morning.

I hunted around to refresh my memory.

This is the gist: Schrödinger's Cat is a thought experiment imagined by famous physicist Erwin Schrödinger that highlights the absurdities of quantum mechanics when lifted from the minuscule scale of atoms into the everyday world.

Imagine, went Schrödinger, a sealed box, and inside the box a cat, a bottle of poison, a Geiger counter and a tiny bit of radioactive substance.

Each second that passes, one atom of that tiny spot of radioactive substance has a chance of decaying. If and when it does, the Geiger counter ticks, a hammer swings, the bottle of poison is smashed, and the cat dies. All straight for an observer on the inside of the box.

The weirdness begins when we step outside the box, because what quantum theory tells us is that, until the box is opened and we discover the cat to be either dead or alive, it is both dead *and* alive.

One word stood out: observation. It was an observation—a peek inside the box—that actually rendered the cat dead or alive. Hiero's fourth sheet stated the means of death to be Observation.

But what the hell did it mean?

Could I *observe* this girl to death or life?

How could I observe if I had no idea where this murder would take place, or who the victim would be?

Then I remembered Hiero's blog. To read his posts, that was a kind of observation, wasn't it? Maybe he was tracking which posts I read—maybe altering his course accordingly? Already I had observed that his plans had some flux to them, some contingency, some reckoning with the real world. He'd had *two* accounts of Chalky's death.

My fingers scrambled to enter the URL for the blog—then halted. What if I was about to observe this girl to death? Well, if Hiero was sticking with the analogy, couldn't I just as easily be observing her to life?

A moment's hesitation, then I finished the URL and hit enter.

The blog banner appeared. I prepared to enter the password, but needn't have bothered. The browser went straight to the latest post.

The title read 'Chapter 17'. And the first line: 'Bunkering Down'.

I glanced at my war bunker—the hotel room, my scant belongings strewn across the bed and scattered beside me on the desk.

Once again, Hiero was writing from my point of view. And I had to hand it to him, he had an uncanny gift for guessing my moves.

I read on—and gagged on the first sentence: 'So I've got myself a bunker, some dive off Hindes Road in Harrow. Time to lie low.'

Hiero had published my current location to the internet. No password.

A kid sitting in Albuquerque or Islamabad could punch up this blog, find my hotel, and give me a cold call.

A *police officer* could get in his car and *drive* here in minutes.

How long had this blog post been available?

The whine of police sirens wafted through the open window. Were they coming for me already? I had a flash of recall: police cars scrunching to a halt below my Hong Kong hotel.

No. I tried to double-psych myself. They knew I knew they were reading this blog. Why would I give away my location? And when they came for me, they wouldn't use sirens, would they?

(Evidently my body wasn't buying it; it was busy scrambling to gather my belongings, and pull up my still-damp jeans.)

No. They thought I was a self-promoting psycho. Those sirens were for me.

36

I said before that *In Cold Blood* was the seminal true crime. But there was another before it.

The non-fiction novel *Compulsion* predates it by ten years. It fictionalises the story of Nathan Leopold and Richard Loeb, both in their late teens, both sons of super-rich Chicago families in the roaring twenties. With exacting prose, it describes their murder of fourteen-year-old Bobby Franks.

The book won a special Edgar, but what made the Leopold and Loeb case stick in the public eye was the apparent motive for the cold-blooded killing. It wasn't greed, or envy, or passion. The boys did not exact revenge. The reason they planned for months in meticulous detail, drove a rented car, picked Franks up from the side of the road, killed him with a chisel, and left him stuffed in a culvert, was *to see how it felt.*

Sure, both Leopold and Loeb had read Nietzsche, and were smart little *Übermenschen*. But one does wonder whether either boy would have gone as far as murder if left to his own devices.

It's funny what humans will do together that we'd never do alone.

Would Charles Starkweather have embarked on a killing spree in Nebraska and Wyoming without his girlfriend?

Would New Zealand teen Pauline Parker have killed her mother without her soul-mate, Juliet Hulme?

Hulme went on to be a successful author of detective fiction, and won an Edgar for her short story, 'Heroes'.

What a world, huh?

37

I walked. No other choice.

Ejected from my bunker, I was in the breeze.

Travel, for J.G. for the foreseeable future, would be by shanks' mare. Not only was I on foot, I was aimless; burdened only with my backpack, and the heavy knowledge that while I ambled, a girl was living her last day.

Difficult thing to imagine, that. Was she, maybe, washing up after breakfast? Putting on lipstick? Last time, my dear. How does that feel? What point, lipstick on a corpse?

But of course, she didn't know.

I tried to imagine what it would be like if I knew this was my last day, this my last morning walk. How would I feel? What thoughts would be swirling through my mind?

Imagine? It could be true. Wasn't such a stretch.

I paused, drew a deep, deliberate breath and took in my surroundings.

If this was my last day, I'd picked a shitty place for a walk.

I'd fled from the hotel, not aware of my surroundings, just focusing on putting distance between myself and the police cars I imagined were en route.

Before coming to the UK, my mental images of it were half-remembered photos from tourist promos or nature documentaries.

This was not one of those places. This was a patch of old suburb gone rotten. Perhaps 'urban decay' tours?

The shells of derelict houses loomed, roofs half stove-in by the elements. Graffiti on graffiti plastered their walls, in a riot of colour and obscenity. Even the weeds poking from the broken asphalt looked delinquent.

I kicked an empty drink can, sent it clanging across the lane, just to connect with the vibe.

A hoarse voice shouted for me to shut the expletive up. It echoed from the dark spaces beneath overhanging roofs and among rusting playground equipment, and I realised the cardboard and cloth lumps in there were habitations. There were people here. Living here. At *home* here.

Home.

I heard Kim's voice again: where is home, Jack? It hadn't quite been a question ...

Home? My thoughts went to my house in Nedlands. Two storeys, 300 square metres, and a sliver of river view.

But it hadn't felt like home for a long time. Not since Kim left. That place, if I was honest, was a museum of a past life, and I was the janitor who ate TV dinners in it, paid for the lawn guy, and slept in its too-large bed.

Home?

If not there, where was my home? Right now I was homeless, lacking only the smell to truly fit into the crowd hanging out in the boxes. But I could see now how short a trip it was, from student, or insurance salesman, or hairdresser—or academic—to homeless, and I pitied them.

Before I had got on the plane to Hong Kong for what turned out to be an abysmal failure (put that thought away), my home, my true home, the place where I burned the candle, fanned the faint embers of life and hope, was ...

The university.

The university had been my home for long years now. That fact was probably the source of the hint of bitterness I'd heard in Kim's voice.

I'd moved out of home before she had, with twelve-hour days full of numbing routine. Only, Kim hadn't thought it was *just* numbing routine, had she.

The Kim I married would never have suspected I could even countenance an affair—that she had, had fuelled my anger enough to let her go. And once again I had learned something. How fear and worry can erode even the best trusts.

I hadn't had an affair. Call it faithfulness. Call it maths. Call it love. The one woman who might have been my wife in another life had left the department and ...

Another life. A *sidewise* life.

The bolt hit me: Jane.

We'd rubbed shoulders at university, colleagues for four years—the university, my home—and then she had returned to her country of birth. To another university. And, yes, she was very much closer to home. Oxford.

The faint roar of traffic reached my ears, and in the distance the silhouette of an overpass sliced through the urban decay. I needed to get to Oxford, and that road seemed my best bet.

I cinched my backpack tighter, quickened my pace. As I walked I turned this question over in my mind: How the hell did Hiero know about Jane?

38

Marten Lacroix scanned the papers perched in her lap as the tube train bustled into London's innards.

She might have scanned the same information more conveniently on a laptop or a phone, but Marten preferred paper. A sheaf of cellulose, tactile, heavy. She had half a ream of email transcripts from the last six months finally unlocked by a warrant, a printout of Jack's blog as of last night, the results of an automated language analysis of his writing, and a much smaller, but more curious, item—a set of photocopied notes entitled *Blood and Ink* by Hieronymus Beck.

Apparently Jack Griffen had posted the notes by snail mail to the Perth police via the other side of Australia before he'd done a bunk to Hong Kong, and the package had been delayed. A sticky note had been photocopied still attached to the top sheet. It said simply: Bloody Australia Post.

Professional outfit, these Perth cops.

Marten held in her hands the cipher of Jack Griffen—crack the code and she might save a life.

The physicality of the paper slowed her down, focused her thinking in a way electronic media could not. She lifted the top sheet carefully, lest the pile slide from her lap and spray across the carriage floor, and slipped it under the bottom.

Secret code? More like cryptic crossword. Lists of facts and details about Jack Griffen's life that somehow had to enmesh and be made to make sense.

For today, this week, however long it took to put this man behind bars, Jack Griffen was Marten's universe. Her challenge was to discover the Unified Theory of Jack—the smallest set of axioms by which he could be explained, and then *predicted*.

This wasn't just a dissection of his history. This game was live. She was hunting a hunter. Could she catch him before he killed again?

Marten took a mental inventory of what she knew about Jack Griffen.

He was middle-aged. Traumatised. Divorced. Alone. Carrying an extremely rare heart condition that kept him at the scenic fringe of death. That was what the years had brought him.

The last few weeks had brought violent assault, murder, attempted murder.

The last few days had put a gun in his hands. And the paper she held in her hands prophesied more to come.

A thinker become a doer.

Marten leaned back in her seat and blinked away fatigue as the train swayed through a bend.

Well, it was a sketch. A line drawing that needed shading to better see the character of the subject, this man.

And in her hands, Marten hoped, were the pages that might offer those insights.

She began again to scan the emails, and soon found they were full of detail. The problem was, none of it fit within the outline she had sketched.

Griffen's work emails were boringly on-topic. The communications of the machine, Marten assumed, of a university faculty. Page after page of administrative queries, meeting follow-ups, timetabling requests, project proposals. The odd thread with fellow academics at institutions in other universities in Australia, and other countries—the US, Europe, a professor in Japan. Occasional banter with office staff. No sniping. No gossip. No two-faced lies. Responses to students for what was, to Marten's eye, a depressingly large amount of pleading for deferred assessment, which Griffen tended to politely but succinctly decline.

But nothing to or from any 'Hieronymus Beck'.

With eyes glazing, Marten took a moment to stretch her neck, before turning to the emails obtained from Griffen's internet service provider. If he had left any trace of his inner self in digital form, it was likely to be here.

A quick survey revealed that Jack Griffen only corresponded with a handful of people. There was a smattering of birthday wishes that were seen by her God's eye view to be all the same, except for the names. But by far the most frequent correspondent was his daughter, Tracey.

Griffen and his daughter spoke of life in California, and of the changes to Nedlands—the river, the bush, the streets of Tracey's childhood. She spoke a lot about her mother, Kim. In the last year she began to sign-off with 'In Christ, Trace'. A rash of recent emails were full of pie-in-the-sky planning on the off-chance Jack could make it to the US for some father–daughter time the following summer.

So he had a good relationship with his daughter. Scratch that idea. That was an anchor, not a pain point.

As for his ex-wife, evidence of direct communication between the two of them was almost entirely missing. The one exception was an email, dated February 15. Marten read it silently, imagining the cadence of Kim's voice:

'I'm not screening calls, Jack. I'm on a cruise. I can hear you laughing at that. What did we used to call them? Day care for adults? Well, for once in my life I'm going to be a child. For two weeks. I think I deserve that. Kim.'

So that relationship was nebulous.

Marten made a mental note to request his phone records to look for other signs of contact with his wife. Perhaps she was his endgame. Kill the Ex?

The train emerged into the half-light of a London afternoon in autumn. A bright red lorry caught Marten's gaze as it matched the train's speed on a side road for moments before turning away.

There had to be something she was missing.

She concentrated, willing a stab of intuition to highlight a connection, to reveal the true force that impelled Jack Griffen.

Psychosis—if that's what he had—was often sparked by trauma. Depression, even schizophrenia, could be triggered by a death, violence, even job threat. One theory held that *Beautiful Mind* genius John Nash's delusional schizophrenia was triggered by his fear of being drafted into the Korean War. In him it manifested as that mix peculiar to schizophrenia, of absurdity living side by side with clarity; of a god complex and persecution; of being caught in momentous history, and of being lost.

And that sounded like Jack Griffen. Such a man would suspect everyone and everything. He would assume his email was being snooped. Was it schizophrenia? He was ticking a lot of the boxes.

But then, he had been holding down a job at the university, apparently quite ably, up until six days ago. And not just any job, a professorship no less.

Could a man be descending into a schizophrenic haze and show no signs of it? Nothing to warn his colleagues or students of the coming crisis?

Marten flicked back to her notes of phone interviews with colleagues of Griffen she had been able to reach. There weren't many, but they all told the same story: he was an introvert, a man who fed off silence, but showed wit and kindness when wrangled into a corner. 'Haunted by loneliness,' said one secretary, but that sounded to Marten suspiciously like wishful thinking from a woman with a crush.

Marten's cheeks billowed with a pent sigh, and she put the sheaves of paper aside, feeling no closer to solving the puzzle of Jack Griffen.

Her hands idly toyed with the pack of business cards that Jack had dropped in the restroom at St Pancras. They were her first tangible link to him. She plucked at the rubber band, peeled it off, and flipped through the cards again. She came again to the card for the engineering consultancy, and realised that her discovery of the medical note on its reverse—*cardiomyopathy*—had distracted her from the obvious question. What was a card for an engineering consultancy doing among a pile of business cards for medical professionals?

Annoyed with herself, she drew her phone and dialled the number on the card.

In no time she was talking to the proprietor. ETN, it turned out, was very small—a mere handful of employees and the owner—specialising in niche automation and design projects.

It was nearing the end of the work day on the other side of the globe in Perth, Australia, but the owner's manner noticeably changed when Marten raised the name of Jack Griffen.

'Yes, I know Jack,' he replied.

'Why would he have your business card?'

'We did business.' He laughed.

'What kind of business?'

'We collaborated on a little device. Jack had some ideas. Called the project his Roald Dahl.'

'Roald Dahl?' This conversation was making less sense than Marten had hoped.

'The children's author, Roald Dahl? Willy Wonka?'

'Yes, of course, I know who Roald Dahl is, but what has he got to do with the project you undertook with Jack Griffen?'

'I'm sorry,' he said. 'Who did you say you work for again, Mrs Lacroix?'

'UK Police. This is above board.'

'Is Jack in trouble?'

'If he is, we're trying to get him out of it.' *And behind bars.*

'It's just that the project is a little sensitive. Jack was referring to Roald Dahl's quest to design medical interventions to combat his son's epilepsy—Dahl hired a miniature steam engine craftsman to design a cranial shunt.'

Marten was still confused. 'Jack doesn't have a son.'

'Correct. We designed and prototyped a device for monitoring his—Jack's—heart. It's a kind of watch that monitors sensors to alert the wearer to imminent cardiac arrest. The hardware is fast becoming consumer grade now—with the Apples and Microsofts of the world—but the algorithms for making sense of the data, and its connection to GPS-based emergency response are still novel. Jack named it the Medline. He wears it twenty-four seven and charges—'

'Wait.' A thought occurred to Marten. 'GPS? Could we use that to find him?'

'Oh, I see. No, no; Jack was always very clear on the parameters there. He's very security conscious, is our Jack.' And he chuckled, perhaps thinking that was uncharacteristically real-world for an academic. 'The only time you'd get a fix on the watch's location by design would be if it fired a distress on the emergency band, if he's in range of a cell tower.'

'That sounds promising?'

'Well, at that point, Jack is having—Wait a minute. I can show you …'

Marten heard the muted clatter of a computer keyboard, then a different voice spoke in her ear: 'My name is Jack Griffen. I am unable to speak. This is a recorded message. I am having a heart attack—'

Hearing the voice of her quarry sent a tingle through Marten, before the recording clicked off. The engineer spoke again. 'We burned that audio sample into the firmware. It would get routed to the nearest response centre with a location attached, just like if you or me dialled emergency. But like he said, at that point he's having a heart attack.'

Minutes later when the platform of St James' Park Station slid into view, Marten was still ruminating. If Griffen hadn't slipped into psychosis, or snapped after a recent traumatic event, what did that leave?

She couldn't escape the depressing conclusion: he was just a homicidal dickhead.

39

'So you're a *librarian*, yeah?'

She said it.

My gaze slid sideways to look at the woman behind the wheel—Iona? Elsa? For a moment I warred with myself over what answer to give. I was tired. It would be so much easier to just nod.

'No,' I said. 'Not a librarian. A professor of literature.'

Her mouth tugged down at the corners in an expression that meant she was sceptical, or else had no idea what I was talking about and didn't want to be rude.

'And you want to visit this Bohemian Library—'

'Bodleian Library.'

'—Bodleian Library because it has good books?'

'It has *all* the books. By an act of parliament in the sixteen hundreds, it's legally entitled to a free copy of every book published in England.'

'Can't they just …' Her fingers flickered above the steering wheel. 'You know, Kindle it these days. Ebooks are so much easier on the hands.' She rolled her eyes in a comradely fashion.

Let it go, came that voice, although even it sounded tired and defeated.

'Some of the books in the library are hundreds of years old. The very rub of their pages tell us about their owners, about technology, society long ago. The oldest is a text on papyrus, preserved in ash from the eruption of Vesuvius. That's nearly two thousand years old.' (Part of me had forgotten that the Bodleian was my excuse; 'You're trying to save Jane's life, remember. This isn't about books.'). 'A draft of Shelley's *Frankenstein*—the germ of the science fiction genre—is in the collection.'

'Uh-huh. And this library is where?'

'Middle of Oxford, on the university campus.'

'I can drop you near Tesco's. Short walk from there, I'd guess.'

Her comment jarred me, reminded me again that I was the recipient of another act of kindness. I promised myself to drop the lecturing tone.

As it turned out I didn't need to. Her left hand scrabbled for the radio dial. Apparently she had run out of questions.

She found the button for a preset station, and a song by Simple Minds filled the tiny car. She ramped the volume until the song drowned the whine of the car's over-taxed engine. She started singing, and for a horrible moment I thought she was going to turn to me and count me in.

The noise washed through me as I stared at a wall of yellow-flecked green streaming past the window. Maybe I dozed. It took a few seconds for the newsbreak to percolate through my hazy thoughts.

'... who the press are dubbing the "Intercontinental Killer".'

She reached over and bumped the volume higher.

'Police have begun a manhunt for Jack Griffen, the Australian man believed responsible for a spate of violent crimes, including the murder of a Hong Kong student. Citizens are advised to be on the lookout for Griffen, last seen entering the UK at St Pancras Station. Griffen is six foot two inches, of slight build, brown hair ...'

I inwardly squirmed, feeling every inch of my six-foot-two-inch frame, my skin tingling. I guessed it was too late to try the dog-food line.

'Hey, that could be me,' I said, alarmed at the sudden desire to giggle.

She looked at me for a heartbeat, rolled her eyes. 'Aren't you from New Zealand?'

What? When did I say that?

'Sure.'

The radio continued: 'The fugitive is considered dangerous, and under no circumstances should he be approached.'

I snorted. Dangerous? Dangerous as a plastic bag.

'I suppose if I was the Intercontinental Killer,' I said, 'I'd be heading to Oxford to kill someone'—a suicidal tide was rising from deep inside me—'that would make you my accomplice.'

'An unwitting accomplice,' she said, her eyes never leaving the road. 'I'm happy for my lawyers to run with that. You're gunna murder the librarian at this Bogeyman Library?'

'Yeah.' I clicked my teeth. Outside the window a man dressed in dirty overalls was peering at the underside of a tractor with obvious confusion. In my best Arnold Schwarzenegger impression: 'She don't know the Dewey Decimal System.'

I glanced at her, 'A little Conan the Librarian joke there.'

And that was that. We drove in silence, and the suicidal tide ebbed within me. It wasn't until she dropped me in the middle of Oxford that it returned. The street was thronged with police cars. A quick tally gave me at least eight chances to suicide by cop.

'Thanks,' I said.

'Any time, Jack,' she said, and winked.

I shut the door, and watched the car move off into a clot of traffic working its way past the police cars.

'Morning, officer,' I said to a bobby, who tipped his hat to me.

Raising my eyes, I scoured the low skyline. Somewhere over yonder would be the Bodleian, and with any luck, Jane.

And, if I played it right, Hiero's corpse.

40

'Oxford?' said Marten Lacroix. 'You're sure about that?'

'Hell no. I'm not sure about anything, but forensics say the perp has put Oxford on the internet as the home of his next victim.'

'And you believe it?'

'Can't argue with a hundred percent hit rate.'

True. Marten sucked her teeth. But ...

'Look,' Collins continued, 'worst case it's damage control. Can you imagine the shitstorm that would land if he *did* hit Oxford, and it was leaked that we knew before it happened?'

'Okay, okay.' Marten waved him off. 'Can I go?'

Collins smiled. 'You want to drive your desk down there?' Marten gave him a withering gaze. 'Peace. I'll get someone to take you down.'

Marten nodded as she made for the door, then paused as a thought occurred to her.

'How about that kid officer, the one who gave his gun to Griffen?'

'Trent?'

'That's him. Can he take me?'

Collins gave her a quizzical look. 'Sure.'

Minutes later Inspector Marten Lacroix watched Trent hold the car door open for her.

She arched an eyebrow at him in what she hoped was an unreadable expression, and slipped onto the cool vinyl seat of the 2015 BMW X5M, the performance cousin of the X5 SUV, and the station's latest response toy.

The grin that kept sneaking onto Trent's face probably had more to do with the car than the prospect of chauffeuring her for a joy ride to sunny Oxford.

As they emerged from the underground parking lot, Trent gave the throttle a prod. The back of the car snapped round and the resulting thrust of raw power sent a tingle through Marten's stomach, and she had to fight to keep her poker face.

They wove through traffic, skirting Churchill's statue. Trent right-angled at speed past Big Ben, and headed for the A40, which would take them to Oxford. He had opted to take Millbank, which offered a close view of the Thames until it curved around the head of Vauxhall Bridge. Marten had the momentary sensation she was on a breakfast date.

Her gaze drifted across the car's dashboard, which said 'money' in at least five languages. Powerful multi-channel, encrypted comms, a DVR connected to cameras facing every direction, and a fish-eye atop the roof just in case. Each could be switched to active night vision if desired. A screen bigger than Marten's first TV not only displayed information ingested from the in-car system, but fused data flowing from the control centre, showing little icons moving through the city like wind-up soldiers.

So much silicon. Was this where the fight to stop psychos would be won? Had she spent those years, that effort, the FBI course, the relentless research, to train grey matter that was already obsolete?

Her gaze slid sideways to Trent, whose smile fell as the patrol car jerked to a stop behind a traffic snarl. The engine's purr faded.

Obsolete? she thought. Let's find out.

'I need your help,' she said.

He glanced at her, sat a little straighter. 'Sure.'

Hook baited.

'I'm having a hell of a time fitting the pieces of this psycho's brain together into a complete picture. So many contradictions. So many pieces that don't seem to fit *anywhere*.'

'Psychos,' he said, with a brief shake of his head, as if the matter of understanding serial killers began and ended with that one word. It would certainly make a succinct profile: Jack Griffen, psycho.

'Can you take me back a couple of days, to the train station. I know it's traumatic.'

Trent was silent, staring into the brakelights of a Ford Kuga that flickered with impatience. For a moment she feared she had laid it on too thick, was too obvious, but—

'No, no. I'm cool. The guy's just some high-paid pen-pusher. I wasn't, like, afraid.'

'Okay. Thank you so much.' *God*, girl. 'What kind of a morning was it?'

'Busy. Never seen the station so stirred up, like a wasp nest.'

'I mean, take it right back. You were lying in bed, opened your eyes. Take me through it.'

She watched his gaze—abstracted for moments. What mental furniture was he shuffling around? The someone lying beside him in bed? The cranial-tolling of a hangover? A yoga mat?

Didn't matter. Marten was internally setting her expectation thermostat, finding the baseline for Constable Daniel Trent.

'First thing when I opened my eyes?'

She nodded encouragement.

'I looked at the clock, saw it was five-something. Way too early for a Tuesday, more depressing than Monday. But I couldn't go back to sleep. Too wired. Day before the station had been full of the rumours of this guy, that he might be coming. That we might be part of it. So I got up.'

'Sheets? Duvet?'

'Sorry?'

'On your bed. What were you sleeping under, or were you on top of your bed, buck-naked for God and all the world.'

He smirked. 'Just a sheet. White linen. Love the feel of it on my skin.' The way he said it left Marten wondering if the confession was inadvertent, or step one in a play for her.

She tugged at the wedding band around her finger absent-mindedly as the car wound onto the M4 and its engine roared back into life.

'What next?'

'Showered, dressed—'

'Listen to the radio?'

'Yeah, in the shower.'

'What was on?'

'That CCR song, "Bad Moon Rising". I think it struck me as right—for *him*, not us. A newsbreak. Some Brexit crap.'

'Breakfast?'

'Coffee. Always. Since I was a cadet.'

'Weather that morning?'

He squinted in concentration. 'Colder than a monk's balls. I had to go back into my flat for a coat.'

'Then you drove to the station?'

'Drove?' He grunted. 'Constable's wage doesn't get you a car in London.' Shared understanding. Tick.

'Took the tube,' he continued. 'Got pinned between a suit that probably hadn't showered for a week and a bunch of school kids—Queen's College, by the blazer. Talking about a YouTuber.'

Marten noticed he was starting to detail without prompting.

Time for phase two.

She let him ramble up to the mission briefing ('A faint aroma of morning sweat; a couple of older officers acting like they were Rambo') then jumped in.

'How was that same room late in the afternoon, after it had all gone sour?'

Trent's jaw hung open comically for a moment, perched, presumably, on the verge of a fine story about how he got to the station. He clamped it shut, then, '*End* of the day?'

'Yeah. I want you to work backwards, until your encounter with the "Intercontinental Killer" starting with how the mission debriefing went down.' She prodded, 'Collins can be a hard-arse. Did he scarify you?'

'Scarify?'

'Give you a proper dressing-down?'

He seemed to consider this. 'Actually?' he said, quiet. 'He was too stressed. Worried that we had …'

'Let a killer into the country?'

The slightest nod.

'What do you remember about the trip back to the station?'

'You know, I think maybe I was in shock.' (More revelation. Step two in the playbook?) 'I drove a patrol car, but was reacting a second too slow to everything—almost hit a pedestrian near the university—a short skank too busy yammering into her phone to pay attention.'

'What was she wearing?'

'Black dress, super-short, super-tight, lotta leg for such a short girl.' His delivery had become monotonic, as if he had entered a trance that echoed the shock of that afternoon.

Marten was on the verge of prompting him again when he continued.

'Collins asked me at the station car park if I was okay to drive, and I said yes, like a hero. Before that, well, it had been chaos. Senior guys running every which way, barking orders. But everyone knew the pooch was screwed, and we were moving so as not to be a target. We searched everywhere. I had to check the ladies toilet near reception, startled a teen redoing her lipstick. Not sure who was more embarrassed.

'Then we started in on the bins, grates, working from the concourse out, anywhere Griffen might have stuck my—the gun.

'Detectives worked the crowd at the same time, asking passengers on the way in, store keepers, anyone, "Seen this man?" Except the photo was wrong. He had shaved his head.

'It was starting to get dark. I had to take a piss. Nearest toilet was the one I'd found *him* in, so I walked five hundred metres to find another toilet.' He glanced at me. 'That's weird, innit?'

'Sounds human to me,' said Marten. It did. 'Who cleaned you up?' she said. 'Your nose, I mean.'

'Nurse,' he grunted.

Marten popped her eyebrows.

He shook his head. 'It was a guy.'

Marten laughed at the disappointment in his voice. 'Sorry.'

'There's a tiny first-aid station over the way in King's Cross. Collins sent me there after I'd made my way onto the main stage and told him the good news.'

They were approaching the entrance ramp to the A40. Trent flicked the shift down, and the engine reacted with an angry whine.

Marten felt the tail of the car sway out as he gunned it around the curve.

'S'pose you want to hear about what happened in the toilet again.'

'I do. But I need you to try something for me. It'll help me work out this psycho. You've been so helpful. We're almost done.'

'Shoot.'

'I want you to imagine yourself in that cubicle again. That's your scene.

Wrap it around you—the harsh light, the touch of cold porcelain, the echo of its tiled walls, the smell. I need you to *live* in it for a moment.'

His gaze slid over to her.

'DCI Lacroix, I do believe you're subjecting me to a forensic sketch interview.' A tight smile. 'I took the class.'

That was to be expected, she thought. But I'll bet you don't know a thing about latent cognitive interviewing technique—need to travel farther than Hendon Police College to get this one, as far as Quantico.

Latent cognitive technique applied pressure to a story the way ice applied pressure to the hull of a trapped ship. Under the gentle but unrelenting pressure of the probe, sooner or later, the liar ran out of fresh detail, and the fabrication began to fall apart. He couldn't help but return to canned sentences like a dog to its vomit.

'Close,' said Marten. 'But I'm not after Griffen's mug. We have that. I want a sketch of the inside of his skull.' Marten observed Trent closely. He was buying it.

'So you're picturing yourself squatting on the crapper, embodying that moment.'

'Oh, the relief,' he joked lamely.

'And you hear the sound of approaching footsteps. They draw near, and fall silent just outside your cubicle. You hear a tap run. You flush, stand up, open the door and ...'

Here goes.

She finished: 'What does *he* see?'

Trent glanced at Marten, apparently checking he had heard right.

'Griffen?'

'Yes.'

'Um ... well, he sees me.' Doubt laced his tone, as if he had suddenly realised he was talking to an idiot.

'Come on, Trent. Put some colour into it. You're allowed to speak the truth. "He saw a handsome young officer, dark-haired ..."'

He smirked. 'Okay,' he said. 'So, I'm at the sink, facing the wall, the mirror. I think I'm crying.'

'You think?'

'I *am* crying. I hear a cistern flush, and see the cubicle door open behind me. I'm rattled; I thought I was alone. Wouldn't have stopped at that sink if I'd known that cubicle was occupied. But then I see, just over the reflection of my own shoulder. Cop's hat. Cop. I turn to face him, and he goes for my gun—'

'You're *Griffen*, remember.'

'Sorry. I go for his gun.'

'How do you go for his gun?'

'I reach over,' he took his right hand from the steering wheel and reached across the dash.

'And you take the gun?'

'Yeah. It's unclipped, lucky me. I grab it, and the cop goes for me—we grapple, spin. I get a finger to the trigger and *bang*! Glass and tile fragments everywhere, taste of propellant in the air.'

'You're still wrestling? Then what?'

'Yeah. No. We're apart. Shock of the discharge, I guess. The cop is still staring me down, but he's afraid—who wouldn't be?'

'So …'

'So I reverse the gun, grab it by the barrel like a hammer, and smash the cop in the face. His nose pops like a tomato, blood everywhere.'

(Wow. The creative juices are flowing.)

'Then I push him back into the cubicle, onto the seat. I take his radio, drop it in the bowl.'

'And leave?'

'Yes. But not before saying: "Move, follow me, and I'll kill you." Then, "*Alley ecka est*"'—He glanced at Marten, a grin on his face—'whatever you said.'

Trent slumped back into his chair, his eyes glittering above the swollen contour of his nose, the storyteller after the story is told, when there is nothing left to do but bask in the adulation.

Marten smiled back. '*Alea iacta est*; the die is cast.'

It was a good story.

Pity for him she didn't believe it.

41

I stood staring at the massive iron gates guarding the library's entrance, the face of Hogwarts to my Harry Potter.

The vast arch of the gates stood in faded limestone. From their edges lines rippled outward, as if the gates had been thrown at wet cement. Their surface was a grid of rectangles, each containing the coat of arms of an Oxford College.

'Alohomora,' I whispered, mindful of the tourists ambling across the quadrangle, and pushed on the wicket gate. It yielded to my touch, and as I passed through, my footfalls echoed on the irregular concrete tiles, bounding off the high enclosing wings of the library. Passing through a smaller door, I was enveloped by the cool, silent gloom of one of Europe's oldest libraries.

I was hunting for Jane Worthington, and it occurred to me now how vague would be the query, 'I'm looking for Jane of Oxford.' I didn't even know if she still went by the same name, or if she was married, or hyphenated, had taken a barcode tattoo, or joined a cult and given up on the Devil's monikers altogether.

In fact, I'd heard bugger-all from her since she left Australia eight years ago. I'd made a point of not contacting her. Maybe I should have been more worried about that, and the kind of reception I'd get.

All these thoughts took time to uncoil in my head, and I'd been standing, staring into space for minutes. Much longer and I would start looking like a thief or a terrorist, or worse, a salesman.

I padded over to what appeared to be a loans counter. A plump woman in a paisley dress peered at me through thick glasses and asked if she could help me. I still hadn't decided how to discretely ask for 'Jane of Oxford' ('Me Jack. Where Jane?') so I stalled.

'I wanted to borrow a book.'

The woman in the paisley dress poked her lapsing glasses a half-inch higher on her nose, leaned forward and said, 'The Bodleian does not loan books, but you are welcome to sit in and use the reserved collection.'

'Wonderful,' I said. 'Can you point me in the direction …?'

'No,' with a mischievous crinkling of the eyes that was unexpected on her matronly face. 'First you must take the oath.'

'The oath,' I said, voice flat. Was this woman gatekeeper of a hitherto unknown sect?

'The borrower's oath,' she said, once again matter-of-fact. 'Here,' and she slid a sheet of paper across the counter to me.

On it were two blocks of text. One in Latin, and the other in English.

'I have to read this?' I said.

'Yes,' she said, and tapped a fake red fingernail on the English text. For a frightening moment I thought she suspected I couldn't read.

Resisting the urge to inform her I was a professor of literature, no less, I began: 'I hereby undertake …'

Somewhere around 'kindle therein any fire or flame' I became aware of another voice, a female voice, echoing my own. I glanced over my shoulder and saw Jane. Or rather, Jane as she might appear in one of those police profiling programs, where they artificially age a missing person. But in her case, it was double the years it should have been. She was beautiful still, but careworn to the point of gauntness.

My shock must have shown, for she interrupted herself to say, 'Not the *Mona Lisa*?'

'Had I but seen you cross the hall, I would have declared myself observer of the transit of Venus.'

She snorted. 'Ford Transit, perhaps—but you're thinking of Thomas Hornsby. He beat you to Venus by two-and-a-half centuries, from these hallowed grounds no less, but then, I guess you knew that, for the Jack Griffen I knew was not one to choose his allusions sloppily.'

'A-hem.'

As one we turned toward the counter to find the lady regarding us. With a glance at the unfinished oath, she set me to task again.

I finished in a hurry, and Jane linked her arm through mine and drew me out into the gloomy spaces of the hall.

'How did you know I was here?' I said.

'I saw you standing in the quadrangle looking like a lost kid. You've saved me from death by a thousand Saxon inflections.'

'Saxon?' I said. She nodded. 'Shit.' And we ambled away.

'Tolkien's manuscripts are here, you know?' she said, lifting an eyebrow at me, a gesture that definitely belonged to the Jane Worthington I had known.

'Are you flirting with me?'

'I don't flirt with Tolkien,' she replied. 'That was a marriage proposal, you idiot. But enough small talk. Why are you here, Jack?'

Noise swelled as a group of tourists came through the doors.

'Is there somewhere private we can talk?'

She looked at me, picking up my mood. 'Sure, sure. Through the staff entrance, this way.' And she led me between shelves piled with brown manuscripts to a door. She produced an electronic keycard, and we exited into a small square of gravel, which was enclosed on all sides by wings of the library.

The door shut automatically with a buzz that sounded out of place among the old buildings. From behind us, above the door lintel, a pair of stone busts with beards like root-tangle stared down with dead eyes. Beneath them ran the text *Schola Moralis Philosophiae*, which my execrable Latin told me meant School of Moral Philosophy.

'So, Jonathan Donald Griffen,' said Jane, and I winced. 'You have me donning my metaphorical cloak, wielding my metaphorical dagger. What's afoot?'

I took a breath and launched in feet first. 'Did you happen to note the, ah, increased police presence on your way to work this morning?'

She nodded, gaze travelling my face.

'They're here for me.'

'Assuming you're not just winding me up, Jack, why would that be?'

'They think I've murdered one, maybe two girls.'

She did me the dignity of not asking the question in her eyes.

I continued, 'And think I'm here to kill another.'

'Another,' she said, voice flat.

'You.'

'Me?'

'Well, I'm not sure if they know it's you yet, but they will.'

'I don't understand.'

'That's because you're sane.'

She looked sidewise at me. 'And you're … not?'

'Jury's out on that one, but it doesn't matter: Here's what you need to know, what you need to *believe*—'

Motion in the corner of my eye snagged my attention, a dark blur. The blur resolved into a bobby in full uniform. He was slinking through the courtyard. My pulse quickened.

I inclined my head at him, eyes on Jane. 'That normal?'

She shook her head ever so slightly.

So the police had narrowed Oxford to the university campus. That had to mean they were looking for Jane, and this cop just hadn't recognised her yet.

'Do you know a way out of here?' I grabbed her hand, but she shook free.

'Let's just go and sort this out, right now.'

I grabbed her arm, tight. 'I can't.'

She pulled away. 'Why not?'

'It's complicated. You have to trust me.'

My pulse beat loud in my ears. A glance at my Medline confirmed my fear: I was orange, pushing red.

'Or you can stand here and watch the Intercontinental Killer have a heart attack.'

Without a word Jane slipped her hand into mine—a lover's touch to my mugger's grapple—and led me toward a shadowed arch.

'How's Kim?'

'Doing well. She's chair of botany at UC Berkeley, San Francisco.'

'Oh.'

The sun's warmth vanished from my neck, and in the sudden darkness the world shrank to the feel of Jane's hand in mine.

When we emerged into the dappled shade of gardens, Jane seemed resolute, but I had no idea where she was taking me. I filled the awkward silence. 'Gotta say, you don't seem surprised to see me.'

'I was surprised to find the 2012 Chezeaux on my doormat'—she tapped her handbag—'but—'

'What?' I halted but she tugged me onward.

'The wine,' she said, 'and chocolates—and don't ask; yes, I ate them—some habits die hard, and you're no sweet tooth. But I *always* share the wine. Let's find someplace quiet to open it, and you can explain to me what you've gotten yourself into.'

Now it was my turn to grab her. Snatching her upper arm, I whirled her to a halt, facing me. For the first time there was fear in her eyes.

'Listen. I did not send you chocolates or wine, haven't done in—what?—a decade? They're not from me.'

She pulled away, but this time I didn't let go. She matched my stare as she drew a wine bottle from her bag. A tag dangled from its neck. I grabbed it, turned it right side up and read the following: 'Save till I arrive. If I don't make it, drink it and think of me. Jack.'

Jane said, 'The wine was always to share, you didn't need the note.'

My voice rose, 'I didn't write the note, because I didn't send the wine!'

'Okay, okay, Jack, I get it.'

'No, you don't. The wine, the chocolates—which you *ate! Shit!*—are from this psycho. The guy who is *actually* murdering people.'

The look on her face then, lasting a split second, no more—I'll remember it forever. It wasn't fear. It was resignation.

'Yes, Jack, I ate them. And I'm fine.' She tugged her arm from my grasp, and twirled on the spot. 'See? Fine.'

Right then my mind chose to remind me of the fourth murder sheet (was that really what we were up to now?). Death by *observation*.

Was I dooming Jane by simply being here?

Was Hiero having a go at me for not having contacted a friend in so long? Was she supposed to die from lack of Jack?

I laughed at the thought.

Jane's brow wrinkled with concern.

'I'm fine, too,' I said. 'But we should get out of here before a cop recognises me.'

'And drink this wine,' she insisted, tapping her handbag.

'No. Toss it. Seriously.'

'It's a Chezeaux. I'm willing to risk it.' Her eyes flashed, and a strange smile lifted the corners of her mouth.

Through a gap in the screen of shrubbery I saw another cop wander past. Their concentration was up. His presence reminded me that I'd been running blind too long. I retrieved my phone, and thumbed open the web browser. Hiero's blog loaded up and I scanned the latest post.

It took three bites; three snatches; three saccades.

Hello Oxford town. Rev. Jack Griffen to administer last rites to Jane Worthington, Oxford University.

Wordlessly I passed the phone to Jane. She read, brow furrowed.

'Why is he writing as you?'

'Why does a monkey play with its faeces? I don't know.'

Jane winced. At first I thought at my quip. But her face spasmed a second time.

'What's wrong?'

'Nothing.'

My expression dared her to repeat the lie.

She sighed. 'Nothing *new*. Forget it.'

'You need to get checked out.' It scared me how quickly she acceded this time.

'Fine. I know a clinic nearby. We'll go there, they can ply me with leeches, then we're drinking this damn wine, Jack.'

She turned about face and that's when I saw not one, but a baker's dozen of cops fanning out in the distance.

'Shit,' she breathed. 'We can't go that way. It'll have to be the Radcliff—' Her voice cut off with a sharp breath.

I examined her more closely. Her face was pale, especially about the eyes. I looked at the cops diffusing through the campus.

'Maybe this is the end of the line, Jane. You need a doctor. Now. We don't have time to play cat and mouse.'

She ignored me, grabbed my arm, and pulled me away at right angles to the approaching cops. Soon a blocky building eclipsed the sun. If I judged correctly, it was the backside of the old Bodleian.

'Isn't this just where we came from?'

She continued to ignore me as we wended through a number of

corridors, leaving me quickly turned around. We descended two flights of stairs.

Half-remembered facts about the venerable campus percolated through my mind.

'Are we heading for Mendip cleft?'

The famous Oxford underground held an aura of skullduggery.

Jane glanced at me dismissively. 'Pshaw. Do we look like a couple of college drunks on an end-of-semester lark?'

We exited a stairwell into a subterranean space filled with bookshelves and quiet reading spaces. A murmur of conversation was the only sound. Jane strode purposefully between the chairs and stacks, and I began to hope that she was okay. Perhaps the chocolate was simply chocolate, and the wine, simply wine.

Sight of the reading room provoked a pang of jealousy. Students were scattered through it in groups of two or three, or sat alone, reading, poking at laptops. What I would have given to sink into that world. I'd lived in that world once, long ago.

'Mrs Worthington!'

The exclamation startled me into the present.

'Fiona,' said Jane, turning to a red-headed woman seated at a table. She had the air of a student, which belied her thirty-something age, and wore a pink woollen cardigan that could not have clashed more with her red hair.

'The Tolkien *Beowulf* you gave me is *divine*.' She held a book up in two hands as if it were a baby to baptise. 'And why are there policemen in the Bod?'

'I'm glad you like it—' A haze of pain crossed Jane's brow. 'Sorry. Did you say police?'

Fiona nodded eagerly, a curious mixture of avidity and disapproval. 'Just a moment ago. Came through the conveyor tunnel like a ...' She paused, her gaze hunting dead air for something. 'Murder of crows. A *blue* murder.' Her mind seemed to catch up with her words. She snorted, then giggled.

'Where did they go, Fiona?' I said, intent.

Fiona's gaze floated to me, seemed to see me for the first time. 'Ooh. You're dishy.'

My cheeks felt hot.

'Which way?' Jane said in a strained voice. Her posture had a strange cant, as if she were fighting to stay upright.

'That way,' said Fiona, waving a hand in the direction we were going, her eyes never leaving me.

Without another word, Jane dragged me back the way we had come.

'Why are they here, Mrs Worthington?' Fiona shouted.

Through gritted teeth, Jane muttered, 'They're hunting the Intercontinental Killer.'

Passing the stairway we had emerged from, we entered an odd, elongated room. It was dark, and the stale air smelled of abandonment.

'They must have started at the far end of the conveyor tunnel.' Jane seemed to be speaking to herself. 'Why would they do that? Why would they even be down here at all?'

With a sinking feeling, I recalled the last time Hiero had outfoxed me.

'Hiero seems to know where I am at all times. It wouldn't be the first time he's played with me. He's writing a story with me.'

Jane raised her eyebrows, but I felt too drained to elaborate. Hiero had probably sent the cops down here. Maybe this was the story's last act. The climax. Jack Griffen filled with lead in a dungeon beneath a library. Add another pinch of spice to the storied Oxford underground.

Was this what it was like to live under Fate?

No. Fate was indifferent. The god of this story was positively malign.

The darkness deepened, and we walked in silence. Beside me, running parallel to the wall, was the half-seen bulk of a conveyor. I knew from past reading that it had once, not long ago, transported books from one library building to another beneath Broad Street. It lay silent now, coated in dust that dulled the shine of its steel.

At the far end we ascended another stairwell. By the time we opened a door to peer into the grounds, Jane was puffing like a steam train.

'Right,' she said. 'Coast is clear. We'll have to circle around, but we can make the clinic now.' She didn't sound as if she were simply humouring me anymore.

I took her hand in mine. She let me.

42

'Just keep driving,' said Marten.

Her eyes were on the lanes seen through the patrol car's windows, but her mind was elsewhere. Mentally, she was turning puzzle pieces about, trying to imagine what kind of picture included Jack Griffen and Jane Worthington and Oxford.

Hasty digging had connected Jane to the University of Western Australia, and Perth. Her tenure had overlapped with Jack's. But why fly halfway round the world eight years later to kill her? This was different to the exchange students; Marten yearned to know why.

Her eyes snagged on a cluster of red bicycles parked on the cobbles of a lane. A couple passed them on the footpath, a bald man and a woman. The man turned to examine the bikes as they passed. They had almost passed out of sight when Marten saw them disappear into a nondescript building.

'We could stop at the station,' said Trent, exasperation leaking into his tone. 'It's a stone's throw,'

'No. We have phones. If I want to talk to the local constabulary, I can. Until then, I don't want to be bombarded with pointless chatter and offers of coffee. Most of all, I need to think.'

Trent did his best to suppress a sigh, and pretended to scan the footpaths and shopfronts.

Marten tried again to place the puzzle piece: Jane Worthington. What would Jack want with her? Why now? Was this a cold grudge brought home?

Nope. Didn't fit.

Unless Jack Griffen was truly falling apart mentally (possible), the grudge motive didn't fit with the other girls. It couldn't be the unifying theme. He had only known—could only have known—the students for at most a year.

Now it was Marten's turn to sigh. So far the only common trait across all four victims was that they were female. Didn't take a genius to spot that. A preschooler could have done it. Heck, her iPhone could have done it.

Maybe it was love spurned? Or any of a number of baseless speculations …

'Shit,' she muttered to herself. 'Anything to catch a break.'

'Sorry?'

Trent was looking at her askance.

'Nothing. Drive on. Keep your eyes open.'

'You think he's just going to be swanning around on the street here after publishing his whereabouts?'

He had a point.

43

I fidgeted.

Next to me, Jane was still as a rock but for the occasional tremor that travelled her body. She was fighting hard to conceal them.

The waiting room was empty. It was lunch hour and the doctor was out. The receptionist had promised he would be back in five minutes.

I retrieved my phone and thumbed it on for something to occupy my hands. I hesitated over the link to Hiero's blog, then noticed a little red notification icon alerting me to an unread email.

A poke of the icon and the email appeared. It was from my IT friend at the university back home, Matt Price. I read it greedily.

> Jack, you didn't ask, but I couldn't help it.
>
> What I mean is, I've been digging, trying to make sense of your situation. I trust you. I know you didn't do these things. Anyway, the thing is, I've found something. I think it's big. I'll write more when I learn more, but I had to get this to you. You sounded kinda hopeless.
>
> This Hiero guy, I managed to intercept traffic travelling via his server. Local email exchange (encrypted, but hey, not everyone is as good as me). I don't understand everything I'm seeing, but it looks like shorthand for exchanges. Handshakes. Took me a while to nail it, but the traffic I'm seeing reminds me most of army dispatches. *Coordinating moves.*
>
> Upshot: Hiero isn't working alone. He might be the trail blazer, but there is another party involved.
>
> More when I can.
>
> Stay safe, Jack. I'm on your side.

Hiero not working alone? The thought was … shocking.

And enlivening.

If Hiero wasn't alone, if there was *someone else*, well that was a conspiracy. Sure, a conspiracy of two, but the more gears in the machine, the more places to jam a spanner.

A loud *clunk* broke my concentration.

I turned to find Jane had placed the bottle of wine on the coffee table. It stood in the only clear spot on the surface, surrounded by year-old magazines.

'You're kidding,' I said.

For an answer, she produced two plastic wine glasses from her handbag, the kind used for camping. She pulled them apart and screwed the stem and base onto each.

'I know you don't feel well,' I said. 'The wine is probably poisoned, too.'

'Are you just going to watch me drink, Jack?'

Was this death by Observation? I was supposed to *watch* Jane die?

She sighed, then gripped the cork in her teeth and tugged it. It came free with a *ploonk*, and she filled the glasses to the brim with a velvety red vintage.

'Poisoned?' She sighed. 'Yeah, probably, so I guess you'd better not drink it. But just pretend for a moment, will you?'

I glanced at my Medline. It was after one o'clock. Where in hell was this doctor?

From the corner of my eye I saw Jane raise the glass to her lips. I reached to restrain her arm, and she stared at me.

'Give me just one moment of pleasure, Jack. Take a look where we are. Take a proper look, and give me a damn moment's normality.'

What did she mean? I scanned the waiting room. What did she expect me to see? Coffee tables, magazines, tired chairs, a fish tank containing a solitary catatonic goldfish. On a board, behind the receptionist, the practitioners were listed. I read the names.

Finally, noticed the pattern.

'Oncology,' I said.

'Got it in one,' she said, and raised her glass.

'Cancer?'

'Terminal. Your pet dickhead wasted some fine chocolate and wine shooting a carcass.' She set the glass to her lips, and closed her eyes.

Part of my mind rejoiced to discover yet another proof of Hiero's narrative fallibility.

But—

My arm whipped out, knocking the glass from her hand. It flew through the air trailing a streamer of blood-red wine, and shattered against a magazine rack.

With a sigh, Jane mimed taking a mouthful of wine. Her eyes remained closed, her chin tilted upward, her lips curved in a faint smile.

'Mmm. So good. It's been so long. Kale, organic quinoa … Why don't they make organic chocolate éclairs? Now that would be some cancer treatment.'

'Cancer.' I didn't know what to say. Eight years. And now this.

At length, I managed, 'How long do you have?'

Pain creased her brow, and she cried out.

'Was three months, give or take. Looks like the schedule's been accelerated.'

Before I knew what I was doing I found myself on my feet, yelling at the receptionist.

44

'No, no. This is the wrong street.' Marten squinted at an intersection. 'Try that one.'

For the third time in a minute Marten cursed herself for being a lackwit, while simultaneously deriding herself for being a hopeful naïf.

She pictured again the memory of the man and woman on the street, and strained to squeeze more detail from it. A bald man and a woman. Why did it *have* to be Jack Griffen and Jane Worthington? (It didn't, you fool.)

What had she seen that had caught at the back of her mind, tickling her awareness until she had paid it attention?

The woman. She had looked normal. Clothes. Handbag. Hair.

The man. He had looked, well, not out of place, exactly. But … he wasn't bald. His head had been shaved, the skin of his scalp shone through lighter than the skin of his face. And his clothes. Shoes, jeans, long sleeve t-shirt. Taken individually, they weren't noteworthy. But together, the ensemble was foreign.

(It's Oxford. They're tourists.)

And he hadn't been holding hands with the woman. He'd been leading her. Tugging her along. Taking her somewhere.

(You're a third wheel here, and you're grasping at straws.)

One way to find out. If she could just find the building she had seen them enter.

Then she saw the bikes. A rank of red bicycles, all tilted at the same angle. Just beyond them, the pale grey door through which the man and woman had disappeared.

'That's it. Pull up.'

Trent swung the car to the kerb, ignoring the double line, and killed the engine.

In moments, he had his belt stowed, and his freshly issued pistol clear of its holster. It surprised Marten. He'd appeared to be barely tolerating her hunt for the anonymous couple. His hand was on the door latch, when her own found his shoulder. He turned, surprised.

'No,' she said. 'You can't leave the car here.'

'Are you crazy?'

'Probably. And you've been a fine help. But it's probably nothing, and we can't leave a patrol car parked on a double yellow.'

He snorted, 'Come off it.'

'Look. If it is him, and we cause a scene out here, he'll disappear. Same as he did at St Pancras.'

Trent's face darkened.

'And if it is him,' she repeated, holding his gaze, 'he knows your face. He doesn't know mine.'

She glanced at the gun gripped in his hand. 'And holster that weapon. I have enough paperwork to do.'

He scowled and slipped the gun back into its holster. She noted he'd forgotten to snap the security loop shut. It was a bad habit that could get him suspended, but now wasn't the time to chew him out.

She opened the door, and stepped onto the footpath.

He leaned across. 'And what are you going to do if Griffen's in there?'

Marten smiled her winning best. 'Why, come and get the cavalry, of course.' She shut the door without waiting for an answer, and strode toward the pale grey door, feeling an equal mixture of anticipation and embarrassment.

A moment later she was inside, peering into what was apparently the waiting room of a medical clinic, and brought to the sudden realisation that neither mood had been right.

She found herself staring at a situation for which she was entirely unprepared.

45

'Forget the doctor,' I shouted at the receptionist. 'Call an ambulance!' Straightaway I knew it was a mistake. My anger seemed to trigger in her a kind of paralysis response, like when a rabbit is caught in the jaws of a wolf, and it ceases to struggle by instinct. I noticed for the first time how young she was. Had Fate given me a trainee receptionist?

Trying hard to moderate my voice, I said, 'She will *die*. Right here in your waiting room if you don't help.'

Slowly, gaze fixed on me, the receptionist reached for the phone and began to dial it by feel. Clearly that instinct was just as fundamental.

Behind me, Jane cried out. An animal noise.

I turned to find her curled into a foetal position on the waiting-room tiles. Through laboured breathing she hissed, 'Like a knife in the guts.' Dropping to my knees, I took her hand in mine. A spasm rocked her body, and her hand clenched.

'Jack.' A voice. I noticed for the first time that someone had entered the waiting room. A woman.

'Are you a doctor?' I said with a glance at her.

'Jack Griffen,' she said.

She was simply standing there, one step in from the doorway, one hand cupped still, as if holding the memory of the doorknob.

'Yes, I—' And then it hit me.

There was only one reason a person other than Jane would know my name here, in Oxford, UK, thousands of miles, and an eternity away from Perth, Western Australia.

'You're a cop,' I said.

The slightest nod.

'I don't care,' I said. 'She's dying, unless somebody does something.'

I heard a murmur from behind the receptionist's desk, then the *clunk* of a handset.

'They're sending an ambulance,' was all the receptionist said. She sat, gaze flicking between me and the newcomer.

'What's wrong with her?' said the cop, gesturing at Jane. She took a step. One hand disappeared into a pocket—going for a phone, a gun?

'Poison,' I said.

'Cancer. Liver. Stage Four,' Jane grunted.

The cop moved two steps closer, then sat on a chair, on the other side of Jane from me. In front of this cop was a woman clearly fighting extreme discomfort, but the cop's eyes never left me, as if I were a tiger in the room. (Tiger, tiger, burning bright …) She withdrew her hand from her pocket. It held a delicate, pink handkerchief wholly at odds with her businesslike mien. Despite everything, I must have smiled. Her brow crinkled with annoyance.

'I've been looking for you, Mr Griffen.'

'You found me,' I said. Jane's face was a white one step above translucence. The veins at her temples were tiny purple squiggles. Her eyes were screwed shut as she strained to regulate her breathing.

'How long till that ambulance?' I asked the receptionist.

'They didn't say.' She sounded like she had dropped acid in an attempt to check out of a day she had not expected.

'Why did you do it?'

Something in the cop's tone made me look up. She spoke as if she knew me.

'Do what?'

Her gaze dipped to Jane's writhing body.

Anger surged through my frame.

'Geez, lady—do you have a name?'

'DCI Lacroix.'

'Sorry, was the question, "When did I stop beating my wife?"'

It was the textbook cliché of a question with an embedded assumption. Either answer—yes or no—and you were damned, and she knew it.

'Okay, if we're trading clichés; you're innocent, is that it?' She sounded pissed, an improvement on 'concerned'.

'Innocent? What a word. But this right here? Take a look. Connect the dots.'

She glanced at Jane, and in what seemed an automatic reaction, placed a steadying hand on her shoulder. 'You expect me to believe this isn't your doing? Want to know how long your rap sheet is right now? And you're the victim? That doesn't make *sense*.'

'Sense?' I hissed. Emotion warped my face. It didn't know whether to cry or rage. 'Sense? Put your bloody logic away for a moment and taste the world where people *live*.'

I turned back to Jane, said, 'I couldn't care less about the little fantasy you guys have got going.'

'So it's all coincidence? You're one unlucky guy, the way murder follows you around.'

'You're confusing cause and effect, lady.'

'It's Marten.' She hesitated. 'I talked to your wife.'

That brought me up short. I didn't correct her, either.

She went on. 'She doesn't believe you're a murderer.'

'Good woman, that,' I said. We were staring at each other across Jane's suddenly still body. Just on the limit of hearing came the whine of an ambulance. Marten seemed to hear it too. She tensed, and looked toward the street.

'Was I just talking to an ex-wife with misplaced loyalty?' So she knew all right.

I didn't reply. I had to lean over Jane's face to see that she was still breathing. Fast, shallow sips of air.

A buzzing noise reached my ears. Marten pulled her phone from her pants pocket, took one look at the screen, and dashed to the door. Then— she locked it.

She spoke to the receptionist. 'Tell me there's a back way out of here.'

The receptionist pointed mutely down a short corridor.

The ambulance whine rose suddenly. It must have turned onto our street. In the same moment, the doorknob rattled, and there came a pounding on the door. A shout came from the other side.

Marten turned to me, reached across and gripped my shirtfront with surprising violence. 'I worked bloody hard to get to where I am today.

You'd better not turn out to be a murdering son-of-a-bitch, or I'll hunt you till you're strapped to the chair.'

Her vehemence surprised me out of the moment. 'You sounded like Sherburn from *Huckleberry Finn*.'

'What?'

'Mark Twain,' I said.

'I haven't read a novel since university.'

Hadn't read a novel? 'But—' The retort died on my lips as Jane's hand gripped my leg. Her eyes were clamped shut, and she spoke with obvious pain.

'Go before this woman comes to her senses. And—' she swallowed. 'Thanks.'

I reached down and took her hand in mine.

'For what?'

'For being a good man. You know what I mean.' Her eyes opened to slits and she looked at me. 'Now get lost.'

'Jane, the melodrama,' I said, numbness stealing over me. 'Just don't die.' I leaned forward and kissed her cheek. It was cold.

'That horse bolted,' she whispered, and her eyes closed again.

Looking up, I found Marten's gaze on me.

'Why?' I said.

'Why what?'

I jerked a thumb in the direction of the back exit. 'Why let me go?'

She stared at me, mute.

The door shuddered with another thump, and this time it was accompanied by a cracking noise.

I leapt to my feet and, with a last look at Jane, raced down the corridor.

46

'Why let me go?'

Jack Griffen's last words echoed in Marten Lacroix's mind as she stared at the end of the corridor, her last sight of the man before he turned and disappeared again.

Why let me go?

God, there were a thousand reasons why not to.

Number one was now sniffling behind the reception counter. How was Marten going to swing allowing—no, positively *abetting*—the escape of Jack Griffen, the Intercontinental Killer?

And number two was about to break down the waiting-room door. Trent would know Griffen had been here, and Marten had let him slip through their net.

Who was going to buy the truth? That Marten thought Trent was a trigger-happy liar, who would have interpreted the waiting-room scene as a homicide about to happen, and shot Jack Griffen point-blank? The same Jack Griffen Marten had now seen in the flesh, and who, if Marten was any judge of character, had been genuinely distraught.

Or an Academy Award–winning actor.

Not according to the woman lying silent beneath Marten's hand.

Marten hauled herself upright, fingers gently leaving the prone form of Jane Worthington, who had lapsed into unconsciousness.

She crossed the room and unlocked the door. It swung inward, and Marten was momentarily stunned. Before her stood Constable Trent, hunched low as if preparing to shoulder-charge. Behind him, two paramedics stood poised with kits. The raw wailing of the siren filled the air before it cut off in a heavy silence. The ambulance was double-parked outside, and through the door its light strobed the white walls of the anteroom. In the distance, police sirens wailed over the top of each other, phasing in and out.

Everyone was staring at her.

''Bout time,' she said, and stepped aside to let them bustle past. Trent came first, gun raised. At the sight of Jane, the paramedics pushed past a protesting Trent, and gathered over her, opening kits. She was lost to sight.

Trent spun on the spot, glancing into every corner, seemingly trying to make sense of the scene.

At last he said, 'Where is he?'

'Gone.'

'Gone where, Marten? And why the hell didn't you answer my call? You promised.'

Marten returned his stare and arched an eyebrow. She let the silence draw out until he averted his gaze.

'DCI Lacroix,' he added. 'Ma'am.'

'He escaped. And I was unable to answer your call as there was a woman dying on the floor at my feet.' She flicked her gaze at the paramedics still huddled over Jane.

Trent persisted. 'He didn't come out the front. So, which way did he go?'

Marten jerked a thumb at the corridor, and Trent rushed down it.

Steeling herself, Marten padded over to the receptionist. A quick appraisal told her the receptionist had slipped into post-traumatic shock in record time. If ever the girl would be clay to mould, it would be now. But all Marten could bring herself to do was offer the woman a hand on the shoulder, and murmur that it was okay now, the paramedics were here.

'You did well,' Marten soothed, while her stomach churned. Had the woman seen her lock the door? Or observed her interaction with Griffen through her stupor? No telling now.

She left the reception desk, as Trent returned.

'No sign of him,' he said, and swore. 'I can't believe we came all the way here, *actually* found him, and he got away again. The captain is going to grind my—'

'Constable.'

He fell silent, expression hunted.

'There's nothing more you could have done. It was *my* call to come in here alone. It was the right call. He doesn't know me.' She gripped his shoulder. 'And, hey, at least he didn't shoot at you this time, right?'

The paramedics were moving Jane. Trent seemed to notice her for the first time.

'And he's done it again. Killed another one.'

'She's not dead,' said Marten.

One of the paramedics caught her eye as they bore Jane out. He shook his head.

47

I'm not crazy, I'm just a little unwell.

The lyric went around in my head, mainly because I couldn't remember the next line, but also because it was—apropos?

Apropos doesn't end with an 'S' sound.

Ah-pro-*poh*, is how you say it.

Ah-pro-Edgar-Allen-*Poe*.

Nevermore.

Sigh.

I'm not crazy …

My legs dangled down the wharf front, a yard above the churn of froth where the waves met concrete. Seaweed mingled with Coke cans. I kicked my legs lazily in time to the music in my head. They felt strangely heavy.

I'd boarded the first train not bound for London, and ended up here. Southport, or Portsmouth, or … None of the signs had sunk in. I kept seeing Jane lying on the waiting-room floor, scrunched into a ball. Not fighting it, just enduring. Waiting.

Looking up, I could see buoys beginning to sway heavily in the rising tide, like upside-down pendulums, ten-foot mechanical metronomes. Gulls wheeled in the sky, crying warning. Much farther out, at the limit of vision, a wall of rain approached.

Why, when at wits end, do I always head for the ocean? Because oceans can take a world of pain. They just keep on sucking it up, bearing it away, pulling it under.

But only because they couldn't give a shit. Not one metric faecal deposit about your problems, Jack-my-man.

My phone buzzed in my pocket.

I withdrew it on autopilot, and cocked my arm to throw it into the ocean.

Then paused.

'What the fuck. In for a penny, in for a pound.'

I pressed the receive button without looking at the screen, and said, 'Hey, dickhead. How's the criminal underworld treating you?'

He breathed once, then laughed. 'Oh, Jack. That is *beautiful*.'

I gazed at the waiting ocean, the spindrift flying from wave tops, racing the coming storm. No. *That* was beautiful. And utterly indifferent.

'You have reached the bottom,' said Hiero. 'Sunk to the bedrock of Jack. Reached the heart of darkness.'

Now it was my turn to laugh. 'Hiero, please don't Marlon Brando me.'

He didn't seem to hear me, just kept going. 'You're at crisis point. It's time to see if the bottom of Jack is really the bottom for *you*.'

'Hiero, hurry the hell up. You're spoiling one of nature's greatest reminders of my impotence, and you're killing my melancholy. You're mixing it up with throat-throttling rage, filling my mind with images of what I'll do to you when I get my hands on you.'

'You're right,' he said, and actually seemed to mean it. 'I'll get off. But, here's what you need to know. Do you remember that book by Forster? It wasn't required reading, but I remember you raving about it, so I unearthed a copy and read it. And you were right. Your taste is uncanny. I loved it. Do you remember it?'

The wind rose, peeling back my salt-damp hair. Gone was the seaweed smell. What remained was pure, deep ocean breath. I sucked in a lungful.

I answered, '*Aspects of the Novel*.'

'Do you remember Forster's argument?'

I snorted. Of course I did.

Hiero continued, 'That every story holds in tension two opposing forces? The freedom of its characters and the demands of its plot.'

Drive your characters too hard to a predetermined plot and they become puppets, one-dimensional props for the author's show; but let them loose, allow them freedom to be and to do the unexpected, and they can derail the story. Destiny versus freewill.

True of story, true of life.

Ever since she'd met God, Tracey loved to remind me that story was embedded in the very word we use to describe the race we humans run: history.

Through the millennia, the arguments were always about the identity of the author.

'Well, Jack, I've decided I've been riding you too hard. Your shoulders must ache from being harnessed to my muse.' (God, what a twat.) 'So, I'm giving you a break. Time to put you in the wind. Give you a chance to see who you are. Surprise me. It's a risk, but great literature—'

'Demands great sacrifice.' I finished for him, remembering our conversation from—when? It would be two weeks ago tomorrow.

'See, you've got it.'

'What do you mean, exactly.'

'You haven't got it.' He sounded so disappointed. 'I'm giving you a break.'

'How long?'

'So businesslike.' He sighed. 'Six weeks. You get forty-two whole days until the next item on my list. The *last* item.' (He was calling lives 'items' now.) 'Time enough to gather your strength, plan your strategy, and come out guns blazing. Give me a cracking scene—strap on a utility belt, load up some magazines. Or … dissolve in a puddle of your own piss and self-pity. But that would be disappointing, wouldn't it? I'm rooting for you, Jack.'

'Okay,' I'd gone monotone. 'Six weeks. Then where?'

'The US.'

'Who?'

'Shit, give a yard take a mile. I'm not telling you *that*, Jack. That's part of the dramatic tension. As Forster would say—'

I killed the call, leaned back and tossed the phone. It arced over the water and struck the face of a wave with a brief flash of white.

Fine. Hiero was giving me freedom. See how he liked his first taste of it.

The rain wall finally landed, and the storm opened up in earnest.

Water ran down the back of my neck, a chill between my shoulder-blades, and seeped into my eyes.

My second act of freedom was to sit beneath the naked sky and soak through.

48

'Forensics report.'

Marten glanced at the speaker, a tan-skinned man, who dropped a large manila envelope on her desk. She couldn't remember his name. He was new, a couple months in the office, still shiny. She thought he might be of Indian or Pakistani extraction. Maybe Persian? He was a gopher between departments, and he said the word 'forensics' like foreign-sicks. Today it didn't even raise a smile.

Probably had something to do with the fear gnawing her stomach.

She pushed the fear aside, and reached for the envelope. Slitting it with a fingernail, she slid the contents—a handful of typewritten sheets—onto her desk. She scanned the text for the vitals.

Jane Mary Worthington had died of cyanide poisoning. She had died relatively quickly, which was put down to a reaction with her cancer medication and complications with her failing health.

That was expected.

The information on the second sheet was not expected.

At Marten's insistence, the lab had also tested the wine remaining in the opened bottle they had found at 'the scene'. One assay had flagged the presence of a substance.

But not a poison.

The wine had contained chemically modified 3-mercaptopyruvate.

Marten's brow furrowed in confusion. It was chemistry. Meant nothing to her.

3-mercaptopyruvate, the report went on, spelling out the implication, might be a fast-acting antidote to cyanide poisoning.

The wine, which Jane had apparently attempted to drink, had contained the *antidote* to the poison in her system.

Marten slumped in her chair and let her gaze wander across the vista of rain-damp Portland stone cladding framed by her window.

Jane Worthington had on the verge of death held in her hands her salvation, and Jack Griffen, according to the receptionist (who, worryingly, seemed to be regaining memory by the hour), had, when she attempted to drink it, slapped it from her hand.

Oh, God. Marten leaned forward and cradled her head in her hands.

'This is not happening. UK profiler the victim of Stockholm Syndrome.'

'Come again?'

Marten shot upright to find Collins looming over her desk. She hastily tucked hair behind her ears, a nervous habit since schooldays, and returned his gaze.

'I'm annoyed I let him get away.'

Collins rounded the desk, and pulled a chair over to sit close. When he didn't speak immediately, Marten's guts tightened.

'Hmm. I've gotta say, that statement isn't squaring so well with the picture emerging.'

'We're too old for games. Just come out and say it.'

Now he looked at her—and was that disappointment in his eyes?

'Why, Marten? You let him escape.'

'You're getting this from the receptionist? She was stone—'

'Stop! Just stop. You *asked* her if there was a back way out of the building. You locked the door.'

Marten's mind spun frantically.

'It was a no-win—No, *listen*!' She stalled his in-taken breath with a hand. She had one shot at this. 'The woman was dying. And any minute Trent was going to come charging in with all the finesse of a bulldog. And there's me. And there's the receptionist. And there's Jack, who according to last known intel has a gun. Do you really want that bomb to go off? I defused it the only way I knew how. I let him go. Hell, I didn't *let* anything. What was I going to stop him with?'

Collins looked at her for seconds that stretched on with those grey eyes that gave away nothing. He was chewing the inside of his cheek.

'Jack?' he said.

'Griffen.'

'But you call him Jack.' He leaned forward, palms on knees. 'I shouldn't even have to ask this, Marten. You're not some green recruit. You're a seasoned cop. Did he get under your skin?'

She suppressed a sigh. 'Look, I did what I could. Rap my knuckles, and let me get on with putting the psycho behind bars. I know what he smells like now. Should be easy to track.'

Collins leaned back in his chair again, and shook his head, the slightest motion.

'No. Not even I can get you off this one scot-free. You'll have to drop below the radar for a while. Take some leave. The media circus will shift to top gear after this fiasco—I'd love to know who fed the "Intercontinental Killer" crap to the press. In the meantime, you'll just clog the gears. Hell, you could do with a break anyway, right?'

Anger took the edge off her fear. 'So, what, I'm suspended?'

'No, that would just bring the dogs. Look, just work with me. Take some time off.'

'Chief Superintendent Collins, if you're not suspending me, I've got work to do.'

He gazed at her for a moment, then rose, returned the chair to its place.

'No one ever accused you of diplomacy, DCI Lacroix.'

'Sir,' she said, and pulled her laptop over. She barely heard the door close as he left.

She was consumed with the drive to see if one split-second decision had wrecked a career built with the sweat of years.

And, far worse: let a murderer remain free.

49

In a little lane, close enough to hear the cry of gulls stirred into the air by a storm closing over Portsmouth Harbour, a young man sat at a café table. His gaze played across the street while his fingers fiddled with the remains of a paper sugar sachet. Sitting on the table before him were a half-drunk macchiato and a sleek black laptop. The laptop was shut, but a white light embedded in its edge slowly pulsed.

The man's thoughts wheeled, a montage of images, sounds, and other sensations. As he watched, an audience to his own freewheeling mind, a smile spread across his face.

'I'll be damned,' he murmured. 'He's doing it. He's actually doing it.'

A flicker of motion in the periphery of his vision disturbed his thought. He glanced that way and caught a glimpse of a bald, middle-aged man disappearing down a laneway.

Without a word, the young man retrieved the laptop and stowed it in a messenger bag, and left the café. His coffee remained half-drunk on the table.

50

Phillip Lau cursed as he reached the automatic doors to the parking lot.

Through the rain-speckled glass he could just make out the dark form of his 2003 Toyota Solara. It had been parked open-air, in a drop-off bay since lunch. He would probably get a ticket. And its door seals leaked.

With a roll of the eyes, he jammed the last piece of sugary donut into his mouth, and returned to the elevator.

Inside, he extracted his keycard from its lanyard beneath his vest, and swiped it over the security pad. He caught a brief glimpse of his own photo beaming back at him from the scratched plastic. Phillip K.T. Lau, mortuary assistant. The photo was five years old, and in it his head sported decidedly more hair. He cursed again, and punched the button for level four.

The door to the coldroom was lit by the green glow of an emergency light. Stepping inside, his fingers scrabbled across the wall for the light switches. With a *clack*, banks of fluorescent tubes clattered to life.

He could do the less-used hallways of Queen Mary Hospital in semi-darkness, but he had to have light, lots of it, to look at the bodies. He thought, not for the last time, that his career counsellor had given him a bum steer. He'd liked biology class. Dissections were fascinating. But human bodies? They were altogether different. They looked too much like him. The power of his imagination was too strong—he saw twitching lips, eyes that flickered open.

He walked along the face of the cold stores, breath misting in the chill, trailing a finger beneath the labels, hunting for 34-B. It was 34-B, wasn't it?

He recalled Connie's orders, as she'd left two hours earlier. Clocking time, and gone for a weekend of depravity, probably. Lobbing make-work over her shoulder without a care for lower-pay-grade Lau. Yeah, no one else had a life. He thought again of his car sitting quiet and cold in the lot.

'Before you leave,' Connie had said, 'can you check something for me? I got a call from a police detective. Wanted me to confirm there was no evidence of tampering with 34-B, that pretty young thing from Sai Ying Pun.'

The pretty young thing from Sai Ying Pun. Sounded like a song title.

Phillip's insides squirmed. They were the worst. The ones that looked like they were asleep. Should be years from death.

His fingers found 34-B.

The latch was stiff under his fingers, but eventually it gave with a snap and he hauled the small fridge-coffin open.

34-B lay, asleep in death.

She appeared to be asleep, but—thought Phillip—thus far invisible to the naked eye, her cells were being broken down into their constituent proteins, eaten, and excreted by a riot of bacteria, despite the three degrees Celsius of the mortuary storage unit.

Hurrying now, he bent over her head, and probed her hair. He had to lean into the coffin and crane his neck. Inches below his eyes, her lips were pale. (Was that a puff of breath? No. Just cursed imagination.) He slid his hands under her head, and gently lifted it away from the steel tray.

'Nothing,' he muttered, and was on the verge of lowering her head when he saw the irregularity. He leaned closer, with her head cupped in his hands, face tilted away from him.

There, faintly visible in the silken flow of her hair—a break in the sheen. A straight cut, such as a knife or scissors would make.

Someone had taken a lock of Li Min's hair, without a care for how it looked.

Phillip smiled as he reached for his phone. He had a legitimate reason to wreck Connie's weekend.

51

My memory gets a bit hazy here.

My mind reaches for recollection like a hand plunging into a dark pool. It frequently comes up empty. The few memories I'm able to fish from that time—the time Hiero left me to sound my own depths—are slick with shame.

Isn't it a rite of passage for every poet to sleep in his own vomit?

But if emptying the contents of my stomach on strangers was the worst my memory had to offer, I'd be happy. On the contrary, it turns out my brain is maliciously adept at retaining the very worst experiences I put it through.

I stole. Really stole. Not just penny pilfering from church money bags.

To begin with I stole food—grapes, beans, apples, straight from their trays. I shoplifted small, expensive items, and pawned them. Razor blades, USB sticks, batteries, perfume.

From the money I made, I bought the cheapest liquor I could find, Captain Morgan, Gordon's London Dry Gin—one step above Pine O Cleen—and got thoroughly smashed.

I like to think of this as my cliché phase. From beneath the alcohol haze, the memories are even vaguer. I do remember vomiting in a public toilet, whose walls were graffitied with layer upon layer of black text. Perhaps it was someone's practice studio. In that toilet a woman pulled her yellow blouse down by the neck to reveal one very white breast. I think that's as far as that went. My fingers were crusty from clutching the toilet bowl. Real mood killer.

Never before had I seen dirt collect in the creases on the inside of my elbows—little deltas of black against my pale skin. I began to be able to smell myself. That lasted for a few days and passed. About this time I noticed the power of repulsion rise. Step into a corridor, and people would slip to the side. Sit at a table, and watch the space around you empty.

I stole clothes too, from Oxfam and Age. Easier than laundering the ones I was wearing. It was curious what I grabbed by raw impulse. Adidas track pants. Bomber jacket (the nights were cold). Shoes were harder. I pawned two pairs before I got the size right. And they were pitch-black joggers with fluorescent orange stripes. My hair was becoming a fuzz as the nap grew longer.

I slept in a homeless shelter. No shit, there was a place in Southhampton where you could lob up and get a cot for the night, and lukewarm porridge in the morning, no questions asked. The building smelled of boiled cabbage, even though I never saw any boiled cabbage, but the bed was soft. I'd never dreamed such places existed.

That was where I got my first fist to the face, and lost my first tooth.

You can steal from the average guy on the street and it's fifty-fifty he'll react from sheer shock and grab you, or else freeze from a weird disconnected sense of propriety and of not wanting to make a scene.

But try stealing from the poor, and be prepared to fight.

I wasn't. I took a blow to the jaw, and stood wondering at the meaning of the sharp pain and the accompanying cracking sound that travelled around my skull.

The tooth, which I found in my mouth like a leftover popcorn husk, was fascinating. The roots were broken off, still in my jaw I guess, but there was plenty of blood on it. I used to dream of losing teeth, of having them all come popping out one morning while looking in the bathroom mirror.

I showed it to the woman who had socked me. My smile might have unnerved her, because she shut up and hurried off.

You'd think I would have shown her my gun. I still had it. But I was keeping that a secret.

I stole other things, too. At the back of my mind was the idea that sooner or later I would need to crawl out of this hole, and I'd need money to do it. But for the time being, I was consumed by an odd combination of a desire to get caught, coupled with the belief I was untouchable. Funny, that. You would think that I would be feeling wretched.

Quite the opposite was true. I felt infused with power. Everything would bend to my will simply because all of their conventions had no hold on me anymore. I could lie and ignore because, at that time, I didn't care for anything or anyone. Not even myself. I was a lump of iron that had been held thrall all its life to a magnetic force suddenly, at the flick of a switch, floating free. The fluxing fields of social convention, of habit, of morality were simply … gone. Had no hold on me.

Understanding this was the turning of a corner on the road back to humanity.

That and overhearing a snotty student refer to me as 'just some sad shit'.

It was a slap in the face far worse than, well, the fist to the face.

There must have been a skerrick of pride lingering at the base of my soul after all.

But the strongest tug back to the land of the living was the memory that came to me one morning, of the fifth and final murder sheet.

I didn't need to pull it out. I could recite it verbatim.

> How: Choice
> Where: A fun house
> When: An anniversary
> Who: The author
> Why: ?

Hiero had told me to head for North America. In less than four weeks, at a fun house somewhere in the US, a choice would be made, and an author would die.

52

Marten didn't know how long Benjamin's hands had been on her hips before she realised. Her thoughts were sunk in the meaning of the curative wine. The wine that, had it been drunk, would have saved the life of Jane Worthington. It was haunting to think the wine's bouquet would have been in her nostrils.

Before Jack Griffen knocked it to the floor.

She stood at the sink, holding a glass, which she had cleaned and dried ten times over with the tea towel in her other hand.

'We getting you back any time soon?' Her husband's voice in her ear was close enough that she felt his breath on her skin.

She placed the glass upside down in the rack. It made a *chink* sound as it swayed against the next. She turned in his embrace and kissed him on the lips.

'I'm sorry.'

A smile tugged at his lips. 'No you're not.'

He hugged her tighter, pulling her body into contact from hips to shoulders. 'And we still love you. Poor saps.'

He said it lightly, but Marten knew from experience that he joked about the true things he found hard to say.

A question rose on her lips, but she pushed it down. It was about the woman and the wine. Compartmentalise. Don't bring it home.

She could feel the warmth of Benjamin's six-foot-five frame through her dress suit.

Don't bring it home. That was the received wisdom.

Why the hell not? Wise men hadn't done so well in her life.

'Why would you poison someone, put the antidote in their hand, then remove it?'

'I wouldn't,' he said, keeping an expertly blank face.

She swatted him on the arm.

'Perhaps I meant to take the poison too, then take the antidote.'

Marten pondered that. 'Seems risky. What if she manages to take the antidote?'

'Then I'd have to kill her another way.'

What other way did Jack Griffen have? His bare hands? She remembered the look of him. The hand touching Jane's had been an academic's hand. Thin, nimble, not abused. It was a ridiculous thought, but they didn't look like hands that could throttle a windpipe.

The gun? He'd fired it once already, a deliberate attempted homicide.

Who was she kidding. No he hadn't. Trent's story stank.

Marten prised herself free of her husband's embrace, and turned back to the sink. Keep the hands busy. Let the mind work.

'Who else could it be?' he said.

'What?'

'You have more than one suspect?'

Oh. She sighed. 'We have a character sheet for a suspect.'

He laughed. 'I have no idea what that means.'

'Jack Griffen, the man with the curative wine, claims he is the patsy'— she smirked at the quaint word—'of the dark and nefarious Hieronymus Beck, who, keeping one step ahead of the poor Griffen, is fitting him up for a series of crimes.'

'The name sounds made up.'

'Doesn't it,' Marten agreed.

She paused, a dripping wine glass frozen in her grip above the cooling water.

Doesn't it, just.

Without another word, Marten placed the still-wet glass on the sink, and left the kitchen.

Benjamin reached for the tea towel and glass, smiling, confused. Since when did his meticulous wife leave the dishes half done?

53

I stood on the weathered planks of a jetty that stretched into a marina on the River Hamble, where it fed into the Solent, a few hours walk from Southampton.

It had been three weeks since I'd tossed my phone into the Atlantic from a Portsmouth jetty, the next port east.

Above me curved a full hemisphere of cold blue sky; my ears were filled with the suck and gurgle of water playing about the pilings, and the *bloomp* of mooring fenders buffeted by boats. In my hand I held a single sheet of paper. It was, by now, much creased, and fluttered in my grasp in the fresh onshore breeze like a caught gull.

Holding it close I read the words I was taking as a motto for the foreseeable future:

How: Choice

I had a choice. Doing nothing was a choice. Wallowing in self-pity and fear was a choice.

So too was getting my arse into gear and trying to stop another murder.

Every man has a choice.

And I'd made mine.

I carefully folded the sheet, Hiero's last 'research' paper, and tucked it into my jeans.

Yeah, I was back in jeans. I'd stolen one last time, but not at random. I'd aimed for a particular look—itinerant journalist, casual to the point of unconcern without being a punk, stick-it-to-the-man. It takes a certain kind of worm to bait a certain kind of fish.

Looking at the fifty-foot yacht moored to the jetty ahead of me, I just hoped I'd guessed this kind of fish right. If I hadn't, I was back to square negative one thousand.

Right on cue, the fish appeared, emerging from the marina office at the head of the jetty: a man, perhaps an inch under six feet—that inch the combined subsidence in his frame of fifty years post-puberty. His head was covered in hair that had probably been a sleek corporate-fox grey, but was now beginning to thin, touched yellow by too much sun or salt. It flamed in the breeze like a halo. His upper body was swaddled in too many layers for the weather. His legs were bare to the breeze, poking from faded cargo shorts, and looking too thin to support his apparent bulk. But he didn't totter. He strode, on those too-thin legs, with a stride that had once walked the earth as a kind of king.

Trailing behind him, a lone little pilot fish, came a boy. He followed the man like an obedient dog, and from the moment he stepped onto the jetty his gaze was pinned to me.

Between us, apart from the stretch of sun-bleached wood, lay the yacht. I waited until the man and the boy were nearly abreast of it before approaching them.

The boy was the first to notice me move. His only reaction was to place a small hand upon the man's hip.

In that instant, the man looked at me, and I knew what so many books had tried to convey: the majesty of a king is in his gaze.

It mattered not that this particular king had abdicated.

'Morning,' he said. His American accent was out of place on those British planks, although it too sounded worn around the edges. He swapped a small tank he carried from one hand to the other, and made to lower it into the yacht.

'Good morning,' I said, my eyes flicking a greeting to the boy who stood behind the man, observing. 'Am I talking to Charles Longman?'

At this, the man stood straight, the tank in his hand seemingly forgotten. 'Who's asking?'

'You don't know me, but I'm after the owner of the *Dawn Treader*.' I glanced at the yacht. Her name rippled with reflected light.

The man's eyes interrogated me. Was he looking for a camera? A notebook?

'I'm here about the advertisement you didn't put in the *Daily Echo*.'

'I *didn't* put. I like that.' The glimmer in his eye—the closest, I was to learn, he ever came to smiling—was there and gone in an instant.

'I forget now,' he said. 'What didn't I advertise?'

'An opening for a deckhand for this year's Atlantic crossing.'

His eyes narrowed. 'This year's?'

I realised immediately I'd made a potentially fatal mistake. Backtracking fast, I said, 'Not you personally. I meant the marina's. Every year a group crosses to Florida in convoy—convoy, is that the right word?'

'That's not what you meant.' He said it deadpan, and turned away, bending to set the tank in his hand onto a bench in the yacht. 'And the group you're talking about doesn't depart for another three weeks.'

The boy scampered over the railing. He too, apparently, thought I'd shot my wad.

Speaking over his shoulder as he worked, the man said, 'The website you're after is crewmates-dot-com. Look it up. It's your best bet.'

In a split-second decision, I changed tack. Dropped the story I'd been about to feed this man, and tried another.

'Look, Mr Longman. You're right. I do know who you are, because I've been researching you.'

A scowl appeared on his weathered brow, and was comically mirrored on the boy's face.

'I've been looking for an opportunity, any opportunity, to spend time with you. Get the great Chuck Longman's story in his own words.'

He grunted. 'So you are a reporter.'

'No, not a reporter. An author. I want to write your biography. What better place than the calm isolation of an Atlantic crossing?'

This is how much this man did not smile. He listened to what I had just said—the calm isolation of an Atlantic crossing—and didn't laugh so hard he sent snot flying. He just stared at me, with those eyes glittering from beneath his leathery brow.

'They already wrote a biography.'

'But not your biography, Mr Longman. Not your words. Not your account. That's what this would be. You tell me, and I'll ghostwrite.'

This was it. My last opportunity. The countdown to the next murder was at three weeks and counting. And if I blew this chance, one I'd sunk so much effort into … well, I was shot.

With difficulty, I returned his stare, not knowing what thoughts were passing behind those eyes. The kid was fidgeting, which, despite my having first laid eyes on him minutes ago, seemed out of character.

With another grunt, Longman heaved himself over the railing and back onto the jetty. He turned, and said over his shoulder, 'I'm not a cruise liner. I don't do passengers. And the biographers already got it right. I'm the depressed old crank who built an empire then blew it on a pair of thighs.'

And with that he walked away, kid in tow.

He'd barely gone three yards when his hand delved into a pocket to retrieve a handkerchief, and I saw something flutter free.

It was a banknote—high denomination. In the breeze it spun and winged its way chaotically across the weathered wood toward the water. By instinct I leapt and clapped a boot at it. Miraculously, I trapped it by a corner. It fluttered angrily above the water. When I stooped to retrieve it, I discovered it was a fifty-pound note.

Longman didn't break step. Didn't seem to have noticed.

I felt a little thrill at the feel of the note; that new hunger for money my weeks of hand-to-mouth had ingrained.

For a moment I battled the urge to thrust it into my pocket. Then, 'Hey!' I hurried after Longman.

He turned, and stretched out his hand for the note, which I returned to him.

'You're hired,' he said. Then, almost an afterthought. 'Know anything about boats?'

'Not a thing.'

That glittering gaze again. 'Well,' he sighed. 'I can handle a know-nothing. But weeks cooped up with a greedy opportunist'—he shook the note—'is another matter.' But then he seemed to think again. 'Really nothing?'

I nodded.

He swore.

54

Marten played a game with herself.

It was a version of let's pretend, and she only hoped she could silence her inner critic long enough to pretend until she had a breakthrough.

The game went like this: let's pretend that Hieronymus Beck is a living, breathing, flesh-and-blood human being. What's more, let's pretend that he is out there in the world, approaching the climax of a self-proclaimed intercontinental killing spree. What kind of a profile of *him* could Marten build? One good enough to put him in custody?

Marten's inner doubter, observing all this like an armchair movie critic, was content to allow: 'This is rubbish. I'll admit the potential usefulness of taking Hiero, for a moment, as a lens through which to better see Jack Griffen. Hiero being the fabrication of an unstable man might yet reveal the contours of that instability.'

But the critic wasn't known for her patience. The movie wouldn't be allowed to play all night. Marten couldn't wrestle with herself forever. She had to move fast.

So working at her desk into the night in a fever of phone calls, and searches on the internet and in the databases of the Metropolitan Police, she hunted for an insight that would shut the critic up.

It soon emerged that no one at the source of this 'outbreak' had done due diligence on the claim of the existence of Hiero Beck. The work was shoddy and presumptuous.

The cops in Perth, Australia, whom Marten now nicknamed Detectives Fish & Chips, had latched onto Jack Griffen the moment he'd come sniffing around the home of the first victim, Rhianne Goldman—the pervert academic snuffling through the entrails of the assault. From that first meeting he became not the primary person-of-interest, but the only person-of-interest.

Then Jack fled to Hong Kong, or raced to save Li, depending on whose version of events you believed. For Detectives Fish & Chips, if there had been any doubt as to Jack's guilt, his flight banished it from their minds.

Then a murder in Hong Kong, as predicted by Jack Griffen (as *perpetrated* by Jack Griffen, again depending on your point of view), and all thought of ground zero, the University of WA, was forgotten.

Next came Vienna (Annika Kreider was still touch and go), and finally … here, the UK, Oxford. And even Marten had gone with the flow for a time, accepting Collins' account without scrutiny.

But it was back there, in Australia where it began, to which she quickly returned. A nagging sense there was a vital clue hiding in plain sight drove her.

She viewed the official website of the Arts faculty at the university, saw its glossy photos of happy students arranged in politically correct racial proportions, artistic shots of campus spaces, cafés, and auditoriums. Bland and useless.

Instead, she dipped into the faculty's social media streams, and from there spidered out into the lives of its students. In the torrents of photos, status updates, and likes—what pundits were calling surveillance capitalism—the real pulse of the place could be felt, however faintly at this distance. Incredible what kids were happy to expose for all to see. But right now Marten didn't lament this naïve oversharing. She milked it hard.

Rhianne Goldman's Facebook timeline was a one-way chat with the world. Up until the date of her assault there was a steady stream of image-shaping factoids. Photos of a university charity event. Breakfast with friends at a fancy-looking restaurant called Matilda Bay. Badges unlocked on a game called Cookie Jam. A new PB on a bridge-to-bridge run. Many photos of sunsets and sunrises across the river, apparently taken mid-jog. (Marten wondered if the attacker had plotted using the photos.)

After the date of the assault, a blackout. Until, weeks later, Rhianne posted a single update that said, 'Time out for me.'

At a loss, Marten foraged through the links to Rhianne's friends. Some had active public pages, and these she pored over looking for the spoor of a young American exchange student with—what was it?—a chestnut fringe and James Dean eyes.

When she found herself looping back onto searched paths more and more she pushed back from her desk and took a break. She knuckled her eyes, made a cup of organic rooibos tea, and sipped it, wondering for the nth time if the packaging was right, if you really were supposed to drink it with milk.

Returning to her laptop, she decided it was time to jump out of Rhianne's Facebook fraternity. Try someone else. She searched for the name of the first murder victim, Li Min, and was disappointed to find that no one matching that name had a public Facebook profile in Perth or Hong Kong.

Grimacing at the pointlessness of it, Marten entered Li Min in a raw Google search, and was pleasantly surprised to find that Plus, Google's own social network, not only had a Li Min, but that it was the right girl—there she was, smiling profile photo and all.

The Google Plus stream proved to be empty, but Li's profile was chock full of links to her virtual presence in specialised social sites—Twitter, Pinterest, Smashwords, Scribophile, Reddit, Flickr. The profile even listed a blog.

Marten clicked the blog's link, but quickly discerned it wasn't a personal journal. Li had followed the market-yourself advice of selecting a theme, and that theme was unfortunately not the inner life of an arts student, but book reviews and commentary on wood-turning.

Wood-turning. Marten nearly cried in frustration.

What had seemed a wealth of information reduced to this: Goodreads simply hosted copies of her book reviews; Scribophile was an online-writers critiquing forum; and the Reddit groups she participated in were all writing-related.

Great if you were literary-minded; useless if you were looking for proof of the existence of the young American.

Marten found herself humming the Bowie song as she scrolled with heavy eyelids through Li's reaction to a critically acclaimed novel, *Freedom*. Li argued against the received wisdom, insisting that the emperor was in fact nude, and likely playing with himself.

On the verge of giving in to the increasingly cranky demands of her body that she put it to bed, or at least reward it with alcohol, she clicked on the last social link in the profile, Li's Flickr account.

Marten had assumed it was like Pinterest, a curated collection of photography Li admired.

How wrong she was.

In no social stream had Li revealed she was an avid amateur photographer. In Flickr, Li documented *everything* in photo. Her account brimmed with documentary evidence of her life.

Adrenaline spiked. Marten skipped off her chair long enough to pour herself a glass of moscato, then began poring over the thousands of photos in Li's account.

Most were location-stamped, and clustered about Perth, Australia, where Li had been an international student. She filled her photos with people—those who were obviously friends, but also those thronging streets, on the beach, in the dusky light of bars, of all moods—candid, thoughtful, and unhappy and clearly waiting for life to become desirable.

As much as she hunted for it, Marten saw no face that matched her expectation of Hieronymus Beck. If Hiero was chestnut and handsome, a gregarious friend, then he was absent from this montage of a student's life in Perth.

Again, doubt tugged at her.

At 3.43 am, for Marten a time out of time when the previous day tipped into the next, and late became early, she clicked on the last photo folder in Li's account.

This folder she had left to last because, according to its summary, it only held a handful of photos, and it was titled *aureus-ambiguus,* which sounded like taxonomic nomenclature.

In the span of a split second, Marten felt the momentary flicker of recognition. In the time it took for the fall of photons on her cornea, and the cascade of biological functions that fired to yield understanding to her conscious mind, she was struck by a frisson of intuition: she'd found it. The face.

The photo was blurry, as though taken in haste, and framed at a severe angle, that if intentional expressed psychological instability. But there was no mistaking the chestnutiness of the handsome young man captured, and features that were somehow an American brand, despite almost four hundred years dilution of the puritan stock.

The only other explanation for the poor focus and framing was that the photo had been taken covertly.

Marten stroked the touchpad of her laptop to place the cursor over the face, and was rewarded with the appearance of a hover text. It, too, sounded like a Latin construction, but here there was a subspecies suffix. It read, *aureus-ambiguus*-beckias.

The knot that had settled in her gut since she watched Jack Griffen leave the cancer clinic in Oxford loosened in one glorious spasm. She stood, snatched up the moscato, and swigged straight from the bottle.

She smiled at herself in a wall-unit mirror. Something had just gone right in the war.

'My God,' she said. 'I think he's telling the truth.'

55

My God, I thought. *I think I'm going insane.*

The gale tore at my body, impelling me to the rail, and the watery death lurking there and everywhere beyond the ridiculously small island of life to which I clung.

Water, water, everywhere, nor … shit, I'm going to die. That's what Coleridge *should* have written.

I was numb with cold, and in that numbness, gripping with fingers I could no longer feel, I remembered how it was I'd come to choose this particular boat for my US odyssey.

Charles Blake Longman.

Not a name known to many, which goes to show how ignorant the average person is of the levers that move the world.

But I didn't start there. I started with my need to get to the US by mid-November, three weeks hence. That was Hiero's generous deadline.

And working quickly down the list of possible means of conveyance for my eighty kilos to US soil, starting with the most comfortable and on down, I in short order ruled out:

Teleportation, as being fictional (Area 51 rumours not withstanding).

First-class air travel, as requiring me to run the gauntlet of way too many cameras and immigration staff on high alert for my mug.

Dirigible, as requiring a dirigible.

Cruiseliner, as requiring money I did not possess, and again falling foul of the problem of too many people trained to spot me.

Ocean freighter. Now this I considered long and hard before reluctantly discarding. In my decision I had to reckon honestly with the gifts life had given me. Physical strength was not among them, and the ravages of the last weeks had left me looking closer to what I actually was, a fugitive. On the other hand, I am blessed (I humbly submit) with a little intelligence, eloquence, and a certain gregariousness, once my introversion has been lubricated with esteem or alcohol.

I didn't think a freighter mess, collected together with a dozen officers, engineers, and gofers, would enable me to ply my gifts enough to divert attention from my need.

So that left …

A smaller craft? But again, my lack of strength and experience with the water would count against me. Was there a context that would allow that lack to be offset by my other qualities?

And here I began to hunt in earnest.

A quick web search led me to Crewmates, which existed for the sole purpose of connecting would-be crew members with yachts. Perfect. I trawled its notices looking for a crew of my age, which also had a bit of 'fat'—that is, was large enough that a deadweight like myself wouldn't send the yacht to the miry bed of the Atlantic to sleep with what was left of the *Titanic*.

One crew-in-the-making seemed tailor-made. A group of middle-aged men and women, probably early retirees, so I'd have to put on some airs, but I could trade with the currency I had—repartee and intellectual sophistication.

I submitted my candidacy to the pool, and began weaving myself into the message threads, which were laced with a disconcerting amount of sexual innuendo or else nautical jargon.

All seemed to be going well until the conversation veered and plunged over a cliff called 'let's go to the Canary Islands first'. Apparently late October was very early for a crossing, and someone complained that they didn't want to 'bump into that grouchy old fart, Longman, setting out'. Another replied that, 'Putting the wind up Chuck was precisely the kind of hijinks to add spice to the crossing'. I piled on that argument with enthusiasm in proportion to my utter lack of understanding.

But the lure of the nudist beaches beneath a dormant volcano of the Canary Islands proved too strong, and that pretty much scotched my attempt.

Annoyed and despairing at the effort I'd wasted entertaining a bunch of adults who hid their world-weariness beneath forced levity and teenage voices, I wondered if my only option was to freeze-pack my carcass and FedEx it to US soil.

Standing in the cold fog wrapping the marina, where I had been spying on the tweeny yacht (appropriately called *Neptune's Flirt*), I remembered that someone had said it was very early for an Atlantic crossing. Perhaps the whole endeavour had been a waste of time. If no one was sailing for another month, I would never make the deadline.

It was a gut punch.

But my mind was not done picking over the Crewmates conversations. On the heels of that first realisation came another: there was at least one yacht leaving this early in the season. And it belonged to a Chuck Longman, whoever that was.

Chuck Longman.

Fine. I'd look him up. It would give me something to do while I worked out another plan. Maybe a cargo freighter, after all.

Chuck Longman, it turned out, had come *this close* to being on the cover of *Time* magazine—'this close' being the distance from the knuckle of his middle finger to its tip, which he had extended, photographed, and faxed to *Time*'s editor, on hearing he was at the head of the cover shortlist.

Chuck Longman, it turned out, was beyond rich. He attracted money by merely existing, like a giant star sweeps neighbouring space clear of gas, asteroids, comets. Planets. By pulling them into its orbit, plunging them into its fire, making them part of itself. He was big enough to be a line item on the US GDP ledger. Could have bought a US election from a standing start, if he'd so desired.

But you've never heard of him. He isn't a Trivial Pursuit answer. It turns out that if you take the total world wealth, some 250 trillion dollars, and subtract the top ten on *Forbes* richest people list, you're still left with 249 trillion dollars—it's Scrooge McDuck's money bin, and there's plenty of room left to swim.

Charles Blake Longman was the youngest son of five born to Herbert and Ann Longman, and into a family empire that already owned hardware stores in three states. By age eight he was selling candy into his elementary school at a healthy margin. At eleven, watching his brothers cash out ahead of him, he proposed to take his inheritance now—less the percentage pro-rata of the early vesting. He then promptly put it back into the family business, which went public two years later. When the Kennedy Flash Crash of 1962 wiped 22.5% from the stock market, and with it the hardware business, Chuck asked his dad why they weren't diversified. He was told, 'It's a solid business. It was my father's before me.' Chuck thought 'Don't put all your eggs in one basket' was probably older wisdom. And when he picked up a book by Benjamin Graham, *The Intelligent Investor*, which advocated buying groups of stocks that were undervalued, and learned of value investing, the fire was lit.

Chuck took nearly all of his money out of the business, at a loss, and diversified on the numbers alone. He never looked back.

His investments grew year on year, and in nearly twenty years he only neglected his own mantra twice to take a punt on two startups. In 1982, while everyone else was backing the big players—IBM and Hewlett-Packard—he bought a ten percent stake in a little company called Compaq, purely on the strength of their thirty-pound 'portable computer' which he toted across the country as he travelled. Twenty years later when everyone was fleeing the internet in the dotcom bust, Longman plumped for 125,000 shares of an online bookseller called Amazon, at $5.97 a share, less than the company's initial price of $18. As of October 2015, his shares were worth 104 times his initial investment, more than seventy-six million dollars of gross return.

But they were just two streams into his river.

And as his wealth grew, his life didn't change. He remained in the modest four-bedroom house in Tulsa, Oklahoma which he'd bought with cash before he married. He continued to drive his first car, and changed the oil himself on schedule.

Prior to the point when uncles, brothers, nieces, and nephews might have thought it worth their while punting on an opportunistic lawsuit for a piece of the family wealth, Chuck created Longman Capital Group, a private hedge fund, and invited any and all far-flung relatives to apply for appointment to the fund management, on one condition—they had to bring skills of value. Needless to say there was a rush to enrol children (and in some cases, parents) in night-school finance courses. But only those that could be appointed on merit were taken. The rest he gave jobs, again on merit, within the collection of private companies wholly owned by the fund.

And his wealth continued to grow, like a tree with its taproot in the water table, which, short of an act of God, can do nothing but reach high and spread wide.

But while he was obscenely rich, he did not, as a rule, attract the spotlight. Unlike Bill Gates, Longman was no geek entrepreneur who had put software on a billion computers. Nor was he the blond hair and Hollywood teeth and the *rockets* of Sir Richard Branson. Even boring Warren Buffett, with his fatherly advice about fiscal rectitude, felt the spotlight. Every one of these world-takers were the portraits on the paper money.

Chuck Longman was the paper.

He didn't make it onto the *Forbes* top ten richest people in the world for the same reason *Forbes* couldn't confirm the suspicion that Vladimir Putin is the world's richest man. The *Forbes* calculation relies on publicly accessible information or self-disclosure—the ledgers of public companies, or the confessions of prideful men will suffice. Beyond that, they're as clueless as the rest of us.

So Charles Longman was simply money. And money, in and of itself, turns out not to be all that interesting if nothing is done with it. He didn't buy fast cars, or fast women. He didn't carve out blocks of Manhattan and erect monuments to himself. He didn't give Africa chickens, or cure malaria.

He simply amassed wealth, and got older.

And that, it turned out, was the one facet of his existence that eventually drew the light.

Every kingdom, however peaceful, must at some time endure the trial of succession.

Even here, Longman had managed so well that the transfer of power would have been entirely peaceful but for the stroke of fate—

A sheet of rain and mingled seawater dashed against my face.

The sudden cold took my breath away and broke my reverie. Somewhere, hidden from my view by the bulk of the cabin and its shroud of spray, Longman swore. Then, more distinctly, I heard: 'Double-lash that dinghy, boy!'

He meant me. The actual boy he called 'Scrub'. But me? I was *boy*. And to reach the dinghy, I would have to let go of the handrail.

Scrub scampered past me, a blur of motion, sure-footed and fleet despite the water-slick deck and the corkscrewing craft. His gaze was a momentary glitter of distrust amid the flying spindrift before he began re-lashing the dinghy. In moments it was done with an efficiency and speed preternatural in one so young. Still he had yet to utter a single word to me. His silence and skill called the lie to his appearance. Perhaps he was a man in a boy's body?

He was also the one who stood in the eye of Fate. The fate I've mentioned that struck Longman's world. Caused him to raise his middle finger and fax it to the editor of one of the world's most powerful publications.

Scrub was, somehow, the boy that dethroned the emperor.

He appeared on the scene not long before Longman announced he was stepping down from the board of Longman Capital. The *Time* article was ostensibly about the retirement of the 'Hidden Emperor', but in reality it was an exposé on the marriage of Charles' youngest son, Thomas, to Alicia Manning. This hint of smut in an otherwise spotless career and life proved irresistible to the editors.

Word on the street was that Alicia had first tried to seduce Charles, as his secretary, and when that failed, had set her sights on the youngest Longman. Thomas divorced his wife and took up with Alicia.

And their son, Scrub, was left to float between his estranged parents.

What he was doing on a yacht in the middle of the heaving Atlantic with Charles Longman I had no idea.

This was the man on whom I was depending to make landfall on US soil by mid-November.

I'm not sure at what point my interest in Chuck Longman as a means to an end turned into a true curiosity.

I could equally ask at what point his interest in *me* became more than a means to an end.

56

Sneaky. There was no other word for it.

Li Min, for all her apparent self-disclosure and commitment to honesty and integrity, had retained, safely hidden away from the world, and particularly from Hiero Beck—thank the Maker!—a vein of sneakiness.

Marten mined that vein with a fury.

She began with the fuzzy photo of the could-be (had-to-be, my-career-depends-upon-it) Hieronymus Beck she had discovered in an out-of-the way folder in Li's Flickr account. She had then looked to see if the photo *went* anywhere.

It had not been shared with anyone from Flickr. Nor, on gaining access to Li's Gmail account, could she find it attached to a sent email.

Marten filtered the sent items to only those containing image attachments. Many emails had attached photos, but there was no sign of the fuzzy snap.

She relaxed the search to include any kind of attachment, and began scrolling through the much longer list. Most were Word or PDF documents. Some appeared to be collaborative projects, shared with a list of university email addresses. One email held an attached spreadsheet, according to Gmail. From the title it appeared to be statistics from an experiment. She clicked on it, and waited for the online spreadsheet viewer to load.

A spinner appeared in the browser and spun for seconds, before a message appeared, complaining that the spreadsheet was unreadable.

Marten would have left it there but for one detail, which her ever-questing gaze noted. The size of the spreadsheet, indicated in kilobytes by the attachment, was exactly the same as the photo for which she was hunting.

With another click, she downloaded the spreadsheet to her computer.

She renamed the file, forcing it to be treated as an image file. Another click, and the image viewer opened.

The screen filled with the fuzzy photo of a young man with chestnut hair.

Sneaky girl, thought Marten. She had hidden the photo in plain sight.

But the photo was immaterial now. She'd pulled on that thread. Marten now rapidly turned to where it led, the recipient. Because whoever that was, had clearly been expected to detect a hidden photo, and know what to do with it. And, more importantly, know what it meant.

Someone out there knew the identity of the young man in the fuzzy photo. She squinted at the lone recipient, the moniker *thereeldeel*.

'Whoever you are, thereeldeel,' Marten muttered, 'you're going to tell me everything you know.'

57

I make it a practice never to look up the author of a favourite book—I mean, who they are in real life. They're bound to disappoint. Turn out to be a raging communist, or white supremacist. Or poodle owner.

I get the same with names, too.

I love the name Marlowe. Roll it around on your tongue. It's a cracker.

It's also a name with literary heft.

Conspiracy theorists insist half of Shakespeare's plays were penned by Christopher Marlowe.

Charlie Marlow (*sans* the 'e') was the narrator of Conrad's *Heart of Darkness*, a tale set during the wax of the British Empire, when every which way lay a frontier. It tells of a steamboat journey up the Congo into the heart of alien Africa, backwards in time to primeval scapes, and a descent into the soul of man. (Incidentally, it was also the inspiration for *Apocalypse Now*, which featured an old, fat Marlon Brando, who nevertheless sweated charisma by the gallon in the jungles of Vietnam.)

Philip Marlowe is Raymond Chandler's wisecracking, hard-drinking, chess-playing detective, brought to the screen unforgettably by Humphrey Bogart. The archetype of the hard-boiled hero.

I looked up the meaning of Marlowe. It means: a bog left by a drained lake.

See? Disappointing.

58

'I told you to take a break from this.'

Collins flicked a hand at the nest of paper in which Marten's laptop rested. A photo of Jack Griffen paperclipped to the top sheet was prominent—a faculty shot from his university, by the look of it.

'Hate to be pedantic—' Marten began. Collins shook his head, indicating he knew she loved to be pedantic. It was part of her job description. 'But you did not. You *advised* me to take a break. I declined.'

Collins stepped back from the desk and squared his feet. Marten tensed and looked up. She could usually read his mood infallibly. Today she had no idea what he was thinking.

'There's going to be an investigation.'

Marten frowned. 'Into ...?' She wasn't going to let him be a coward. She'd make him spell it out.

'You. Your conduct.'

The floor of her office dropped away. 'You're kidding.'

'Dammit, Marten. I gave you every kind of warning I know how to give, and you couldn't drop it.'

Her gaze narrowed. Investigations cost money and were bad press. They didn't start of their own accord. 'Who?'

'No. You're going to have to let it—'

'Trent,' she said, no longer looking at Collins.

His silence told her she was right.

Gradually her office pulled itself back together. She glanced at her watch. It was a quarter to noon.

'Okay. If I'm suspended—'

'You're not suspended,' he sighed. 'But you are taking leave. As of now.'

'Good,' she stood and began collecting paper from her desk. 'And the first thing I'm doing on leave is being taken to lunch by you.'

Collins glanced at his watch. 'Bit early isn't it? And you don't want to have lunch with me. You want to throw darts at my face.'

'Why can't I do both? I'm not taking no for an answer.' She batted her eyelashes hideously at him.

He chuckled roughly and stalked out of the office, pausing at the threshold to hold the door open.

Marten gathered her laptop into her bag and passed him, saying, 'And they say chivalry is dead.'

'Hurry up,' he muttered. 'Bloody woman.'

Minutes later they were seated at a window of The Feathers, barely a block from Marten's office.

She had drunk half a martini, steeling herself, then plumped her phone down on the table. A phone number was already loaded into the keypad, just needed the touch of a button to enact the call.

Collins glanced at it and swore. 'An ambush. I should have known.'

'Just be quiet and listen.' She thrust one half of her earbud headphones at him. He sighed, then leaned forward to insert it into his ear, resting his elbows on the table and bowing his head.

Marten inserted the other earbud and touched the call button.

The call blipped three times before it was picked up.

'*Wei.*'

Collins lifted his head, frowning.

'Alexa?' said Marten.

A pause. 'Miss Lacroix?'

'Mrs, yes. You said call back at eleven, but something came up.' She flashed her eyes at Collins, who pretended to ignore her. 'It's only half-twelve. I hope it's okay.'

'Sure, sure,' said Alexa, sounding unconvincing.

'Oh, great.' Marten raised her eyes to the ceiling, saying a silent thank you, and tried to arrange her thoughts.

Alexa spoke. 'You wanted to talk about … about Li?' Marten didn't need her psychology degree to interpret the broken sentence. Li and Alexa had been long-time friends. And Li was barely four weeks cold.

'Yes and no. I'm after information about someone Li might have known.'

One of Collins' hands appeared on the table at the edge of Marten's view. Its fingers began a slow, rhythmic undulation—*tap, tap, tap …*

Shit. She had a minute, perhaps, to pique his interest before she was busted back to the academy.

'Can I confirm something first? I need to know if you're thereeldeel?'

Marten took a moment to realise how stupid that sounded, but before she could clarify, Alexa spoke.

'That's me. Double-e, double-e. The other was taken, but I don't care anymore. I kind of like it the way it is now.'

Collins' fingers drummed faster.

'Do you remember getting an email from Li on the twelfth of September? The subject line was "Sub-population stats", and she attached a spreadsheet.'

The silence that followed sounded pregnant to Marten. She strained to interpret the fuzz in the line over the clatter and murmur of the café's ambient noise.

About the time Marten began to hear the throb of her own pulse, Alexa responded. 'I remember the email. But I'm guessing you know it wasn't a spreadsheet, and I'm guessing that's why you called.'

Smart girl, thought Marten.

'Let me cut to the chase then, Alexa. The spreadsheet was in fact a photo of a young man. What I want to know is: was that man Hieronymus Beck?'

A pause. Then—

'I don't know.'

Marten stared at the phone. She couldn't have heard that right.

'What I mean is,' Alexa continued, 'I don't know for sure. I never met him in person, and Li never sent me another message.'

Of course. The message was sent twelfth of September. Li was murdered shortly after.

But Marten clung to the words 'I never met him in person'.

'But I think that was him. I'm sure that was him. You see, all I had to go on was her *word*. He didn't let anyone photograph him. Ever.'

That explained why the photo was so obviously covert, and the only one.

Marten slumped in her chair, and the earbud popped from her ear.

As she scrambled to replace it, Collins gestured at a waitress for another Coke. The fire had taken.

'—think she doubted I believed her, even though I assured her again and again that I did. So I think she sent the photo as proof.'

Marten pressed. 'Proof of what?'

'That her boyfriend wasn't imaginary.'

Marten placed both hands on the table, palms down, fingers splayed, and fought her wheeling thoughts for clarity. She felt as though this call, Alexa, were a buffet but she had only seconds to eat. She strained to distil her need to the essentials. Alexa was her only source on Hiero, beside Jack and a comatose girl lying in a Viennese hospital. What could Alexa tell her?

'Alexa, there was no one enrolled at the university by the name Hieronymus Beck.'

'You think Hiero had something to do with her ... with—'

'That's what I'm trying to find out. Think.'

A pause, then, 'Li said he was an exchange student studying linguistics, but attending lectures in literature. He was meeting with a professor—I forget his name.'

'Jack Griffen?'

'Griffen, that's it. I remember; it reminded me of Harry Potter, which is silly. So Hiero wouldn't have been on the enrolment for Li's course.'

Or *any* course, thought Marten, but didn't press the point.

'When did she first start talking about him?'

'Oh, not long after the start of semester she started dropping hints that there was this guy hanging around. She spotted him a couple of times at a café off campus, watching her. She couldn't stop talking about his eyes, how they made everything else around her pale. I laughed with her; she had it bad to be spouting that crap.'

There was a smile in her voice at first, before reality seemed to catch.

'Then one day when she was alone he sat down at her table. He said, "Hi," full of confidence, and she blurted, "I knew you were American!" She was so embarrassed, but she was right. He looked straight out of California.'

Marten risked a glance at Collins. His gaze was abstracted, but he wasn't bored. His fingers had stilled. He was listening intently. She swiped into the phone's photo gallery and found the image of Hiero. Collins' gaze twitched toward it, then grew unfocused again.

Marten said, 'After that, their relationship became steady?'

'Steady. But thin.'

'Thin?'

'They met regularly—cafés, museums, the beach—but maybe once a week? It was high-octane. She filled the other days with fantasy. But Hiero—it sounded to me like he was spread too thin. Or ...'

'Or?'

'Had more than one iron in the fire.'

'Did you ever say as much to Li?'

Alexa made a surprised noise. 'Oh, no. Pure speculation on my part. And besides, she seemed so happy. Hiero might have been on drip-feed, but he was potent. More than enough for Li right then. Who was I to intrude on that?'

Marten changed tack. 'When did you learn that Hiero didn't want Li to photograph him?'

She laughed. 'Immediately, of course. A photo was the first thing I asked for when she told me she was seeing someone.'

'Did that seem odd?'

There was a pause, and a rustle of motion. 'You know, what she told me then, his reason for not wanting to be photographed? That was the first hint that he might be shitting her. Benefit of hindsight and all that.'

'Why?'

'Well, it sounded so far-fetched.'

Marten sensed Collins drawing down over the phone, as if to better hear, despite the wire dangling from his ear.

'Li said that Hiero hinted at a dark past.'

Marten's eyes flashed at Collins—see!—but he appeared to be studying the grain of the tabletop.

'Li said he was the great-great-grandson or something of the single surviving member of a murdered family. Hiero said there were kooks who looked up people like that, hassled them, even stalked them. He'd had it in the US, and didn't want it in Australia.'

Marten sat back in her chair, momentarily unsure what to make of the revelation. It wasn't at all what she had expected to hear. She wasn't sure she believed a word of Hiero's story, but to keep Alexa on the line while she tried to sort through it, she said: 'Is that all Li said about his ancestry, this murder?'

'I don't remember, I'm sorry. Nothing, except—except it was Christmas. The family was murdered at Christmas.'

Alexa went on, unprompted. 'Li was a journalism student. And here was this handsome, charming American navigating the fallout of a tragic past. I mean, wow. You can see why I wanted a photo. *Potent.*'

From the corner of her eye, Marten saw Collins move like a robot suddenly activated. He retrieved a pen from his pocket and scribbled on a napkin. He slid it next to the phone, and tapped it once with the pen.

He'd written: Jack Griffen.

Marten suppressed a sigh. 'And did Jack Griffen's name ever come up in these conversations, other than that Hiero was meeting with him?'

'Oh, the professor? Of course. They were planning to play a prank on him.'

Marten found herself inches from the phone.

'I'm sorry, did you say a prank?'

'Yeah. A prank. That's all she said. She was very secretive about it, but she and Hiero were going to prank him. Li at heart was a gentle soul, despite the front she put up. If she was pranking a teacher, I was sure it was in good humour. I didn't press her on it.' A sigh. 'And then, well, soon after, I couldn't press her on anything ever again.'

Minutes later Marten and Collins were staring at each other across the table. They broke the silence simultaneously:

'Hiero,' said Marten.

'Griffen,' said Collins.

59

Longman's boat, it turns out, is what some salts call a stinkpot. Part sailboat, part trawler, all floating apartment.

When I learnt this, I finally understood that half of the gibes in the Crewmates forums were oblique references to Longman not being a real sailor. Yes, the boat had sails, and could pull above five knots in a thirteen-knot breeze on sail alone. But if the wind failed, or the sailor simply felt like taking a quiet finger of Scotch over the paper in a rare afternoon of sunshine on the cusp of the hurricane season, he could reef sail and fire up the diesel motor, point the bow, and let the screw carry him over the waves.

This was what Longman was doing now, and my delight was unseemly. I lay back in a deckchair like a cat, a notepad and pen resting in my lap, and tried to arrange my thoughts for the interview that would soon come.

Despite myself, my interest in how it was that a reclusive tycoon and an eleven-year-old kid had come to make a habit of crossing the north Atlantic unfashionably early in the season had grown until it overwhelmed the festering dread I felt for what awaited me on the far shore.

Unfashionably early in the season. *Psychotically* early in the season. In November the Atlantic was still frequently scoured by hurricanes, and I wondered what business Longman had dragging a kid into it. If he wanted to pit himself against raw mother nature in a burn-out-rather-than-fade finale to life he was welcome to. But why put the kid in harm's way?

I voiced the question before Longman put his paper away—the customary signal he was ready to submit to interview.

He said, 'The "kid" is old enough to make up his own mind.'

Scrub still had yet to speak. I was surer than ever that he suffered from some kind of mental disorder. I tried to delicately put this to Longman:

'Perhaps he doesn't know how to refuse?' The boy clearly doted on the man.

Longman lifted his head and yelled. 'Scrub! Come here and urinate on the reporter.'

A shadow fell over me. The kid had an uncanny knack of being everywhere, silent as a mouse. His dark eyes stared at me for a moment, and a hand strayed to the waist of his shorts—which he wore at all times, despite the chill.

I tensed. Then Longman waved him away. The kid turned and disappeared into the cabin.

'I'm not a reporter,' I said, embarrassed at my fear.

'And he ain't a kid,' said Longman. Then, barely audible, 'They stole that from him.'

In the silence that followed, all I could hear was the deep *chug, chug* of the diesel motor, and the faint susurrus of the wind in my ears. The deck thrummed with the beat of the motor, and the slap of a slight swell across our line.

The ocean was clear to the horizon in every direction. All the world might have sunk beneath the waves. The sight gave me a peculiarly claustrophobic feeling.

The rustle of newspaper pulled my attention back from the vastness. Longman spoke, his voice gravelly at the edges. Sitting there with his hat jammed over his ears, a fringe of exposed hair feathered by the wind, and squinting from beneath his deeply creased brow, he looked so much the salt-bitten sailor that I had to force myself to remember the same voice had spent most of its strength commanding boardrooms rather than decks.

'You think I have a death wish and don't care if he is collateral?'

Chuck Longman, I was beginning to learn, valued directness. I nodded.

'Hurricanes don't run on a timetable. They're subject to chance, and if you're not willing to accept that, you might as well not get out of bed in the morning.'

'Wind is fickle,' I said, in a lame attempt to build the conversation.

He turned his squint on me. 'Wind is about the only thing you can rely on out here.'

'But I thought you just said—'

'For a reporter, you need to pay more attention to words. I was talking about hurricanes, not wind. Hurricanes blow up on the beat of butterfly wings on the other side of the world, right?' A wry tug of his mouth revealed he didn't buy this wisdom. 'That's a chance event. A broken spar. A cracked fuel pump. A chaffed line. All chance events. But the wind, this time of year, this place—it's blue chip. It'll flux, but the trend is steady. That's an investment in the long run.'

I should have been prying for details of his life, but I couldn't let this go. 'Fickle wind—it's a cliché. I'm not a sailor'—he grunted in agreement—'but clichés are clichés by force of truth.'

He sighed. 'You know why all those nice yachts in the marina back there don't convoy out and make a beeline for Miami—that's a beeline from the UK or Spain to the US?'

This was news to me. That's precisely what I thought they did. What *were* we doing?

He answered his own question. 'Because sitting slap-bang in the middle of the North Atlantic is the Azores High—a high-pressure zone a thousand miles wide. Sure, it wobbles around, sometimes makes it as far west as Bermuda, where it's called the Bermuda High. You're making the same mistake most folks make about the wind, thinking of it as a two-dimensional thing. It's not. That deadzone is the bottom of a massive cauldron of wind reaching into the atmosphere, and around it, always clockwise in the northern hemisphere, races the wind. It's driven by an ocean current that drags the air within it until the whole lot is moving. That cauldron starts to churn late November and keeps on until May. It's so regular, people used to trade on it.'

'Tradewinds,' I said. He nodded.

Something else occurred to me. 'So if you don't head straight for the US coast, where are we headed, exactly?'

'If you're a sailboat heading for the US, you head south until the butter melts, then ride the wind to the Caribbean.'

Sweat began to cool on my neck. 'And how much further than a beeline is that?'

He leaned back, casting his eye over the empty sea. 'Oh, about three thousand miles.' He looked at me then, and seemed to be reading my thoughts. 'Give or take.'

I swore out loud. Couldn't help it. My back-of-the-napkin calculations had put me on US soil conservatively by the seventh of November. I hadn't factored in a lazy cruise via the Caribbean. I felt stupid and angry.

Longman said, 'All the more time to plug me for my dirty secrets.'

Desperate, I said, 'Isn't there some way to get there sooner?'

'Sure,' he said equably. 'We're powered, full tank of fuel. We can head for Florida right now.'

'We have to do it,' I spoke with more force than I intended. Longman's eyes flashed, but he was no longer looking at me.

A shadow fell over me, and I turned to find Scrub staring at me. His arms were outstretched before him.

In his hands he grasped my gun.

The shock of it drove me upward, but before I gained my feet, something caught me a blow behind my right ear, and I fell as if shot.

60

Criminal profiling, when it comes down to it—for all its technical complexity and nuance—reduces to answering one, simple question: who are you?

Who are you, Hieronymus Beck?

Everything else builds on the answer. Where he is. What he has done and why, and what he might do next.

But how on earth could Marten answer that question sitting in the study of her flat in Wood Green? She had so little *material* to go on. Even an alchemist needed lead.

She had spent so much time amassing and arranging the facts of Jack Griffen's life and soul. At least she'd spoken to him—confirmed he was a living, breathing human being.

Hiero was an overheard story. A ghost. And that relentlessly sceptical part of her brain that was prerequisite for her line of work kept whispering doubt to her. Perhaps this was all the work of an exceedingly cunning mind—Li's friend, Alexa, notwithstanding.

Marten had seen the sincerity in Jack stooped over a dying woman, but psychopaths excelled at empathy. It was the lever that gave them such power over others—to think their thoughts and so manipulate them.

Marten remembered reading about the experiment Elliott T. Barker conducted at Oak Ridge in 1968, called the Total Encounter Capsule. Barker treated Canadian spree killer, Mathew Charles Lamb. It turned out that if you stuck psychopaths naked in a lighted room for days, fed them through straws in the door, and dosed them on LSD, what you got was cleverer, more self-aware psychopaths. It had been, effectively, professional development rather than cure.

She didn't know why she so desperately wanted to believe that Jack was a good guy. Somehow she thought she owed it to him to try. She owed it to one mental image of him—she corrected.

It wasn't true she had nothing to go on. She had one thread. One small lump of lead that might transmute to gold.

Riffling through the papers in her lap she found the transcript of her phone conversation with Alexa. Scanning the document, she at last found the detail, slim as it seemed, on which her hope now rested. She re-read it for the umpteenth time to make sure she had it right.

Hiero claimed to be a descendant of the single surviving member of a family that was murdered at Christmas.

Marten arranged her laptop in her lap and, feeling like a student cramming an essay, entered her first search in a web browser: Christmas mass murder.

Of the results, Marten quickly dismissed the first, the Covina massacre of 2008 in Los Angeles—where a recently divorced man dressed as Santa had raided a party with a gift-wrapped flamethrower and killed nine. That was too recent to be the one Hiero meant.

The second result was about Ronald Gene Simmons, and over this Marten had to pause. Simmons, an ex-serviceman, had begun killing on December twenty-second, 1987. After first killing his wife, son, and granddaughter, he waited for the rest of the family to arrive at his Arkansas home, and took them alone to the back of the house with the promise of a present, whereupon he strangled them one by one while holding their heads in a rain barrel. Simmons buried the dead in a cesspit dug by the children. He finished a week later, leaving sixteen dead—shot or strangled—including all of his family, and two strangers.

My God.

Simmons was executed in 1990, his death warrant signed by Arkansas governor Bill Clinton. That family was extinguished; Hiero was too young to be connected to Simmons.

Finally, the Lawson family.

A week before Christmas Day, 1929, Charlie Lawson took his family from their tobacco sharecropping farm into Germanton, North Carolina. He bid them buy new clothes—whatever you want, knock yourselves out—then visited the local photographer for a family portrait.

Then on Christmas Day, he shot them all with a twelve-gauge shotgun, before turning the gun on himself.

Another family extinguished from the earth in one stroke.

All? No. All but one—the eldest son escaped.

A tingling sensation crept up from the base of Marten's neck. She read on. She leaned in closer to look at the family portrait displayed on the Wikipedia page. Marten scanned the faces, looking into the eyes of each for an inkling of the fate that awaited them. She settled on the father. *Those eyes knew, didn't they.*

The son, the sole survivor, stood next to his father in the portrait. He had escaped by virtue of being sent on an errand to town. (Had the father meant for him to escape?) What had become of him on hearing his entire family had been killed, and his home become a museum to murder? Had he lived to father his own children?

Another internet search yielded the answer: he had died just years later in an automobile accident. Marten mused. The son died, apparently childless, but how could one be sure?

The faces of the doomed stared out at Marten across eighty-six years, and she felt a pang of pity that surprised her.

Every man, every moment, stands at the brink of eternity—and for some the plunge is swift and unexpected.

Pushing herself back from the laptop, Marten tried to assess her night's work. Had she made any progress? She had found one story of murder that might fit with what thereeldeel, Alexa, had related to her of Hiero's secret. Maybe. But she felt way out on a limb here. Even if it were true, of what good was the knowledge that Hiero had a psychotic ancestor? If Hiero were indeed responsible for the murders of Li Min and Jane Worthington, his sanity stocks had already tanked. No need for further confirmation.

Feeling like the fisherman at the end of a fruitless night casting the line one more time, Marten pulled the laptop close and entered a search. She searched for mentions of the Lawson murder.

The first page of results was about the murder itself—newspaper articles on special anniversaries of the murder; a *Rolling Stone* magazine mention of the most creepy songs, including a bluegrass ballad recorded a year after the murder.

She clicked past one page of this, then another. On the verge of giving up at the fourth page of results, her eye was hooked by a photograph.

There, peering through a window of 320 by 240 pixels, was the face of a younger Hieronymus Beck.

Breathless, she leaned close to read the summary: 'Teen author draws on family skeletons for inspiration.' The article appeared to be a local publication, the *Winston-Salem Journal*. Beneath the photo, a caption in small font said: 'Randall Todd'.

'Got you,' breathed Marten. With a twist of her lips, she added, 'Randy.'

61

'I can explain,' I panted.

My vision squirmed from the blow that had sent me to the deck, but I was pretty sure the blur to my left was the boy, Scrub, and he still had the gun trained on me. All it would take would be a twitch and he would spread my brains over the polished hardwood.

Longman laughed without humour. 'Just once, one of you squibs is going to say, "You know what? I can't explain."'

I chewed my lip. 'I can't explain?' I said, hopefully.

He stopped laughing.

'No, you're going to explain, alright. To a jury of two—me and Scrub here. And if we don't like what we hear, well …' He glanced at the ocean that spread in every direction to the limit of vision. 'Quick execution. No one knows you're here, right?'

The appalling truth of what he'd said sank into my stomach like a stone. 'You wouldn't.'

His gaze pierced the fog. 'You've got no idea what I would or wouldn't do.'

'So tell me,' I said, grabbing at the self-disclosure like a drowning man a passing plank.

He grimaced in annoyance, then spoke to Scrub. 'Into the cabin.' Scrub stepped closer, close enough for me to see a speck of pocket lint snagged on the head of the Glock's recoil spring. He held the gun outstretched in his hand, pointed at me. A vision of the last time it had been pointed at me filled my mind—a toilet in St Pancras Station, and above the gun, the fearful, hungry eyes of a young police officer. I heard again the impossibly loud crash of its discharge. I jumped up as if stung, and bent to enter the cabin.

Darkness pressed at the edges of my vision like a pathogen fighting my body. Nausea tickled the underside of my jaw. I hoped the blow hadn't knocked anything permanently loose. In the cabin, I groped for the raised lip of its small table, and half-fell onto the couch that stretched in an L-shape around it.

Longman followed me and sat on the perpendicular segment. The boy swivelled the captain's chair to face us and clambered onto it. He trained the gun on me. Behind him, the electric glow of a depth map limned his small frame. The sea was so calm I could hear the thrum of the AC unit labouring under the couch.

Longman placed his hands palm up and spread them briefly in a gesture of expectancy.

My mind worked furiously. What came out of my mouth in the next moments held the power of life or death, unless this was all a bluff. Looking into the eyes of Longman, who returned my gaze with grey steel, I didn't believe he was bluffing. There was a hardness there.

Okay. Let it all out. 'I'm wanted for murder.'

'I know,' he said.

'You *know*?'

He flicked his gaze at the boy. 'Scrub.'

Scrub shifted the gun to his left hand, leaned over and from a stowage compartment next to the console retrieved a laptop. With an expert twitch of one hand he flipped it open. Light from its screen lit his face, and he turned it toward me.

Staring back at me was my university Faculty of Arts staff photo. Scrub had found it in the international news section of the *Telegraph*.

All the air went out of me. I slumped in my seat and buried my head in my hands.

'You know what,' I said. 'I can't explain it. Any of it. I barely understand it myself. But I can tell you one thing, and you can believe it or not. I haven't murdered anybody.' Not yet, anyway.

'Boy,' said Longman, and it took me a moment to realise he was addressing me. 'You're on a boat in the middle of the Atlantic, wanted for murder, carrying a gun, maybe thinking to add a couple more to your tally, and we have the power to *disappear you*'—said with a Jamaican accent. 'So, it might not be poetry, but you better bloody well have a go at explaining. Give it your best shot. You've got nothing to lose.'

So I gave it my best shot. Recounted everything I could remember from the night I first found Hiero's folder in the green half-dark of the corridor outside my office, of seeing the assault on Rhianne Goldman in the paper the next day—the *kyoketsu-shoge*—of my flight to Hong Kong, and the first dead body I'd ever seen.

I told them about my race to find Annika Kreider in Vienna, only to arrive minutes late, to hear her shoved in front of a train.

I recounted how I'd made it to the UK, and reached Jane, talked to her, only to watch her die in front of me.

Skipping over how I wallowed in a slough of self-pity after Jane, I told of my plan to crew Longman's yacht, and of meeting him and Scrub on the jetty just days prior.

Longman listened with an unnatural stillness, face betraying nothing of his thoughts.

As I approached my narrative's conclusion, to that moment there in the cabin, spilling my guts to the inscrutable Longman, while Scrub watched me over the Glock's sight, swivelling his seat back and forth ever so slightly, I strained to think of the most powerful supplication for life I could construct. What might move this man?

I failed. My monologue petered out with a pathetic, 'And the gun, I never …'

Silence and the slap of water on the hull.

Longman just gazed at me. Charles the Inscrutable. Sounded like a character from a sixties fantasy adventure.

Longman glanced at Scrub. I turned, an arm rising involuntarily in useless defence.

The boy simply stared at me with his gaze like lightning, then, with a motion almost too slight to see, nodded.

'Well,' said Longman, and he slapped his thighs and rose. 'I need a beer.'

'What about me?' I said, rising.

He looked me over. 'You need a beer, too.'

Something prodded my back. I turned to find Scrub holding the gun toward me, butt first. I took it. For the first time since I'd met him, he smiled.

None of this went a long way toward convincing me of my sanity. I rode a ship of fools.

Just visible through the cabin portal was the high white slash of an airliner contrail. I wondered if anyone looking down from the plane at its tip would be able to see us, a tiny bobbing cork in a vast ocean.

62

We're unaccustomed to mystery.

Somehow the success of science at harnessing the natural world has diffused the idea that the human mind can crack all mysteries. All we need is time, and the universe will yield like stone to a hammer.

'Well,' Marten mused, 'more people should try unpicking the human heart. That would cure them of that delusion.'

And where the hell was Jack Griffen? What she wouldn't give to talk to him right now. She glanced through a window at the Atlantic Ocean spread thirty-thousand feet below in a glittering, swell-wrought texture, and idly wondered if he was somewhere down there.

Just another mystery.

His destination, though, was clear: the US. Randy Todd was a US citizen. And the most recent post in the blog simply said, 'Nearly done. Time to book my unicorn to New York.'

Add to that the odd email she had received from Jack, relayed by the university IT employee, Matt Price. It implied Jack was headed to the US. He'd signed off the email with some nonsense about a poop-deck, and 'Arr!', which Marten took to indicate he was at sea or losing his marbles.

On the strength of it, Marten had booked a flight. Collins didn't argue. He wanted her to disappear for a few weeks, until the smoke from the botched Oxford operation cleared.

But New York didn't narrow her search all that much. The tri-state area held twenty million people. Enough to hide a gaggle of serial killers.

With a sigh, Marten retrieved the sheet of paper on which she had bullet-pointed her itinerary, and glanced over it again, as if it were not etched on her brain already.

The first item on her list she anticipated being the most difficult. It said

'Get Grover Jackson, Assistant Director of the FBI's New York Field Office, onside'. Somehow she had to parlay what small cache of intercontinental goodwill remained between London's Police and the FBI—still a tension fifty years after the Cambridge Five, somehow baked into the FBI's DNA by the irascible J. Edgar Hoover—into transport and provincial authority to find one Hieronymus Beck.

This was problematic, given that the last time she had set foot in New Jersey, she had been marched out, accused with killing the state's case. The memory made Marten frown. Nine years and the injustice still stung.

The case had revolved around the death of a young girl—and it was right there that Marten had underestimated the depth of emotional charge she was dealing with. Years later, now equipped with the experience of motherhood, it was clear she should have trodden more carefully.

But, she'd been *right*, dammit.

The accused, Cory Wayne, a factory worker for a biopharma company, had matched the half-remembered sightings of a few key witnesses. He'd had no alibi for the time of the assault. For opportunity, the presence of the girl alone near the woods had been judged sufficient for the state to bring a case.

And motive? That was anchored to records obtained from Wayne's internet provider, which included a torrent of pre-pubescent porn. Mr Wayne had simply crossed the line from voyeur to participant—or would have, had the girl not run and fallen.

The case fell under the purview of the FBI by virtue of being both a violent crime and a crime against children. The discovered child pornography sparked its own investigation, but it was the murder case that saw Marten attached—a soft ball for a recent graduate from the FBI's profiling program. They'd found the murderer; just needed to confirm the fit so there were no 'accidents' when it went to trial. No one counted on their star pupil upending the case.

Marten's crime was to assert that porn did not a murderer make. It could, of course. God knew, it did plenty of harm—reduced sex to recreation, and the female body to the recreational equipment par excellence. It wrecked marriages, and was busy twisting up the self-worth of a generation of girls by removing the inner life from the concept of beauty.

But it didn't prove murder precisely because of its ubiquity.

The closer she looked at the evidence against Wayne, the flimsier it appeared.

For starters, the girl had run almost a mile into densely forested Appalachian foothills pursued by her attacker. Mr Wayne, when brought into custody, was three hundred pounds with the VO2 aerobic score of a seventy-year-old. Her pursuer had to have kept on her heels to not lose her as she tick-tacked through the dense woods.

The physical facts alone should have thrown doubt on the guilt of Cory Wayne. But to young Marten's profiler's eye—albeit freshly minted—Wayne was thirteen kinds of wrong for the crime.

And the man Marten's deconstruction of the case pissed off the most? That was Grover Jackson. He was the one to suggest the assignment of Marten Lacroix, the star product of the FBI's International Criminal Investigative Analysis Fellowship—a young, black firebrand, now on faux secondment from the UK. A marketer's dream.

Grover. She sighed. He was definitely a Grover. His parents must have consulted an oracle who peered into the mists of time and saw the hard-arse in the womb.

This Grover was now the head of the FBI in New York. He was the guy she would have to convince to give her the resources and the latitude she needed to find Hiero Beck.

Her current boss, Collins, had told her how to get Grover onside. Thinking about it made her mouth curl as if she had tasted something sour. But he was right.

She had to sell Grover on the Devil coming ashore on his beloved US—one Jack Griffen, the Intercontinental Killer.

63

Date: 2015-31-10: 2015-10-31T13:53:29-02:00XX
From: JackTheKipper <jkipp3r.70@hotmail.com>
To: Big Daddy <rapture_the_mattysphere@gmail.com>
[9 threads inlined, reverse – emacs/Mu+]

Matt, can you forward this to our friend? 'Did you get off your arse and start looking for Hiero Beck?'

> You're lucky I found this, Prof. It was thrown into spam, but being the anal guy I am, I check. Forwarding… I'll relay any response from our friend. Cheers, The Blackbird.

> She says: 'Beck? No. I'm busy hunting Jack Griffen.'

> Oh, that's hilarious. Can you pass on my burner number? Email is too slow. I want to talk to her when I make landfall. (PS: 'The Blackbird'? I like it. Very Spy Who Came In From the Cold.)

> She says you should consider yourself lucky she's even acknowledging your emails. No phone calls. (PS: What's a Spy Who Came In With A Cold?)

> She wants deniability? Shit, there are more important things at stake than her career. She should know. She held Jane as she died. Could do with some perspective. Tell her Beck is heading for the US. (PS: 'What's the Spy?' Sheesh, Matt. Get an education.)

> She says she knows. And—get this—his real name is Randall Todd. (PS: You should be more polite. Remind me again, how many people in the world *don't* think you're a serial killer?)

> Fair. I repent in sackcloth and ashes … Hiero is a Randy? That's gold. I take it all back. Tell her she's doing a plum job. I'll call him Randy next time I'm talking to him with anything other than the muzzle of a gun.

> A gun? Jack …

64

I watched Longman's leathery fingertips poke at the laptop keys with their incongruous delicateness. If pirates had carried laptops, this would have been a pirate's laptop.

It took me a moment to discern what was wrong with the beaten-up laptop, aside from the obvious age of the device in the hands of a billionaire. Its keys were in alphabetical order. Where normal keyboards spell QWERTY from the top left, this one spelled ABCDEF.

And Longman was the slowest typist I have ever seen. Paint dries quicker than he types. He seemed to return to 'A' before scanning to find the letter he wanted each time, as though his finger were the head of an old dot-matrix printer.

'Why don't you dictate,' I said, 'or get a PA?'

'I had a PA,' he grunted. His gaze flicked to me. 'She destroyed my life.'

He knew how to destroy a conversation before it began, too.

Visible through the cabin portal were the swells making the boat pitch. After a day of green gills and retching over the side of the boat, I now felt only mildly nauseous, something about which I felt quite proud.

We were just days from the Florida coast, making good time on the beeline Longman had charted since I'd spilled my guts. The engine chugged away night and day, a constant background noise added to the wind and wash, like another force of nature.

Machines that just keep going amaze me. I can't help anthropomorphising them, imagining them flesh and blood. The analogy falls down when I consider my own flesh and blood. My own traitorous heart.

With a start, I realised I hadn't checked my Medline in over a week.

I twisted its face toward me and saw the heart icon blipping along at a steady, safe 60 bpm.

The sailor's life for me.

But actually, the cause was living with someone who trusted me. *Two* someones who trusted me. Heck, Scrub had sat by my feet every day this week listening to me read aloud. I'd found a tattered, salt-stained copy of *The Neverending Story* in a bedside drawer. I experimented by reading the first chapter aloud when he was near. After that he was hooked.

My calm also came from the fact there was nothing I could do but wait. For the moment, I was a passenger of life.

I glanced at Longman. I couldn't let his comment about the PA who destroyed his life pass.

'You seem full of life to me,' I said.

His finger paused, hovering above the keyboard.

'I had resolved,' he said, and the slow *clack, clack* of his typing resumed, 'to spend what was left of my strength on someone other than me for once. That woman nearly took even that from me.'

The clacking ceased again, and I watched his gaze follow Scrub as the boy passed by the outside of the cabin carrying a book.

'Scrub?'

The typing resumed again.

'Justin Charles Hunt.'

'Your grandson.'

'*Your*,' he muttered. 'Such an elusive thing, ownership of a person. *My* grandson. His mother's son. His sister's brother.' He paused. 'The state's ward.'

I let the silence stretch, waiting to see if he would continue. He did.

'Do you know anything about US prisons?'

'Only what I learned from *Shawshank Redemption*.'

He grunted. 'In the US, prisons are a business.'

'Like Walmart?' I said, dubiously.

'Like Walmart.' My doubt must have registered on my face. 'I'm not joking. One of my investment advisors tried to convince me to invest in CoreCivic—their shares are classed as a "real estate investment trust". Shortly after, they were investigated for maltreatment of prisoners and a higher than acceptable death rate of detainees. But in any case, I wasn't buying. It's repugnant.'

'And this is connected with—' I gestured in the direction of the prow, where Scrub had been heading.

'It would have been his future, if left to his mother and father. My son, and his ex-spouse.'

He returned to his typing—*clack! clack!*—a simmering anger bending his frame. I let him pound away with measured wrath, and waited.

'The boy was being shuffled between institutions while his parents played ping-pong with their child, the prize being the freedom to live like children themselves. A perverse irony. His own parents failed to recognise what was patently obvious to one grumpy old man—he wasn't rebellious, or antisocial, or "authority-averse"; he was special.'

He waved away my response. 'A horrible word, I know. But from age two the boy had been different. He didn't speak a word. He would arrange his toys in lines, by size and colour. He remembered things. Incredible detail. They used to call these kids *idiot savants*. It's the autism spectrum these days, but even that implies we know what the hell we're talking about.'

'So you tried to, what?'

'I tried to point out their bloody responsibility to their child, and to actually look at him, and consider his needs. In the end, their needs were money. A lot of it. Controlling interest. In business terms, I showed too much.'

'That you loved him.' It slipped out. But Longman just nodded without looking at me.

'And would you believe that slime at *Time* had the gall to pretend the cover was just about my *money*? *People* had the follow-up story of my "Secret crusade: a grandson's guardianship" already warming their presses.'

'So you faxed them the bird.' I couldn't help smile.

He grimaced, almost a smile, and I saw his gaze kindle for a moment with relish. 'I faxed the bastards a flock. Threatened a legal shitstorm if they ran with the cover.'

'Then you bought a boat,' I joked.

'Yes. Before he became the mayor of Providence, Vincent Buddy Cianci joked he had enough cash to either become the mayor or buy a boat. He did the sums; becoming mayor was cheaper.' He paused. 'He didn't do his sums right.'

I had heard of Buddy Cianci. 'He paid in pounds of flesh to the mob. What did you pay?'

Longman watched the ocean tilt a degree through the cabin portal a moment, then said: 'That's just it. I've paid nothing. It's taken me four years to be able to say it, but I'm the most blessed man alive.'

65

'Ms Lacroix.'

Marten shook the proffered hand. 'It's "Mrs", and you bloody well know it. Start how you mean to finish.'

A perfect smile split the face of Grover Jackson, but did not touch his eyes. 'Would you prefer "Cadet Lacroix"?'

'Would you prefer to keep your teeth?'

'That time of the month, Marten?'

Marten seethed for a moment, before remembering who she was. 'You might have grown up some in seven years.'

They walked in silence through the terminal exit and into the haze around JFK. The air was still and neither warm nor cold—like a bath at body temperature. Marten tasted engine exhaust at the back of her throat.

Grover's eyes disappeared behind aviator shades as he slipped behind the wheel of a black Cadillac. Marten dumped her hand luggage—all she had brought—onto the rear seat before sitting in the front passenger seat. Her door was barely shut before Grover wedged the car in front of a taxi and headed for the exit ramp.

The Cadillac had settled into the flowing metal river of the Van Wyck Expressway before he spoke. 'Tell me this story about Griffen is crap, and you're just here because you needed a break from the ball and chain.'

'His name is Benjamin, and we have a son now—David.'

'Congratulations,' said Grover automatically. 'And it also wouldn't have anything to do with fleeing the stink you put on in Oxford?'

How did he know about that?

'No, and no, Jack Griffen is real, dangerous, and probably on US soil.'

'Why do I care?'

'Because if he kills again and it gets out that the FBI knew he was here and did nothing about it ...'

Marten felt Grover's eyes move behind the mirrored lenses.

'Shit, Marten. What do they put in the water in London? You'd talk to the media?'

Marten watched the traffic in silence.

'What do you want?' he said.

'I told you. A car. A jet, if I need to get interstate. And access to NCIC databases.'

He laughed. 'You don't want much.' Then, 'Done.'

'Done?' It slipped out. Marten had prepared herself for a long argument, and was ready to call Collins back in London for support, and even then hadn't been sure of getting what she needed. But, 'Done'?

Warning bells were just beginning to ring when Grover said, 'On one condition.'

'What condition?'

'You apologise—full and frank.'

'Apologise for what?'

'All of it,' said Grover, and he flashed that full smile. Marten knew without seeing behind the mirrored lenses that his eyes were smiling now.

'Look, Grover, I'm sorry—'

'Not to me,' he said, and Marten's heart sank.

66

Call me Ishmael.

Actually, text me, Ishmael. The reception here is crap.

My brain played absurd games. It was trying to distract me from the anxiety cramping my guts. From my hideaway in the owner's cabin beneath the bridge, I heard voices rise and fall over the gurgle of water against the hull. Longman was having a conversation on which my freedom hung.

A sudden clang of iron startled me, and I remembered Scrub was loose topside. From the constant pad of his feet on the deck, and the frequent scrapes and thuds that overlaid the conversation I was straining to hear, I got the impression he was trying hard to make it appear the boat held no secrets. I smiled despite my churning guts.

Another minute of holding my breath in the dark, and I heard a sound that frightened me to my core. The heavy clump of a man's tread. Longman had said he was known here, trusted. He would sign the customs forms on the jetty, or in the officer's booth if it was cold. The officer would not come aboard.

Timber creaked directly above my head. I was inches from a customs officer, at that moment the embodiment of civilisation—the thing I'd stepped outside the day I tore open the door in a Hong Kong high-rise. The night I first laid eyes on a dead body.

The tread passed over my head and away. I heard the officer call, I assumed, to Scrub. The boy made no response, of course. Longman's voice rose in explanation, and I heard his feet land heavily above me, and follow with what my imagination told me was nervous haste.

The sound of the latch on the cabin door opening, a sound that had welded with my new familiarity with the ocean, told me the officer was homing in on my position.

The customs officer's voice came clearly through the hatch, which was all that sat between where I squatted and the bridge above.

'That's the new Garmin multibeam sonar, right?'

'Yeah,' Longman's voice, sounding breathless. 'Not so new now.'

'But top of the line, right? These puppies can see three-sixty degrees, school and bed in real-time, huh?'

Longman grunted agreement.

'And this—' I heard the slight squeak the captain's chair made when it moved. 'A man could sleep in this thing.'

'Hardly,' said Longman, but I could hear a little pride seeping into his tone.

There was a click, and a slight tremor shook the boat as a pump pulsed.

'Where's De Hayes, anyway?' Longman again.

'Got croup, would you believe it. At his age.' The chair squealed again, and the radio crackled. 'He said you called him direct, but his answering machine took it. Said you were early this season, and he regretted not being able to catch you for that "pint".'

'De Hayes doesn't need me for an excuse to drink,' said Longman. To my ears his levity sounded forced.

'Why are you so early this year? He said you'd normally come through the Caribbean, and take your time tooling around the islands.'

'Something came up. I set straight course a few days south of the Azores.'

'You wouldn't believe what people try to smuggle in these days.'

There was a pause. I willed myself to be a stone.

'Want a look through the cabins?' said Longman. I almost wet myself.

More silence, broken only by the rhythmic squeaking of the captain's chair.

'No, I'm done. I just wanted to check out your sweet ride. I've seen these Nordhavns, but never one tricked out like this.'

The chair squealed one last time, and I heard the clump of the man's weight coming down on the cabin floor, and then he was leaving.

A minute later I bustled out of the stowage into the cabin. The cabin light was off; Longman's head and shoulders were silhouetted against the marina lights.

'Give it a minute, Jack. Don't waste a year's care for the want of a moment's patience.'

I froze, and peered through the cabin portal at the jetty, and the retreating back of the customs officer. Beyond him, where the jetty ended, lay solid ground. Only dark parking lot, but a sudden hunger for earth took me. I fought to wait.

We waited in silence, motionless for what felt like hours. Scrub slipped soundless into the cabin and stood by his grandfather's side, kept vigil with us.

The jetty had been empty for minutes, and at last I could stand it no longer. I stooped to pick up my backpack, but Longman laid a restraining hand on my shoulder. With his other hand, he thrust something toward me.

'For your journey.'

He held a bundle the size of a thick book. I took it without examination, and tucked it into my backpack beside my meagre belongings.

My hand was on the cabin door handle when his hand grasped my arm again. The thought of landfall was a fire in me now, and I had to suppress the urge to tear away.

'You know, Scrub never took to anyone before. Except me.' Longman's eyes glinted in the darkness. 'And I'm not getting any younger.'

I turned to look at the boy.

Only days ago, he'd been holding a gun on me. Now his eyes were shining.

'If I come out of this, I'll drop you a line. Promise.' I didn't say it, but deep down, I'd been thinking for a while now that those chances weren't good. 'And, thanks.'

The cabin door whooshed shut behind me as I stepped onto a deck scoured by a rising wind. The tide-run beyond the marina on St Johns River glimmered with white chop, and the night was riven by the occasional lonely gull's cry.

Adrenaline fizzed in my veins as I vaulted over the rail and onto the jetty. I made my way, swift but as casually as I could manage while my heart hammered in my chest. The faint orange light of my Medline strobed the planks. The jetty seemed to sway, but I knew it was my sea legs that were lying to me. The thick planks were rock solid.

Soon dry land was a stone's throw away.

Metres.

At my feet.

I stepped onto the grit gathered at the kerb of the parking lot and breathed in. Did the air taste different at that threshold?

After almost three weeks at sea, I had made landfall. US soil. Somewhere out there, treading the same soil, was Hiero. He had another woman in his sights, no doubt.

I'd left the lifeless body of a neglected friend in the UK. I wasn't going to let that happen here.

67

A Californian redwood shifts four tons of water to its canopy every day. It can pull with the force of a John Deere tractor, through vessels a millimetre wide.

Kim told me this once as we sat beneath an oak on the grounds of the University of Western Australia. Not bad for something lacking a nervous system.

It had been spitfire season, when you could find hairy caterpillars clinging to the sides of trees in great, writhing lumps. When she told me the redwoods achieved their water feat with capillary action, I joked that it was more efficient than *caterpillar*-y action.

She didn't think it was funny, but she laughed anyway, because I'd had a story rejected that day.

That's Kim.

68

Marten sat, to all appearances patiently, while Grover delivered her bio.

Top cadet of her intake at Hendon Police College, London. Awarded the Queen's Police Medal in her second year of service. One of the youngest to make the rank of inspector, a feat that earned her a place in the five-man shortlist—the entire 'special dispensation' quota for the UK in the FBI's own training apparatus—sponsored by the International Criminal Investigative Analysis Fellowship.

'Where the world comes to learn to profile the criminal mind. Marten liked our country so much she stayed to take a degree in forensic psychology from Harvard.'

She'd never seen Grover in salesman mode. He was uncannily convincing. He had put her on a pedestal, and was jacking it to the roof.

She waited for the cue he was about to push her off it, and all the while, the second hand of the clock at the back of the hall wound around its face.

'It's fair to say Detective Chief Inspector Marten Lacroix has taken the ladder of success three rungs at a time. Her calibre was obvious from the first day she arrived at Quantico, her record during her time here almost spotless.' He paused. 'Almost …'

Here we go, thought Marten, and braced for impact.

Standing at the lectern, he turned toward her, as if including her in a shared understanding. 'There was that one case, her first in New Jersey, just a few hours drive from here.'

From the number of smiles that appeared in the audience, Marten knew they were primed. This was a full-tilt set-up. She was going to eat grass, and they were ready to enjoy every bit of it.

'But far be it from me to steal her thunder. Much better heard from the horse's mouth. Marten?' Grover inclined his head, inviting her to the lectern. He was smiling, but the crease in his brow said, 'Remember: an apology, for everything. That's the deal.'

She stood, and walked to the lectern with a calmness she did not feel. She had to tug the mike down; Grover was a big guy. She tapped it once. 'This thing take estrogen?'

The laughter quickly petered out and she was left with a yawning silence.

Her gaze wandered across the ranks of agents. She noticed a few had notebooks open in their laps, pens poised. On a hunch, she said, 'I'm fresh off the plane. Assistant Director Jackson didn't even give a girl a chance to powder her nose, so I need a little help. Somebody jog my memory; which lesson are we talking about? Which rung, to labour the analogy, did I slip on?'

A hand shot up, predictably belonging to one of the note-takers.

'I think Director Jackson is referring to the Wayne case.'

Marten's brow creased in mock confusion. 'You're all too young to have heard of it, surely?'

In answer, the agent who had spoken raised his book.

'Are you telling me it's required reading?' She pivoted to look at Grover, put a hand to her breast. 'I'm flattered,' she said, and noted that his smile had been replaced by a look of faint suspicion.

'Well, let me turn this around then. Nothing worse than listening to a lecture. Allow me to test the mettle of the agency's up and coming. The future. The brains trust.'

She tilted her head at Grover, seeking permission. A curt nod indicated she had it. He couldn't politely do otherwise.

Another breath. Her gaze raked the audience, all faces upturned and expectant.

'We had a motto, mantra even, when I was a cadet. I wonder if any of you know it?'

A handful of arms shot into the air. Marten nodded at a young woman in a severe black suit.

'Fidelity, Bravery, Integrity?'

'Straight from the crest. But no, I'm referring to a less-than-official motto. Perhaps it has fallen out of favour in these times.'

Marten observed the young agents trade glances.

'So polite.' She glanced at Grover. 'A regular tame flock you've husbanded here, Director.'

A voice was raised tentatively. 'The truth stinks?'

Marten laughed. 'Close enough, if Grover Jackson's house rules won't abide no cussin'. The truth is indeed a pile of crap. The point being, of course, that it will out in the end—declare its presence to all who have noses and aren't too delicate to hunt for it.' She pinned them with her eyes. 'The truth. Not convenience. Not simplicity. Not pragmatism. Not expediency. Certainly not beauty.'

She paused to allow her words to sink in.

'So. The truth. Grover invited me up here an hour ago. I asked him to assist me in the capture of Jack Griffen, the Intercontinental Killer, who even now has likely made landfall on US soil. He agreed, on one condition. That I apologise for my part in the collapse of the case against Cory Wayne.'

Grover's expression shifted. In no time he'd assumed the look of one in on it. So smooth.

'So,' Marten said, 'the truth is construed from facts. Let's try lining a few up.

'First, the prime and only suspect in the State's case was a Mr Cory M. Wayne. I don't remember what the "M" stands for; let's assume "Molester"'—a few laughs—'Now, who can tell me on what evidence the case was built?'

Hands began to shoot up.

'No need to be polite. Just call it out.'

A voice called out. 'Wayne was seen near the scene of the crime.'

Another said, 'Coworkers reported he'd been agitated in the days prior.'

More voices chimed in, speaking over each other.

'Internet records indicated his porn consumption spiked in the weeks preceding the murder.'

'Dirt from the embankment where the victim was found matched traces taken from his boot treads.'

On and on it went. Everyone, it seemed, was eager to show they knew the material. Marten waited patiently.

When the flow finally began to ebb, she raised a hand for quiet.

'You really are good students. So, honouring my deal: Grover. Everyone. I'm sorry.'

Silence.

'I'm sorry for pointing out the case against Corey Wayne was built entirely on circumstantial evidence, targeting a man with no demonstrable motive nor relevant history. For that, I apologise.'

Marten continued over the murmurs.

'I apologise for finding fault with every cliché of criminal profiling trotted out to explain what motivated Wayne to get off the couch one summer day and go hunting for a real, live little girl—a need to reassure himself of his fading manhood, to seize control of his life, to find some outlet to vent his anger.

'Never mind that he had plenty of opportunity to do all three routinely in the bars of his home town, as revealed by numerous witnesses. Not to mention the money he was making from his cut of black-market OxyContin.

'Folks, Cory Wayne's manhood was alive and well; he felt in control of his life.'

She watched the anger glint in eyes as it travelled the room like unseen lightning. But then, too, she thought she saw mental cogs turn behind those eyes as minds rehearsed the list of evidence she had recounted. The hostility faded from some faces.

'Second,' she said, 'when these concerns were discreetly pointed out by a certain young agent to her senior colleague, what action did he or she take?'

No one leapt to answer. They were gun-shy now. Apparently, Marten Lacroix was not the cardboard cut-out they'd assumed her to be.

At last, the woman who had first given Marten the FBI's motto spoke up.

'The senior officer provided the media with the key evidence, and asked the local sheriff to organise a public forum where community members might come forward with further information.'

'Brave girl. Yes, it was indeed that agent's response to call the equivalent of a *townhall meeting* to pump more hot air into the case, rather than admit what was obvious to everyone involved—that it was bullshit—and begin the painful task of raking over other leads that were now that much colder.'

From the corner of her eye, Marten saw Grover refold his arms like he was snapping wood. How much further could she push it, before it backfired? Not enough, and he'd pay her request for help lip service and get away with it. Too far and he'd simply freeze her out, reneg on his promise.

'So, I apologise for taking a fresh look beneath the mountain of grief and anger, rightly felt, but unhelpfully piled upon the first-hand facts of the case.

'And while I'm at it'—an olive branch, a real concession—'I am sorry for grossly underestimating the depth of grief and anger generated by the death of a young girl in a small town—which can't have made this investigation easy. If I'd been a mother then, as I am today, I would have trodden more carefully.'

For some reason, the memory of Jack Griffen bent over the prone form of a dying woman in a waiting room flashed across Marten's mind. It was a moment before she gathered up the threads of her thought.

'But who then?' This from a hard face with a crew-cut. 'Who murdered Jennifer Nicolls?'

'We don't know. I don't know. And, it's okay to say I don't know. Takes a man to say it,' she joked. And, she thought, there's one more truth that smells like shit.

'But time is wasting, and there is a killer loose on US soil right now. The textbook for this case hasn't been written yet. I—we, with your help— could be writing it now, instead of taking points from an old grudge.' She spread her hands. 'What do you say?'

Finally, she turned to look Grover full in the face. His expression was unreadable.

'Before these witnesses, Grover. Have I apologised for "all of it"? Fulfilled my part of the deal? Will you let me help you catch Jack Griffen before he murders again?'

Motionless a moment, Grover stood and strode to the lectern.

'Please join me in thanking Detective Lacroix.'

The applause was louder than she had expected. When she turned to speak with Grover, he had already left the stage.

69

Any fool can hold a gun.

For proof, I offer myself. Crouching in the shadowed stoop opposite the café, I held the Glock raised before me, gripped double-hand. Easy.

Fully loaded, a Glock 17's steel, brass, plastic and propellant totals nine hundred grams. Weighs less than a can of beans. And any fool can hold a can of beans.

What's more, if the Glock is typical—built, as it was, by a man with no firearms experience to win a contest by the Austrian Ministry of Defence—any fool can design one too.

But to fire one at a human being?

That, it turns out, takes a devil.

It's like they say: pressure can make a diamond, or a stain. It all depends on what's being squashed.

Squatting there in the shadow, one shoulder braced against a dirt-encrusted brick wall, trying to keep the Glock's sight trained on the kid's chest as he sauntered to the café entrance, I was beginning to fear I was from Stainsville.

The problem wasn't the occasional yellow flash of a taxicab, or the stink of rotting trash wafting out of the gutter. I had clear sight across the street. There was no wind to speak of. I knew the chambered hollow point round would expand when it punctured his flesh with a good chance of smearing an artery or organ.

Everything was ready.

Except me.

My hands were jittering like a junkie in withdrawal.

Maybe it was nerves? I know it wasn't guilt.

No, I wanted a tight bead on his chest. I wanted my bullet to tear him a new hole. Was *giddy* to see him ragdoll to the ground, and watch his blood sluice onto the street.

Those are the perks of an Angel of Death on an avenging mission.

My real fear was that my body was falling apart. That the stresses of the past weeks had caught up with me, and the flesh-machine named Jack Griffen had finally thrown a cog. That deep down, part of my constitution had ruptured. Now, when I needed it one last time.

Maybe murder took more than a professor of literature had— particularly a forty-five-year-old professor of literature with a diabolical heart condition and a fear of needles.

Why not? Everything else had broken.

I strained again to still the tremble in my arms. Just one more shot.

Because—*oh, boy*—I meant to murder. Just once. First and last on my scorecard.

My one hope was that before he died, he had the presence of mind to look for me. I wanted him to know I made it. Me, Jack Griffen. I played his game. And he lost.

… Would lose.

If I could tug the trigger back a mere centimetre.

But with murder, how wide is the chasm between saying and doing?

Murder. The oldest crime. Stuff of books and movies, and news headlines of not-quite-near places and unfamiliar faces. Not something encountered during school drop-off, or grocery shopping, in the office, on the beach. Murder is a beast from a different dimension. Scary, sure, but ultimately unreal, because it belongs to another world.

But have you ever wondered what it would take for *you* to cross that chasm? What circumstances? What passions? What failure of logic? What temporary insanity?

In Ross Macdonald's novel *The Instant Enemy*, his hard-boiled detective Lew Archer says of the murderer, 'The second self that most of us have inside us had stepped into the open and acted out its violence. Now he had to live with it, like an insane Siamese twin, for the rest of his life.'

Think about it. Who do you love most in all the world? What would you do to the person that brought violence into your loved one's experience?

I'm not talking about an accident. I mean an act deliberated over. Relished. Lacking even the mercy of death, because the perpetrator plans to violate your loved one again. And again. And again.

How are you feeling? Get anything? A little flutter deep, deep down of a kind of rage that would throw down every ingrained inhibition and put primal bloody murder into your hands?

That little flutter is a long way from murder, but it's there, isn't it. You felt it. And the thing is, it's alive. All it needs is a little sustenance and it will grow. It feeds on scraps that fall from the table of your emotions.

For me it took a simple discovery to crystallise the desire to murder— really make it *become*.

And that discovery was learning Hiero's next target.

Hiero had sat down, by a window. Perhaps I wouldn't have to wait for him to exit the café after all. I imagined a bullet striking the window glass. Saw it turn white and fall like shattered ice. How much force would the glass sap from the bullet? Enough to render its killing power iffy?

Not if I plugged him in the head.

As I watched him fuss with his hair, I rued the fact that the human body is decidedly more mobile than the tree trunks I'd abused learning to aim the gun.

How had the long, twisting—at times, twice-walked—path of my life led here, to this moment, in a foreign city, on the other side of the world, with a gun in my hand, and murder in my heart?

Memories of the previous week were a mixture of blurred boredom and shattering revelation. Gold flecks amid the pan's dross; tacks in the mud.

The first thing I did after I left Longman and Scrub was purchase a burner phone in Jacksonville, using some of the cash Longman had given me. The next was hit Hiero's blog. The most recent entry was short:

3PM, with the best cheesecake in New York.

Straightaway I knew it was a cipher. Put that way to keep the police off, but enough for me to decode.

I had only ever travelled to the US once before. Hiero knew it because he had asked. The trip was for a conference in New York. A member of the conference's review committee gave me a tour, which included a little café in Chelsea for, he claimed, the best cheesecake in New York.

I should say, the part of the blog post that was *legible* was short. Because beginning immediately after 'New York', the text turned into garbage. Trash. Random letters and symbols, like the blog had passed its expiry date and begun to rot.

But I paused over that oddity only briefly. I had my target. A café in New York, at 3.00 pm on the thirteenth of November.

Driving north, I covered a thousand miles in three days in a second-hand peanut-brown Dodge Avenger 98 that wallowed along the lanes like a walrus on ice, but which had come with no questions asked and no formal registration switch. Finally I could say I felt okay on the right side of the road, if not comfortable. A fear still lurked in me that in a vehicular crisis, my reflexes would fire the wrong way in a split second, and send me into onrushing traffic. But I wouldn't need to worry about driving soon. Wouldn't need to worry about anything.

I started with five boxes of ammunition—five thousand rounds of hollow-point 9 mm Parabellum—bought from a gun shop on my way through Savannah. Many times I drove an hour off the interstate looking for a barren place to fire the gun, took out a box of ammunition from the trunk, and paused to marvel that in one of those boxes lay the bullet that would end Hiero's life. And a darker thought: in there, too, lay one for me.

I will never forget the first time I chambered a bullet, aimed the gun, and pulled the trigger.

The explosion was like discovering a new colour. A new primal force in the world. It was as different from when the cop shot a mirror in the St Pancras Station restroom as watching fireworks is to *being* fireworks. I was the killing force; the killing force was me. Because I had caused it. Squeezed the trigger and brought the angel of death to life.

Well, angel of noise. Which is mostly what I achieved for the first thousand rounds of ammunition. My first target was a spruce pine in South Carolina. Recoil snapped my arm away from the tree each time, and my brain was slow to catch on. By the time I'd finished that day, I was plugging it reliably at ten paces. Next day, different tree, I was sinking rounds into the same head-sized knot reliably at fifteen.

After the trees, I graduated to setting empty soda cans on the hood of a rusted Ford Ranger, which had once been puke yellow, barely twenty paces from my feet.

This practice became routine, and I soon learned I need not find so secluded a place to train with the weapon. I stacked empty cans on burned-out cars, rotting fence posts, and once, a cracked toilet cistern and bowl that had somehow grown moss. In a place just south of the Virginia border, kids appeared and watched me take potshots at my cans lined up on the edge of a wrecked dumpster. They cheered when I finally obliterated Dr Pepper at forty paces. I grinned at that, blew the air from the end of the barrel like a cowboy, spun the gun by its trigger guard and holstered it.

On the rare times I couldn't find empty cans, I shot up trees like the hippie Antichrist.

All this time I never forgot Hiero's deadline. The clock was ticking at the back of my mind with an insistence that crept into my dreams. But I'd had enough of blindly rushing in. This time I would arrive eyes wide open.

I sighted along the barrel at Hiero's head.

If anything, the tremor in my hands was growing worse. There was no way I was going to get a clean killing shot from across the street. The cover of the shadowed stoop I had so assiduously chosen would have to be abandoned. The wind eddying in my hiding place chilled the sweat on my neck, and I acknowledged something I'd known for days now. In order to put an end to this, to kill Hiero—make sure of it—I would have to get up close, do it point blank. This really was the end of my life.

Adrenaline surged as I uncoiled from my hiding place. It propelled me forward so fast I felt I was watching someone else dash across the street. It was another man whose shoes slapped on the asphalt, then the cement footpath, ducked beneath the bough of a plane tree, and took one last look at the target before raising his gun. That man was surprised how light the gun felt now. How light *everything* felt.

The gun settled, finally stood rock-still in my grip.

A memory of a hallucination—the ghost of a ghost—picked that moment to assault me: 'Dad, you're no killer.'

I hesitated—could I hug my daughter again with these hands if I pulled the trigger?

Two things happened at once that shocked me back into the moment.

A girl emerged from further inside the café, passed in front of Hiero, spoiling my shot, and sat across from him.

And a voice spoke in my ear. 'Act Three, Jack.'

The first signal of something deeply wrong was a spreading sensation moving from my bowels to my throat. My brain was just beginning to catch up with my body as I turned dumbly to find a face grinning at me from beneath the peak of a New York Yankees cap. His face caused a tug of recognition, but before I could place it, he said: 'Give me the gun.'

Ignoring him, I twisted to see if the girl had moved, if I had a clear shot at Hiero, and the realisation finally hit home.

The girl at his table was Tracey. My daughter.

She was facing the street through the glass. Her expression was of complete surprise. Her mouth framed one word: 'Dad?'

'Come on, Jack,' said the voice, breath warm on my skin, and its owner laid a hand on my shoulder. 'Do I need to spell it out? Think of the children.'

I tore my eyes from my daughter, turned to the man—boy. Through the welter of colliding thoughts, I marked his jeans, jacket, cap. And a laptop bag hanging from a strap over his thin shoulders.

The smell of cigarette smoke clung to him. It evoked a memory of swaying carriages and autumnal fields. For a moment I was back on the train from Vienna to Paris, when Jane had still been alive, and I had been so close to Hiero.

Or so I had thought.

It was the laptop that closed the final circuit in my mind.

In a flash I remembered a passenger seated alone in a compartment, a New York Yankees cap, bent over a laptop.

'Who the hell are you?' I breathed, even as he took the gun from my numb fingers.

He smiled, and it had a bit of Hiero in it.

'Me? I'm no one. I guess you could say I'm Hiero's ghostwriter.'

A phone buzzed, and he retrieved it.

'Slow?' he said into the phone, irritated. 'How about I just let him shoot you next time? No one would see that ending coming.'

70

Marten had always thought humans were strange, from as far back as kindergarten, when Joey Baldwin had earnestly informed her that his penis had a name, and he would talk to it in the toilet cubicle.

But for a town to take pride in a mass murder—even a mass murder older than living memory. To turn it for tourist dollars. 'Strange' no longer covered it.

This happened in the immediate wake of the Lawson family murders of Christmas 1929, when entrepreneurial Germanton residents opened the Lawson home to tourists at twenty-five cents a pop. Visitors souvenired sultanas from the Christmas cake Marie Lawson had baked, which would never be eaten.

Fast-forward almost a century and things weren't so crass. Now you could visit the Lawson Family Murders Museum, twenty miles over in Madison, housed on the second floor of what was once the funeral home where the bodies of the Lawson family were embalmed. You could sit in a recreation of the main room and imagine those frantic last moments of life, quivering with terror as you sought a hiding place from your father and his shotgun.

Marten sighed, and swallowed the last of her coffee, warming her hands on the mug. Her gaze flicked between the empty main street and the face of Hiero Beck staring up at her from the photo by her saucer. What the hell had she hoped for here, anyway?

She remembered Grover's reaction once she caught up with him after her 'apology'. It had been touch and go—'Fine, Marten. Your bridges are burning. What do you want?'—but here she was. In the end, the extent of the help to Germanton was an upgraded ticket on Delta from La Guardia to Charlotte and permission to carry her Glock, itself a legacy of her time with the FBI.

And when she'd finally driven into Germanton, a 'town' of 827 folk, what had she hoped to find? A kind of lodestone, calling its child, Hieronymus Beck—Randall Todd—home after all this time?

The place added a visceral jolt to the imaginary world of a mass murder, but not much else. She was able to confirm that Arthur Lawson, the only surviving member of the family, had four children before he died in a car accident at age thirty-two. But they were all accounted for, and none bore the surname Todd.

That left a child born out of wedlock, who would be nearly impossible to track down in formal records. This is where living memory became the only resource, but—and Marten gazed at the forlorn street—there wasn't a lot of living left in this town.

'Can I get you anything else, honey?'

'I'm fine, thanks,' Marten said, and twisted to meet the waitress' eyes. The habit was a human touch she cultivated in herself. It helped her to not see people as cogs.

But the woman's gaze was transfixed by something on the table.

Grasping, Marten asked: 'You know this boy?'

'He's no boy,' she said, and took Marten's cup from her fingers.

Marten rose and followed her inside.

The inside of the café was empty like the street outside, save for an elderly lady propped in a chair by the window, scratching with a pen at a crossword. A solitary ceiling fan beat futilely at the tepid air, fighting with a steaming bain-marie.

Marten followed the waitress until she passed through a flip-counter and disappeared with Marten's dirty dishes into the kitchen.

'You piss my niece off?'

The old lady's words so shocked Marten she lifted a hand too late to hide a smile.

'I can tell,' the lady continued without looking up from the crossword. 'She drops her heels on the floor like river stones.'

'I didn't mean to,' said Marten, coming over to the table. 'She saw this.' Marten placed the photo of Hiero on the table beside the crossword.

The lady glanced at it. The only response Marten noticed was a slight deepening in the creases gathered above her brow. Her pen moved again, scratching in missing letters.

The waitress returned. 'Go on then.' She stood leaning against a wall behind the counter, arms crossed, gaze fixed on her aunty.

The pen stilled, and the old lady looked up properly for the first time. She gestured with one hand for Marten to sit.

'What did she tell you?' said the old lady. 'You can call me Rose.'

Marten shook the proffered hand, feeling the flesh curiously soft beneath dry skin. 'Nothing, really. Only that Randall was—is no boy.'

'Ah. Well, it's right there, at the start, where we differ.' She put the pen down, and lowered her glasses to peer at Marten over their rims. 'And why are you interested in the boy?' placing an emphasis on the last word.

'You have to ask, Rosie?' said the waitress, and she scrubbed angrily at the counter with a rag. 'Trouble. That's why you're sniffing after him, isn't that right, Miss …?'

'It's Marten. And, yes, there's been some trouble.' *Trouble.* That didn't begin to cover it.

Marten felt Rose's gaze settle on her, calculating. 'What do you do, Miss Marten, if I might ask?'

Intuition told Marten that the truth would play best. 'I'm a profiler for Scotland Yard. I construct psychological profiles from crime scene evidence, or of persons of interest to better predict their behaviour—'

'I know what a profiler is, Miss Marten.'

'I'm working alongside the FBI'—A slight stretch. Marten squirmed— 'to find Randall before …'

'More trouble,' offered Rose.

Marten nodded.

'Kid's middle name,' muttered the waitress, worrying at the countertop without seeming to realise her confession.

A car trundled up the main street, reminding Marten that while time might flow like treacle in Germanton, North Carolina, it still flowed. She couldn't skirt the true nature of her visit any longer. She weighed her next words—

Rose beat her to it. 'It's murder, isn't it? Not just one.'

Marten's mouth hung open, and she stared at her.

The old woman pressed on, her sclerotic grey gaze somehow piercing. 'For the FBI to be involved, it's terrorism, or children, or serial murders. And I wouldn't imagine profilers travel across state to profile *witnesses*.'

'The FBI,' said Marten when she finally gathered her wits, 'to the extent they're interested, are looking for a man named Jack Griffen. I'm a little off the reserve here.'

'You think it's Randall,' Rose stated, matter-of-fact.

The waitress appeared at Marten's shoulder, wringing the rag in her hands.

'Murder, Rose? I mean, he was an arrogant, self-absorbed little son of a bitch, but …'

Rose's pen was scratching again, and her head was down, but— marvellously, to Marten's mind—she began talking as though her concentration were wholly on Marten.

'I knew he was trouble the moment I laid eyes on him. I remember it clearly. He was standing over the bar of a bicycle at the gas station. He pulled a plastic wine glass from his backpack, poured from a bottle, and drank. He tipped his head back and must have swallowed half of it in one go. Then he took a good hard look at the place, and saw me watching. He winked at me.'

A chuckle like rustling leaves escaped the bent-over head. 'You can call it wise after the fact, but maybe it was intuition.'

'If you thought he was trouble,' said the waitress, 'why the hell did you invite him back here for lunch?'

The force in her words made Marten look up. Tears stood in her eyes.

'Because, Jessie, the world would be a better place if less people did something with trouble other than always running from it.'

'Yeah, well maybe you shouldn't get to make that decision for everybody.' Jessie stormed into the kitchen. Only Marten saw Rose's arthritis-swollen finger lift to her face and come away wet.

'Could you tell me where Randall lived? Short of canvassing the streets, I'm lost. And time is short.'

'Randall didn't live in Germanton,' said Rose, filling crossword squares with her neat capitals.

'But—'

'That first day I saw him, he'd ridden from Winston. His mother had moved them there weeks before, got herself a job with R.J. Reynolds, Big Tobacco, and Randall had enrolled at a film school in Winston. It took him that long to learn of the Christmas murders.'

'So you know about Hiero—I'm sorry—Randall's history?'

'From before he and his mother moved to Winston? Can't say I do. Only that he came with a tan, and a mongrel accent.'

Exasperation sharpened Marten's tone. 'But it can't be a coincidence that Randall is related to the Lawsons.'

'No, it's no coincidence,' Rose said equably. 'It's not true.'

'But—'

'You know, Miss Marten, for a profiler you do a lot of talking and not a lot of listening.'

Marten suffered the rebuke with a silent nod.

'Randall Todd,' Rose went on, 'appeared on the streets of Germanton, and tried that story on a few of us. Most didn't believe him. And at first it seemed he'd just made it up from whole cloth to impress Jessie's daughter, my great-niece, Kelsie. They became thick as thieves.' For the first time, Rose hesitated. 'And, that part, I don't understand.'

'What part?'

'Why he had to involve Kelsie at all. There must have been plenty of girls at the university. Why did he pick her to play out his fantasy? What did she have to do with his father?'

'His father?'

'He was fascinated by the Lawson murder. The murders—how a father could kill his own family in cold blood, his own children. But even more, how the same father could spare one son. Randall was desperate to know what about that boy, in his father's eyes, had caused his father to send him to town that Christmas day while he obliterated his family.'

'I'm sorry,' Marten felt a headache beginning to pulse at the back of her neck. 'Whose father? The Lawson boy or Randall's?'

Rose laughed unhappily. 'Both, I guess. He talked about the Lawson father, but his own father was a hole in every conversation I ever had with that boy. The bruise you don't touch. The question in his eyes.

'He confessed to me once—very out of character. Perhaps I reminded him of someone he'd trusted, that he would be so vulnerable. He told me his father once said to him, "I didn't marry to have children. I married to have a wife." How about that?'

Rose's eyes were wide with remembered shock.

'I got the rest from Randall's mother. His father had given over his job altogether to go hang around police stations in Los Angeles, listening to the police radio, pestering journalists. Looking for the next serial killer maybe. Randall was just another inconvenience.'

Rose filled the last clear squares of the crossword with her crisp capitals and laid her pen down.

'Terrorism, child abuse, fraud. None of that fits Randall. But murder? He wrapped himself in it. I wish it surprised me. But it doesn't.'

There was meaning here, connected, twisting, just beyond Marten's grasp. She could sense it. But right then, all she could think was: Griffen, what the hell are you tangled in?

'So,' Marten said at last. 'What exactly did Randall do here?'

Rose leaned forward. 'You've heard of YouTube?'

71

The first words out of Hiero's mouth when I met him were, 'I feel like I already know you.'

People say that if they're being glib. They might also say it if they have an intimate view into your life.

Hiero is many things, but he is not glib.

72

'It's Marten, Kim. Please don't hang up. I'm clutching at straws. The more I learn, the less I know.'

'Oh, you came around, huh?'

She didn't sound smug. Just resigned.

'If you mean, do I think Jack is telling the truth: yes. But he can only tell what he knows … It's the rest of this mess I can't understand.'

'I'd love to help, Inspector Lacroix, but what do you think I know that you don't?'

'You know *Jack*, Kim.' Marten sighed in exasperation. 'It has to be something about him. I'm looking for a motive, any motive—even one that makes sense to a psychotic mind. What would drag Hiero halfway round the world to attempt such an elaborate sting. I mean, what is it about Jack?'

'I don't know what else I can say. Jack? Well, he gave me the greatest gift in my life: Tracey. And then, he left …'

Marten heard a muffled thump behind Kim's words.

'Look, someone's at the door. I'm sorry I can't help more. I'm worried for Jack. But I have to go.'

73

It turns out that fury and fear don't mix.

They're oil and water. They don't smear together to create excitement or apathy. They slip and bobble against your mind, tugging all of your will first one way and then the other.

'Dad, what are you wearing?'

Tracey. All of my fear.

We were seated at a table in the café that served the best cheesecake in New York, all four of us, and it was the first thing Tracey said after she gave me a rib-creaking hug. The smell of her shampoo hung in the air.

'And, what happened to your hair?'

I swept a hand over my stubbly head, rubbed at the beard collecting on my chin. Its touch was surprising.

She reached across and plucked gently at my shirt.

'You look like something straight out of Greenwich Village. And—oh, my gosh!' She leaned forward, gaze intense. 'Are you missing a tooth?'

'He's a gypsy poet.' It was the first thing Hiero had said. 'Aren't you, Jack.'

'Are you okay, Dad?' Tracey's eyes squinted with concern. 'You look piqued.'

And still my mouth refused to speak. My thoughts were a tornado of questions, and lying at its centre, a single question: How? How could it have come to this? How was it I was sitting in a New York café across a table from the person I hated the most in all the universe, and next to him, the one I loved the most?

Out on the street, before the ghostwriter had guided me to the café entrance, he instructed me. 'Play along, Jack. Play nice. Give it away and your daughter dies.'

I looked properly at my daughter, in the flesh, for the first time since she had visited me in Perth three years ago.

She had grown. She was a woman. Not even I could see the child in her now. Her brown hair was its natural colour, and fell in a curling cascade past the back of her chair. She wore a simple floral-print dress over tights—always spring for Tracey, no matter the true season. A sweater lay in her lap. Her skin was clear and tanned by the California sun, the constellation of freckles over her nose long faded. Her mouth quirked in an odd way, and her eyes rested on me, alive with the question of what I was doing there.

Saving your life, was the answer. For the moment. But as soon as I'd seen to that, the next priority would scream for attention.

My gaze flicked to the ghostwriter, to his laptop bag in which he'd stowed my gun. Could I snatch it away before he got the gun? He sat there, cap pulled snug and low, his fingers flickering away on his mobile, seemingly oblivious to the rest of us. If I failed to snatch the gun, would he use it? Perhaps it was all a bluff. We were sitting in a café on a busy New York street in daylight. Surely he wouldn't risk it.

But then, the ghostwriter was a completely new player. I knew nothing about him.

He was a little-d Deus Ex Machina.

I felt a momentary twinge of regret: what if, on that train from Vienna, I had stormed his compartment, knocked him out, ransacked his laptop? What might have changed? Might that have been enough evidence to convince Collins that I wasn't the bad guy? Would Jane still be alive? Would Tracey have been kept out of it?

Perhaps this ghostwriter was insane. Or maybe Hiero had some hold on his 'Ghost' stronger than a lifetime behind bars.

My gaze drifted to Hiero.

Hiero. All of my fury.

I knew what he was doing. Writing the novel of a lifetime. With my life. And now he'd drawn Tracey into the plot, tangled her life in the skein of his narrative.

Hiero—Randall Todd, according to the London profiler. But to me he would always be Hieronymus Beck. US exchange student. Sharp of tongue, and gold of looks. Writer wannabe.

I took my first proper look at the boy I'd been chasing for seven weeks, and tried to square that experience with the person seated across from me now.

His hair was cropped shorter than usual. He wore brown chinos, and layers in different shades of green in place of his usual white t-shirt. But the smile and the gaze that kept finding me, they were the same I had faced every week in my office, as we talked novels, and lambasted or worshipped their authors, sometimes both in the same breath, and generally spouted crap.

But was he the same?

No, not the same. Our journey had wrought change on Hiero, too.

Maybe the differences were all in the eye of the beholder; I looked now with hatred.

Beneath his eyes were half-moons of faint purple. A speckle of stubble glinted in the café's retro electric-bulb light where his razor had missed it. And his smile—it wasn't quite the same. It needed attention. If for a moment he was distracted, it fell away, leaving his face mannequin-blank.

So the writer-strain is telling on you, eh, Hiero? The thought, curiously, buoyed me.

Act Three, the ghostwriter had said. Act Three was the climax, the resolution. The end.

Well, that ending wasn't written yet.

And while every book has an author, he is not the only one able to effect which words ultimately lie on the pages of the final manuscript.

Hiero had decided to edit my life. But two could play at that game.

What was Hiero's climax? What denouement did he have in mind? What was the perfect resolution for his magnum opus?

Putting fear and fury aside, I concentrated, tried to spin up the wheels of an entirely different part of my mind. It took willpower that felt physical in its strain.

I tried to invoke again the author's mind. Conjure the muse. Think Hiero's thoughts after him. That I might anticipate, that I might reshape.

—And struck again the bane of every writer, the thing that had dogged my own novel down through the years: writer's block.

What the hell did Hiero have in mind? I drew a big fat blank.

Act Three. It is the ratcheting up of the stakes to eleven. The final assault on the mountain summit. The dip of despair as the would-be-lovers are sundered and the against-all-odds reunion.

Act Three is a hopeless rebel assault on a planet-sized battle station, its destruction, and the birth of hope; it is the drawing back together of a sundered fellowship and an act of bravery that breaks an ancient evil; it is the showdown with a serial killer, in his domain, in the dark, when all hope of help is gone.

Hiero had left bloody fingerprints halfway around the world.

Rhianne Goldman in a bed in Perth, body bruised and mind enshadowed.

Li Min, lying cold in a stainless steel box in Hong Kong.

Annika Kreider plumbed into life-support in a Viennese hospital. Vegetable or vital young woman awaiting a coin toss.

And Jane Worthington. Stainless steel box number two, Oxford.

Student in my school.

Student in my faculty.

Student in my class.

Old friend …

Daughter.

The trajectory should have been obvious.

What an idiot.

The day I understood that Hiero's next target was Tracey was the day that murder, having fully gestated, cracked from its egg, and took roaring possession of my heart.

Of course Hiero's final prey would be my daughter. What higher stakes were there? Yet another of Aristotle's inevitable surprises.

If I had seen this coming sooner, I could have spent my energy getting Tracey the hell away. At my urging, Kim would have done it. Come to New York herself, and dragged Tracey away. That woman has diamond bones and molten blood when she needs to, and she learnt she possessed them long ago, when Tracey fell prey to a different kind of evil.

I must have grimaced. 'Are you sure you're okay, Dad?'

'New York coffee,' I said, turned it into a smile.

'Won't have to stomach it much longer, eh, Jack.' Hiero's smile was back, looking a little less effortful.

I raised my eyebrows, noncommittal. I had no idea what part I was acting here. It felt like playing tag on a minefield.

'Don't tell me you forgot?' said Hiero. 'Road trip was your idea. You can't beg off now.'

Road trip?

'Why didn't you ask me earlier?' said Tracey. 'I'll miss the last day of lectures, but of course the answer is yes.' She beamed. 'I still can't believe it. I didn't think you had a devious bone in your body, Dad—talking about next summer, when you knew you were coming to the US this year. *And* you cooked it up on the sly with—' She glanced at Hiero. 'It's "Hiero" now?' He nodded, and her shrug told of a frightening familiarity with his eccentricities. 'Anyway, you didn't need Hiero for leverage. You know I love to hang out with you.'

Hiero smirked. I read more than simple amusement in the depths of his pupils.

Thinking fast, I said, 'This screenwriter guy, McGee? Travis McGee?'

'McKee.' She knew I didn't forget names, was used to bad dad jokes.

'McKee. Is he that good?'

She nodded, and thumped a stack of what I assumed to be seminar notes in her lap.

'I don't mind waiting a day or two,' I said.

'But you were adamant,' said Hiero. The smile had gone. 'If we don't leave today, we risk not making the date.' He emphasised 'the date'.

Playing tag on a minefield—*in the dark*, I amended.

Ghost glanced up from playing with his phone, and gave me a dead stare, daring me to protest.

'*The date*,' said Tracey with a mock shiver. 'It's kind of exciting.'

The bottom dropped out of the world.

My subconscious has been rolling on ahead of events and finally chose that moment to reveal to me what Hiero's endgame was.

74

Breaking her own rule, Marten thumbed the number into her phone.

She listened impatiently to background fuzz as the network sought to make the connection, willing someone to pick up. She had never called this number. She had to hope the geek in Perth, Australia, wasn't lying to her.

The call tone cut out. The other end had picked up, but answered only with silence.

'Griffen?' said Marten.

'Here.'

Hallelujah.

But the lassitude in his response gave Marten pause. She didn't know what she expected from this man, contacting him again directly, but it wasn't apathy.

'It's me, DCI Lacroix. Marten.'

'Uh-huh.'

'I have—wait. You're not alone?'

'Uh-huh.'

So he couldn't talk. Adjusting quickly, Marten took the story she had been about to spill to Jack in its entirety, and shook it until only the branches remained.

'I'll make it quick. Just let me know if you need something repeated. Pretend I'm your boss, and switch to autopilot.'

'Okay, Kim.'

Fainter, a voice said, 'Hi, Mum!'

Marten couldn't believe her ears.

'Is that your *daughter*?'

'Uh-huh.'

Why wouldn't Jack be able to talk in front of his daughter? If she was with him, she either didn't know he was a fugitive, or had accepted his explanation.

Marten resisted the temptation to ask, and continued. 'I'm in the US, and I've been digging into the life of our friend Hieronymus Beck, aka Randall Todd.'

'Sure.'

'You remember he was peddling some story about being descended from the Lawsons of Germanton, the famous Christmas murder. Well, I visited Germanton. He's no Lawson. But—get this: he's tried it before. Playing make-believe for real. At least once.'

There was a pause as Marten waited for a response, but there was only silence punctuated by the occasional car horn.

'Are you in traffic?'

'Manhattan. We're in a taxi.'

'Anyway, he's done it before. There was a girl in Germanton, and she got mixed up with Hiero.'

A cough. Male.

'Wait—who's that—?'

Marten didn't finish the sentence. She was interrupted by a *ping* from her phone, announcing the arrival of a message.

She thumbed it open to find a single photograph. She enlarged it and tried to make sense of what she was seeing.

The image was taken at an angle, with one corner obscured by a dark blur, perhaps a thumb or finger. Three people sat on a seat, silhouetted by an overexposed blaze of light filling a window behind them. The back seat of a car, Marten saw. To be precise, a taxi. Jack had snapped a shot, presumably over his shoulder from the passenger seat, of those riding with him in the taxi.

Marten held the phone close and peered at the poorly exposed figures on the seat. In the middle sat a young woman. Her resemblance to Jack Griffen confirmed her to be his daughter. To one side of her sat a young man in a New York Yankees cap. It was pulled low, but his head was tipped back, and his eyes were closed as if he were resting. He was unfamiliar.

On the other side of Jack's daughter, eyes open and fixed on the camera, was a face Marten did recognise, albeit by second-hand experience. Hieronymus Beck.

The sudden confirmation of his existence shocked Marten. She recoiled from the photo as if his gaze projected physical force.

'Kim?' said Jack.

Mentally, Marten assembled the pieces, conscious of the silence and the need to speak. Jack Griffen was riding a taxi in New York with his daughter, an unknown man, and the man he accused of murdering two women and attempting to murder two more. He was on the other end of the line, calmly pretending that she, Marten Lacroix, was his ex-wife, and they were having a chitchat catch-up, while *she*, Inspector Marten Lacroix, was trying to tell him that she had found prior evidence of Hiero doing precisely what Jack had accused him of—warping reality to fit a sick fantasy. Only this time, the fantasy was as dynamite to a firecracker.

She took a deep breath, and spoke. 'Message received, Jack. Hang in there. Good luck.'

A pause, then, 'Eight years divorced, Kim, and your nagging will be the death of me.'

He chuckled, perhaps to lighten the remark, and hung up.

75

The burner phone was plucked from my grasp, and I twisted my neck around to find it now in Ghost's hand.

'Sorry,' he said. 'I forgot to fix your battery. I know what's causing it now.' With the hand not holding my phone, he unzipped his laptop bag, and from it produced a cable, which he plugged into my phone. Whatever he was doing, I had to assume the phone was his thing from now on.

If Tracey thought anything strange about it, she said nothing. She was looking through the window at something Hiero was pointing at.

'Park and one twenty-eight,' the taxi driver grunted. It was the first thing he'd said in the fifteen minutes it had taken him to drive us from the café to the RV hire. The mountains and foothills of Manhattan skyscrapers had fallen away to an uneasy plain of pawn shops, and laundrettes, and cookie-cutter apartment blocks. Harlem.

The taxi came to a stop on the kerb, at a slant, to the noise of honking traffic. Hiero, Tracey and Ghost piled out of the back. The taxi driver's dull brown eyes rested on me, while the cab bounced slightly as the luggage was pulled from its trunk. Apparently I was paying.

For a moment I considered trying to alert the taxi driver to my predicament. But I couldn't think of what to say—certainly not anything that would bring the cops aiming for anyone but me. So I fished into my wallet and pulled out two crisp notes depicting Ulysses S. Grant, a hundred-dollar tip, in the faint hope he might remember me fondly.

He took the cash, the brown gaze not even flickering, and was already gabbling to dispatch. Uber has done nothing to improve the mood of taxi drivers the world over.

On the pavement I found the others collected around our pile of backpacks. Tracey turned to me, and said over the scrape of the taxi's tail on the kerb, 'Really, Dad? A Winnebago?'

The corner of Park and East 128 was a car and RV hire yard. Behind a chain-link fence sat a motley fleet of cantankerous-looking rust buckets and aging Winnebagos. Hiero turned from gazing at the RVs, smiling like a kid who'd been told he was going to Disneyland, and gave me two thumbs up. I wanted to punch his white teeth down his throat.

Ghost coughed, reminding me of my part.

'Got to hit all the American clichés, right?' I said.

Ten minutes later, with the image of the manager's hands full of a prodigious tip and face full of astonishment lingering in my mind, I was behind the wheel of a 2000 Winnebago Rialta. It had eighty thousand miles on the clock, a grumble in the low end, and manoeuvred like a dump truck down roads that seemed like shopping aisles.

The feel of the wheel under my hands was grainy and sticky, but it answered to my command, if sluggishly. It gave me a small satisfaction. This RV was the only thing left in all the world that answered to my will. Everything else was going to hell while I watched.

Beside me, three feet away on the passenger side of the continental bench that was the front seat of the RV, sat Hiero. His manner seemed easier, the tightness around his eyes had faded. I guessed he was feeling pretty good about himself.

His master plan was nearly done, his narrative nearly told. All the main characters were finally together, on the other side of the world from where the story began—no mean feat. A wonderful talent, demonically applied.

Myself, Tracey, Hiero … and Ghost, although I had no idea how he fit into this. A ghostwriter normally didn't enter the story, unless it was a novel by Philip Roth.

We were on the road to the final destination. Nothing stood in the way of the climax. And still I had no idea what shape it would take.

No. That's a lie. I had an idea of its contours. I simply quailed from examining them too closely.

My grip tightened on the wheel. I suppressed a momentary urge to plough the Winnebago off the road and into a streetlight or shopfront.

But Tracey was loose back there. A crash could kill her.

And if it didn't, Hiero had made the situation painfully clear: if I did anything to threaten the forward progress of his story, any attempt to harm them or escape; if there was even one whiff of police. He would kill Tracey. Kill her and frame me. He and Ghost had a failsafe way to do it, he told me, and there was nothing I could do about it.

If it was a bluff, it had succeeded. I was terrified it was true. It might as well be. I could not risk it.

Unless I could take them both out with one stroke.

'Take a left here.' Hiero's voice broke me out of my daymare.

Obeying, I saw we were entering a highway that in the distance arched up into a bridge. We were leaving Manhattan.

We passed under a gantry on which electronic boards listed traffic speeds at what I guessed were points along the route. The current temperature and date were displayed in the top left. Fifty-three degrees Fahrenheit. Thirteenth of November, 2015. A Friday.

Dusk was drawing down.

In two days it would be the fifteenth of November.

My mind hit the date and careened off it like a bullet.

My thoughts drifted inexorably to the other side of the world ...

November in Perth, Australia.

Late spring, according to theory. But Australia for the most part, Perth in particular, doesn't do spring—except perhaps for an afternoon in September on occasion.

School would be letting out. Graduating students flocking to Rottnest Island, west of Perth, or south to Dunsborough. Letting their hair down, drinking, hunting for hijinks that at least someone frowned at.

The campus of UWA would be breathing a collective sigh, even the lawns, the trees, the koi in the pond beneath Reid Library. Researchers and staff would stretch their legs in the cafés, take their time, stroll between appointments without looking where they were going.

The days would seem somehow slower. Afternoons taking a little longer to come, and a little longer to cede to twilight.

I could picture myself in my office, frowning over supplementary exams that needed marking, for students who had received sudden diagnoses of incidentalomas. But for the most part, my thoughts would be turning to the novel that sat to hand, enticing me, condemning me. Reaching for the bottle in the bottom drawer, I'd take a steadier. Then another. What was good for Hemingway …

I pushed away the memory of a chat with Hiero that threatened to intrude on the flow of memory and imagination.

My mind slipped further into the past.

November was a month that held its store of happier times.

My first communication with Kim that lasted longer than ten seconds happened in November. She told me not to stand on her saplings, so it was probably a twenty-second conversation, but they got longer after that.

Walks along Leighton Beach with Kim. The water chattering over our toes still crisp, clinging to winter's cold, but the breeze racing over the sand now warm. The sun falling into the Indian Ocean in an apocalypse of purple, orange, yellow, and casting the massive freighters plying the port of Fremantle in silhouette. Days that each felt like the earth had been forged anew.

It was fourth of November 1993 that Kim showed me the pregnancy test with its three little bars that as good as spelled 'Tracey'.

Tracey.

Distant past.

And now, in the near future, Hiero was going to draw a line through the life of my Tracey. For a novel.

I failed her nine years ago. I wasn't about to fail her again.

What could I do to screw with Hiero's novel?

He must have caught the look on my face.

'You know, Jack, there's a bed back there.' He jerked his head in the direction of the RV's living space, where Ghost was parked at the table with his ever-present laptop open before him. Tracey was seated in the cross-angle.

'Hey, Trace,' Hiero called. 'You feeling sleepy?'

'No?' she replied, confused.

I stole a look at Hiero. In reply, he simply raised his eyebrows. The implication—there were worse punishments he could inflict on me than the death of my daughter.

The smile I forced in return was a rictus.

'Imagine how this is going to spur your novel,' he said. 'You've been stalled forever, admit it. I'm doing you a favour. Think of all the experiences you would have missed without my goading.' He ran an appraising eye over me. 'But look at you now. You began a starchy, buttoned-down academic. Now you're a card-toting gypsy poet.'

'My novel hasn't been front and centre.' All thought of it had vanished the moment I realised Hiero had drawn Tracey into *his* novel.

'But it has to make you laugh,' he said. 'I've read your early drafts, remember? It used to be some literary wank. But then you recast it as a murder mystery, and planted your family in the middle of it under a lens.' He chuckled. 'You were the one who told me bad books tell us more about their authors than their characters.'

A sign passed out of sight above us. It had read: 'Hackensack ¾ mile'.

Not exactly the Oregon trail, but we were heading west. And like true pioneers, some of us would soon be dead.

Well, that was Hiero's plot.

With a glance to check he wasn't watching, I laid a hand on the metal lying flush against the skin of my inner thigh. The RV's spare key. It had lain there since I'd scooped it into my pants—and sweated through waiting for Hiero to ask for it—only minutes before, but somehow it still felt cold. Perhaps it was because it was the repository for my hope. Such a small vessel for such a mighty hope. I touched it gingerly, as if it were a seashell that might shatter at my touch.

Thirty seconds alone in the RV, and we would be free.

Just thirty. The time it takes to tie a full Windsor. Was that asking for too much?

Thirty seconds versus eternity. Would Hiero give us thirty seconds? You could flip a coin.

Yeah, fifty-fifty some of us would be dead before we made the Rockies.

I still didn't like the odds.

76

'I'm telling you, it was Jack Griffen. Here, in Manhattan.' Marten looked in Grover Jackson's eyes for a spark of recognition of what she was telling him, but he was barely listening. 'He's wearing a bow, Grover. Winding a klaxon. Carrying a placard that says, "The FBI is incompetent."'

Grover paused in the corridor of the FBI's New York field office, 26 Federal Plaza, to hand a folder to a clerk, and turned to face Marten.

'Marten, you've been running on my meter for days.' He held up a hand to forestall her reply. 'And before you start calling me a bean counter, let me put you in the picture. Things have changed a little since your stay with us.'

Stay with us? Marten chose not to be offended by the slight. There was a time Grover hadn't assumed Marten was simply visiting.

'There's that little thing that happened sometime before you headed back to the green isles called Nine Eleven. *Thousands* dead? Or maybe you heard of Fort Hood 2009? Boston 2013? The FBI has doubled the number of agents assigned to counterterrorism, tripled the number of analysts. Are you getting the picture?'

Leaning away from him, Marten framed an imaginary headline in front of him: 'FBI intercepts intercontinental ballistic missile, Jack Griffen.' He twitched. 'Subheading: Assistant Director Jackson lauded for tenacity in the follow-up of murky leads.'

'Fine. I'll give you a pass on data and intel.' Marten raised her hands in mock ecstasy of supplications answered. 'But I'm not flying your sorry ass anywhere else. You can hitchhike from here.'

Five minutes, two elevators, and seven doors later, Marten was leaning over the desk of an FBI data analyst, musing at how fifty years had turned typewriter pools into digital intel pools. Not much had changed, except the twenty-odd heads bent over keyboards belonged mostly to males barely past the cusp of adolescence instead of women.

The particular head bent over a keyboard before her was covered in black hair that curled tightly over the scalp except for a round bald spot near the crown. The pattern reminded Marten of how her son, when an infant, had rubbed away a patch of hair on the back of his head. She quickly pushed away a pang of guilt. The intel operative that Grover had sent her to was Nick Alvero. She hoped this wasn't some joke, and that the similarity to her son's infant head didn't portend difficulty.

'Good afternoon—'

This was met with an upraised hand, while Nick's head remained bent over the keyboard, gaze flicking out at intervals to inspect the effect of his rapid-fire typing.

'Nowhere on this chance-kissed rock is it "good".'

Momentarily taken aback, Marten thought again of her son, who was probably tucked up in bed, the memory of her husband's lullaby echoing in his ears.

'My name is—'

'I know who you are. It *is* afternoon, I'll grant you that.'

Still he did not look at her. His fingers were a blur on the keyboard.

'I need—'

'I know what you need. Satisfaction. Does this look like a place that serves satisfaction, Detective Chief Inspector Marten Lacroix?'

For the second time in bare seconds Marten was struck dumb. Nick didn't seem to notice nor care. Then, in one swift motion, she bent over, seized the plug of the power board beneath his desk, and yanked it from the socket.

'Jeez!' Nick sprang away from the screen, rolling to a stop on his chair, and finally looked at Marten. 'Ten seconds. Ten seconds and that auction was *done*!'

Placing each hand on the lip of his desk with deliberateness, Marten leaned over them and said, 'In a moment I'm going to reach down and plug your toys back into the power. When I have done so, you are going to greet me with joy and listen to my instructions with the solicitude my rank and experience deserve, and then follow them as if your life, your eternal happiness, depended upon it.'

A smile quirked the corner of Nick's mouth. 'And if I don't?'

Marten's eyes narrowed. 'I will hand you your arse in front of your colleagues.'

He swept a hand across a fringe that had long since receded.

'Chill. You can chill, Marten.' He jumped up from his chair, stole a chair from a nearby desk, ignoring the barbed glance of the young man behind that desk, and trundled it in front of his own by the standing Marten. He gestured for her to sit, then promptly prevented her sitting by bending over the seat cushion to peer at nothing Marten could see, and sweeping its surface with the palm of his hand.

Marten was still squinting at him as he returned to his seat, trying to gauge if he was mocking her. He had made her smile, so she decided she didn't care.

'Jackson said it's crap,' he began, 'but to get what you wanted and move on to real work.'

'Wow,' said Marten drily. 'Customer service is a real priority for the FBI's IT section.'

Nick tapped at his keyboard again, gaze fixed on the centremost of three large flatscreens that curved around him like the cockpit of an airliner.

'We're very customer-focused. Director Jackson just has narrow criteria for who our customers are.'

'Jack Griffen—'

'Dr Jack Donald Griffen of Nedlands, Perth, Australia, forty-five years, six-foot-two, until recently sporting mid-length brown hair, with a penchant for expensive jeans and supermarket shirts.'

'Wait,' said Marten, suspicion solidifying into certainty. 'That's *my* profile.'

Nick smiled tightly. 'Plagiarism is the truest form of flattery,' he said. 'But that's just my intro. This isn't from your profile: Jack Griffen entered the US sometime between the ninth and tenth of November, likely landfall a water rat tie-up at Jacksonville, Florida, or St Augustine. He bought an old model brown Dodge, unregistered, probably from a dealer where he made landfall, and then drove an average of five hours a day until he entered Manhattan via the Holland Tunnel yesterday, double-parked the

Dodge in Midtown, locked the keys in, and walked away. The Dodge was towed. Subsequent to that, we know he met with three people at a café in Chelsea this afternoon, and had something from the dessert counter and a coffee—we're unable to determine if it was a latte or a cappuccino. The vision isn't great.'

'Holy shit,' breathed Marten, earning her a scowl from the seat-owner opposite.

'Everyday shit,' returned Nick.

'How did you do that?'

'His daughter.'

'His daughter?'

'She held a Hell's Kitchen hotel room with her credit card two weeks ago.'

'So?' said Marten, feeling like a wet-behind-the-ears cadet, but compelled to ask anyway.

'Well, you said Jack Griffen was here in the US. What were the chances he would be so close to his daughter and not see her? Worth checking at least.'

Okay. That was normal investigative grunt work, but—

Anticipating her next question, Nick continued. 'We traced her phone's handshake with the hotel's free wi-fi network leading up to today. The first two days were erratic—probably sightseeing. After that, her phone left the hotel sometime around quarter past nine every morning, except for the weekend, and one other time—'

'Today,' said Marten.

He nodded. 'So I poked around the anomaly. CCTV from the cross-streets south and north found her heading down Tenth Ave at quarter to three. I lost her two streets later. Cameras were out. She must have taken a lane.'

Marten felt a shudder of disappointment, forgetting that she already knew this story had a happy ending.

'Fortunately for us, she allowed her phone to connect to the café wi-fi in Chelsea. We spotted its MAC address.'

'MacAddress?'

Nick laughed. 'Not a burger. It's M-A-C, media access control address. Every phone on the planet has one, and it's unique. Baked into the silicon.'

Marten smiled. 'The FBI must be on better terms with the spooks these days.'

'NSA needs all the friends they can get since Snowden pulled their pants down, and revealed they're tapping everything.'

Everything. No, not that. Not yet. They had access to virtually every phone record in the US, every single phone call into or out of the Bahamas and Afghanistan, and via a program called XKeyscore, could interrogate anyone's internet browsing history, searches, emails, and online chats for good measure—and all without a warrant. So far, they hadn't cracked reading minds. That was the CIA's bag.

'From there I found a camera capturing a sliver of café window. Miss Griffen ordered at the counter, then disappeared. I guess she found a table in the back. After half an hour I nearly gave it up as a solo breakfast, when a young guy appeared. He took a table in plain view, and a minute later she joined him. I figured it was a date after all, and a waste of time.'

'Until Jack showed.'

'Yeah.' Nick's brow wrinkled. 'It drew my attention straightaway, because Griffen was with another guy, and they appeared to be arguing—it felt off. But—why am I telling you?' Abruptly he peppered the keyboard, and angled the screen toward Marten. 'You can see for yourself.'

Marten leaned toward the screen. Four videos were playing, tiled within a window that filled most of the screen. Each offered a vantage covering part of an intersection, a slice of footpath, and shopfronts that shrank with foreshortening before they were occluded by a welter of tree canopy and shop signs. Cars sporadically raced down the street in one video, and sprang with mind-bending physics onto another, racing away at right angles. In the top corner of each video a string of digits marked the time, the last digits flickering in a white blur.

Motion in the corner of the bottom-left video caught Marten's eye. A young woman stepped onto the footpath. Marten's gaze flicked to Nick.

'Uh-huh,' he said.

The young woman on the video entered the café. Visible through the sunlight reflecting from its window was a short counter, a table and chairs. The young woman, Tracey Griffen, hovered at the counter. She didn't fidget or play with a phone. She glanced a few times at the streetscape visible through the window, ordered, and moved farther into the café, out of sight.

Without asking, Marten reached past Nick and grabbed his mouse. She placed the pointer on the video skip button and prodded it forward in thirty-second jumps. She ignored the lone figures, pairs, and groups that seemed to materialise whole onto the footpath from another dimension, until—

There! Another figure appeared. Caught for a moment in freeze-frame, one hand outstretched toward the café door, head turned, gaze seeking over his shoulder, almost as if he knew he was being watched.

That face. Despite knowing it was coming, seeing his face was still a shock. Marten's breath caught.

'You know this guy?' said Nick.

Does anybody know this guy?

'His name is Randall Todd. I'd dearly love to talk to him.'

'Oh,' said Nick, and something in his tone drew Marten's attention.

'Oh, *what?*' she said, steel in her voice.

'Nothing,' said Nick, but a blush spread up his neck. Marten continued to stare at him as the seconds ticked by until, 'Director Jackson said …'

'Yes?' but Marten had already guessed.

'That you … and, well … That you were desperate for someone to pin the murders on other than—'

'Other than Jack Griffen, because—what?—I have a crush on him? I'm carrying his baby?'

Nick laughed sheepishly. He seemed to want to join Marten in her joke. *Problem for you, Nick: this isn't funny.*

Now it was Nick's turn to lean toward the keyboard and prod the skip button. The video jittered forward until two figures leapt into the foreground. A young man with a Yankees cap pulled low, and a middle-aged man with sparsely-cropped hair.

'I don't know who the Yankees fan is, but—' With a click of the mouse, Nick framed the pair and zoomed. 'There's Waldo.'

Nick seemed relieved to offer a different target for Marten's ire.

Silent a moment, Marten studied the grainy image of Jack Griffen's face. She had come to know it with a kind of intimacy—the intimacy the hound has with the rabbit. Or so it had been. She hunted different prey now.

Nick said, 'That ain't no cigarette lighter he's holding. It looks like your man was going to fire that gun, until the other guy intervened.'

Marten's eyes shifted to Jack's right hand. It was almost hidden by his trunk, twisted as he was toward the other man, but poking clear were two inches of the unmistakable blocky profile of a Glock barrel.

It didn't look great for Jack, true.

The only movement Marten made was to press play, and release the two figures back into motion.

They disappeared through the doorway, and appeared a moment later framed by the café window. Words were exchanged, and the newcomers took seats.

Even at this distance, Marten could tell Jack Griffen was shell-shocked.

From the corner of her eye, Marten noted the smug smile on Nick's face.

'Wonderful,' she said. 'Now can you show me something useful?'

The smile fell from his face so quickly Marten had to suppress a laugh.

'But—'

'Maybe you think profilers are failed screenwriters who ended up behind police desks, whose definition of a good day is to churn out a fun character. I don't know you. But right now, I couldn't care less about Jack Griffen's past.' She flicked a hand at the video still running. Coffees had just arrived. 'I need to know where he is now, or another person is going to die.'

To his credit, Nick didn't attempt to cover his embarrassment with a joke. His fingers went to work on the keyboard. The video jumped ahead, and Marten watched the four surveilled people file out of the café, and walk off screen.

'From here, CCTV pegged them on the sidewalk two intersections over, and then they vanished.'

'How could they vanish? What about the cell towers?'

'Tracey's phone fell off the world soon after the guy in the cap sat down.'

From the look on Nick's face, Marten assumed this was not an ordinary phenomenon. She let it lie, turning her mind instead to the problem of where Jack might have gone with his daughter, Hiero Beck, and the unknown fourth man.

Had Jack slipped a clue to her when he called from the taxi? She raked over the conversation, which had been necessarily, frustratingly one-sided.

Then she remembered—he *did* give her something. A photo. She whipped out her phone and thumbed open her messages, hoping the photo would be worth a thousand words.

She found it, and laid the phone down on the desk between two Rubik's cubes and a stained coffee mug.

Nick peered at the metadata attached to the photo. 'Taken at fifteen fifty-three. The GPS coordinates give us one fix on their location, but it doesn't really help.'

'The photo gives us direction of travel.'

'What?'

'The sun?' said Marten. 'The big ball of burning gas in the sky that explodes vampires and gives life to our lonely ball of rock? Squint your eyes. Where are all the light values in this photo?'

'The what?'

Forced patience. 'Where's the sunlight coming from, Agent Alvero?'

'Oh.' He didn't need to say it. Every one of the three faces was limned clearly from the left of the image. It was taken in Gramercy Park, between Midtown and Downtown, where the skyscraper ranges momentarily broke, before the up-thrust ranges of Midtown.

'That doesn't really help us, either,' he said. Beyond the faces on the back seat of the taxi, the world was a blur in the rear window.

'How about the taxi number, would that help?'

She didn't need to explain this to Nick. He plugged the number, which was silhouetted in reverse amid the rectangle of light, into his databases.

Soon they would have a drop-off location for this fare. And then what?

If Hiero was taking cover in New York City, Marten knew there was a chance of piquing Grover's interest. If not …?

Marten glanced at her watch and sighed. Back home in London it was 1.00 am. Her son, David, would be sleeping. Benjamin, if he was being naughty on a Friday night, would be reviewing a case that had squeezed out of the work day, or curled up on the couch reading a book.

She felt a pang of homesickness. Then, almost in the same moment, she wondered if Jack Griffen felt homesick.

No, she decided. If she was any profiler, she knew what emotion gripped Jack Griffen's heart at this moment. Fear. Fear alloyed with rage.

The kind that doesn't sputter out before it reaps a soul. She just prayed it wasn't his.

77

It happened at a farmhouse on the outskirts of Holcomb, Kansas—a pin drop in the vast Great Plains, slap-bang in the middle of the US of A, almost exactly halfway between San Francisco and New York.

They came at night.

In the early hours of November fifteenth, 1959, when the chill prairie night had driven folk to bed, and drink or fatigue had left those awake with blurred senses.

They brought a knife and a shotgun, but this was just in case.

They entered by a side door. It was unlocked, and led into an office. The moon shone through a venetian blind, revealing the dark bulk of a desk, a bookshelf, the glint of a letter opener. Closing the blinds, they made a furtive search by flashlight, the whisper of paper and creak of floorboards covered by a breeze rustling the leaves outside the window. Their search yielded nothing. Behind the desk stood a panelled wall, books, framed maps, a fine pair of binoculars (which were taken and later sold in Mexico)—but no safe.

So the short one with shoulders like a bull, Perry Smith, ripped out the telephone wires. It was time to rouse someone.

They began with the man of the house, softly spoken Herb Clutter. They roused him from his bedroom on the ground floor. Standing there in his pyjamas, his eyes revealed fear, but he was polite. 'Safe? There is no safe.' No ten thousand dollars. He always paid by cheque. Had only thirty dollars in his billfold, and they could take it and go. Just please, *please*, don't bother his wife. She's been ill so long. Please don't hurt his family.

Thirty dollars? That just wasn't going to cut it. The taller one, Dick Hickock, hadn't driven all day for thirty dollars. And thirty dollars wasn't going to buy food and women and a lifetime of diving off the coast of Mexico for sunken Spanish treasure, no sir.

So they tied Herb up, the only real threat, and began to wake the family one by one.

The mother, Bonnie—a waif of uncertain sanity.

The boy, Kenyon, a strapping all-American lad of fifteen summers, whose only blemish was the glasses without which he struggled to coordinate his lanky frame.

The daughter, Nancy, the epitome of country youth and beauty. Smart, pretty, helpful, accomplished, well-rounded and—amazingly for all that—humble. Smith couldn't leave Hickock alone with *her*.

Each was secured with rope, apart. Mother and daughter were tied to their own beds. The boy was tied to the playroom couch. The father was tied up on a mattress in the furnace room. God only knew how it felt for each to be alone with their thoughts as these men ranged through their house at night, and did who knew what to the other members of their family.

At last it became clear that there really wasn't a safe. Dick's jail mate from Kansas State Penitentiary had been wrong, had mistaken Herb Clutter's generosity for real wealth.

Smith, meaning to call Hickock's bluff that he could kill a man, said, 'All right, Dick. Here goes.' And he cut Herb Clutter's throat. There was a sound like a drowning man might make. But Herb Clutter wasn't dead. So Smith shot him, turned the room blue.

Then came a succession of shots—burst of noise, then scramble after the discharged shell. After the first, the mother and daughter knew what was coming.

The men left, departing into the darkness from which they had emerged. Thirty dollars richer, and the new owners of a radio and set of binoculars, which were later found by a KBI agent in a Mexican pawn shop.

An entire family murdered for a fantasy spawned by a jailhouse rumour.

Four lives blotted from under heaven in cold blood.

In Cold Blood.

Truman Capote's book invented the true crime novel in one swoop.

I ran over it again. Couldn't believe it. Had to believe it.

Hiero was taking us into *In Cold Blood*.

No, not quite. Hiero was taking us into his novel, *Blood and Ink*.

But, shit, the model was clear now.

The date, the fifteenth of November, was tomorrow. An anniversary of the murders.

It was the dead of night. The temperature had dropped close to freezing east of a place called Buckeye Lake. The lights of Manhattan seen last night now seemed a dream.

We were some miles west of Zanesville, Ohio, on Route 70, heading for Kansas, and Holcomb. We had long since traversed the gently winding road that ran crosswise through the worn folds of earth that were the Appalachian range.

Memories haunted me, of conversations with Hiero about *In Cold Blood*. The novel had figured more than any other in our weekly catch-ups. Hiero was besotted by its sense of place, its sculpted pacing, and, above all, the knowledge that it was true. The gut didn't dip as Capote evoked scenes of disintegrating panic and fear because they were *like* something that had happened once upon a time; it dipped because the events described *had* happened. It was appalling. Fascinating.

Hiero wanted a novel. A great novel. A true novel. And he was going one better than Capote. Capote had simply recorded old facts stuck like flies in amber. Any dumb mechanism like a tape recorder could do that. But Hiero was creating the facts.

The lights of an approaching car filled the dirty windscreen. It passed, plunging us back into relative gloom. The Winnebago's poor lights strained to push back the night, and the lane markers came on and on, as if they were rails and we were a train riding them. Last stop, murder.

How could I derail this absurdity?

At our last gas stop I'd steeled myself, extracted the spare key from my underwear and swapped it for its twin. It started the engine, but I was paranoid it might have a distinguishing mark, a scratch or notch on its black lozenge or metal tongue that would snag Hiero's gaze and give the game away.

Ahead, a corona of light silhouetted the dark mass of a hill. Probably another gas station. They were strung along the highway at intervals like so many fake pearls.

My gaze flicked to the tank dial on the dash. Still a third full, but if Hiero wanted to push on …

'We should fuel up,' I said. Hiero, who by his stillness might have been asleep, but for the glint of his eyes, was silent. 'Plus, I need to take a piss. I think I'm getting bedsores.'

'You're cute when you're trying to be hip.' Hiero's words were slurred as if he really had been sleeping with his eyes open. Perhaps the strain was telling.

We crested the rise, and the gas station's dome of light spread before us. Without asking again, I flicked the indicator, and lurched off into the gas station's slipway.

'We're stopping?' It was Tracey. She leaned an arm on my shoulder. 'I'm busting.'

'We stopped for the toilet half an hour ago,' I said.

'We're in the US, Dad. It's "restroom". And we've also been having this argument since I was three. Girls have smaller bladders.'

I lifted my right hand from the steering wheel to hold my thumb and forefinger a pea's width apart. I didn't trust my voice for a comeback. My gaze hunted the parking lot for the ideal spot while my gut twisted. Hiero's promise was echoing in my head: 'Try anything, and she's dead.'

But don't try anything, and she's dead.

It was Russian roulette. Spin the cylinder and hope to hell the lucky prize didn't swing up to the hammer. At least in Russian roulette there were empty chambers. *In Cold Blood* didn't end well for anyone.

Not even the killers. They were hanged six years later—Hickock hung strangling and spasming for minutes; it put the ghost into the witnessing chaplain. I wondered if Hiero had thought of that. Probably. His research had been impeccable thus far.

The Winnebago crunched to a halt on the pockmarked asphalt, and our wake of exhaust wrapped the vehicle before swirling up into the night. The parking lot lights threw out weird coronas, like alien ships landing. I sat for a moment while the cooling engine ticked. Everything was a clock now. Tracey's voice broke me out of it, unfroze my will.

'Back in five,' she said. 'You boys want some empty calories?'

'I've gotta go, but it's dark out. Any of you guys want to hold my hand?'

Not waiting for an answer, I opened the door on its protesting hinges, and stalked toward the toilets.

Tracey disappeared into the shop. My mind worked frantically at how to get a moment alone with her. I reckoned I had two minutes at most before Hiero or Ghost came sniffing. And how the hell was I going to convince her that we were in the hands of psychotic killers, a whisker from death (or worse, Hiero's voice taunted).

I slowed my steps, heading for the men's. If I made it, there was a chance I could wait and listen for Tracey's arrival, and slip into the women's. If anyone was watching—anyone—it would be game over. If there was already someone in the women's, it would be game over.

Inside the men's I found yellow light washing a tiled floor whose grout was the colour of clay. I fancied they hadn't been cleaned. Ever.

I entered the cubicle nearest the entrance on the theory it would allow me to hear Tracey pass by on her way to the women's. I lowered the lid and sat. My heart was thumping, but I didn't bother checking my Medline. Perhaps passing out on a toilet was a novel solution to this nightmare. It occurred to me that some of the most exciting times in my life had taken place in toilet cubicles.

The cubicle next door was occupied, but the thought was faintly encouraging. The proximity of another human, even one defecating or staring at the cubicle door, was comforting.

And then I heard a whisper. 'Dad?'

Tracey's voice.

My sanity was cracking up again. Back in Vienna I had imagined her into Annika Kreider's apartment. Then again, on the train to Paris. Each time, despite knowing she was not there, her presence had comforted me.

Now I'd imagined her into the men's toilet, when the real, living, breathing version was a stone's throw from where I sat, buying snacks in the shop. Perhaps I should introduce them.

'Dad.' More insistent.

I couldn't help myself. 'Tracey?'

'No, Dad.' The sarcasm confirmed it.

'What the hell are you doing in the men's toilet?' I said. Then, into the silence, crashed the realisation that I'd got my chance. We were alone.

But for how long?

'Tracey,' I hissed. 'You've got to listen to me.'

'No, Dad—' There was a bang, and my cubicle door shuddered. 'Let me in!'

I unlocked the door, and she flew into my arms and buried her head in my shoulder. Wrapping my arms around my little girl, I felt a momentary—ridiculous—happiness. The world was going to shit, but here was my daughter.

Too soon, she shoved me back and glared at me. Her finger jabbed me in the sternum. 'Listen. And don't you dare not believe me.'

We spoke at once:

'Hiero—'

'Hiero—'

Shared understanding crossed the gap between us like a spark.

I shut my mouth. Tracey gulped air, visibly steeled herself, and spoke. 'Hiero is planning to kill someone. Really kill.' Her hands balled in a crushing gesture of helplessness. 'Maybe *you*.'

I gripped her by the shoulders and made sure she could see my eyes. 'I know.'

'You know,' she said, as if to herself. And then she buried her head again and her body heaved with wave after wave of sobbing. I had to strain to make sense of what she was saying through her spasms.

Hiero had played the same game with Tracey that he had played with me. Kept her toeing the line with the threat of violence to me. He had bumped into her with seeming serendipity, and who knows how long he'd intended to keep up the pretence of a chance rendezvous in a city of over eight million, but something had forced his hand. Struck fear into him. Or perhaps he did it for the joy of it. Why torture only one when you could torture two?

Fury took me. I had been nursing the lone consolation that Tracey—my little girl—wasn't aware of the threat hanging over her. And here she was telling me I was wrong. She knew. And she'd been lying and playing a part just as much as me. Worse. Protecting *me*.

My blood boiled.

'I'll kill the—'

'Dad,' she sighed, pushed me away, wiping tears from her cheeks with the backs of her hands. 'You could never kill anyone.' Memory of a conversation we'd never had in a Vienna hotel room flashed through my mind.

Over her sniff, I could just hear her mutter, 'Besides, it's all my fault.'

Gently, I pushed her to arms-length. 'How on earth could any of this be your fault?'

The tears that rolled down her cheeks now were different—she looked forlorn—and it terrified me.

'Simple, Dad. If not for me, Hiero wouldn't even know you exist.'

'But—'

'Just shut up, and listen. Please!' She set her head, and, not quite looking at me, began to speak as if by rote. This was a prepared confession. Biting my tongue, I set myself to hear her out.

'One time, one time only have I let myself drink too much—'

'Jesus, Tracey, if you think—'

'Dad!'

I made a zipping motion across my mouth, tried again.

'I was tired. Stressed. Probably self-pitying. It was end of semester, party season. Any number of excuses, but there you go.' She slid a finger across her cheek and rubbed idly at the moisture with her thumb.

'Hiero was there, except his name was Randall Todd then. He'd been at the university maybe half the semester. I think maybe he liked me, maybe not. Either way, I wasn't interested. I mean, I liked him—in a kind of kindred spirit way. He'd lost his parents, and—' Her eyes darted to mine, and in them I saw the rest of that thought. 'And I guess it all poured out of me. Picture every crappy, clichéd, coming-of-age sob fest, and there's me.' Her nose crinkled in self-disgust. 'I kept coming back to the holiday we took to Exmouth. How the tension in the air between you and Mum was so thick I could see it, and I had this weight in my stomach that knew—just knew—there was something deeply broken in our family, and there was nothing in all the world I could do to fix it.

'Hiero told me how one day when he was thirteen, his mother just up and dragged him off to New Mexico, leaving his father, a private detective, in Los Angeles. How for years it had been another term, another move, another school.

'I told him how Mum thought maybe you were having an affair with Aunty Janie.' Heat flashed through my body. *God, that's how Jane got twisted into this.*

'I knew that wasn't true, Dad.' Her fingers gripped my wrist—mistaking my emotion. 'And I argued with her. Convinced her. She didn't really believe it. She was just hurting and confused.

'And to Hiero I tried to describe how you just … disappeared. You didn't go anywhere, but you were just going through the motions. Like you'd been cast in the role of "Dad" but didn't want the part.

'But at some point during this mutual catharsis with Hiero—I didn't notice at the time—he stopped talking. And when I finally ran dry, I looked up and found him just staring at me, with a look in his eye I couldn't name then.

'I can name it now, though,' she said, resigned. 'Avarice.'

She fell silent. I could have picked up the story. Some time after that drunken conversation, an email had popped into my inbox. A cold call from a Hieronymus Beck, wanting to do honours, self-funded, on exchange from the US. He wrote, 'I've read every one of your short stories I could get my hands on.' He loved story. He lived and breathed story.

He'd had me at 'I've read every one of your short stories …'

But Tracey's fault?

That's ludicrous, is what I wanted to say to Tracey. But a calmer, wiser part of me just took her in my arms again and hugged her tight. It would have to do for an apology for now. My confession wasn't a luxury we could afford right then.

'What are we going to do?' Her eyes cast about as if a door of escape might open miraculously in our stinking cubicle. She had the look of a hunted animal. 'Or we just stay here? Right here. What are they going to do, drag us out past …'

I watched the cogs turning in her mind. She was probably totalling up the number of people within three miles of us. The guy behind the shop counter. One. Four or five in cars pulled up at the pumps? Another one eating a microwaved heart attack at the dinette. Seven souls?

Hiero wouldn't have let us out, particularly let us out together, if he wasn't prepared to pull the pin here and now, and run the risk of not getting away with it.

Perhaps he was happy to give his novel an abortive ending. My gut told me he wasn't, but what if I was wrong? I thought of Huck Finn and Jim, and that made me think of Marten Lacroix who didn't read novels.

Tracey must have recognised my grimness for what it was.

'We could run for it. Or, or—barricade ourselves in the shop behind the counter. This is the US, Dad. The owner is bound to have a gun.'

It took every shred of willpower in me to say, 'No.'

She recoiled, but I said it again. 'No. We can't. Not here, at any rate. It's too isolated. He would take the risk and shoot. I know he would, if he thought we were finished playing his game.'

'But how do you know he's not going to do that anyway?' The strain pulled at her face, threatened to make it a mask of madness, but it subsided.

'He won't.' How much could I tell her? Enough to calm her. But not all of it. 'Trust me. Please. He has a destination, and we're not there yet. He won't try anything until we reach it, because he has way too much riding on it. He's invested to the core.' Down payment, one soul.

I felt the metal teeth of the RV's key pressing into the soft skin of my thigh. Part of me said that had to stay secret, too. But I had to give Tracey something concrete.

'We've got this,' I said, and slipped the key from its hiding place. She glanced at it sitting snug in my palm, and understanding lit her eyes. 'If they give us just thirty seconds alone in the van, we're gone and they'll never catch us. Just keep your head down, and be ready.'

'In five hours, Dad, they haven't left us alone in the RV once.'

Without a word she reached into her jeans pocket. She grabbed my hand and over the key placed a mobile phone.

All my resolve nearly crumbled in that moment of recognition.

'How did you get this?'

'I stole it.' A blush spread up her neck. I nearly hugged her again. Standing cramped in the men's toilet plotting for our lives and my little girl felt shame at having stolen someone's banged up, low-end phone. 'It's why I've been stopping every opportunity to go to the restroom. Looking for an unguarded handbag.'

Holding the phone up closer I saw that it appeared to be dead. My heart sank. 'Battery's dead.'

'No. I turned it off. I couldn't be sure if I'd silenced it.'

I gave her a quick hug. She smiled with the ghost of pride. My thumb hovered over the power button.

'Call the police,' she said.

The police. 'First sniff of police and she dies. And you go to jail for it.' That's what Hiero said. Probably bluffing. But what if he wasn't.

'No,' I said with deep reluctance. 'Not the police—not the US police. But I know someone. She's a friend.'

'A friend.' Tracey's voice was flat with an emotion I couldn't read.

'I hope so.'

78

Marten stared through a grimy window of the little office at ranks of Winnebagos for hire. The FBI's IT wizard, Nick Alvero, had made short work of finding the taxi fare that had picked up Jack et al. a few streets over from the café, and dropped them here, a rust-bucket RV emporium.

The manager of the emporium was right now out there plying his charm on a would-be customer. Either that or he was having a showdown with a local gangster and they were about to brandish sidearms and begin a shootout. It was hard to tell. She guessed you had to be a hard case to keep a business going in this neighbourhood.

When at last he came inside, without having exchanged shots, but also without having secured custom, he had plastered on his face what was meant to be a winning smile. After all, he probably thought Marten was another customer.

Marten was about to disabuse him of that notion.

'That guy,' he said, jerking a thumb over his shoulder at the man in the lot, who was now talking on a phone, 'does not know his shit. It's like he came here to convince me a caravan is a better bet than an RV. Like, "Yeah, I want to spend my hol-i-day backing the frickin thing." Know what I'm saying? Like telling me Batman would beat Spidey.'

Marten couldn't resist. 'He would.'

He stared at her. Then his face split in a grin. 'Feisty lady.'

The coquettish smile Marten dredged up seemed to encourage him, but before he could dig himself any deeper, she said, 'Feisty *police officer*.'

'Oh. Shit, eh?' He began to fidget, moving notes for no apparent purpose, and rearranging the strangely large number of mobile phones that were scattered across the counter.

'I'm not interested in whatever other businesses—legitimate or otherwise—you have going here. I just want to know about a hire you made yesterday. Okay?'

'Sure, sure,' he said, still playing with the office debris. 'Which van? I'm a successful businessman. Had plenty of business yesterday.'

Marten frowned, and spoke slowly. 'I don't know which van. That's what I'm trying to find out.'

He suddenly turned and fixed a penetrating gaze on her. 'You didn't show me a badge. You might only be a feisty lady.'

Marten felt a tingle of unease and flashed her London badge.

'Feisty, *naughty* lady,' he said, and Marten again saw the intelligence betrayed by his gaze. 'Your badge don't amount to much but a Halloween costume here in the borough. And that mongrel accent? A guy could say you were trying to impersonate an officer.'

Hoping that her uneasiness didn't show (Grover, after all, was just as likely to drop her in it if pressed), she said, 'I'm conducting an investigation with the full co-operation of the FBI—'

'On your own,' he stated, making it sound like an accusation.

This guy was a rock.

And the clock was ticking.

In a flat tone, she said: 'You have a lovely range of RVs. I would like to enquire about the possibility of hiring one.'

Raising both arms in the air, he said, 'Ah! Welcome, welcome, lovely lady,' and emerging from behind the counter, 'step this way.'

Minutes later Marten stood on the kerb at the point where, sixteen hours ago, Jack Griffen had alighted from a yellow taxi. In her hand she held a note, on which was scribbled in pencil the licence plate of the RV that Jack had hired.

She was also the holder of a three-day hire of her own RV, which nevertheless was not going to so much as leave the lot, and the advice that no New Yorker could ever imagine a sulky, rich man beating Peter Parker.

She retrieved her mobile and was at the point of calling Grover Jackson to inform him that Jack Griffen was at large in a hired RV, when the phone rang in her hand. The sudden vibration startled her.

The caller number was unfamiliar, but she accepted the call and held it to her ear, curious.

'Marten?'

'Speaking. Who is this?'

'Oh, God, thank you.' And she recognised the voice of Jack Griffen.

'Griffen! Where are you?'

'Sitting on a crapper, with my daughter, Tracey. Tracey's here.'

'That makes no sense, Jack, but whatever. What is your location? We had you at the café in Chelsea, then lost you. I have the registration of the RV you hired and was about to put it through to the FBI—'

'No, no, no!' His shout was painfully loud. 'You can't do that. Whatever you do: Do. Not. Involve. Police.'

'Jack,' said Marten reasonably. 'I'm police.'

'You're also a friend.' A pause. 'Aren't you?'

'Of course,' she said.

'Good. Then, as my friend, know that if Hiero detects the faintest whiff of police he will start shooting. Do you understand?'

'Jack, I understand, but cops deal with this sort of thing all the time.'

'Not like this.'

'Jack—'

'Not ever with *my daughter*.'

Marten swallowed what she had been about to say. It was too easy to imagine how she would feel if her son were caught up in this.

'What do you want me to do?'

'God, I don't know. We're stopped at a gas station. It's all my fault.'

'It's not, Dad.' A girl's voice.

Jack went on. 'I'm a fool. The hours we spent talking about it. I should have guessed sooner.'

'What, Jack?' Marten wished she could reach down the line and slap him. 'Talking to who?'

'*In Cold Blood*—'

The call died.

Marten couldn't believe it. She stared mutely at the phone, before attempting to call back. But each time an automated voice said the number was unavailable.

79

Fourteen hours since Tracey and I had crept like guilty kids from the gas station restrooms, apparently undiscovered, and sharers now of a common burden. The knowledge that both of us were in thrall to murderers.

To me the shared burden, despite age-old wisdom, felt doubled.

In that time we'd stopped three times to replenish the RV's miserly gas tank. We had crossed into Indiana, Illinois, Missouri. Watched the green fade from the land, and the horizon withdraw into a distance haze.

We'd hit Kansas City three hours ago, at midday. The sun could barely raise a glitter from the brown Kansas River.

Kansas. Fate state. Emblem a lonely farmhouse.

Behind me, Tracey slept on the camper's couch. Next to her, Hiero sat upright, eyes shut. Beside me, Ghost was at the wheel, driving in a trance. A half-hour ago he had begun to shrug his shoulders and straighten his arms. Every so often he would drag a palm across his face.

'Tired?' I said.

'Not my first all-nighter,' he said without shifting his gaze from the white line forever unwinding just beyond the RV's hood from the sun-haze on the dusty windscreen.

In the distance a gas station sign stood like a sentinel, poking above a rare rise in the road.

'No good you planting this thing into a light pole from fatigue. Why don't we stop. Stretch our legs. Grab a Coke. I need a leak.'

A digital bleeping intruded. Twisting to look into the cabin, I found Hiero fully awake. He silenced the alarm with a flick of his finger upon his watch.

He spoke to Ghost. 'Go ahead. Pull in at the next stop. Fill up. Everyone could do with a drink.'

We hadn't drunk anything for hours. The last stop Ghost had bought only salted crisps and peanuts.

Our RV laboured up the last reach of the hill with a whine of its 2.8 litre engine, crested it, and curved down, following the highway as it skirted a tumble of rocks. A cluster of buildings hove into view, and just beyond them, the gas station. Ghost had already left the highway and was in the slip lane when the white bulk of a county sheriff's SUV appeared, parked out front.

My heart skipped a beat.

The briefest grab of the brakes was the only evidence Ghost had seen it. Then he executed a smooth turn into the pump bay directly across from the sheriff's car and killed the engine.

Ghost tugged the brim of his cap lower and got out. For a moment I feared Hiero would make me stay. The cop was visible through the dirty plate glass brooding over a mug and a newspaper.

But Hiero raised no call as I opened my door and slipped out.

Inside, I found Ghost staring at a wall of candy. The cop was still wedged into a booth not twenty feet away.

A little fantasy played in the cinema of my mind: me, walking calmly over to the policeman. Stooping, I whisper in his ear, 'We're being kidnapped. Please help. But quiet.' The cop turns to look up at me, his gaze serious, believing. 'Two men,' I say. 'One behind me.' I jerk my head in the direction of Ghost, who is still pondering the sugar wall. 'One outside. He has a gun. And my daughter ...'

My daughter.

I look in the direction of the RV. Hiero's face fills the cabin window, then disappears. A gunshot explodes in the dry air. The fantasy falls apart.

Back in reality, Ghost had moved to the soda station. He had four tall cups lined up, and was filling them assembly-line style.

While I was fumbling in my mind for the right sequence of words, Ghost beat me to it.

'I thought you needed a piss?' He pushed the fill button and premix Coke cascaded into a cup.

'I'm clenched tight,' I said. 'Probably will never urinate again.' The stream of soda continued to hiss into the cup.

'Do you mind if I sit down with the cop?'

He twisted his head to look at me from beneath his cap, then shrugged. 'Your funeral.'

Fighting to master fear and anger, I said quietly, 'Whatever he's got on you, we can work it out.'

'What makes you think it's like that?'

'You seem sane.'

He turned back to the soda. The shushing noise had risen in pitch, the cup was almost full. Two empty cups remained.

A pretty young clerk appeared, toting a fresh stack of cups. As she refilled the dispenser she glanced at Ghost and his cap. 'Don't get many Yankees fans here.'

Maybe it was a flirt. A blush rose up the sides of Ghost's neck, but his gaze remained fixed on the cup he was filling. The girl pushed the last cups home into their slot and left.

I tried, 'We were never properly introduced.'

Silence.

'Ghostwriter, huh?' I continued. 'Orchestrating, laying it out. Getting it down. But you know what ghostwriters never get?'

'No, but you're going to tell me. You're the ghost whisperer.'

'Glory,' I said after a forced laugh. 'They never get any glory, even though they're the ones with the real genius. The real artistry.' I leaned closer. 'If you help me, you could be the hero.'

Soda hissed. From behind me came a rustling and a slap. The cop had folded the paper and thumped it on the table. He coaxed the last drop of whatever was in his mug into his upturned mouth, preparing to leave.

'I'm rich, you know. Whatever he's paying you, I can double it. Treble it.'

'No you can't; I checked.' He grimaced. 'Shit, I had to make a *deposit* into your account when you were in Hong Kong. Couldn't have you redlining when you needed to get to Vienna.'

Of course he'd checked.

'I forgot. You're the IT whiz.'

'No one says "whiz" except old guys.'

The back of his skinny neck screamed at me to throttle it.

'I've hacked grad students,' he said. 'I've hacked journalists. Doctors, bankers, cops. I hacked my mom's boyfriend—and he was an ex-marine. But you guys, you'—he turned to air-quote at me—'"academics" are the worst. It's like you guys think the net isn't there to eat you. "Knowledge should be free!", huh?' He laughed and slid the last cup under the nozzle. 'You have no idea,' he said, 'but when I looked through your department's email I found a woman, a lecturer, who thinks you have nice eyes. She's been emailing an admin about you, who said forget it, he's married.'

It occurred to me that this was the longest utterance I'd ever heard him make.

'But you got owned, yourself, didn't you?' I prodded.

'By your pet tech? The guy who tried to hack my server?' He shook his head. 'Man, I bounced that douche. He didn't get anywhere.'

Except, he did, I thought but didn't say.

'Why did you get into it? Computers.'

He flicked the fill switch off and half-turned to me. 'You kidding? The world is getting eaten by software. Any idiot can see that. Netflix, Amazon, Uber, Google, Betterment. Software streams your movies, brings you dinner, takes you where you want to go, tells you what to buy, sets your thermostat, manages your investments, and pretends to listen to your complaints. We don't make *things* anymore. If you don't speak the digital language, you're a caveman.' He turned back. 'Actually, no. It started with the porn. The best stuff is always behind a wall.'

'That's where you met Hiero, huh? Behind a wall.'

'Come on, Jack. Give me some credit.' Hiero had slipped silently behind us. I had no idea how long he'd been listening. Speaking to Ghost, he said, 'You get those. I'll pay for the gas.'

Ghost put the drinks on a disposable carrier, gave me an inscrutable glance, and left for the cashier.

Hiero watched him go. 'No point trying to make a deal with that one, Jack. You don't hold the right currency. It's funny though,' he said, 'that he's more embarrassed about how we met than about his porn habit. Says a lot about our friendship.'

'Friendship,' I grunted. 'Is that what you call it?'

'Partnership, then, you ol' stickler,' and he gave me a nudge in the ribs. 'But I like to think of Wheeler'—was that his name?—'as a friend. What's mine is his, what's his is mine.' He moved, and I had to follow to hear what he said next. He came to rest before the plate glass looking out on the pumps. Right before us, the cop was seated behind the wheel of his patrol car, apparently engaged in a monosyllabic conversation with someone on the other end of a call.

I willed the call to be about us; for a photo of me to be dispatched to him; for him to glance up, make the match. Above all, to take responsibility for navigating this nightmare out of my hands.

But he remained on his call, eyes staring into the middle distance, unseeing.

Hiero went on. 'Wheeler is a prime example of how much of life's narrative can be driven by chance encounter. He's a Forster curveball through and through. Pitched into my life when I got involved in a little make-believe with a girl.'

My ears perked up.

'Do you remember lonelygirl15?' he said.

A vague memory of controversy floated just beyond my reach.

He said, 'Lonelygirl15, Bree Avery, a sixteen-year-old girl who appeared one day in June 2006 talking into her webcam, just one more random video amid the growing avalanche of cat videos and lip-syncing that was YouTube when Google bought it for one point six-five billion. Over the next few months we heard her teenage angst, met her boyfriend, learned her parents were part of a cult—'

'Wait. Wasn't she a fake?'

'Fake? Oh, there was no girl named Bree—the actress was nineteen-year-old Jessica Rose of Mount Maunganui, New Zealand. She was a character dreamed up by filmmakers. Fooled everyone. The scoop was made by a Silicon Valley journalist, and his son, Matt Foremski. But fake? The creators said she wasn't really a fiction, as she was part of every one of us. And while it lasted, that was some great storytelling.

'And through all that, as the suspicion built, you know who was hanging out on the forums, a lonelygirl fanboy?' He chuckled. 'Our friend, Wheeler. He wished so much that he'd been the one to make the scoop—his little dream of being a Pinkerton.

'Lonelygirl was a great idea, but it was so … tame. It took me a year to gather the material, the GoPros, a police scanner for early warning, a willing girl from a two-dog town you've probably never heard of in Nowhere, North Carolina. The thing about lonelygirl that ultimately failed is that it didn't interweave with the real world; it was hermetically sealed. It lacked verisimilitude. The cult Bree's parents belonged to didn't exist. But the fires *we* lit, the things *we* stole, they burned something, bit someone.'

A sardonic laugh erupted from Hiero. 'We were small fry, though— only managed to pull off a handful of episodes. But one amateur sleuth, a would-be Matt Foremski, set himself on our case, I think because he thought the girl was genuinely under compulsion.

'Wheeler's first email to me began: "You don't know it, but you just got owned." Ha! Melodramatic punk. It was too late anyway. The law had squashed us, took down the videos, slapped cautions on me, blah, blah. But I liked his style. Sent him a case of beer. Something told me—my Muse?—that he would be a good friend to have one day.'

The deep grey of Hiero's eyes found me. He seemed to be looking into me, looking for some sign of a deeper understanding, a deeper connection.

It didn't explain how Ghost had switched from vigilante to villain. For all his apparent candour, Hiero wasn't telling me everything. Ghost didn't seem like a true believer, the type to buy into Hiero's art. Was Hiero dangling a pot of cash that I didn't know about?

'You still don't get it, how beautiful this thing you're a part of is.'

Outside, the sheriff's car backed out of its bay, and left.

Hiero followed it with his eyes. 'Were you tempted? Or do you trust me?'

'I trust you.' Like I trust a mosquito to bite, or a leech to suck.

Ghost had been my last shot. Who ya gunna call? … pretty much anyone but Jack Griffen.

I could feel the press of cold steel on my thigh.

There was nothing left now but to take the next opportunity and gamble.

80

Marten wrote Jack's phone number by hand into her notebook, leery of trusting her own phone not to explode and take the precious link to him with it.

She stood a moment on the Harlem kerb like a lost tourist.

What on earth did he mean by 'I should have guessed sooner'?

She took stock. After nearly seven weeks on the trail of first Jack Griffen, then Hieronymus Beck, then Randall Todd, her cache had expanded then dwindled to a phone number, a licence plate, and a petrol station somewhere on the continental US.

Even if the FBI mobilised whatever agents they had in the area, or flew them in, would it be soon enough? Hiero was just as likely to slip the noose. Or worse, if he sensed the hounds closing in, murder Jack and Tracey and disappear.

'In cold blood,' as Jack had said.

Weariness settled on Marten, and she moved the three feet it took to sit on the kerbside. She felt paralysed, pulled in opposite directions by choices of equal force. Call in the FBI, disregarding what Jack said; or take her scant clues and meagre resources and hunt them down herself.

She ached for her husband's embrace. Just to be near him, to have him listen and to know that whatever he said, it would be good.

With effort Marten stood. Across the street was a dime store, and out front a bench seat. A tramp sat propped at one end as if he was part of the seat. Triple-checking for traffic, Marten crossed the street and went into the store. A minute later she emerged with a can of Coke and a chocolate fudge donut. She sat on the bench at the opposite end from the man and bit into the donut. She gave herself a moment to savour the sugar on her tongue, then swallowed.

Then, comfort food taken, she pulled out her mobile and dialled her husband. The tramp grunted once, his gaze fixed on a point halfway across the street.

She held the phone to her ear, while she munched. The Coke sat beside her. Someone picked up.

'Marten?' Benjamin's voice, slurred. 'What time's it?'

'That's my line,' she said, then did the mental math and worked out it was late evening. She had probably roused him from bed. 'I'm sorry. I need your ears. I've got no one else.'

The tramp grunted again, and from the corner of her eye Marten wondered if his hand had inched toward her unopened Coke.

'You can have my ears, honey,' said Benjamin. 'I'll mail them. But the brain isn't a going concern right now.'

'That'll have to do,' and she smiled despite herself.

Motion caught her eye, and this time she definitely saw the man's hand move another inch toward her Coke.

'You want it?' she said, nodding her head at it.

'Coke,' he said, and clearly took her question for an offer, because he snatched it away, peeled open the top, and had it to his lips in one sweep of his arm.

'Coke,' Marten echoed, struck by the guy's dexterity.

'Pepsi,' he said.

'Marten?' Benjamin's voice was tinny in her ear. 'What's going on?'

She clutched the phone to her ear. 'I'm here.'

'Doctor Pepp-ah!' said the tramp, like an old-fashioned train conductor announcing a station, then belched.

'Did Grover welcome you with open arms?' said Benjamin, seeming to want to get the conversation in some order.

'I don't have time for that.'

'Mountain Dew!' the man bellowed.

Marten summoned her concentration in an effort to screen out the noise.

'Jack Griffen and his daughter are being held hostage, and I have two problems.'

'Oh,' said Benjamin. All attempts at levity fell away. 'Line them up, hon. Knock them down.'

'First: I don't know where they are.'

'What *do* you know?'

'I just got off the phone to Jack. Hiero has them, somehow. I think he's armed.'

'Wait a minute, Marten. Armed? What are you getting yourself into? I thought this was strictly profile work.' Anger now, her husband's cover for worry. 'You're there on a break, for heaven's sake. The whole reason you went for the profiling—'

'It's fine. I'm fine. Just …'

Marten touched the Glock in its holster. It was a legacy of her time in the US, still chambered with the larger than standard .40 S&W.

There was silence. Marten imagined Benjamin wrestling himself to calm. The tramp took that moment to calmly announce, 'Sprite.'

'Okay, okay,' said Benjamin. 'What did he say, in this phone call?'

'That he was at a gas station, with his daughter, and he should have known.'

'Should have known what?'

'Precisely.'

'Soda,' barked the man with an air of finality.

There was a rustling sound that Marten guessed was Benjamin finally sitting up in bed.

'Okay. Let's back it up. What did he say, *exactly.*'

Marten repeated as much of the short conversation as she could remember verbatim.

'In cold blood?'

'In cold blood,' repeated Marten.

'Against slavery!' The man's outburst shocked Marten.

'Amen, brother,' she said vaguely, then raising her voice to be heard over a surge of traffic on the street, continued. 'Planned. Malice aforethought. And, for some reason, Jack is killing himself that he should have known that Hiero was gunning for him.'

'Tell me again who these people are, Marten.'

She sighed, wiped a lock of hair from her eyes, and rehearsed her own profile.

'Jack Griffen, somewhat jaded and world-weary academic; Hiero, young charismatic American, whose youth Jack has been feeding on, and in return giving of his experience. Perhaps Jack considered Hiero a protégé? I imagine it stroked his ego to unload his wisdom on the young man, even live a little vicariously through him. See his passion, his easy success.' She paused, listened to her own voice echoing in her memory.

'I'm listening,' said Benjamin.

The tramp appeared to be mumbling at the passing cars. His mouth was going nonstop now.

'And perhaps that picture is complete garbage. I mean, who am I kidding. This isn't an episode of *Criminal Minds*.'

'I'll be your Watson, Ms Holmes.'

'You're a darling. But I don't buy my own speculation.'

'What do you know for sure? Facts, Marten.'

She laid out for him again what she had pieced together from her fact-finding of those who knew Jack in Perth, what she had learned from the man himself, and more recently, what she had discovered about Hiero Beck, or Randall Todd.

'But it sounded like Jack was angry at himself for something he should have known all along, something between them, or … I don't know. How could I know? I wasn't there in Jack's office when they were chewing the fat, talking books, reading, writing, life.'

She flicked a flake of icing and watched it arc onto the pavement, and be swept away by a passing car.

'And then he couldn't even tell me where he was. "A gas station." Thanks, Jack.'

'The idiot.' The man had assumed a musing cant.

'You got it,' she said. 'Maybe I'm the idiot.'

'I didn't call you an idiot,' said Benjamin.

'An idiot to think I'd be any use here. This isn't my turf anymore. I could do just as poor a job at home.'

'Confessions,' said the tramp.

'Well, I'd love to see you home,' said Benjamin. Marten's eyes stung, and she angrily brushed at them. 'You know,' he continued, 'when you said "in cold blood", know what it made me think of? That Attenborough documentary we watched last year. You remember it? *Life in Cold Blood*.

We couldn't get over the baby turtles that deep-freeze through winter and thaw out in spring.'

'Documentary,' she whispered, and in the depths of her memory, just beyond her reach, lay something Jack had said. It sparkled on the tip of her tongue.

Then she had it. And she felt elated, and horrified.

'Books,' asserted the man.

'Book,' corrected Marten. One in particular. One book that created the genre of true crime. *In Cold Blood*, by Truman Capote.

She should have known.

'Ben,' she said slowly, her voice sounding like a stranger's in her own ears. 'Did you ever read Truman Capote's *In Cold Blood*?'

'Oh, sure.' A pause. 'Oh, God.'

'Yeah. Where did that happen?'

'Someplace in the mid-west, I think. Oklahoma or Kansas. Here let me—' A muffled noise filled the silence. 'Looking it up. Kansas, Holcomb. Four dead.' The sound of air sucked through teeth. 'Marten, the date.'

'What about it?'

'The murders took place on the fifteenth of November, nineteen fifty-nine.'

Fifty-six years ago tomorrow.

'Marten. Honey? Are you there?'

'Here.'

'So maybe that's where they are? Or where they're headed? But you said you had two problems. That was the first. What was the second?'

'And Ben, I love you.'

'Marten. The second. What was it?'

'Never mind.' She hung up.

'Bat out of hell,' began the man.

Marten dropped him a twenty-dollar note and left him to it.

81

The inside of the back of the Winnebago swam into view.

Only, the cabin was on its end, as if the back of the van was planted on the ground, with its headlights pointed at the stars.

Did we have an accident? I couldn't remember.

With a shock I saw Tracey stretched out across from me, and only then did I realise we were both lying down on the cabin's couches.

For a moment I was certain she was dead. The shock of it blasted my mind to pieces. Hiero had run out of patience and terminated the experiment.

Then I saw her chest rise and fall. She was breathing. Asleep not dead. Relief flooded me.

Her eyes were closed, and her mouth sagged in a way that spoke of more than sleep.

I tried to raise myself from the couch. The side of my face was dimpled with the pattern of its material. Its musty taste was in my mouth. As my head rose pain lanced my neck, and nausea swept my stomach. I collapsed again on my face and took stock. That decided it; we'd been drugged.

As memory began to sift back into my awareness, I strained to listen for any sound that might help me fit the pieces back together. The tick of the cooling engine floated in from the forward cabin. The build and fade of the noise of a passing car. In the silence that followed, I heard the rumble of voices.

Something tickled the back of my mind.

Cokes. The last stop, Ghost bought four Cokes. Hiero had been the one to share them out. Both Tracey and I had wrinkled our noses a bit. They'd tasted as if the pre-mix was slightly sour, but we'd both been so thirsty we'd drunk them anyway. Hiero hadn't allowed us a drink all afternoon, and food had been limited to salty snacks.

Rolling enough to pull my arm clear, I dragged my sleeve up and looked at my Medline. On its face a slow green light pulsed. Forty-nine bpm, a few notches above catatonic. Whatever they'd put in our drinks, that was some good stuff.

I attempted to rise again, and pain tolled in my skull. Worse than any hangover I'd ever had. I was glad Tracey was sleeping. Maybe she'd sleep through the worst of it.

While I waited for my head to clear, I strained to hear what the voices were saying. The occasional passing car blanketed the conversation, but slowly I was able to make sense of it.

My ears sifted out two voices. Their cadences revealed who they were before I could make out distinct words. They belonged to Hiero and Ghost. And they were arguing.

The thing tickling the back of my mind began to scratch like a cat wanting in.

'It's a risk, is all I'm saying.' That was Ghost.

Hiero laughed. 'Most of my fucking life has been a risk, Wheeler. Man up.'

'Call me that again, Randy, and I'll break your face.'

A car passed, and there was silence but for a scuffing sound. For a moment hope flared, as I thought they might be fighting in earnest. But it soon sounded more like feet scuffing in gravel. When Hiero spoke again he was calm.

'You know what? You're right. Maybe it was a risk I didn't have to take.'

'We.' Ghost corrected, flat.

'A risk *we* didn't have to take.' Another scuffing sound, then a metal ping somewhere further away. Was Hiero taking pot shots with stones at a sign? 'It's possible they know—' Another car swallowed the rest of the sentence and I swore under my breath in frustration.

When it passed, Ghost was speaking. 'Count on it. They were gone way too long at the stop before the last. Had to be twenty minutes, for a shit?'

'Livin' on Coke and fries binds a man.' The humour fell flat.

'Why did you let them out together when we're so close?'

So close? The sweat froze on my neck. I thrust my arms into the couch and managed to rise into a sitting position. Tracey slumbered on.

How close? What day was it? I groped through my memories, picking them up and putting them down as though my mind were a room full of objects from someone else's life.

Something hard pressed against my stomach. With hands that weren't quite following orders, I pulled a phone from where it was slotted into the top of my underwear, just below my belt.

Sight of that phone snapped my memories into place.

Of course. The phone.

Tracey had handed it to me in the toilet cubicle at a gas station. When? Yesterday evening.

I leaned to peer through a crack between the curtain and the top of the window, barely breathing lest I reveal I was awake. It was dark; the only light washing the curtains was the orange of high-pressure sodium lights.

If my timeline was right, Hiero had bought us the fries and Coke mid-afternoon. Sometime after that the lights had gone out. That made it evening of the fourteenth, unless I'd lost an entire day.

Almost zero hour.

I gripped the phone in my palm. So Hiero hadn't taken the opportunity to frisk us. Or maybe he had, and was playing a double game.

Bloody phone.

After all the self-control Tracey had exerted to carry it, keep it hidden until an opportunity to use it arose. I'd got through to Marten, and was about to tell her what our best play was. The battery indicator was a healthy twenty-eight percent, and then—bang, dead. We were staring at it, incredulous, when Ghost banged on the cubicle door. 'Time's up, Jack.'

I'd made some joke about him wanting to come in and help me. He called me a name, and exited the restroom, leaving Tracey to run the gambit of getting out unseen.

Now I squeezed the power button, as that was about the measure of my impotency. And was shocked when the phone vibrated back to life.

This time I was watching as the battery indicator read first twenty-nine percent then, a flicker later, three percent with a helpful pixelated exclamation mark. Then it died again. There was no response to my repeated squeezing of the power button. The last squeeze produced a cracking noise, and popped the back off the phone.

More than the last battery level stood emblazoned in the semi-dark. The screen had told me the carrier was AT&T. It had also told me the cell tower region.

Holcomb.

Hiero and Ghost must have tag-team driven for four hours straight after we were drugged. They had driven us deep into Kansas. Right into the heartland where the Clutter family were murdered.

To the county.

On the date.

Finally, the cat scratching to get into my head pulled out a bowie knife and sliced the back of my head open: the key.

The spare key to the RV.

I stood in a rush that collected my head on the plastic light fitting, but didn't feel the pain. My hands groped around my groin like a drunk. I felt a lurching sensation of loss. The key wasn't there.

No. It was. It had slipped farther down and made a hammock of my underpants.

I delved into my pants and came up with the key.

Thirty seconds is what I'd asked for. Thirty seconds, the distance between here and eternity.

Swivelling on the spot I planted a kiss on Tracey's forehead. Her face was still slack with the drug. I paused for a fraction of a second and stole that image of her, stowed it in my memory. Not pretty. Not something she would want for her social media. But to her father, beautiful.

The distance from the back of the van, where the twin bed lay, and the driver's seat was a scant fourteen feet. But half-drugged, in the gloom, trying to move swiftly and silently, and all the time fearing the door latch's rattle, it felt like a hundred metres.

I made it. Laid my shoulder against the driver's seat's leather, and slipped my bottom down its back like a hand into a glove. I swung my legs into the footwell, and froze, hearing the suspension creak.

From behind came the rumble of voices I hoped was Hiero and Ghost still in conversation. Body set like a statue, I looked askance, but caught no sight of motion. No way to tell if they'd seen me. No way to tell if Hiero wasn't now levelling the gun at me from over my shoulder.

How many of my thirty seconds had I used?

My pulse hammered in my throat.

My hand darted forward. The key slotted into the ignition in one go. Practice makes perfect.

Have you ever wondered what a tenuous miracle is a car's ignition system? That twitch of the wrist, the roar to life of the perpetual bomb that is the combustion engine? Tens of components chained together— at one end the key, a lump of metal and plastic shaped to fit your hand, at the other, smaller than the eye can see, solid state circuits, doped semiconductor, operating between one microsecond and the next. This assembly takes the energy stored in the car's battery, a mere fourteen volts, and compresses it, goads it, *blasts* it into a whopping fifty thousand volts— all for a tiny spark.

Our lives were hanging on the motion of less than a billionth of a gram of electrons.

Child's play compared to the nerves that fire the human heart.

I pleaded for both miracles, just one more time, and turned the key.

The dashboard indicators lit, and the cabin filled with a noise that to my frayed nerves roared like a tempest. The floor vibrated as the starter motor strove to spin the engine into life. My right hand gripped the shift, ready to jam it into drive the moment the engine caught.

But instead of the normal, smooth ramp into vitality, the RV coughed, refusing to start. Did I pump the accelerator too hard? Had I flooded the engine?

Night pressed on the windshield. At any moment I expected Hiero or Ghost to appear.

Then, louder than the labouring starter—an explosion.

'Dad!' Tracey's voice, fuzzy, alarmed. 'What's going on?' Her hand found my shoulder, and I felt her steady herself.

The RV continued to cough as I held the key clockwise, tight against its limits.

Headlights, not ours, swept the artificial twilight outside. It lit the asphalt, a rubbish bin, a solitary light pole. A pull-off indistinguishable from a thousand others spotting US highways.

The world was fragmenting. I strained to hold my senses together.

At last, I saw the motion I'd expected from the corner of my eye. A shape approached the driver side window from behind.

'Tracey,' I hissed. 'A car just pulled in. The cabin door. Go.'

'But Dad—'

'Get out, and GO!'

Her hand slipped from my shoulder, and I heard the latch on the door turn.

I had to trust that the darkened interior of the RV would hide her passage.

A moment later there came a tap on the window. I turned to find Hiero holding the gun. He tapped the window again with its barrel and gestured for me to stop the car, then pointed the gun at me.

A flicker of shadow moved across the headlight wash from the other car. If Hiero noticed it, he showed no reaction.

He prodded the window again with the gun, and I reluctantly killed the motor and withdrew the key. He opened the door and motioned for me to get out.

I did so. Glancing to my left, I saw Ghost appear, silhouetted by the yellow headlight pouring past the back of the RV. He hurried toward us.

Hiero turned to acknowledge his approach for a moment.

But a moment was all I needed.

I grabbed the gun barrel with my left hand, pushing its aim wide, and punched Hiero on the broad side of his jaw.

He staggered back, but regained his balance quickly. The gun remained in my hand. I switched it to my right, and levelled it at him. To Ghost I said, 'Stop.'

The crunch of his sneakers on the asphalt fell silent. I felt wetness spread beneath my grip on the gun handle. A split knuckle was weeping blood. But inwardly, I was ecstatic. Adrenaline coursed in my veins. I knew I could pop Hiero's head from his shoulders. No doubt about it.

Without taking my eyes from him, I ordered Ghost to join him where I could see them both, and with a twitch of my wrist, shoot either.

One thought kept rolling around and around in my head. A mania. 'Free. We are free.' I couldn't believe it. The thought was too large to settle, to encompass.

Our two captors stood before me, and I held the gun.

And Tracey … What was she doing? I'd told her to go.

My peripheral vision registered shadow flicker again in the headlight wash. But my eyes didn't leave the boys in front of me. Never take your eyes off the snake.

'Dad!' Tracey's voice, only …

'Jack.'

I'd thought the idea of freedom too big a thing to grapple with, to understand.

That thought shattered and drifted away like a dandelion on the wind in the face of my realisation.

Kim. My ex-wife, Kim. It was her voice I heard.

I looked away from the snake, compelled by an involuntary impulse.

My eyes saw; corroborated the evidence of my ears.

Kim. Wife of fifteen years. Wife no longer. Was here, stumbling across the tarmac of a crappy highway rest stop in the middle of Bloody Nowhere, Kansas, USA.

Behind her came another. A woman. A girl.

'Hi, Prof.' Rhianne Goldman. Hiero's first victim.

I laughed. The third Fate had arrived, and she had red hair and big breasts.

Weeks ago, when I'd been trying to convince myself Hiero wasn't a murderer, I'd reasoned that if he had meant to kill Rhianne, she'd be dead. I'd been right after all.

'You need to put that gun down,' she said. 'Mine's bigger, and it would make a real mess of the fruit of your loins here.'

82

'We had a deal, Marten. You broke it.'

Grover sat on the concourse bench. Behind him a security detail of two men hovered, ear pieces conspicuous. It was a typical reverse power play. 'I'm very disappointed.'

'Cut the crap, Grover. You're ecstatic,' said Marten. 'Don't ever play poker.'

'Now is not the time to get cute with me. I made your operating parameters very clear, but you seem to have taken particular delight in flouting them at every opportunity.'

'You're just pissed about the meeting, admit it. How was I supposed to know "don't embarrass Grover Jackson" was a "parameter"?'

Grover paused as the departures concourse filled with the blare of a flight delay announcement. The smell of cinnamon and roasting coffee wafted from a takeaway counter. Marten knew she should be hungry—when had she last eaten? She also knew it was anxiety smothering her hunger.

The clock was ticking. Her American Airlines flight to Garden City, Kansas, via Fort Worth—the nearest airport to Holcomb—was already boarding. If she missed it, she missed the beginning of the fifteenth of November entirely.

'You still haven't told me why you're here,' she said. 'I have a plane to catch.'

Grover seemed to come to life. 'Yes, but not the plane you intend to catch.'

Marten's eyes narrowed. 'You wouldn't.'

In response, Grover spread his arms, the reluctant disciplinarian.

'I'm getting heat—'

'Huh,' said Marten. She leaned away from him, and appraised him afresh. 'Grown man's clothes, grown man's voice.' She darted a glance at the two security officers hovering nearby. 'But those are babysitters, Grover. You're behaving like a child.'

In a flash, Grover pressed a finger to Marten's chest bone.

'A child, Marten?' For a moment, she feared he would strike her.

'I told you: sniff around, but do it *without* official FBI sanction. Instead, you tried it on not once, but twice—first in Germanton, and then right here in New York, at the RV hire in Harlem. I could slap a charge of impersonating a federal agent on you for that alone.'

How on earth did he hear about that?

'And I asked you for a full and frank apology for your behaviour nine years ago. But you couldn't give it, could you? And do you know why? Because now, as then, you are the child, Marten. Your only concern is yourself.

'Look at me with all the disdain you like, but I'm busting your *arse*'—he emphasised the 'r'—'back to the UK, and you can thank me for going easy.'

He turned. The two guards took the cue that the meeting was over, and moved to flank him.

Marten stood stunned, furious, helpless. The part of her mind playing out Jack Griffen's movements raced into the next hours. Saw him shuttled to Holcomb. Felt the clutch of fear as he laid eyes on the lonely farmhouse, felt his daughter tremble beside him. She imagined the impotent rage he felt to be in the hands of a man missing some elusive ingredient of humanity.

While, in the movie in her mind, her future self sat useless, thirty thousand feet in the air. She was returning home to her family, but her thoughts remained on another family, a man and his daughter, and her own failure.

'Grover, wait.' She grasped his shoulder. 'Please.'

Perhaps her tone made him hesitate. He raised an eyebrow. Marten hoped it was an invitation to petition.

'You're not just angry because I made the FBI look like idiots. You pushed hard all those years ago to bring me in. It was a gift, and it exploded in your face. And I'm guessing it set your career back. And ...' Dangerous ground. 'You didn't always look at me like that.'

Grover's expression was unreadable.

'Say you're right—' she said.

'*Say*?' He began to move again.

'Okay, okay.' Marten clenched her fists. She needed a reset or Grover was gone. 'You're right. But hear me out.'

The guards moved to intercept her, but Grover waved them off.

'You've got one minute. Then, if you're not queuing at immigration, I'm slapping you with charges.'

'Jack Griffen—'

'Your bit on the side.'

Marten refused to rise to the bait, despite the smirks that rose on the guards' lips.

'I know the place and time of his next murder.'

'So you finally admit he's just a run-of-the-mill homicidal piece of trash?'

Crossing her fingers behind her back, Marten gave everything to the lie. Damn Jack to save him?

'There's nothing run-of-the-mill about Jack Griffen. The reason I know his plan is he's killing by the book.'

Grover's chin dipped in disbelief. 'By the book?'

'By *a* book, to be precise.'

'I'm listening.'

'Everything up to this point has been a dress rehearsal, support acts to the main event.'

'Which is?' Grover held his watch up pointedly.

'*In Cold Blood*.'

'Capote.'

Trust an FBI man to get it in one.

'He's en route now to Holcomb, Kansas, to the house where fifty-six years ago—'

'November, wasn't it,' said Grover. A gleam entered his eye.

'Tomorrow,' she said.

He glanced at his watch. Marten saw the gleam grow brighter.

'Think about it,' she said. 'Hickock and Smith murdered the entire Clutter family in cold blood. Griffen's collected two young men, and his own daughter.'

At this, Grover's brow creased.

'This is … This is …'

'Dynamite,' said Marten. 'More cerebral than the Zodiac Killer, sexier than Paul John Knowles, more countries than, well, anyone.'

'And you wanted it for yourself,' said Grover. 'Nothing if not true to form, Marten.'

For a moment she feared he would break the deal and send her packing.

'I've given him to you on a platter.'

'On a platter,' he repeated. His gaze abstracted. Then it snapped back into focus. 'Fine. Get on your plane, go to Kansas. I'll have agents on the ground there before you.

'Oh, and Marten. You know what platters always make me think of? Turkeys. Happy thanksgiving. Or did you forget that Jack Griffen tried to kill a cop?'

83

The happiest day of my life?

I remember the happiest *moment*. It remains in my memory, stubborn as a diamond in the dust.

If you guessed my wedding day, you would be wrong. Nor was it the birth of the squirming, dribbling lump of flesh that turned out to be Tracey. My two girls never competed for my affection.

The moment welds both. I'm seated on a picnic blanket. Beside me, nestled into my side, sits Kim. The remains of a cold chicken lunch lies on our plates, and half-empty wine glasses of cleanskin shiraz sit in our hands. Above stretches the last electric blue of an early-spring day, and the air carries a hint of clean chill. Before us a grassy bank dips down to meet Serpentine Dam. Wild oats sway in the breeze. The artificial lake's surface glints like a billion diamonds in the fading light. From the far side comes the roar of excess water pouring through the overflow, and a wall of mist stands above its suicidal rush.

Capering across that dazzle is the silhouette of Tracey. Her stubby three-year-old midriff outpaces her feet. I can't see her face, but I know she is breathless and smiling. It's all too much for her senses to take in at once.

The happiest moment of my life. I had no words for it then either.

But you know what? It could have been burgers and Coke at the weedy playground down the street. What made it special wasn't the where and the what. It was the who. For the first time in my life, I *got it*.

Now I lifted my gaze to find Kim and Tracey seated opposite me on the RV couch. Mother and daughter, so alike in their haunted looks.

'So,' I said, 'we finally get the family road trip you always wanted.'

I didn't expect laughter, but Kim didn't even have scorn. That scared me more than anything Hiero had done or said.

'Jack,' she whispered, glancing feverishly toward the front of the RV, where Hiero and Rhianne sat murmuring. Headlights from the car following us, driven by Ghost, slid in shifting bars on the ceiling above us. Kim leaned toward me in the half-dark. 'What is this?'

'This?' I racked my brain for an answer. I couldn't say, 'I told you so.' 'This is the delirium of a very ill boy.'

'The exchange student?' She looked sick with disbelief. I nodded.

'I think that's his girlfriend you arrived with. How …?'

Her story was depressingly short.

Rhianne had arrived at Kim's South Berkeley house just after noon the previous day.

All morning Kim's head had been full of the arguments she would put to the faculty board that afternoon to allow her to fail four of her bioinformatics students. They'd scored below forty percent on their final, but the board was putting up a fight.

Then DCI Lacroix called and worry over Jack erased all that.

Then a knock at the door interrupted the call.

Through the spyhole in the front door, Kim eyed the young woman on her doorstep, and was disarmed by how unlike a saleswoman or charity collector she looked. The nattily dressed young lady peered into the spyhole and said, 'Ms Sparkes?'

'Ms, huh?' I interjected. 'Stuck dynamite under your Captain Crunch.'

Kim fell silent. I couldn't read her mood under her fear. It was then I realised she was still dressed in grey sweatpants and a faded khaki hoodie. She wouldn't be caught dead on the street in her house clothes, yet she'd come halfway across the continent wearing that. That fact, curiously, scared me most of all.

'Mum?' Tracey spoke softly, but seemed to share my conflicted fascination with how Kim had come to be here.

'So I opened the door,' Kim went on. 'The first words out of her mouth were not a PhD proposal, or a misconduct complaint, or any of a billion things I'd now give—' Her voice caught. I thought she was on the verge of breaking down.

'Kim,' I coaxed. 'You're no lamb to be led silent to the slaughter. What happened?'

Visibly steeling herself she continued. 'She said, "Your daughter is dead if you don't do *exactly* as I say."'

The next thing Rhianne did was pull out her phone. She said if she failed to check in every hour, even once, gave the wrong code, indicated she was under duress—anything to indicate all was not *peachy*—Tracey was dead.

And her first command? Take a pee, and get in the car.

What followed sounded like a cross between *National Lampoon's Vacation* and *Fargo*. They stopped twice at bland McMotels to sleep for about four hours. Rhianne paid with cash for doubles, and slept like a cat both times. Kim managed a fitful slumber at the edge of exhaustion at the second stop. Her red eyes and pasty skin told better than words how weary and overwrought she was.

'Halfway across the country, and I thought we were going all the way to New York, to Tracey, and she made me pull off. She walked out of earshot, and had the longest phone call yet.'

'Where was that?'

'I'd lost track. Too many names on too many signs. But I remember this one, because we pulled off right under the sign—Garden City. Ironic name, but then I guess it would seem a garden coming from the west.'

'You don't remember passing'—it was hard to say—'Holcomb?'

She shrugged.

It didn't matter. Why did I even ask?

'Oh, Mum.' Tracey wrapped her arms round Kim, as if she were the mother comforting her child.

But Kim stared at me with an intensity that belied her fatigue. Maybe she was running on rage, too.

'This girl,' she said. 'You've seen her before.'

Had I?

I remembered a house in Nedlands, and Rhianne Goldman's fraught limbs hugged to her like a scared spider. That image didn't reconcile with the woman who had stridden from the darkness toting a gun. But they were one and the same.

'Yeah. Rhianne, if that's her name, was the first "assault" perpetrated by Hiero. She was the hook Hiero set. But I don't know her. I have no idea how she fits into this.'

I glanced at Kim. 'You were jammed into a car with her for twenty-four hours. You must have talked. Who is she?'

Kim sighed. 'She was a rock. I tried everything. Told her we could turn around any time, no cops. We could pretend it was a practical joke. I told her she was beautiful. I told her I didn't have a daughter (bit late). She gave me nothing but silence.' Kim paused, and made a curious gesture with her naked ring finger. 'Then I noticed she wore a ring. It looked like an engagement band, but its setting was empty. Just a claw, good for nothing but catching threads and scratching skin. And I asked her what it was …'

A faint rumble of laughter came from the driver's cabin. The silhouette of Rhianne's head obscured my view of the onrushing road lines as she leaned over to kiss Hiero.

Kim lowered her voice further. 'Her reply didn't make sense. She said the ring was her *embellishment*. She said it was for her hero. That her own quest had taken her into Hades, whatever that means. And on a hunch, I said, "Are you ready to go to jail for the rest of your life for this hero?"'

Kim fell silent.

'And?' I said, impatience making my voice harsh.

'She said, "Yes."' A gentle shake of her head, like an echo of her first response to hearing that reply. 'She turned to me, and her eyes dared me to call her a liar.

'I tried another tack. I said her parents must be worried about her. That made her laugh. Her mother organises dog shows in Hollywood, she informed me, and would be more upset if two prize dogs rutted on stage than if her daughter kidnapped someone. Her father, she said, is a hedge-fund manager, and if a thing didn't divide into the categories of profit and loss, risk and reward, it didn't enter his mind.

'"But you're taking a heck of a risk," I told her. "For what reward?"'

'"Risk?' she said. 'Great art demands great sacrifice. It's a writer's job to turn blood into ink."'

'—Hiero,' I groaned.

'—T.S. Eliot,' said Tracey.

Rhianne was a true believer.

'Tell me what's going to happen, Jack. What do these children want with us?'

She said it with her look of old. Not nasty, just the look that brooked no crap. She knew I was scared to the core. No point in lying.

I swallowed, and opened my mouth, ready to introduce her and Tracey to the real nightmare.

—When the RV turned sharply and crunched to a stop.

The engine died and a vast silence swallowed us.

The side door flew open, and Hiero poked his head in.

'Let's go, campers,' he said, a huge grin winking in the dark.

Kim and I shared a mute glance, then we all filed out of the RV.

My shoes met the telltale grip-and-slide of gravel. The night was silent but for the hiss of wind in a sea of grass. Above me the Milky Way blazed in a band across the sky. The moon hadn't risen, the galaxy was our only light.

Even so, I was pretty sure the squat shed twenty paces away was no Holcomb farmhouse.

'Where the hell are we?' I said.

'*Acte trois*,' came Hiero's voice out of the dark. 'Climax.'

'Ah.' I nodded sagely. '*Merde*.'

A rattle of chain broke the silence. A tiny light shone against the shed door, revealing Rhianne and Ghost bent over. There came a clatter and a creak, and a dark hole appeared in the shed wall. The light disappeared as they moved inside.

A moment later it reappeared, and in it I saw Ghost pull a thumbs up.

'Inside,' said Hiero, and he prodded me in the side with the gun I'd stolen from the British bobby. Kim and Tracey followed without being asked, and I was relieved to see Hiero let them.

A tiny hope flared inside me. Was he going to lock us in and leave?

We reached the shed, and Kim entered, hands out front, walking like a blind woman into the darkness. Tracey clung to her side.

'Wait,' said Hiero. We froze. 'Professor,' he continued, and something in his tone raised my hackles. 'You hate novels written expressly to spark controversy. You pilloried *Sophie's Choice*, *American Psycho*, *The Da Vinci Code*. But you know, for a while now I've thought you're wrong. Dead wrong.'

He leaned close. His face seemed to hover before me in the darkness.

The world was silent a moment, but for the sighing of wind in the grass. Then he spoke.

'Who says fiction can't blend the real world in any way it sees fit? It spawned an idea, and the irony is you're the one that gave it to me. Let's call it Jack's Choice.'

My hands were clutching at his throat before I knew it. Hiero moved fast, brought the gun smashing down on my brow. Sparks burst behind my eyes, and I found myself sitting on the ground in the doorway.

I had to blink away the quick, hot flow of blood. Tracey screamed, and I felt Kim crouch over me, hands on my shoulders in a vain attempt to pull me away.

'What's he talking about, Jack?' Her voice was hoarse in my ears.

Drops of blood tickled my chin as they fell, and not for the first time I wished for my comfortable hobbit hole and a pipe of Longbottom leaf.

Hiero bent over me and looked into my eyes. 'Shit, Jack. Don't fall in a heap now.' He straightened and said, 'Mrs Griffen. Kim. Three enter this shrine tonight, but only two may leave. The choice of who stays is Jack's: wife or daughter.'

Kim didn't correct him.

'But no matter what, one dies tonight.'

He kicked me in the chest, and I fell through the door into darkness, piled atop Kim. The door creaked shut.

84

Profilers are trained to spot anomalies.

Marten knew she was supposed to feel the grit in her eye, and want to pluck it out. The trouble is, life is a sandstorm, and without a filter, grit is all there is.

She needed that filter if she was to get the jump on Hiero, but had no idea where to find it. She'd turned over every clue from the last few weeks, every detail—however inconsequential it seemed—and found nothing.

She rubbed dry eyes, and squinted down the aisle of the 737 carrying her to Fort Worth, on her way to Garden City, Kansas. She looked for inspiration, but all she saw were ranks of chairs as far as the bulkhead, and here and there a head jutting above a chair back, or lolling into the aisle.

Sleep. If only.

Glancing to her left, she counted four of the six occupants of her row asleep. One man's chair was tilted back as far as it would go. A baseball cap was tugged down over his face, and his Adam's apple jutted conspicuously in the dim light.

Marten had wondered why on earth a person would want a baseball cap in a plane, at night. Mystery solved; the cap was just another way to hide.

Caps can be used to hide.

That was another bit of grit.

Because the next connection Marten's restless mind made was to the young man tagging along with Hieronymus Beck. Hadn't the FBI tech, Nick Alvero, even called him Cap Guy?

She saw again the security camera footage of Cap Guy forestalling Jack Griffen on the pavement outside a café in Manhattan. He took the gun from Jack's hand, and all the while, seemingly by accident, his face lay hidden in the shadow of his cap's brim. In the café, he sat with his back to the street camera.

Pretty astute.

But the guy wasn't a machine. He was human, and to err is human.

Marten pulled her phone from the seat pocket in front of her and swiped her way through the photo gallery to the one she wanted.

She scanned it and smiled.

'You erred your butt off barely a half an hour later when you let your guard down.'

She was looking at the photo Jack had snapped over his shoulder of the three on the back seat of the taxi, Tracey, Hiero, and Cap Guy—whose head was tipped back enough to reveal his face.

It was a young face. Thin lips. Strong nose. Dark brows arching over darker eyes. No hint of crow's-feet.

With the photo, it would only be a matter of time and she would know his name. But it struck Marten that she hadn't asked what should have been the most obvious question: what was he doing in this picture in the first place?

This wasn't his show. This was the Hieronymus Beck show. He was writing a novel, according to Jack Griffen. Not that Marten fully understood that, but she trusted his judgement.

Cap Guy was like a puzzle piece that had fallen into the wrong box.

But there was an even more fundamental question, the real piece of grit: why is this guy, whoever he is, taking pains to hide his face when Hiero is not?

Two conspirators. But did they have the same conspiracy?

Moments later Marten dialled Perth, Australia, silently thanking Nick Alvero for his quasi-legal wi-fi filter workaround. She scrunched lower, and waited for Matt Price to pick up.

'Marten? It's really—'

'Shh. No time. I have maybe a minute before I'm busted, but even more, Professor Griffen's life expectancy is down to hours unless you can help me.'

There was silence. Then, 'That's my inviting silence. Are you going to fill it?'

Marten quickly told Matt what she knew of the new player. He was of similar age to Hiero and Tracey. Always toted a laptop. She was attaching his photo to an email, and Matt's job was to find anything he could on this guy.

'Can you do that? In'—she checked the in-flight channel for the estimated arrival time—'seventy-eight minutes?'

Matt's only response was, 'A laptop, you said? I'm all over it.'

When the plane landed, an excruciating seventy-*nine* minutes later, and the all-clear for cell telephony was given, she found an email from Matt waiting for her. It began, 'Does this guy strike you as a nature lover?'

85

A silence like no other I had ever heard.

Two pairs of eyes glinted in the dark, fixed on me. I couldn't bear it any longer.

'We have ourselves a three-body problem,' I said.

'Call him in.' Kim's voice. 'Do it now. Tell him it's—'

'You? Forget it, Kim. I'm not playing his game.' I held up a forestalling finger, a useless gesture in the dark. 'Not even if I thought for a second he would honour his word, and let the rest of us go.'

'It's worth a shot.'

'No, Mum, it isn't.'

I silently thanked God for Tracey's support. It held the man, Jack Griffen, in the room; banished the child threatening to enter.

'We need a light,' said Kim, and I caught the faint relief in her voice. It made her all the more a hero in my book.

'Dad, your arm.' It took me a moment to understand Tracey meant the faint orange glow leaking from my sleeve, my Medline. I rolled my cuff up over it, and its little beating heart blazed crisply in the darkness. Eighty-seven bpm. Not chilling, it said, but not redlining either, which is what I expected. Maybe I was experiencing that calm before inevitable death, the peace gifted to creatures with eyes to see its approach.

Lifting my forearm before me like a burning brand, I played the Medline's light over the shed wall. It revealed bare sheets of corrugated iron, and the pale blur of a spider scrambling up a thread toward the roof. Its shadow loomed crazily across the wall. Dust hung in the air, tickling the back of my throat. Tracey gave the wall an experimental rap with her knuckle. It sounded solid.

'What are you looking for?' With a crunch of gravel, Kim squatted cross-legged in the dirt. 'He won't have left anything useful. He'll have thought of it. He thinks of everything.'

I returned to my search, stepping crabwise along the wall. 'You only just met the guy. Don't buy Rhianne's propaganda. I want to know where we are.' Under my breath, I added, 'And Hiero doesn't think of everything. Not even close.'

My foot rapped something that gave off a hollow bang, and I nearly tripped. A fifty-five-gallon drum sat against the wall. A crust of dried liquid surrounded the rim of its lid.

I heard a sniff, and Tracey left my side. A quick glance told me she was squatting by Kim, with her arms wrapped around her. The two women shuddered together as though one body, sobbing in time.

Intent on my search, I didn't notice at first when Kim's tears became laughter. I stared, dumbfounded. Tracey rose, and felt her way to my side. Eventually Kim found breath to speak.

'I remember, once, saying you would be the death of me, Jack Griffen.'

'I remember.'

I returned to my search, reached a corner of the shed, and played the light over the steel beams that met there. They were draped with cobwebs and constellations of dried-up moths. 'Long, long ago, in a land far, far away.'

'And this lunatic wants to write a story,' Kim said. 'And we're the lead characters.'

'He does, and we are ...'

So why, after all the trouble he had gone to, was he not here now?

Why miss the last words of antagonist and antagonist's estranged ex-wife? It didn't make sense. Locking us in here, out of sight. Out of earshot.

'Dad.' Tracey was pointing at the roof. I leaned, twisting my neck to see where she pointed. I saw nothing at first, then the faintest patch of red, not-quite-black touched the underside of a rafter. But it was only visible if you stood where we were standing, and only if you were looking for it.

Bingo.

Quickly I tipped the drum and walked it, scrunching through the gravel, to the spot directly below the light. Reading my intention, Tracey steadied me as I stepped onto it and gingerly reached a hand up. The touch of cobweb sent a tingle down my arm, but I pushed through it, sent my fingers spidering along the upper side of the rafter until I found what I was looking for. A small, blocky object was stuck to the top of the rafter. I tugged, and it tore free.

I jumped down from the drum and examined my find by the Medline's light.

'What—?' began Tracey, and I held a finger to my lips.

Her gaze returned to the phone cradled in my hand. Its little red need-charge light winked plaintively.

I wonder to this day how differently this might have all turned out had I been a fraction faster to display my find to Kim.

But before I could show her, she spoke.

'Seeing as how it's time for honest talk, Jack. How about you tell me what the hell happened to you.'

Wow. You pick your moments, Kim.

I glanced at Tracey, repeated the shushing gesture. She nodded. (Who was this mature young woman?)

I clicked the Medline display off, and covered the phone's telltale light with my thumb, before I turned to Kim.

The orange ghost-image of the shed faded from my vision into utter dark. For a moment, the only sound was three sets of lungs pumping air. Sense-starved, we could have been transported anywhere in the world. A limestone cave in Western Australia. A submarine listing slowly into the Marianas Trench. Beneath the covers of a couch-tent—lacking only the marshmallows for a midnight snack.

The darkness, so often my crutch for difficult conversations, removed one stimulus too many. I couldn't gather the threads I needed to keep my girls alive when my last glimpse of Kim before the light died had seen a woman looking so lost, crouched in the dust, hair in disarray, wearing yesterday's clothes, eyes glinting with unshed tears.

'I got owned by an exchange student.'

A sigh in the dark.

'I know,' I said. 'Not what you meant.' I groped my way forward, found Kim's shoulder, slumped down next to her. Tracey settled against our backs, silent.

'Last will and testament, huh, Kim?'

'You were the one with the chronic aversion to communication, Jack. The most open you got was on morphine. I used to joke if I wanted to get inside your head I had to get your body into emergency.' She paused. 'But this? I don't know what this is, but I'll take it. So—you left us nine years ago. Where did you go?'

'Can't we discuss this later, over a sirloin and a nice red?'

Her only answer was a faint sigh.

'You want an answer?' I said. 'What makes you think I communicate any better with myself?'

She snorted. 'The writer can't communicate.'

The writer? The writer was outside with a gun, no doubt watching the time. How much longer would he let this play out?

But weren't there *two* writers here tonight? Could I call myself a writer?

After a decade suffering the open wound that was my novel, I think I'd earned the title. Yes.

So I'd be damned if I was going to let Hiero have it all his way.

Time to rewrite. To edit. To redact.

'I'm going to tell you both something, but I need you to promise you won't freak out.'

They waited for me to go on.

'I mean it. You have to promise.'

'I promise, Dad.'

'Kim?'

A sigh. 'Sure, Jack, I promise.'

This didn't need to be the whole truth. Just enough for them to trust me.

'Good.' I cleared my throat, and plunged in. 'The novel Hiero is writing with our lives is *In Cold Blood*.' No need to give either Tracey or Kim a synopsis. A full second later, Tracey's gasp told me she'd got it. Kim pulled away from me.

'Jack, you asked me if we'd passed Holcomb. You meant *that* Holcomb?'

I rushed on. 'When we got out of the RV tonight, we might have found a Kansas farmhouse, a mile out of Holcomb. Assuming weeks—maybe years—of meticulous orchestration, I wouldn't have put it past Hiero to have arranged to get the old Clutter house all to himself, ready to reprise some version of that bloody night of fifty years ago as the climax of his novel.'

'But we're not at a farmhouse.' Kim's voice was flat with stress.

'No, we're not.'

'Then you're wrong,' she said.

'No, I don't think so. Or—no, you're right.' How much could I say?

'To expect the Holcomb farmhouse, that would be wrong. But it's just surface detail. I haven't stopped turning it over in my head. We're in Kansas. There are six of us. It's night, on the anniversary of the murders …'

The crisis loomed. If Kim and Tracey could absorb one more blow, and keep it together, we had a chance.

I dredged my will to continue.

'But the real *In Cold Blood* isn't about the murders at all. It's about the *murderers*. Two of them, alike in their crime, but so very, very different in nature. The kind of difference that spawned a new branch of criminal psychology.'

'Two murderers,' Kim echoed. My eyes were slowly adjusting to the dark, and I watched her square off to me, squatting in the dust. 'Hiero is one.'

And he would make me the other. Kim got it.

I felt the phone, warm beneath my hand, and wondered if Hiero was getting it, too. Outside, crouched around the phone with Rhianne and Ghost, maybe sipping hot chocolate, was he happy I was connecting his dots?

'But why you?' said Kim.

I had my suspicions.

'How do the other two fit,' said Tracey. 'Ghost and this Rhianne?'

What were the chances of a nexus like this, three terminally unbalanced twenty-somethings with the means to prosecute their shared delusion? In a world of billions, it was a downright certainty. Add to that another equally ineluctable truth—it's the easiest thing in the world to murder. The human body is such a fragile organism. The hard bit is getting away with it.

All I said was: 'U2 would be nothing without roadies.'

We were silent, each with our own thoughts. Outside, the mournful creaking of loose sheet-iron told of a rising wind.

Plucking up the courage before we ran out of time, I circled back to the beginning.

'The answer to your question, Kim—your first question—is: I didn't go anywhere.'

I gripped her wrist to stall a retort, but she spoke anyway. 'Sure, every day when we got home your body was there, or something like it let itself in late at night. Its keys jangled like yours, and it smelled of your aftershave. But *you*? The ghost had left the machine, Jack.'

'Don't you get it?' My hands found her shoulders. 'I didn't *go* anywhere, because there was no me left to leave. I fell apart. One day I turned a corner in my mind and didn't recognise the place.'

'I don't know what that means! But you could've—'

'Could've? Life narrowed to a choice between three appalling options: I could be there but not there, not there, or *nowhere*. I chose door number one. Maybe I should have taken door three, checked out completely.'

She leaned close, right up in my face. Her breath touched my skin. She still smelled like Kim. She spoke one word, drawn out, pleading. 'Why?'

But I fancied her eyes asked, 'Was it *me*? Was there someone else?'

Someone else.

Someone else. The fear of a rival. Deep waters, those. Powerful currents. Did Hiero even know they were twisting through his narrative? Of course he did. If I guessed right, it was he that had unleashed them.

But sometimes the falling tree kills the beaver.

I had to believe that Hiero's coterie was not three true believers, but two believers and one amoral opportunist.

And the panic and despair I'd seen in Kim's eyes that threatened to drown her had finally given way to anger—at Hiero or me, I didn't know. It didn't matter.

Time to commit.

'The truth?' I said. Kim nodded. 'Hiero still wets the bed.'

A flash of horror registered on her face, as if she thought I'd gone mad.

Raising the phone to my mouth, I said, 'I'm not choosing, you colossal arsewipe, so the ball's in your court.'

Silence followed, broken only by the crackle of static.

'Dad.' Tracey's hand touched my shoulder, and pointed. There, beneath the door, a fringe of light. It grew brighter.

Someone was coming.

86

In the silence, the sudden screech of rusted door hinges was startling. A shaft of light speared the gloom, leaving me momentarily blind.

The sound of footsteps. Puffs of dust rose and drifted through the stark light. A shadow moved above a high-power Maglite. My forehead felt the cool kiss of a gun barrel.

'Got that?' said Hiero. 'Remember it. Now—*empathise,*' drawing out the last word with a sibilant hiss.

Rhianne and Ghost had followed Hiero into the shed. They moved apart and watched in silence. In the reflected light I noticed Rhianne's alabaster neck bore no mark of the wounds contrived with the *kyoketsu-shoge*.

With an economy of motion, Hiero took the gun away, and planted it on Kim's temple. 'The time of choice has arrived. What's it to be? Contestant number one, the ex-wife, estranged yet stretching for more, and—' He interrupted himself, seemed genuinely annoyed with me. 'I mean, come on. The woman asked why you left. She wants you, you dolt. Isn't it obvious? And you can't muster up one straight answer for the mother of your only child?'

He stepped sideways, and planted the gun on Tracey's temple. 'Contestant number two. Young woman of grit, who, bucking the trend, doesn't hate the father who left her, but strangely holds some affection, even love, for him. How about that? You guys are writing this yourselves. It's a thing to behold.'

He glanced at me. 'How's it feel, Jack? *Wet?*' He laughed. I remembered the night in my office an eternity ago when he laid a knife blade to my hand and asked me how it felt. Asked me to choose between fingers and thumb.

'You need to choose, but if you refuse, I will "glut the maw of death, until it be satiated with the blood of your remaining friends".' He was quoting *Frankenstein*. Cute.

'Choose.' He whipped the gun back to Kim's head. She flinched. 'Wife.' He planted it on Tracey again. 'Daughter.' His arm switched back and forth. 'One. Two. One. Two.' Then, faster. 'Thumb. Fingers. Thumb. Fingers. Man up, and do the humane thing, or I will. Eeny, meeny—'

'Stop!'

'—No. Choose. Miny, mo.'

'I'll choose, I'll choose, goddammit! Just put it down.'

He fell silent, but the gun continued to travel, back and forth, tick-tock, from Kim to Tracey. The Maglite still gripped in his left hand made a blazing circle in the gravel at our feet. The reflected light carved shadows in all the wrong places on his face.

'I *promise*,' I pleaded. 'I'll choose. But, please, just give me a minute. I have to know why. This novel—'

The gun halted midair, poised between Kim and Tracey.

'I'm listening.'

In a rush, I went on. 'I have to know if this is all my fault.'

He laughed. 'Jack, you're the antagonist. *Of course*, it's your fault.'

I felt rooted to the ground, and I couldn't think rooted to the ground. I needed to pace. It's what I do when my plot is in knots. But I doubted Hiero would indulge me tonight, so—

'I can't think while you're pointing that thing.'

'Oh,' he said, and raised the gun to point at the roof. He pulled the trigger and the report crashed against my eardrums. 'Hey, it works. Unlike Rhianne's stage prop—another bluff you bought.'

Stage prop? There was only one gun here, and I'd *willingly handed it over*.

Hiero continued. 'But go on.'

Through the hole torn in the iron roof by the bullet's passage, a tiny star glinted. From outside, far away, came a sound like a low, hoarse scream.

'Where the hell are we?' I said.

'We're—wait. What's this place called, Wheeler?'

'You know very well.'

'Oh, Sandstone Ridge or something. Bison reserve. A few miles from Garden City. That noise was probably a bison, or maybe a golfer with a triple bogey. There's a golf club around here, too.'

'You're not going to get away with it, you know.' I was speaking to Hiero, but cast my eyes at Ghost and Rhianne in turn. 'Your plot is full of holes.'

'Do tell,' he said, smirking. I'd hoped to ruffle him, but pressed on.

'In your version, I'm the predator. You're the hero, fleeing the rabid professor, ready to put him down if necessary.'

He nodded. A fair assessment.

'You tease me into showing up at Rhianne's—the almost rape victim. I'm nearly arrested right there, at her bedside, snooping out the damage.'

'You were a darling,' whispered Rhianne. 'Your concern set my heart aflutter.'

'Next I'm in Hong Kong, seen moments before the discovery of the body of Li Min. Then Vienna, running from attempted murder—'

'Actual, not attempted, Jack. Fatal brain herniation. Your news is stale.'

Rhianne actually *smiled*.

I grasped for something to wipe the smile from her face. 'Hiero probably told you it didn't mean anything when he kissed these girls—just like the movies, right?'

Her eyes darted at Hiero. It was a small satisfaction.

Of course, it had been Rhianne who had visited the bedside of Annika Kreider, Chalky, and taken a lock of her hair, God knows why. Maybe it was a perverse kind of trophy? Detective Thomas had accused me of doing it, called me a psycho, and I wondered if he'd taken my advice and checked if Li Min had all her hair.

'Then the deranged professor is blogging his exploits to the world, like the clichéd megalomaniac you've cast him to be.

'On the train from Vienna, you played a dangerous game. But, maybe not so dangerous. You'—I jabbed a finger at Ghost—'were there, head down over your laptop, making sure I didn't screw up the narrative.'

The laptop, ever present, sat snug in a leather messenger bag slung over his shoulder.

'I had to keep my head down,' Ghost said. 'One look at your face when you were padding up and down the corridor like an asthmatic bloodhound playing hot and cold, and I nearly shot coffee out my nose.'

Hiero flicked the gun in my direction. 'When are we getting to the holes, Jack? Dawn is coming, and you promised me a decision.'

He was getting impatient, but I hazarded a guess I could play him for more time.

'Your IT genius here isn't as good as he thinks he is. The blog made me see I couldn't do it alone, so I called in help. And the first cracks began to appear in your façade.'

Ghost snorted. 'The hack from your home town?' He was trying to appear confident, but was clearly irked at the suggestion his work had a weakness.

'Hack?' I laughed. 'He tore your walls down. Showed me what you were up to. And he has a copy of all of it. He recorded the hosting account—I wonder who owns the attached credit card? You said that was all you, right?'

Hiero glanced at Ghost, but oddly didn't seem upset that the entire contents of his fictional blog were safely copied away, ready to be given to the police.

'That's your first problem,' I said. 'But not the last. Here's what you'll have to talk yourself out of when you're tried for homicide, Randall Todd.'

The only sign my use of his real name had registered was the gun barrel dipping to point at my guts.

'Your history at Germanton, home of the Lawson family Christmas massacre? There's a young woman happy to tell all.'

Rhianne shot a sideways glance at Hiero.

'Want me to keep going?'

Hiero's smile returned. He nodded, gracious.

'You and Rhianne must have overlapped somewhere before coming to Australia. A university perhaps, fishing like you were with Tracey? Another massive coincidence.'

'My laptop password was removed. I didn't remember until later. Ghost tells me he stuck money in my account. That's all got to show up, right?

'Chalky's landlady in Vienna; I was the second guy asking after Chalky that day. The first had an American accent. You willing to bet the landlady can't pick you out of a line-up?

'No matter what happens here tonight, you're not walking away from this. Not one of you. But you can stop it now. We'll testify to your remorse. Whatever it takes.'

Hiero turned to Ghost. 'Please tell me you're still recording. That was pure gold.' Ghost nodded.

'I'm serious,' I pleaded. 'Smith and Hickock *hanged* for the Clutter murders. They won't hang you, but they'll lock you in a cell and throw away the key. Let us go—*all* of us, and you have a chance at a life.'

'Jack, you do realise the body count for *In Cold Blood* is four. If we were still doing *In Cold Blood* do you think I'd have given you a choice? *In Cold Blood* leaves you *all* dead. The job lot.'

'Choice or no choice, Hiero, it's not going to work. Alone, maybe you could have slipped away.' I glanced at Rhianne and Ghost. 'But you had to cast the roles of Bait and Rigger. You couldn't do it alone.'

Hiero said, 'In the end, we're all alone.' He drew nearer. The fire of a strange intensity burned in his gaze. 'So make your choice. *Please*. The mother or the child. Or your choice is both.' And he raised the gun.

I let my shoulders slump. 'I choose—'

Mentally rehearsed a hundred times in the last few minutes, it had been smooth, swift and powerful. My right arm, cutting down on Hiero's forearm, knocking the gun clear; my left swinging my fist into the side of Hiero's skull. The force of the combined blows sending him reeling sideways into Rhianne and Ghost.

In reality, my right arm tangled with his outstretched arm when it collapsed at the elbow. The blow spun him to face me, and the fist, meant to club him away, caught him in the throat. He retched and collapsed *towards* me.

So I improvised.

I lifted my right knee. It met his chin as he fell, and propelled him backwards onto his rump. The Maglite fell with a *clunk* to the ground. Its light sheared the gloom at a crazy angle, and for a heartbeat froze everyone in place.

Good enough. The way to the door was clear.

I bolted through it.

87

From its perch atop a power line, the owl gazed out over the dark prairie.

An immense hush filled the world. Above, the last stars were yielding night to the dawn. Clouds drifted west in ranks, ponderous as buffalo, limned in moonlight. Below, the land was a mosaic of shadow and deeper shadow.

All was quiet, save for the hiss of wind in the grasses, and the skittering of a mouse, a sound only the binaural ears of the owl detected.

First one then another form resolved from the gloom. Far away, but moving fast. They ran in a line.

But the owl had no interest in these creatures.

Save only that in their flight they might scare prey from cover.

The mouse skitter erupted. A small shape bolted. The owl plunged toward the grass.

It tasted blood.

88

My lungs worked like bellows.

My breath came in with a gasp, went out with a wheeze. The cool air was sandpaper on my oesophagus. Grass whipped my shins. Each footfall was a whole-body jolt.

My senses were Lego pieces. I was falling apart.

But something else was rising in their place. From below, rising like a kraken from the deep, was the pain in my chest.

Not the normal pain, these sharp little jabs that arced off at random from a point behind my rib cage. This pain was a slow-building fire. A runaway maelstrom. A locomotive boiler fed too much coal, leaving nothing to do but to stand well back and watch it buckle steel.

And through it my legs pumped like pistons. I flew over the sea of grey grass as a glow rose in the east.

Voices spoke in my head, repeating lines. A question: 'What are your legs?' An answer: 'Steel springs.' Dredged from a movie the name of which escaped me. They went round and round as if stuck on loop.

And I ran.

Morning was bringing dewfall. The spicy scent of sagebrush filled my nostrils.

I felt the thump of footfalls that weren't mine. They fell faster than mine, were gaining. A cry fluttered above the noise of wind in my ears, indecipherable.

Surprise had given me a lead, but Hiero's younger legs were closing the gap.

The fire in my chest grew. It consumed all other senses—all the Lego pieces of Jack Griffen burned, melted, disintegrated. I was a fireball flying over the grass with one desire: go far.

'What are your legs?' Steel springs.

I ran.

I must have blacked out for a split second, as grass suddenly reached up to embrace me. My head collided with the hard ground beneath, and sparks skittered across my vision.

I sprawled, and lay panting, burning.

Hands grabbed my shoulders and with savage strength rolled me onto my back. Hiero's face loomed above me. Sweat glinted on his brow in the rising light.

'Coward!' he yelled. Flecks of spittle struck my face. 'You *coward*!'

I struggled to speak. My lungs hauled air in, but couldn't seem to get it out.

A wild determination took his eyes. He gripped my shirt and hauled me into a sitting position. 'You're coming back. You have to choose.'

At last I managed to croak, 'I chose.'

Hope wiped the anger from his face in a moment. The abrupt change was childlike in its purity. It was the face I'd seen across my desk so many nights—chestnut hair and eyes that glittered with excitement over the promise of Story.

'You did?' He let me go, turned to gaze back over a low rise in the direction of the shed. 'You did. You gave me your promise.'

He looked at me again, must have seen me struggling to speak. 'No. You don't need to tell me yet.'

He sat back on his haunches and gazed out at the wilderness emerging from night. When he finally spoke, it was with a quiet voice.

'Just me and you, Jack. I'm glad it's just us, here at the end. No more masks. Everyone wears masks.'

Nausea stirred my guts. I wondered if I might vomit on the dry grass.

'God, I'm just exploding with …' His hands made vague gestures in the dark. 'Do you have any idea how hard this has been? And I've had to keep it all in here.' He tapped his forehead. 'No one to share it with. No way to let out the building pressure.'

He rested against a sagebrush. Its branches crackled in protest.

'I saw you in Hong Kong, you know. At the airport. Wheeler's flight was delayed, and we missed our handover. So I had to risk snatching your luggage, putting it on the wrong carousel. Couldn't let you get to Li's when there was even a chance she could be resuscitated.'

He was staring at his hands, palms open.

'You were haggard, standing staring at the empty carousel in disbelief. I saw a man desperately trying to cling to *normal*. As if you needed spare jocks. A girl's life was ebbing away. And I yearned to pull you aside, take you off stage for a moment. To compare notes, savour the journey. Encourage you.'

My arms resting in my lap had begun to tingle. Felt like they belonged to someone else.

Hiero kept talking, oblivious.

'Late nights. Poor internet. McDonald's. Just real-life shit, settling on me like dust in the crawlspace of my head. Give it time, and it'll break you. And then the mother of all worries: I let you go. For weeks I let you roam somewhere in the UK, in Forster-space. Gave you time to surprise me, not knowing who would emerge on the other side. That worry nearly brought it all crashing down. We didn't pick you up again until Wheeler found you poking around in yachting forums. Then, in New York, to see you on the pavement outside the café ... I could have hugged you.'

He looked at me as if he would hug me now.

'What kept me going? *The choice*, Jack, the choice.'

He sat back on his haunches and appraised me.

'You're a good man. And Tracey, she's a lovely girl. I don't know your wife, but from what Tracey tells me, she's also quality. Quality family.'

He planted a hand on my chest—I marvelled that the furnace beneath my skin didn't burn him—and leaned toward me again. 'But even a good man can do bad things. Even Job cussed out God. Press him hard enough. Take away his friends, his work—his health. Strip him down to the chassis, and you no longer have the same man, do you, Jack? That's just a man that *looks* like your dad, but isn't any more. It's not your fault.'

Jesus. Pity now? After all I'd been through, my heart was going to betray me with pity for this boy?

This boy is a murderer, my mind counselled me. And he hasn't finished.

There would be time for pity, but it wasn't now.

I lifted a hand that weighed the earth, and beckoned for him to lean closer. I whispered into his ear. 'You said choose a loved one.'

He nodded, expectant.

I said, 'I did. I chose me.'

He recoiled, confusion wrinkling his brow. I twisted my wrist toward him so he could see the face of my Medline. Its crisp red light carved the hollows of his face in sharp contrast, black on red.

One hundred and sixty-three beats per minute. Sustained.

'My choice was *me*, Hiero. What man doesn't love himself? I'm having a heart attack.'

He stared at me like I was the crazy one.

My hand found the strength to grip his shirtfront.

'It. Is. Over. You can't fix this. Can't edit it. My girls are safe. Anything else would be melodrama, and you would hate that.'

The dawning realisation that he would not get the ending he wanted, that his experiment with my soul—the abominable choice between wife and daughter—was void, was fascinating to watch. It seemed to war with his exultation, crept over his features as if his very skin resisted the idea.

Darkness was irising in from the edge of my vision. I guessed I had moments of consciousness left. With the last of my strength, I rolled the Medline toward me and strained to focus on its face. There, beside the solid red heart was a flashing symbol, a phone.

I smiled.

'And if I were you, I'd leg it. Right now, a nine-one-one dispatcher at the Garden City Police Department is listening to a younger version of me tell her that I'm having a heart attack. An ambulance is on its way, here. You've got maybe five minutes.'

Tears glinted in his eyes.

A little of that pity must have stolen back into me, because I whispered, 'Your line is: "The horror! The horror!"'—pity because only a good student would get the reference to Conrad. But only a little; it was the villain's line.

He let me go and I slumped back on the ground, staring into the sky. The last stars glittered, holding out against the tide of light.

My chest rumbled with a chuckle that lacked the strength to get out.

I was laughing at the fact that we were both wrong about *The Killing Joke*. Batman suicided.

Darkness swallowed my vision. In the last moment of consciousness, I remembered which movie had the line, 'What are your legs?' It was *Gallipoli*. The heroic, tragic Australian campaign of the First World War. That man had died running too.

The very last thing I heard was the unmistakable sound of gunshots. Two, in the distance. *Puck, pock*.

The very last thing I thought was the horrible doubt that I had somehow miscalculated.

89

Marten studied Professor Jack Griffen.

He'd come a long way from the musty halls of academia; his flesh was etched with the rigours of the journey.

He had fallen asleep in the time it took her to fetch a glass of water. She took a sip and set the glass down beside her chair. The noise woke him.

'You perving on me?' he said, slurring a little.

'Trying to decide what to make of your face. It's a toss-up between Rocky Balboa—the fourth movie, when he gets the snot beaten out of him by the Russian—and a turnip.'

He grunted, but didn't ask which she'd settled on.

A nurse entered the room, hovered over him a moment, scrutinising the machine beside his bed. She left without a word, stopping only to glance at Marten with a look that said she had overstayed her welcome.

Jack seemed to notice. 'If she glares at you again, just shoot her.'

'They took my gun. Standard procedure.' *And I don't want it back.* 'That reminds me, though. I think these are yours.' Marten placed a pack of business cards held by a rubber band on the bedside table. His eyes settled on them, and lit with recognition.

'Old friends,' he said. 'Where did you find them?'

'You dropped them in the restroom at St Pancras Station after you left that young officer on the toilet with a blood nose.'

'He tried to shoot me, you know.'

'I know,' said Marten. 'A lesser man would relish the news that the young officer was busted back to traffic duty for leaking case details to the press.'

'His gun made it all the way to the Armpit of Kansas.' He passed a hand over his eyes, and sucked air through his teeth. 'I'm sorry. I shouldn't joke about it. I'm just ... There I am, with the light leaking away, thinking I am done. And I hear shots …' His voice trailed into silence broken only by the muted piping of the machine.

Marten reached for her glass and found it empty.

'Old hand like you, Jack. Thought you would have known the difference between the discharge of different calibres—my Glock is chambered with the larger .40 Smith & Wesson.'

'Old hand was having a heart attack,' he retorted, irritated.

Marten took it as a healthy sign.

'How on earth did you find us?'

'A bit of sleuthing, with some help from Matt Price, your IT chum.'

'I owe that boy.'

'You do. He was on your side from the beginning.' *Unlike me.* 'But the key was Mitchell Cooper.'

'Mitchell Cooper?'

'Hiero's helper.'

'Oh,' said Jack. 'I only ever called him Ghost, as in Ghostwriter. After Matt alerted me to exchanges between Hiero and another party, I figured someone was helping him orchestrate things. It explained how he knew things he shouldn't have known, like that I took Li Min's journal. But I didn't lay eyes on Ghost until New York, when he confiscated the gun. Hiero only ever called him Wheeler, which I guess must be another nickname. Who is he?'

'Mitchell Cooper, twenty-three, listed address a trailer parked at the back of his parents' home in Lansing, Michigan. Bought bitcoin early because it was cool, and made enough money to spend his days playing online poker badly, and nights phishing for information to blackmail schmucks. But I didn't find that out till yesterday. I was so focused on who these kids were, I missed the obvious. Unlike Hiero, Mitchell was very much concerned with his future—about it not being behind bars. He studiously did everything possible to hide or erase his presence from the record of this affair. Hid from cameras, covered his digital tracks.'

'*Tried* to,' corrected Jack.

'Yeah. Turns out he wasn't quite as good as he thought he was; Matt was better. Starting with Hiero's blog, which was run from a server maintained by Mitchell, Matt was able to fingerprint his digital presence, which included a number of online identities.

'From the beginning, he was booking flights for Hiero and Rhianne, surveilling you—in Perth, Hong Kong, Vienna, London. Hiero was always ahead of you, but Mitchell was your shadow, constantly feeding your movements to Hiero.'

'Made me feel like an idiot, is what he did,' mused Jack.

'You? I'm the one who waited until the eleventh hour to ask the right question. I put Matt on his trail, asked him to concentrate on the US, and he discovered Mitchell nosing about in a forum—last year, mind you—asking about night tours of the Sandsage Bison Reserve. The forum was for the Kansas Outdoor Adventure Club. Kansas, the state of *In Cold Blood*, which was the bomb you dropped in your last call to me. I couldn't believe it was a coincidence. Matt hunted for more digital traces in and around the area, and found transactions for one-way flights out of Garden City and Wichita, even Colorado Springs. One-way flights for *two*. Mitchell was working on the getaway contingencies for himself and one other.'

'Rhianne.'

'Right.'

'Do you think Rhianne knew?'

'She didn't seem that upset Mitchell was shot. She kept asking for Hiero after she came to.'

'Came to?'

Marten smiled. 'Tracey didn't tell you?'

He shook his head.

'Your girl laid Rhianne out with a right hook a prizefighter would be proud of.'

Jack laughed and winced in the same moment.

'Best as I can arrange in my head,' she said, 'Mitchell was the third wheel on this hell trolley, and put all the contingencies in place to bear away the object of his infatuation if the plan failed and Hiero got caught in his own web.'

'Makes me wonder,' Jack mused, 'if Mitchell was as bad at locking his back door as Matt thinks.'

'Oh, I think he got owned fair and square. Rhianne or no Rhianne, Mitchell has a strong sense of self-preservation.'

A silence gathered. Marten wondered when the nurse would return. Next time she would probably bring security.

'You know,' she said, 'it's a good thing it wasn't Holcomb. If it had been, you'd probably be dead. Grover—the Assistant Director of the FBI in New York—as good as told me his agents would be gunning for you. They staked out the farmhouse in Holcomb. When you didn't show, they set up watches on emergency traffic. Your Medline pinged their bell loud and clear. But by the time they arrived at Sandsage, you were already down. Would have been hard to explain shooting an unconscious man in the throes of a heart attack.'

His eyes found hers. They held a twinkle of mischief.

'It's a good thing you wandered into Hiero's novel, Inspector Lacroix. You were a complete chaos ball. Perpetrated all sorts of mischief.'

Marten spoke her growing suspicion: 'When did you know Hiero wasn't taking you to Holcomb?'

'Oh, a couple of weeks back.'

'What!'

An orderly bustled into the room pushing a wheelchair.

'Physio, Mr Griffen,' he said. 'Got to keep you moving.'

Marten rose, with her hand outstretched in a stalling gesture. She glared at Jack.

'You knew?'

He smirked. 'Well, to be fair, I didn't know Hiero was reprising *In Cold Blood* until—what day is it?'

'Tuesday,' said Marten.

'I didn't know for sure it was *In Cold Blood* until four days ago. But I've known that Hiero wouldn't let anything happen to me before his climax; he was wrapping me in cottonwool until the very end. That meant Holcomb, or *any* place I might have let slip, or the police could sleuth, was out.'

'That's a hell of a gamble.'

'No gamble. Holcomb was too pat,' Jack said, and eased his legs off the bed. 'Too many clues pointing in that direction. So I thought back over my time with Hiero, raked over the memories. My time at a loose end on your sunny isle gave me a chance to reflect. Forster-space.' He tilted his head, and for a moment Marten felt she was being schooled. 'You forget,

Inspector, you're looking at all this—at Randy Todd—with the eye of a criminal profiler. I'm looking at it as a *writer*. And Hiero's *narrative* didn't make sense.'

'You mean his alibis weren't watertight?'

'No, they weren't—and you can bet I began desperately to catalogue them so that when I got caught I wasn't going to jail. But that's not what I'm saying. Hiero began this odyssey with a set of notes for his immortal novel, *Blood and Ink*. Each held a description—not particularly enlightening before the fact, mind you—of a murder.

'And there I was stumbling along, always a step behind, while he pinned each one on me. Worried about stopping him, I missed the most important clue of all. It was winking at me in the blog entry for Annika Kreider's murder, when Hiero wrote that Annika was always first to class, despite him never having attended my lectures—a reminder I *knew* this girl, unlike Rhianne or Li Min. It was blindingly obvious at Oxford, when he set Jane up telling me the next murder would be 'closer to home'. Narrative has to have a progression, and all along it was that each murder hit closer to *me*.'

The wheelchair's tyres squealed on the floor as the orderly pivoted it to face Jack. The man was studiously attempting to appear uninterested.

'He foreshadowed it the night he set the plot in motion, an hour before he left the notes on the tiles outside my office. That night he gave me a choice. It was play-acting, but the choice was lose fingers or a thumb. Flesh of my flesh.'

Marten frowned. 'You're saying you should have realised he was targeting you?'

'More. Man is pulled from normal life into unfamiliar waters is Narrative 101, turning point, Act One. But if the rest of his novel was simply a rising body count, rinse and repeat, barring that I was just further from home or closer to the victim ... well, to Hiero's mind, that's no immortal novel. It's an airport novel. Worse: it's melodrama. Surface detail with no depth.'

'I still don't get it,' said Marten, rising from her chair. 'Why isn't it enough that you're the last body? How could you assume Hiero would protect you until the very end?'

'Because he needed something from me that my corpse couldn't give.'

Jack scrunched forward with a grimace, ready to launch at the wheelchair.

'But why me? Why my fingers?' He raised his hand and examined his thumb and forefinger as if the answer was written on them.

'I've thought about this a lot. I cast my mind back over every encounter with Hiero since the start of the year. There had to be more to his fixation with me than my simply being a ready patsy.

'He always seemed to want my approval, of an idea, a piece of writing, a novel review—I guess it's natural for a student to want the approval of a teacher. But it was more than that. He would talk about his father—a version of his father, filtered through his fantasies—as if the memories he described were somehow *shared* memories. As if I just needed the highlights, could fill in the gaps myself. When he talked to me about those times, it was as if we were reminiscing.'

'You know,' said Marten, 'the old lady I spoke to in Germanton said Hiero's father was a hole in every conversation she had with him.'

Jack grunted. 'Seems he saved it all for me.' He slipped across the gap from bed to wheelchair, but the orderly made no move to wheel him out.

'I was a man who had already walked out on his family. I'm about the age of Hiero's father when he walked out on him and his mother.'

'So Hiero was punishing you?'

'Punishing? No. Experimenting, although he felt sure of the outcome. And he thought the result would hold true for every father, every man. Hence immortal. That when crushed in the vice of physical necessity— when forced to choose between Kim and Tracey—I would make the choice.' He passed a hand across his brow. 'I mean, can you even?'

It beggared the imagination. What would Benjamin have done if jammed into that dark shed with her and David? Could she have chosen between her husband and her little boy?

'And if a man could do that?' said Jack. 'Anything—*anything*—from the smallest white lie on up, was just normal life. Expected. Explained. It wasn't Hiero that caused his father to leave. It wasn't his fault. His father just got squeezed too hard by life and bailed out.'

'What did Kim make of this,' said Marten, 'finding herself in the middle of Hiero's experiment?'

'Kim?' A half-smile twisted his lips. 'After telling me to choose her, she took the opportunity to ask why I left nine years ago.'

My God. The guts of the woman.

'And what was your answer?'

A nurse appeared. 'I'm sorry, Mr Griffen really must begin his physiotherapy.'

Marten ignored her. 'Jack, what did you say?'

'You heard the lady. Torture time.'

Marten decided her hands could hold a gun one more time.

90

The breeze blowing across Fremantle Harbour carried the clean smell of countless miles of open Indian Ocean.

I could inhale that every day of eternity and never grow tired of it.

Above, a gull beat its wings to hover in the cloudless sky and complained.

'I think he's aiming for you, Jack.'

I turned to Kim and smiled. Even bird shit wouldn't dent my mood today.

'Is that them?' she said, squinting and pointing to the mouth of the groin that protected the harbour.

Between the tumbled rocks of the walls a small vessel had appeared, silhouetted against the setting sun. The yacht's sail was reefed, and it was entering the harbour under power. A handful of gulls flocking above it looked like a swarm of midges at this distance.

'Know in a minute,' I replied, and descended the steps to the wharf to shed nervous energy.

The craft that pulled alongside the jetty minutes later was unmistakably the stinkpot, Chuck Longman's yacht. The boy, Scrub, leapt from the still-moving craft with the mooring line as soon as the gap closed to a few feet. The figure behind the wheel was intent on manoeuvring the yacht and didn't appear to have noticed us yet.

'Has he had a growth spurt?' Tracey had come up behind us, and was looking at Scrub. 'I thought you said he was small for his age.'

Scrub hadn't looked small when pointing a gun at me, I remembered. But that seemed like an aeon ago.

'Come on. Let's see if they need help,' I said, knowing full well they'd done this a thousand times, and certainly did not need our help. I suddenly felt nervous. Longman and Scrub were going to be staying with us for two weeks, and I feared it was too much, too soon.

Longman greeted us with a gruff hello and invited us onto the boat.

'I wasn't expecting a party,' he said, and I noted his troubled gaze settle on Scrub. The boy had tied off and now squatted motionless by the bollard, coiled like a cat, his gaze flicking restlessly between us. 'No offence,' Longman finished, with a glance at Kim and Tracey.

Kim smiled to set him at ease. 'I told Jack he should have stayed home.'

'Hi Scrub,' I said.

In answer, he pointed at me. 'Why does your t-shirt say "L"?'

Hiding my shock at the first words I'd heard him utter, I glanced at Longman. His eyes twinkled, and the barest smile touched his lips. For him, it was a burst of pride and joy.

I dipped my chin to peer at my shirt front, as if I'd forgotten I was bearing a one-foot-tall black letter 'L' on a yellow background. 'Oh, this? It was a present from my daughter, Tracey,' and I indicated her. 'I'm a professor. It stands for "Learned".'

Tracey walked smoothly over to Scrub and squatted to whisper in his ear. To my surprise, he let her. His brow crinkled in concentration as she spoke, and then all at once he burst into gales of laughter.

I turned to Longman. 'You probably want a proper shower and something to eat that doesn't come out of a can.'

'To be honest,' he said, pausing to lock the cabin door, 'I could kill an ice-cold beer followed by a scalding-hot coffee.'

'Sail and Anchor?' I suggested.

'Then Gino's,' said Kim.

Longman climbed from the yacht with an agility that belied his spindly legs and improbably large torso. Somehow, he looked older and seemed younger.

Scrub rose and followed his grandfather as he headed for the marina office. Tracey gave us a surreptitious thumbs up and followed.

Ever since I had suggested Longman and Scrub visit for a couple of weeks, my mind had constructed disaster after disaster for how this would play out. As usual, all that the worry had done was eat tomorrow's energy. Again, my anxiety had not fully reckoned with a Tracey on a mission.

Feeling the little fizz of adrenaline, I twisted my wrist toward me and out of habit looked for my Medline, fearing to see its sullen orange—or worse, its angry red.

But all that met my gaze was my naked wrist. A crisp tan line on the edges of a band of white skin.

I took a deep breath, conscious of Kim regarding me.

'You okay?' she said.

It had been Kim's suggestion that I leave it home today. I nodded.

'Good,' she said, and shoved me over the side of the yacht.

I tipped overboard like a tin soldier, rigid with surprise. The marina's salty water embraced me, cold enough to take my breath away. I swallowed water before remembering to shut my mouth, and thrashed to turn upright as fleeting thoughts of sharks filled my mind.

My head broke the surface, and I blew a geyser of water from my mouth.

When I'd knuckled the water from eyes, I looked up to see Kim standing on the jetty watching me. One of her hands gripped the top of a corroded metal ladder that descended into the water, the other was caught halfway to her throat, betraying a hesitancy uncharacteristic in Kim.

Half-floundering, half-stroking I made my way to the bottom of the ladder. Kim's silhouette loomed above me. My mind returned to that night months ago, in the dark of a shed on Sandsage Bison Reserve, half a world away, and the scene for the climax of Hiero's novel. And to Kim, and her question: 'Why did you leave?'

It had taken me forty-eight hours to give her an answer, from a hospital bed the morning of the day Marten visited me.

I'd had a day of semi-waking, and then another of fevered lucid thought to compose my answer. I say 'compose', because I'd known the answer for years. Just needed to find the words for my ex-wife.

Why did you leave?

The answer: I broke my life before it could be broken. Like the tigress who devours her cubs rather than let another predator take them.

Tracey's illness was the last and biggest; the straw that broke this camel's back. And if I couldn't have my life in the shape I wanted, then no one could.

Kim's response? She had said, 'Jack, life is fragile. If you play with it, yes, it might break. The alternative is, well … there's a name for a place where you don't touch things: a museum. Is that what you want your life to be?'

Fragile. Lying on a hospital bed, my face bruised with the pattern of Hiero's boot, my chest stiff from the rough handling of a heart-attack patient. The irony did not escape me. That there of all places I was talking to Kim, really talking, for the first time in years.

I climbed the ladder, water cascading from my sodden clothes. At the top, I found her outstretched hand and took it.

'You okay?' she said, her expression a curious mingling of concern and a smile that wanted out.

Okay?

Visible at the end of the jetty, emerging from the office, were the forms of Longman and Scrub and Tracey. I had invited them into my life. Longman pushing seventy, and fragile. Scrub, beginning to bud. Fragile.

Tracey appeared beside Scrub, talking animatedly.

What did she think of me? Her dad, who had disappeared down a hole when she was twelve. Could it have been a worse time? Fragile.

And Kim. Standing there on a jetty on the other side of the world from the life she had begun again, holding the hand of her one-time husband, getting wet for the privilege.

Fragile.

I could offer a prayer of hope for Hiero. Snarled up as he was now in legal proceedings that would sooner or later commit him to life behind bars for decades. I could thank him, too, after a fashion.

Without him I wouldn't have written my book.

The one you're holding.

'I'm okay,' I said to Kim. 'But handle with caution.'

EPILOGUE

A month after Longman and Scrub sailed out of Fremantle Harbour, almost a year to the day after I made it back to Australia, I got a call from my young IT friend, Matt Price.

I knew from the first moment he was excited.

'Matt?'

'You won't believe it,' he said, breathless, 'but I did it.'

'Did what?' I grunted. It was after midnight. 'I have no idea what you're talking about.'

'Cracked the code.'

'What code?'

'The rest of Hiero's blog.'

That woke me up.

'Wait,' I said, dragging myself upright in bed. 'The rest of Hiero's blog was a hash of random garbage.' It turned to junk right after '3PM, with the best cheesecake in New York'. Just before I finally caught up with him. And found Tracey.

'No,' he said, barely containing his glee. 'It was a code, and I cracked it.

'Underneath that junk, it begins: "The All-Concealing 'I'" ...'

The skin at the nape of my neck prickled. Because The All-Concealing 'I' is a narrative trope, a term for when a first-person narrator—normally a candid sharer of their inner world—subtly withdraws that intimacy. Begins to omit things and play on a reader's false assumptions.

The technique is often used in detective fiction to put distance between the narrator and the reader, to allow a plot twist without the reader feeling cheated. Like when your spouse appears not to hear you ask how their afternoon went, only to reveal the next day—your birthday—that their afternoon was spent hunting in bookshops for your present, a first edition of *The Demolished Man*.

Matt was still speaking. I tuned in again.

'Don't ask me how much time I put into this. It's embarrassing. But when you mentioned the blog turning to garbage, I couldn't help taking a look. There was no good explanation for why the data should become corrupted. So I hit it with every kind of code-cracker I could get my hands on: I tried simple ciphers, Caesar, Null, Vigenère—you know, spy stuff. Then heavy-duty computational encodings of the shared secret kind— Triple DES, Blowfish—and got nothing. After two months of brute-forcing top-of-the-line AES, still nothing. And it just gripped me tighter.'

'Matt, I don't know what those things are.'

He barrelled on. 'Well, finally, I thought, this thing is uncrackable. But there's only one kind of code that is uncrackable—truly, theoretically, all-computing-power-to-the-end-of-time uncrackable, and that's a one-time pad.'

'One-time pad? Isn't that back to spies and dead-letter drops?'

'Right. A one-time pad takes an enciphered text—that's the blog garbage—and a secret cipher, some text that tells you which letter to substitute for which, and *voila!*, you get back your plain text: the rest of Hiero's blog.

'Technically a one-time pad requires a random cipher, and I searched for that, but came up empty. That's when I began trying other chunks of writing. I tried earlier blog posts. I tried the murder sheets. I tried the text of email correspondence between Hiero and Rhianne, Hiero and Mitchell. But all those cipher texts did was turn the garbage into different garbage.

'Finally, knowing your history, I began piping novels through it. Then one morning I woke to find The All-Concealing "I", and I knew I'd cracked it. Want to know what it was?'

We spoke over each other:

'*In Cold Blood*—'

'*In Cold Blood*.'

'To be precise, part one of its serialisation in the *New Yorker*, September nineteen sixty-five,' he said. 'Sending the fully decoded blog now.'

The feeling of reading the rest of Hiero's blog, which until that day had been hidden beneath a layer of encryption, was like discovering a photo of yourself in a place you've never visited.

I read it in one sitting. Then reread it. Then read it again. Then sat at my desk, staring through the window at the river as the sky paled and the stars disappeared.

Hiero had carried on in the same vein, faking the perspective to be mine—me, Jack Griffen.

So much was spot-on, if skewed. Our long-haul drive into the middle of nowhere, Kansas. Only in Hiero's version, I was the one holding Tracey and Hiero in thrall. Rhianne showed up on cue, with Kim, at the pull-off south of Garden City.

Then came the dark shed in the middle of Sandsage Bison Reserve.

Hiero's version was prescient on a number of points.

In Hiero's version, too, when it came to the crunch, Ghost had lit out. Apparently Hiero had always known Mitchell Cooper had the heart of a mercenary. Hiero had dangled Rhianne in front of him—this smart guy whose smarts disappeared in front of girls—but when things started falling apart, he'd decided his own hide was priority number one.

But we'd already figured that out.

As for Rhianne, she was cast as the student 'Jack' had secretly seduced in Perth. She had then dragged Kim into it, the older model she suspected Jack still loved. But when it came time to shed blood, she'd folded. Rhianne was no Barbara Ann Oswald, to crash and die in a helicopter attempting to break a hijacker like Garrett Trapnell from prison. Hiero's fictional Rhianne claimed she was under compulsion, and threw herself on the mercy of the victims, Hiero, Kim and Tracey.

Real life mirrored this, albeit with the sluggish pace at which the wheels of justice turned in Rhianne's court case. She ultimately pled duress and accused Hiero of forcing her to aid him against her will. Her infatuation had broken in the face of the visceral reality of three people fearing for their lives.

But just last week her case had been damaged by the arrival at her parents' home of a one-carat diamond. The diamond was the product of a company called SoulDiamond, which specialises in artificially growing gem-quality rocks from organic material. The diamond of course could not be interrogated for DNA, and SoulDiamond had not kept any residue of the original material provided by Rhianne—loved ones, humans or pets, just needed two-thirds of a cup of ash, or half a cup of hair. They were, however, able to tell the court that the sample had been human hair. The prosecution was not lax in pointing out that both Li Min and Annika Kreider had hair taken from them post-mortem, and that Rhianne had contacted a number of orderlies at Queen Mary Hospital, which held Li Min's body, with an offer of five thousand dollars to do 'a favour' for a grieving friend.

It seemed Rhianne would suffer no rivals to Hiero's attentions, despite his assuring her they were make-believe for the true crime of the ages. She had exacted a kind of revenge on these girls who dared to get into Hiero's bed. She, too, had made sacrifices for art.

But Hiero …

To finally see the endgame clearly through his eyes.

In his version, there was no choice. Jack Griffen simply murdered his ex-wife and daughter in cold blood. It left Hiero and Jack together at last, ready to write the first chapter of a new story.

The final revelation was that Hiero was 'like a son unto Jack'—his words. And Jack had now demonstrated the depth of his love for the boy.

Deeply twisted.

And deeply human.

A couple of days later I wrote Hiero my first email. He responded the same day, and it's become a regular thing.

It's probably hopeless. But the author in me wonders if it's possible to recover some part of the man Hiero could have been before the boy was derailed at age eleven when his father left.

And I even told Kim.

See? I'm learning.

ACKNOWLEDGEMENTS

Blood and Ink was made possible by a lot of theft.

Special thanks to David Williamson for his kind permission to use an iconic moment from his screenplay *Gallipoli*. I'm grateful to Penguin Random House for permission to use excerpts from *The Simple Art of Murder* by Raymond Chandler, *The Instant Enemy* by Ross Macdonald, and *The Iliad* (Book XX, page 507), translation by Robert Fagle. Lyrics from the song 'Unwell' by Robert Thomas are used courtesy of Sony Music Publishing. I'm indebted to the following works in the public domain: Mary Shelley's novel *Frankenstein,* and William Blake's poem 'The Tyger'.

Write what you know is an old saw. I guess the corollary is *Know what you write*, which this year turned out to be how to keep vigil at the bedside of a desperately sick child. More than once Jack's recounting of Tracey's battle with meningococcal septicaemia spooled through my mind with an odd force, a kind of doubly false déjà vu. Slippery things, maxims.

But while I do not want to repeat this year, I hope never to forget it. In the scariest hours, it imparted a laser focus—relationships trump pretty much everything. While trying to polish this manuscript, the biggest acknowledgement is of the many folks—too many to list—who helped us through this time, offering lifts, providing dinners, cleaning sinks. For messages, and prayers, and shoulders. Thank you so much.

To my editor, Georgia Richter, thanks for taking an interest in the manuscript, then letting the deadline slide. I love novels that bear scratching below the surface, and you brought a marvellous mix of unlooked-for expertise to the task—forensic etymologist, investigative journalist, insurance claims assessor. I assume you were bitten by a radioactive copy of Strunk & White when young. (We can argue about the received spelling of *arrgh* ...) But seriously, thank you for making it a better book. What errors remain are all mine. A big thanks also to the rest of the folks at Fremantle Press: Claire Miller and Chloe Walton for marketing chops, and for answering my dumb questions. My thanks also to Jane Fraser, CEO. Accepting unsolicited manuscripts is gutsy and refreshing.

A number of intrepid beta-readers braved the typo-blizzard that was the first manuscript. Thank you Anders, Aranda, Tristan, Matt, Jeff, Jono, Esther, Steven, Pete and Bronwyn. A special shout-out to Belinda Mellor. You were the first stranger to grok my stuff, and are a gifted author. It encouraged me that there might be enough weirdos out there to make an audience. Because of you all, *Blood and Ink* is a better book.

It's well established that methylxanthine alkaloids are vital to the writing process. I'm grateful to my suppliers near home and Freo, for good coffee and a licence to camp at a table. Cafés were ahead of the remote-work curve by centuries. Special mention to the Deckchair in Augusta. I recommend their weaponised muffins; these muffins are what you see from Plato's cave.

Without teachers who love story for story's sake, it's easy to miss that fiction holds power. I'm indebted to many who helped fan my love of books. Mr Yates, you were one, and I'm sorry we baited you with trout-fishing stories so much, but even so. You all helped give truth to Chesterton's claim that 'Fairy tales do not tell children the dragons exist. Children already know that dragons exist. Fairy tales tell children the dragons can be killed.'

To Mum, Dad and Cathy, thanks for the enduring encouragement. You left a copy of *Lord of the Rings* propped against the TV long enough for me to discover it wasn't a biography of a monomaniacal jeweller. Thank you for reading. Elisha, Cayley and Jos—thanks for putting up with Disappearing Dad at weekend lunchtimes. In answer to your question, 'Can we read the book?' I say yes. (When you're fifty.) Tara, thanks for not just giving me the time to write, but for being an advocate. You should complain more. I am blessed. I love you all very much.

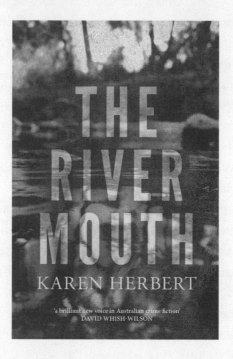

Fifteen-year-old Darren Davies is found facedown in the Weymouth River with a gunshot wound to his chest. The killer is never found. Ten years later, his mother receives a visit from the local police. Sandra's best friend has been found dead on a remote Pilbara road. And Barbara's DNA matches the DNA found under Darren's fingernails. When the investigation into her son's murder is reopened, Sandra begins to question what she knew about her best friend. As she digs, she discovers that there are many secrets in her small town, and that her murdered son had secrets too.

'… tautly plotted, brilliantly characterised, and laced with venomous moments that lay bare the town's racial and criminal histories. *The River Mouth* marks the debut of a brilliant new voice in Australian crime fiction.' *David Whish-Wilson*

FROM FREMANTLE PRESS

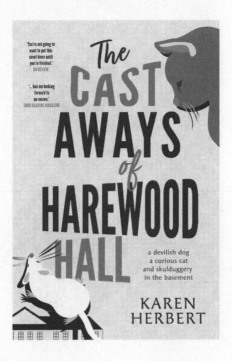

Josh is a sweet, well-meaning university student with a big heart. After he impulsively steals two research mice from a campus laboratory, he hides them in the basement of the retirement village where he works. The mice are happy and so is Josh, until he discovers that the lab mice could cause a deadly disease.

Enter a cat called Harley, a dog called Bobby, the arrival of some mysterious packing boxes, and a strange spike in the village's water bill. As the clock ticks, and disaster looms, can the efforts of the Harewood Hall residents save the day?

'You're not going to want to put this novel down until you're finished.'
AU Review

AND ALL GOOD BOOKSTORES

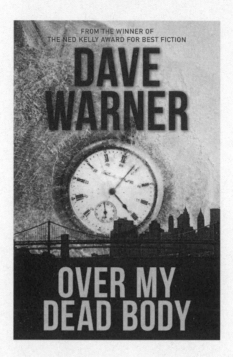

Cryogenicist Dr Georgette Watson has mastered the art of bringing frozen hamsters back to life. Now what she really needs is a body to confirm her technique can save human lives.

Meanwhile, in New York City, winter is closing in and there's a killer on the loose, slaying strangers who seem to have nothing in common. Is it simple good fortune that Georgette, who freelances for the NYPD, suddenly finds herself in the company of the greatest detective of all time? And will Sherlock Holmes be able to save Dr Watson in a world that has changed drastically in 200 years, even if human nature has not?

'… *Over My Dead Body* is a witty, enjoyable tale that provides a new take on the Sherlock Holmes canon.' *Murder, Mayhem and Long Dogs*

Journalist Alex Grant is enjoying the last days of her summer holiday in Croatia when she is accosted by an old school friend, Marie Puharich, and her odious brother, Brian, both there to attend the funeral of their fearsome grandfather's two loyal retainers. The only upside of the whole sorry business is meeting Marco, the family's resident adonis. An incorrigible foodie, Alex is unable to resist Brian's invitation to visit the family creamery in Australia's south-west to snoop around for stories and eat her body weight in brie. But trouble has a way of finding Alex, not least because her curiosity is the size of a giant goudawheel. What begins as a country jaunt in search of a juicy story will end in death, disaster and the destruction of multiple pairs of shoes.

'A rollicking, delicious and chaotically disastrous mystery.' *Readings*

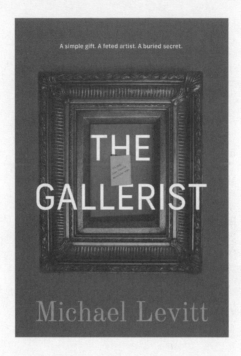

When Australian expat Simone moves to London to start a career, getting pregnant is not on her agenda. But she's excited to start a new life with her baby and determined to be a good mother. Even though her boyfriend Paul's cold and grey apartment in the Barbican Estate seems completely ill-suited for a baby. Even though Simone and Paul have only known each other for a year. Even though she feels utterly unprepared for motherhood. The arrival of Paul's cousin Rachel in the flat should be a godsend. But there is something about Rachel that Simone doesn't trust. Fighting sleep deprivation and a rising sense of unease, she begins to question Rachel's motives, and to wonder what secrets the cousins share.

'… a quietly unsettling portrait of new motherhood and how we should always trust our innermost instincts.' *Reading Matters*

First published 2022 by
FREMANTLE PRESS

Fremantle Press Inc. trading as Fremantle Press
PO Box 158, North Fremantle, Western Australia, 6159
www.fremantlepress.com.au

Cover illustration and design by Nada Backovic, nadabackovic.com.
Cover images: Nada Backovic; Alina Humeniuk, Funkey Factory, Marek
Trawczynski, istockphoto.com.
Printed by McPherson's Printing, Victoria, Australia.

 A catalogue record for this
book is available from the
National Library of Australia

9781760990879 (paperback)
9781760990886 (ebook)

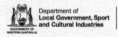

Fremantle Press is supported by the State Government through the
Department of Local Government, Sport and Cultural Industries.

Fremantle Press respectfully acknowledges the Whadjuk people of the
Noongar nation as the traditional owners and custodians of the land
where we work in Walyalup.